O9-BTO-839

RED WOLF

ALSO BY LIZA MARKLUND

Prime Time

Paradise

Studio 69

The Bomber

RED WOLF

A Novel

LIZA MARKLUND

ATRIA BOOKS

NEW YORK LONDON TORONTO SYDNEY

A Division of Simon & Schuster, Inc.
1230 Avenue of the Americas
New York, NY 10020

This book is a work of fiction. Names, characters, places, and incidents either are products of the author's imagination or are used fictitiously. Any resemblance to actual events or locales or persons, living or dead, is entirely coincidental.

Originally published in Sweden in 2003 by Piratförlaget as *Den Röda Vargen.*

First Atria Books hardcover edition February 2011

For information about special discounts for bulk purchases, please contact Simon & Schuster Special Sales at 1-866-506-1949 or business@simonandschuster.com.

The Simon & Schuster Speakers Bureau can bring authors to your live event. For more information or to book an event, contact the Simon & Schuster Speakers Bureau at 1-866-248-3049 or visit our website at www.simonspeakers.com.

Designed by Jill Putorti

Manufactured in the United States of America

10 9 8 7 6 5 4 3 2 1

Library of Congress Cataloging-in-Publication Data

Marklund, Liza, date.
[Röda vargen. English]
Red wolf / by Liza Marklund. — 1st Atria Books hardcover ed.
p. cm.
"Originally published in Sweden in 2003 by Piratförlaget as Den Röda Vargen"—T.p. verso.
1. Bengtzon, Annika (Fictitious character)—Fiction. 2. Women journalists—Sweden—Fiction. 3. Criminal investigation—Sweden—Fiction. 4. Serial murders—Sweden—Fiction. 5. Terrorism—Sweden—Fiction. I. Title.
PT9876.23.A653R6313 2011
839.73'74—dc22 2010050508

ISBN 978-1-4516-0206-7
ISBN 978-1-4516-0208-1 (ebook)

RED WOLF

PROLOGUE

He had never been able to stand the sight of blood. There was something about the consistency, thick and pulsating. He knew it was irrational, especially for someone like him. Recently this revulsion had crept into his dreams, taking expression in ways he couldn't control.

He looked down at his hands and saw they were covered in dark red human blood. It was dripping onto his trousers, still warm and sticky. The smell hit his nose. He jerked back in panic and tried to shake it off.

"Hey, we're here."

The voice seeped through the thin membrane of sleep, making the blood suddenly vanish. The intense feeling of nausea remained, the sharp cold rushing in through the door of the bus. The driver hunched his shoulders in a vain attempt to escape it.

"Unless you want to come down to the garage?"

All the other passengers had got off the airport bus. He stood up with an effort, bent over with pain. He picked up his duffel bag from the seat, muttering *merci beaucoup.*

The jolt as his feet hit the ground made him groan. He leaned against the frosted side paneling of the bus for a moment, rubbing his forehead.

A woman in a crocheted hat, on her way to the local bus stop a bit farther on, stopped next to his duffel bag. There was genuine concern in her eyes, her back bowed as she leaned toward him.

"Are you all right? Do you need help?"

He reacted strongly and immediately, waving his hand in her face.

"*Laissez-moi!*" he said, far too loudly, panting from the effort.

The woman didn't move, just blinked a few times with her mouth open.

"*Êtes-vous sourde? J'ai déjà dit laissez-moi.*"

Her expression crumpled in the face of his aggression, and she backed away with an offended look in her eyes. He watched her go, heavy and thickset, plodding toward the number 3 with her bulging carrier bags.

I wonder if this is how I sound, he thought. When I speak Swedish.

Realized that his thoughts were actually formulating themselves in his mother tongue.

Indépendence, he thought, forcing his brain back into French. *Je suis mon proper maître.*

The woman glared at him before getting on the bus.

He stood there in the diesel fumes as the buses slid away and the street emptied of people. Listening to the silence of the cold, absorbing the shadowless light.

Nowhere on earth was outer space as close as it was at the Polar Circle. When he was growing up he took the isolation for granted, not realizing the significance of living on the roof of the world. But he could see them now, as clearly as if they were engraved on the streets, the buildings, the frozen conifers: isolation and exposure, endless distance. So familiar, and yet so alien.

This is a harsh place, he thought, in Swedish once more. A town that's frozen solid and only exists on state subsidies and steel.

Then:

Just like me.

He carefully lifted the strap of the bag over his shoulder and chest and started to walk toward the entrance of the City Hotel. The exterior, from the turn of the last century, was just as he remembered, but he had no way of knowing whether the interior had changed. During his time in Luleå he had never had any reason to enter this citadel of the bourgeoisie.

The receptionist welcomed the old Frenchman with distracted politeness. Checked him into a room on the second floor, told him when breakfast was served, gave him the plastic card with the magnetic strip that would open the door, and promptly forgot all about him.

You're least visible in a sea of people, he thought, thanking her in broken English and heading off to the elevators.

The room was ingratiating in an insecure and shameless way. The ambition and cost suggested luxury and tradition, indicated by cool tiling and replicas of fashionable furniture. Behind the façade he could see dirty windows and grubby fiberglass walls.

He sat on the bed for a moment, looking out at the twilight, unless it was still dawn?

The sea view that the website boasted about consisted of gray water, some wooden buildings next to a harbor, a neon sign, and a large black roof.

He was on the verge of falling asleep again and shook himself to clear his head, once again noticing the smell emanating from him. He got up and opened his bag, then went over to the desk where he lined up his medicines, starting with the painkillers. Then lay down on the bed as the nausea gradually eased.

So, he was finally here.

La mort est ici.

Death is here.

TUESDAY, NOVEMBER 10

Annika Bengtzon stopped at the entrance to the newsroom, blinking against the sharp white neon lighting. The noise crashed against her, chattering printers, whirring scanners, the faint tapping of trimmed nails against keyboards. People feeding machines with text, images, letters, commands, signals, filling digital stomachs with no hope of ever finishing the job.

She took a few deep breaths and sailed out into the room. Over by the news desk the only activity was of the focused variety that was for the moment entirely silent. Spike, the boss, was reading some pages with his feet crossed on his desk. The temporary head of news was skimming the shimmering computer screen with increasingly red eyes, Reuters and French AFP, Associated Press and TTA and TTB, domestic and foreign, sports and financial, news and telegrams from all over the world, an endless stream. The exultant shouting hadn't yet started, no noisy enthusiasm or disappointment about stories that had either come off or blown up, excited arguments advocating one particular approach or another.

She slid past them without looking, and without being seen.

Suddenly a noise, a challenge, a voice breaking the electronic silence.

"So you're off again?"

She started, took an involuntary step to one side. Let her gaze swing toward Spike's voice, and was blinded by a low-energy lamp.

"I read that you're flying to Luleå this afternoon."

The corner of the morning team's desk hit her in the thigh as she tried to get to her glass box too quickly. She stopped, shut her eyes for a moment, and felt her bag slide down her arm as she turned around.

"Maybe, why?"

But the editor had already moved on, leaving her all at sea, caught between people's stares and digital sighs. She licked her lips, hoisted her bag onto her shoulder again, feeling their skepticism stick to the nylon of her quilted jacket.

Set sail, away, home. The aquarium came ever closer. Relieved, she slid the door open and fled in through the tired curtains. Slid the door shut behind her, resting the back of her head against the cool glass.

At least they had let her keep her room.

Stability was becoming more and more important, she knew that much, both for her personally and for society as a whole. As chaos broke out and the nature of war was changing, it was more important than ever to look back, to learn from history.

She dropped her bag and her coat on the visitors' couch and switched the computer on. News reporting felt increasingly distant, even though she was sitting in the middle of its pulsing, electronic heart. Things that led the front page today were forgotten tomorrow. She no longer had the energy to keep up with AP's ENPS, the news beast of the digital age.

She ran her fingers through her hair.

Perhaps she was just tired.

She sat patiently with her chin on her hands as all the programs loaded, then opened up her material. She thought it was looking pretty interesting already, but the suits in charge weren't so enthusiastic.

She recalled Spike out there, his voice above the waves.

Gathered together her notes and prepared her presentation.

The stairwell was dark. The boy closed the apartment door behind him, listening intently. The loose window on the stairs up to old Andersson was whistling as usual, the old boy's radio was on, but otherwise it was quiet, completely quiet.

You're useless, he thought. There's nothing here. Wimp.

He stood there for a few moments, then set off determinedly for the front door.

A real warrior would never behave like that. He was almost a master; Cruel Devil was about to become a Teslatron God; he knew what mattered—that you must never hesitate in battle.

He pushed the door open, the same plaintive creak. The endless winter snow meant that the door only opened a fraction, seeing as no one had cleared the steps that morning. He forced his way out, squeezing through the gap. His rucksack caught on the door handle, though, and the unexpected jerk almost made him weep with annoyance. He tugged and pulled until one of the seams split, not caring.

He stumbled down the steps, waving his arms madly to keep his balance. At the bottom, he peered through the falling snow above the fence and stopped still.

The whole sky was illuminated by a blue light swirling against the black backdrop, coming and going, coming and going.

They're here now, he thought, feeling his throat tighten. This is for real.

He set off, but stopped next to a broken lawn mower that was hardly visible under the snow, hearing his heart hammering once more, faster and faster, thud, thud, thud, thud. He screwed his eyes shut.

He didn't want to see, didn't dare go up and look.

He stood there, his ears pricking, feeling his hair gel stiffen in the cold. Hard flakes landed on his nose. Every sound was wrapped in the cotton wool of the snow, the sound of the ironworks barely audible.

Then he heard voices. People talking. A car engine, maybe two.

He opened his eyes as wide as he could, looking over the fence toward the soccer field.

Police, he thought. Not dangerous.

He waited until he had calmed down before creeping toward the road and leaning carefully forward.

Two police cars and an ambulance, people with confident postures and broad shoulders, with belts and uniforms.

Weapons, the boy thought. Pistols. Bang, bang, you're dead.

They were standing there talking, walking about and pointing; one man had a roll of tape that he was unwinding; a girl closed the back doors of the ambulance before getting into the passenger seat.

He waited for the sirens, but they didn't come.

No point rushing to the hospital.

Because he's already dead, the boy thought. There's nothing I could have done.

The sound of a bus accelerating grew louder down the road; he watched the number 1 go past the fence, annoyed that he had missed it. His mom got so angry if he was late.

He ought to hurry. He ought to run.

But he stayed where he was, his legs refusing to move, because he couldn't go onto the road—there might be cars, gold-colored cars.

He sank to his knees, his hands shaking, and started to cry, wimp, wimp, but he couldn't stop.

"Mom," he whispered, "I didn't want to see anything."

Anders Schyman, the editor in chief, unfolded the graph of the circulation figures on the conference table in front of him. His hands were twitchy, a bit sweaty. He already knew what the columns showed, but the conclusions and analysis affected him in a way that actually made him blush.

It was really working. It was going to be okay.

He took a deep breath, put his hands facedown on the table, leaned forward, and let the information sink in.

The new direction for the news team was making a clear difference, both to the circulation figures and to the finances. Here it was, in black and white. It was working, the bitterness from the latest round of cutbacks was dying down. The reorganization was complete, people were motivated, working toward a common goal, in spite of the cuts.

He walked around the shiny walnut table, his fingers stroking the wood. It was a beautiful piece of furniture. He had deserved it. His high-handed treatment of the staff had turned out to be exactly the right thing to do.

I wonder if anyone else could have done it, he thought, even though he knew there was no one else. He had finally been able to prove himself.

The deal he had worked out with the printers had cut their print costs by 8 percent. That was saving the owners millions each year. And the recession meant that the cost of paper had gone down, which of course he couldn't take any credit for, but it all added to the successful development of the business. The recruitment of a new sales manager had helped attract advertisers, and in the last three-quarters they had taken market shares from both the morning papers and the broadcast media.

And who was it who had fired the old fogy who was still selling advertising space like he was working on some small-town local paper?

Schyman smiled to himself.

But the most important thing was probably his continued development of sales on the front page and flyers. He wasn't counting his chickens, but, fingers crossed, it looked like they were going to catch The Competition during the next financial year, or possibly the one after.

The editor in chief stretched, massaging the small of his back. For the first time since he arrived at the *Evening Post* he felt a sense of real satisfaction. This was how he had imagined his new job would be.

It was just a bit of a fucker that it had taken almost ten years.

"Can I come in?" Annika Bengtzon asked over the intercom.

He felt his heart sink, the magic fade. He breathed in and out a couple of times before going over to his desk to press the reply button and say "of course."

He stared out at the Russian embassy as he waited for the reporter's nervous steps outside the door. The newspaper's success meant that he had finally started to get some respect out in the newsroom, which was most noticeable in the fact that there was less traffic through his door. This was partly explained by the new way the newsroom was organized. Four all-powerful editors worked shifts, running the various departments, and it was working just as he had planned. Instead of making him weaker, the delegation of power had actually made him mightier and more powerful. He had handed the responsibility down, and instead of having to argue constantly with the whole of the staff, he imposed his authority through his cardinals.

Annika Bengtzon, the former head of the crime team, had been invited to become one of the four. She had declined. They had fallen out badly. Schyman had already revealed his plans for her, seeing her as one of three possible heirs, and wanted to get her involved in a larger program of development. Becoming one of the editors was the first step, but she had turned the offer down.

"I can hardly punish you," he had said, hearing exactly how that sounded.

"Of course you can," she had said, her unreadable eyes fluttering across his. "Just get on with it."

Bengtzon was one of the few who believed they still had open access to him and his office. It annoyed him that he hadn't done anything about this. In part, her special treatment stemmed from the big media storm last Christmas, when she had been taken hostage in a tunnel by a mad serial killer. That had certainly helped break the paper's downward spiral; the market research proved that. Readers found their way back to the *Evening Post* after reading about the night the mother of two had spent with the Bomber. So there was good reason to treat Bengtzon with kid gloves for a while. Her way of dealing with the situation and the attention that followed her release had even impressed the board. Maybe not her as a person, but the fact that she had insisted on the press conference being held in the newsroom of the *Post*. The chairman of the board,

Herman Wennergren, had practically turned cartwheels when he saw the paper's logo live on CNN. Schyman had more mixed memories of the press conference, partly because he had been standing directly behind Annika in the spotlight during the broadcast, and partly because of the countless repeats that had been shown on every channel.

He had been staring down at the tousled back of her head, noting the tension in her shoulders. On screen Bengtzon had been pale and giddy, answering the questions clearly but curtly in decent school-level English. "No embarrassing emotional outbursts, thank God," Wennergren had said on his cell phone to one of the owners from Schyman's office afterward.

He could well remember the fear he had felt at the mouth of the tunnel when the shot rang out. Not a dead reporter, he had thought, anything but a dead reporter, please.

He stopped looking at the bunker of the embassy and sat down on his chair.

"It'll collapse beneath you one day," Annika Bengtzon said as she closed the door behind her.

He didn't bother to smile.

"I can afford a new one. The paper's on a roll," he said.

The reporter cast a quick, almost furtive glance at the graphs on the desk. Schyman leaned back, studying her as she carefully sat down on one of the heavy chairs for visitors.

"I want to do a new series of articles," she said, looking at her notes. "Next week is the anniversary of the attack on the F21 air base in Luleå, so it would make sense to start there. I think it's time for a proper summary of what happened, all the known facts. There aren't many of those, to be honest, but I could do some digging. It's over thirty years ago, but some of the employees from those days will still be in the Air Force. Maybe it's time for someone to talk. You don't get any answers if you don't ask the questions . . ."

Schyman nodded, folding his hands on his stomach. Once all the fuss had died down last Christmas, she had spent three months at home. A sabbatical, they had agreed to call it. When she got back to work at the start of April she had insisted on being an independent investigative reporter. Since then she herself had chosen to focus on terrorism, its history and consequences. Nothing remarkable, no revelations, routine reports from Ground Zero and 9/11, a few follow-up pieces about the bombing of that shopping center in Finland, and interviews with survivors of the Bali bombings.

The fact was that she hadn't really done much lately. Now she wanted to go even deeper in her retrospectives of past acts of terrorism. The question was just how relevant this really was, and if it made sense to embark on that battle right now?

"Okay," he said slowly, "that could be good. Dusting off our old national traumas, the hijack at Bulltofta, the siege of the West German embassy, the hostage crisis on Norrmalmstorg . . ."

". . . and the Palme murder, I know. And out of all of them, the attack on F21 is the least written about."

She dropped her notes in her lap and leaned forward.

"The Defense Department has kept the lid on this, applying a whole arsenal of secrecy legislation. There were no media-trained PR people on the defense staff in those days, so the poor bastard in charge of the base up there had to stand there in person shouting at reporters that they had to respect the security of the nation."

Let her run with it a bit longer, he thought.

"So what do we know?" he said. "Really?"

She looked dutifully down at her notes, but he got the distinct impression that she knew all the facts by heart.

"On the night of November 17–18, 1969, a Draken fighter plane exploded in the middle of the F21 base at Kallax Heath outside Luleå," she said quickly. "One man was burned so badly that he died of his wounds."

"A conscript, wasn't it?"

"That only came out later, yes. He was transferred by air ambulance to the University Hospital in Uppsala, and hovered between life and death for a week before he died. The family was gagged and kicked up a real stink a few years later because they never got any compensation from the Air Force."

"And no one was ever arrested?"

"The police interrogated a thousand people or so, the security police probably even more. Every single left-wing group in Norrbotten was pulled in, down to their least significant members, but nothing was ever found. It wasn't as simple as all that, though. The real left had managed to stay pretty tight knit. No one knew all their names, and the whole lot of them used code names."

Schyman smiled nostalgically; he himself had gone under the name of "Per" for a short period.

"You can never keep stuff like that secret, though."

"Not completely, of course not, they all had close friends in the groups, after all, but as far as I know, there are still people in Luleå who only recognize each other by the code names they used in left-wing groups at the end of the sixties."

She could hardly have been born then, he thought.

"So who did it?"

"What?"

"Who blew up the plane?"

"The Russians, probably. That's the conclusion the armed forces came to, anyway. The situation was completely different then, of course, we're talking about the height of the arms race, the deepest freeze of the cold war."

He closed his eyes for a moment, conjuring up images and the spirit of the time.

"There was a huge, great debate about the level of security at military bases," he suddenly remembered.

"Exactly. Suddenly the public, or rather the media, demanded that every single base in Sweden had to be guarded better than the iron curtain itself. Which was completely unrealistic, of course; it would have taken the whole of the military budget to do it. But security was certainly stepped up for a while, and eventually secure zones were established within the bases. Dirty great fences with video cameras and alarms and what have you around all the hangars and so on."

"And that's where you want to go? Which one of the editors have you spoken to?"

She glanced at the time.

"Jansson. Look, I've got an open plane ticket for this afternoon. I want to meet a journalist on the *Norrland News* up there, a bloke who's found out some new information, and he's going off to Southeast Asia on Friday, away until Christmas, so I'm in a bit of a hurry. I just need you to give the okay."

Schyman felt the irritation rising again, maybe because she was excusing herself so breathlessly.

"Couldn't Jansson do that?"

Her cheeks started to go red.

"In principle," Annika said, meeting his gaze. "But you know what it's been like. He just wants to know that you're not against it."

He nodded.

She closed the door carefully behind her. He stared at the space she had left, understanding exactly what she meant. She works without boundaries, he thought. I've always known that. She hasn't got any instinct for self-preservation. She gets herself into all sorts of situations, things normal people would never dream of doing, because there's something missing there. Something got lost long ago, yanked out, roots and all, the scar fading over the years, leaving her exposed to the world, and to herself. All she's got left is her sense of justice: the truth like a beacon in a brain full of darkness. She can't do anything else.

This could get really messy.

The editorial team's euphoria over the sales figures for the Christmas holiday had come to an abrupt halt when it emerged that Bengtzon had got an exclusive interview with the murderer while she was being held captive. It had been typed on the murdered Olympic delegate's computer—Schyman had read it—it was sensational. The problem was that Annika, like a real pest, had refused to let the paper publish it.

"That's just what the bastard wanted," she had said. "And because I've got copyright I can say no."

She had won. If they had published without her consent, she had promised to sue them. Even if she might have lost the case, he wasn't prepared to challenge her, considering the amount of good publicity the story had already got them.

She's not stupid, Anders Schyman thought, but she might have lost her bite.

He stood up, went over to the graphs again.

Well, there would be further cutbacks in the future.

The sunset was spreading a fiery glow in the cabin of the plane, even though it was only two o'clock in the afternoon. Annika looked for any gaps in the whipped-cream clouds beneath her but found none. The fat man next to her drove his elbow into her ribs as he spread out his copy of the *Norrland News* with a sigh.

She closed her eyes, shutting herself off. Pulled the shutter down against the hiss of the plane's air-conditioning, the pain in her ribs, the captain's reports on the temperature outside the cabin and the weather in Luleå. Let herself be carried at a thousand kilometers an hour, concentrating on the pressure of her clothes against her body. She felt dizzy, shaky. Loud noises had begun to startle her in a way she had never experienced before. Open spaces had become impossibly large; cramped spaces made her feel suffocated. Her sense of spatial awareness was warped, so that she had difficulty judging distances; she was always covered in bruises from where she had walked into things, furniture and walls, cars and the edge of pavements. Sometimes the air seemed to vanish around her. The people her vicinity used it all up, leaving nothing for her.

But it wasn't dangerous, she knew that. She just had to wait until it went over and the sounds came back and colors became normal again; it wasn't dangerous, wasn't dangerous.

She suppressed the thought, letting herself float away, feeling her chin drop, and suddenly the angels were there.

Hair like rain, they sang, *beings of light and summer breeze, danger-free and cherry trees . . .*

Fear made her sit bolt upright in her seat, she hit the folding table, spilling orange juice against the wall of the cabin. The racing of her heart filled her head, shutting out all other sound. The fat man was saying something to her, but she couldn't make out what.

Nothing scared her as much as the song the angels sang.

She didn't mind as long as they kept to her dreams. The voices sang to her at night, chanting, comforting, meaningless words with an indefinable beauty. Nowadays they sometimes carried on after she was awake, which made her mad with anxiety.

She shook her head, cleared her throat, rubbed her eyes.

Checked that she hadn't got orange juice on her laptop.

As the steel tube broke through the clouds on its final approach it was surrounded by swirling ice. Through the snowstorm she caught a glimpse of the half-frozen gray of the Gulf of Bothnia, interrupted by dark gray islands.

The landing was uncomfortably rough, the wind tugging at the plane.

She was last out of the plane, restlessly shuffling her feet as the fat man heaved himself out of his seat, got his luggage from the overhead compartment, and struggled to pull his coat on. She ran past him on the way out and noted with some satisfaction that he ended up behind her in the queue for rental cars.

Key in hand, she hurried past the crowd of taxi drivers by the exit, a cluster of dark uniforms that laughed and made shameless evaluating judgments.

The cold shocked her as she walked out of the terminal building. She gasped carefully for air, tugging her bag higher on her shoulder. The lines of dark blue taxis sparked a memory of a previous visit here with Anne Snapphane, on the way to Piteå. That must be almost ten years ago, she thought. God, time flies.

The parking lot was down to the right, beyond the bus stops. The gloveless hand holding the laptop was soon ice cold. The sound her feet made reminded her of broken glass, making her cautious. Her forward motion left doubt and fear behind it; she was on her way, she had a purpose; there was a reason for her being here.

The car was at the end of the row, she had to clear the snow from the license plate to make sure.

Dusk was falling incredibly slowly, taking over from a daylight that had never really arrived. The snowfall was blurring the outlines of the stunted pines that edged the parking lot; she leaned forward, peering through the windscreen.

Luleå, Luleå, which way was Luleå?

In the middle of a long bridge heading into town the snow suddenly eased, giving her a sense of the river beneath her, frozen and white. The structure of the bridge rose and sank around her in soft waves as the car rolled onward. The town gradually crept out of the snowstorm, and off to the right dark industrial skeletons rose toward the sky.

The steelworks and ore harbor, she thought.

Her reaction as the buildings enclosed her was immediate and violent, a déjà vu from childhood. Luleå was like an arctic version of Katrineholm, colder, grayer, lonelier. The buildings were low, in varying colors, built of cement blocks, steel-and-brick panels. The streets wide, the traffic thin.

The City Hotel was easy to find, on the main street, next to the Town Hall. There were free parking spaces outside the entrance, she noted with surprise.

Her room had a view of the Norrbotten Theatre and Stadsviken, a strangely colorless picture in which the leaden gray water of the river swallowed all light. She turned her back on the window, and rested the laptop against the bathroom door, putting her toothbrush and extra clothes on the bed so she didn't have to carry them with her in her bag.

Then she sat down at the desk and used the hotel phone to call the *Norrbotten News*. It took almost two minutes before anyone answered. She was about to hang up when a sullen female voice answered.

"Could I talk to Benny Ekland please," Annika said, looking out of the window. It was completely dark now. She listened to the mute hum of the line for several seconds.

"Hello?" she said. "Benny Ekland, is he there? Hello?"

"Hello?" the woman said quietly.

"I'm meeting him this week, my name's Annika Bengtzon," Annika said, getting up and hunting through her bag for a pen.

"So you haven't heard?" the woman said.

"What?" Annika said, taking out her notes.

"We don't even really know what happened," the woman gulped. "Only that there was some sort of accident. Everyone on the paper's just shocked."

Annika stood there, her notes in one hand, the phone and pen in the other, staring at her own reflection in the window; for a moment she was floating through air.

"Hello?" the woman said. "Would you like to talk to anyone else?"

I . . . I'm sorry," Annika said, swallowing. "How did he die?"

"I don't know," the woman said, now almost in tears. "I have to take another call now, then I'm done for the day. It's been a terrible day, a terrible day . . ."

Silence on the line again. She hung up, sat down on the bed and fought a sudden feeling of nausea. Saw that there was a local telephone directory under one of the bedside tables. She pulled it out, found the number for the police, dialed, and ended up talking to the station.

"Ah, the journalist," the duty officer said when she asked what had happened to Benny Ekland. "It was out in Svartöstaden somewhere. You can talk to Suup in crime."

She waited, one hand over her eyes, as he transferred her, listening to the organic noises of the hotel: water rattling through a pipe in the wall, a rumbling ventilator outside, sexual groans from pay TV in the neighboring room.

Inspector Suup in the criminal investigation department sounded like he had reached the age and experience where very few things actually shook him.

"A bad business," he said with a deep sigh. "I must have spoken to Ekland every day for the past twenty years. He was always on the phone, like a dog with a bone. There was always something he wanted to know more about, something he had to check but which we really couldn't tell him, and of course he knew that. 'Listen, Suup,' he used to say, 'I can't make sense of this, what about this, or that, what the hell do you lot spend your time doing, unless you've got your thumbs rammed up your backsides . . .'"

Inspector Suup gave a quiet, sad little laugh. Annika stroked her forehead, hearing the German porn stars faking a noisy orgasm on the other side of the wall, and waited for the man to go on.

"It'll be empty without him," Suup eventually said.

"I was supposed to be seeing him," Annika said. "We'd arranged to meet up and compare notes. How did he die?"

"The postmortem isn't done yet, so I don't want to speculate about the cause of death."

The policeman's measured note of caution unsettled her.

"But what happened? Was he shot? Beaten to death? Stabbed?"

The inspector sighed once more.

"Oh well," he said. "It'll get out anyway. We think he was run over."

"A car accident? Run over?"

"Hit at high speed by a vehicle, probably a large-engined car. We found a stolen Volvo down in the ore harbor with some damage to the bodywork, so that might be the one."

She took a few steps, reaching for her bag, and pulled out her notebook.

"When will you know for sure?"

"We brought it in yesterday afternoon. The experts are checking it now. Tomorrow or Thursday."

Annika sat down on the bed with the notebook in her lap; it bent and slid away from her when she tried to write in it.

"Do you know what time it happened?"

"Sometime during Sunday night or early Monday morning. He was seen in the pub on Sunday and seems to have caught the bus home."

"Did he live in . . ."

"Svartöstaden, I think he may even have grown up there."

Her pen wouldn't work, she drew big heavy circles on the paper until it started again.

"Where was he found, and who by?"

"By the fence down by Malmvallen, opposite the ironworks. He must have been thrown quite some distance. A bloke finishing his shift called early yesterday morning."

"And there's no trace of the culprit?"

"The car was stolen in Bergnäset on Saturday, and of course we found a few things at the scene . . ."

Inspector Suup fell silent; Annika listened to the silence for a while. The man next door had switched the channel to MTV.

"What do you think happened?" she eventually asked quietly.

"Junkies," the policeman went on in the same tone. "Don't quote me, but they were high as kites. It was icy, they hit him and drove off. Death by dangerous driving. We'll get them. No question."

Annika could hear voices in the background, people working in the police station demanding the inspector's attention.

"One more thing," she said. "Were you working in Luleå in November 1969?"

The man gave a short laugh.

"Well, I'm old enough," he said, "so I could have been. No, I missed the explosion at F21 by a few months. I was in Stockholm at the time, didn't start up here until May 1970."

* * *

Once she had pulled her jacket on and found her gloves in her bag, her cell phone rang. The display said "number withheld," which meant one of three things: the paper, Thomas, or Anne Snapphane.

She hesitated for a moment, then took the call and closed her eyes.

"I'm sitting on my Operativ office chair from IKEA," Anne said, "and I'm about to put my feet up on my Prioritet desk. Where are you?"

Annika felt her shoulders relax in relief, no guilt, no demands.

"In Luleå. Do you mean to say that you're actually in your new office?"

"Name on the door, everything. This is my first call on my new Doro telephone. What's my number?"

"Withheld," Annika said, letting her coat and gloves drop to the floor again. "What did the doctor say?"

Her friend gave a deep sigh.

"He seemed even more tired than me," she said, "but perhaps that's understandable. I've been seeing him for almost ten years, after all. That would wear anyone out. But at least I'm tuned in to my health: I know I'm a hypochondriac."

"Yes, but even hypochondriacs can get brain tumors," Annika said.

The silence on the line solidified into fear.

"Shit," Anne Snapphane said. "I've never thought about it like that."

Annika laughed, full of a warmth that only Anne could give her.

"What the hell am I supposed to do, then?" Anne said. "How do I get less stressed? The press conference is tomorrow and I've got to do the whole ownership profile, all the technical crap about permits and stuff."

"Why?" Annika said. "You're head of programming. Let the managing director sort that out."

"He's in New York. What do you think of this? 'TV Scandinavia is owned by a consortium of American investors who all have many years experience owning and running television channels. We will be broadcasting across the terrestrial digital network in Finland, Denmark, Norway, and Sweden, with our headquarters and studios here in Stockholm. The proprietors believe that the Scandinavian countries and Finland, with a combined audience equivalent to a tenth of that of the U.S.A., represent an unexploited television market. In the ministry of culture's proposal in January, Minister of Culture Karina Björnlund will indicate that the terrestrial digital market should obey the same competition rules as the rest of the market, so the Post and Television Committee will be awarding licenses to companies that fulfill the broadcast requirements. . . .' What do you think?"

"I lost it at 'consortium,'" Annika said. "Can't you liven it up a bit?"

Anne gave a deep sigh.

"If you knew the fuss this is going to cause," she said. "We're challenging the established broadcasters in an entirely new way, because we'll be using the terrestrial network to reach every household in the Nordic region. Everyone's going to hate us."

"So don't tell them, then," Annika said, looking at the time. "Tell them about your kids' programs and how you're going to prioritize educational broadcasting and culture, serious news, and home-produced documentaries about people in the Third World."

"Ha ha," Anne said sourly. "Very funny."

"I have to go," Annika said.

"And I have to get a grip," Anne retorted.

The main office of the *Norrland News* was in a three-story office block between the Town Hall and the County Governor's Residence. Annika looked up at the yellow brick façade, estimating that it had been built in the mid-1950s.

It struck her that it could have been the *Katrineholm Post*, it looked just the same. That impression only grew stronger when she leaned against the glass door, shielding her eyes from the lamp above with her hands to get a look at the reception area. Gloomy and deserted, just an illuminated emergency exit sign casting a dull light on green newspaper racks and chairs.

The speaker above the doorbell crackled.

"Yes?"

"My name's Annika Bengtzon, I'm on the *Evening Post*. I was supposed to be seeing Benny Ekland this evening, but I've just found out that he's dead."

The silence radiated out into the winter darkness, accompanied by some crackles of static. She looked up at the sky, the clouds had cleared and the stars were out. The temperature was falling rapidly now; she rubbed her gloved hands together.

"Oh?" the voice from the newsroom said, its suspicion clearly audible over the poor connection.

"I was going to give Benny some material; there were a few things we were going to discuss."

This time the reply came immediately.

"In return for what?"

"Let me in and we can talk about it," she said.

Three seconds of static hesitation later the lock clicked and Annika opened the door. Warm air smelling of paper dust enveloped her. She let the door click shut behind her as she blinked to get used to the low green light.

The stairs up to the newsroom were to the left of the door, worn gray linoleum with rubber edges.

A large man in a white shirt that was hanging out at the waist met her by the photocopier. His face was flushed, his eyes painfully red.

"I'm really very sorry," Annika said, holding out her hand. "Benny Ekland was a legend even down in Stockholm."

The man took her hand and nodded, and said he was Pekkari, the night manager.

"He could have gotten a job at any of the Stockholm papers whenever he wanted; he turned them down often enough, preferred to stay up here."

Annika tried to smile to compensate for her white lie.

"So I gather," she said.

"Do you want coffee?"

She followed Pekkari to the staff room, a tiny windowless room between the Saturday supplement and the letters desk, containing a small kitchen unit.

"You're the one from the tunnel, aren't you?" he asked, sounding confident of his facts.

Annika nodded quickly, taking off her coat as he poured thick tarlike liquid into two badly washed mugs.

"So what were you two going to talk about?" Pekkari asked, handing her the sugar.

She waved it away.

"I've written quite a bit about terrorism recently. Last week I spoke to Benny about the attack on F21, and he said he was on the track of something new. Something big, a description of what actually happened."

The editor put the sugar bowl on the table, digging among the lumps with nicotine-stained fingers.

"We ran that last Friday," he said.

She was shocked, not having heard anything about new revelations in any of the media.

Pekkari dropped three lumps in his mug.

"I know what you're thinking," he said. "But you're on one of the biggies—you don't know what it's like for locals. The agencies only care about Stockholm. As far as they're concerned, our scoops are worth less than cats' piss."

Not true, she thought to herself; it depends on the quality of the material.

Suppressed the thought; looked down at her lap.

"I started out on the *Katrineholm Post*," she said, "so I know just what it's like."

The man stared at her, eyes wide open.

"Then you must know Macke?"

"On sports? Of course I do. He's an institution."

Out of control and alcoholic even when I was there, Annika thought, smiling at Pekkari.

"What did you have for Ekland?" the man said, slurping his coffee.

"A few historical summaries," she replied quickly. "Mostly archive material from the seventies, pictures and text."

"Must be on the net," Pekkari said.

"Not this."

"So you weren't trying to get his story?"

The man's eyes stared fixedly at her over the edge of the mug, and she calmly met his gaze.

"I have many good qualities," she said, "but mind-reading isn't one of them. Benny called me. How else would I know what he was up to?"

The editor took another lump of sugar, sucking on it thoughtfully as he drank his coffee.

"You're right," he said, once he had swallowed with an audible gulp. "What do you need?"

"Help to get access to Benny's articles on terrorism."

"Go down to the archive and talk to Hasse."

Every newspaper archive in the whole of Sweden looks like this, she thought, and Hans Blomberg looks like archivists have always looked. A dusty little man in a gray cardigan, glasses, and a comb-over. Even his bulletin board contained the anticipated prerequisites: a child's drawing of a yellow dinosaur, a noisy "Why aren't I RICH instead of BEAUTIFUL?" sign, and a calendar counting down to an unspecified goal with the words "NEARLY THERE!"

"Benny was a stubborn bastard," the archivist said, sitting down heavily behind his computer. "Worse than a mule, never gave up. Wrote more than anyone else I've come across, sometimes at the expense of quality. You know the type?"

He looked at Annika over the rim of his glasses, and she couldn't help smiling.

"Not to speak ill of the dead," the man said, conducting a slow waltz on the keyboard with his index finger, "but we might as well be honest."

He blinked cheekily at her.

"His death seems to have affected people here badly," Annika said tentatively.

Hans Blomberg sighed.

"He was the star reporter, the darling of the management team, the union's hate figure, you know, the boy who dances into the newsroom after one job and cries: get me a picture byline, because tonight I'm immortal."

Annika burst out laughing; she had actually seen someone do precisely that.

"Well then, young lady, what exactly are you looking for?"

"Benny's series about terrorism, especially the article on F21 that was published the other day."

The archivist looked up, his eyes twinkling.

"Aha," he said, "so a nice young girl like you is interested in dangerous things?"

"Dear Uncle Blomberg," Annika said, "I'm married and I've got two children."

"Yes, yes," he said. "Feminists . . . Printouts or cuttings?"

"Copies, preferably, if it isn't too much bother," Annika said.

The man groaned and got up again.

"This business with computers," he said, "everything was going to get so much easier, but it hasn't. Twice the work, that's what computers have meant."

He disappeared in among the cabinets, muttering "T, T, terrorism . . . ," opening drawers and huffing and puffing.

"Here you are," he said a few moments later, triumphantly holding out a brown envelope. His hair had slid backward to reveal his bald scalp. "Terrorism à la Ekland. You can sit over there. I'm here till six o'clock."

Annika took the envelope, opening it with sweaty fingers as she went over to the desk he had indicated. Cuttings were infinitely superior to computer printouts. On screen all the headings were the same size, all articles the same size, every picture just as small. On the page the articles could live and breathe beneath noisy or subtle headlines: the typeface alone could tell her a lot about what the editors were hoping to achieve, what signals they wanted to send. The number of pictures, their layout and technical quality told her even more: how important the item was deemed to be, but also how important this picture or article was in the general torrent of news that day. The skills of an entire profession of editors had been wiped out by the electronic archive.

But she had serious stuff to study here.

The clips were arranged in date order, oldest at the front. The first text had been published at the end of April and provided tasty details from the history of Swedish terrorism, including the story of the inventor, Dr. Martin Ekenberg from Töreboda, who really only succeeded with one invention: the letter bomb. She paused when she recognized several phrases she herself had used in articles on the same subject published just weeks before. She concluded drily that Ekland had evidently allowed his colleagues to inspire him in a very direct way.

She leafed through the pile of cuttings, a lot of it was old padding, but some of it was new to her. She read with growing interest about the fuss in Norrbotten archipelago in the spring of 1987 when the military spent days searching for submarines and Spetsnaz brigades that had been landed on the islets. A stubborn fifteen-year-old rumor had it that a Russian frogman had been shot in the leg by a Swedish officer. The officer's dog picked up a scent and started barking; the officer shot into some bushes, where bloody tracks were later found, leading to the water. Benny Ekland had been more interested in retelling the rumor as entertainingly as possible than in getting to the bottom of what had really happened. There was a brief quote from military command in Boden, to the effect that the atmosphere was completely different in the late eighties, that everyone misjudges things sometimes, even the Swedish military, and that it had never been ascertained that there had ever been any submarine encroachment in northern Swedish waters.

At the bottom of the pile was the article she was interested in, containing information that was entirely new to her.

Benny Ekland wrote that during the late sixties the old Lansen planes of the Norrbotten air defenses were being switched for more modern Drakens for search and reconnaissance purposes. The air base was subjected to numerous acts of sabotage against the new planes, mostly in the form of matches being inserted in the planes' pitot tubes. These tubes sat like small spears at the front of the planes, and were used to measure airspeed, pressure, and so on.

It was thought fairly obvious that left-wing groups from Luleå, probably Maoist groups, were responsible for the sabotage. No damage was ever done, and none of the match wielders was ever caught, but the article cited anonymous sources in F21 claiming that these acts were the basis of the more serious attack that followed. The Maoists were believed to have discovered something that had catastrophic consequences.

After each flight, when the plane was on the tarmac, absorbent material had to be spread on the ground, or a stainless-steel container placed behind the plane. Not all of the fuel in the engine was burned off, and had to be drained after the engine had stopped.

On the evening of the attack, the night of November 18, 1969, the whole base had been involved in a large night exercise. Afterward the planes remained on the tarmac, and that was when the terrorists struck.

Instead of sticking the match in the pitot tube as usual, they lit it and tossed it into the container of surplus fuel behind the plane. The explosion was instant, and massive.

Ekland wrote that considering the air group's lamentable history, it was easy to conclude that it was the local leftists who were behind this act of sabotage as well, even if it did have fatal consequences this time.

He writes like an idiot, Annika thought, but the theory was very interesting.

"Can I have a copy of this one?" she asked, holding up the article.

The archivist didn't look up from the screen, not wanting to interrupt his fingers' slow waltz over the keys.

"So you found it readable, then?"

"Of course," Annika said, "I haven't seen this information before. Might be worth looking into."

"The photocopier's out by the stairs. If you give it a knock it might work."

The man glided soundlessly through black streets. The pain was under control; his body vibrated with energy. His thoughts echoed between the frozen walls, giving answers that were alien to him.

Luleå had shrunk over the years.

He remembered the town as big and brash, full of self-confidence, rolling in glitter and commercialism.

Tonight the self-confidence was gone, way out of sight—it had probably never really existed. The place felt impotent. The main street had been closed to traffic and turned into a long, windswept playground, lined with sad little birch trees. This was where people were supposed to make their living; this was where they were meant to consume their way out of depression.

The curse of freedom, he thought. The bastard Renaissance man who woke up one morning in twelfth-century Florence and invented capitalism, sitting up in bed and realizing the possibilities for his own ego, realizing that the state was an organism that could be controlled and manipulated.

He sat down on a bench outside the library to let the worst of the morphine rush leave his body. Knew it wasn't good to sit still in this sort of cold but didn't care.

He wanted to sit here and look at his cathedral, the building where he had founded his dynasty. The ugly extension on the corner of Namnlösa gatan, "nameless street," was one of his old haunts.

The lights were still on, there were probably meetings going on right now, just as they had all those years ago.

None of them like ours, though, he thought; there'll never be any like ours.

Two young women were on their way out; he saw them stop in the lobby and read the notices of cultural events on the board.

Maybe it's unlocked, he thought vaguely. Maybe I can get in.

The girls glanced at him as they passed each other a few meters from the door, the sort of unfocused glance that you only get in small, narrow-minded places: we don't know him, we'll ignore him. In larger towns no one noticed anyone at all. That suited him much better.

The library was still open. He stopped in the middle of the lobby to let the memories come, and they rushed in, overwhelmed him and took his breath away. The years were erased; he was twenty again; it was summer, hot; his girl was beside him, his beloved Red Wolf who was to succeed better than anyone ever dared imagine. He held her to him and smelled the henna in her copper-colored hair, couldn't help sniffing a few times.

A sudden draft hit his legs and pulled him back to the present.

"Are you all right? Do you need help?"

An old man was looking amiably at him.

The standard phrase, he thought, shaking his head and swallowing his French reply.

The hall came back into pretentious focus again; the old man went into the warmth and left him alone with the notices on the board: a storyteller session, a carol service, a concert by Håkan Hagegård, and a festival of feminism.

He waited until his breathing had calmed down, ran his hands over his hair. Took a cautious step toward the internal door, checking discreetly behind the glass. Then he quickly crossed the hall and went down the back stairs.

Good grief, he thought, I'm here, I'm actually here.

He looked at the closed doors, one after the other, conjuring up the images behind them, he knew all of them. The cheap oak-colored plywood panels, the stone steps, the folding tables, the bad lighting—he smiled at his shadow—the young man who booked rooms in the name of the Fly Fishing Association, then held Maoist meetings until long into the night.

He was right to have come.

WEDNESDAY, NOVEMBER 11

Anders Schyman pulled his jacket on and drank the dregs of the coffee. The lingering darkness made the windows look like mirrors; he adjusted his collar against the image of the Russian embassy. Stopped and stared at the holes where his eyes ought to be.

Finally, he thought. Not just a useful idiot, but the driving force. At the board meeting that began in a quarter of an hour he would not only be accepted, but respected.

So where was the euphoria? The twitchy happiness he felt when he looked over the graphs and diagrams?

His eyes didn't answer.

"Anders," a voice said over the intercom. His secretary sounded nervous. "Herman Wennergren is on his way up."

He didn't move; daylight crept closer as he waited for the chairman of the board of the newspaper.

"I'm impressed," Wennergren said in his characteristically deep voice as he sauntered in and grasped Schyman's hand in both of his. "Have you found a magic wand?"

Over the years the chairman had rarely commented on the paper's journalism, but when the quarterly report was 14 percent over budget, official circulation figures showed steady growth, and the gap between them and The Competition was shrinking, he assumed it had to be magic.

Anders smiled, offering him one of the chairs and sitting down opposite him.

"The structural changes have settled down and are now working," Schyman said simply, careful not to mention Torstensson, his predecessor and a close friend of Wennergren, by name. "Coffee? Some breakfast, perhaps?"

The chairman waved off the offer.

"Today's meeting will be short because I have other business to attend to afterward," he said, glancing at the time. "But I've got a plan I wanted to talk to you about first, and it feels rather urgent."

Schyman sat up, checking that the cushion was supporting the small of his back, and fixed a neutral expression on his face.

"How active have you been in the Newspaper Publishers' Association?" Wennergren asked, looking at his fingernails.

Schyman was taken aback, he had never really had anything to do with it.

"I'm a deputy member of the committee, but no more than that."

"But you know how it works? Gauging the mood in the corridors, that sort of thing? How the different interest groups fit together?"

Wennergren rubbed his fingernails on the right leg of his trousers, looking at him under his bushy eyebrows.

"I've no practical experience of it," Schyman said, sensing that he was walking on eggshells. "My impression is that the organization is a little . . . complicated. The proprietors who spend most of their time in competition with each other are supposed to agree and work toward common goals. That can't be particularly easy."

Wennergren nodded slowly, picking at one nail after the other.

"A correct evaluation," he said. "The A-Press, the Bonnier group, Schibsted, the bigger regional papers, like Hjörnes in Gothenburg, *Nerikes Allehanda*, the Jönköping group, and us of course—there's a lot of different priorities to try to unite."

"But it sometimes works, like the demand that the government abolish tax on advertising," Schyman said.

"Yes," Wennergren said, "that's one example. There's a working group up in the Press House that's still dealing with that, but the person responsible for pushing that through is the chairman of the committee."

Anders sat quite still, feeling the hair on the back of his neck slowly prickle.

"As you probably know, I'm chair of the Publishers' Association election committee," Wennergren said, finally letting his fingers fall to the seat of the chair. "In the middle of December the committee has to present its proposals for the new board, and I'm thinking of proposing you as the chair. What do you think?"

Thoughts were buzzing around the editor's head like angry wasps, crashing against his temples and brain.

"Doesn't one of the directors usually occupy that post?"

"Not entirely. We've had editors before. I don't mean that you would forget about the paper and just be chair of the association, which we've seen happen before, but I think you're the right man for the job."

An alarm bell started to ring among the wasps.

"Why?" Schyman asked. "Do you think I'm easily led? That I can be managed?"

Wennergren sighed audibly, leaned forward, hands on his knees, ready to stand up.

"Schyman," he said. "If I was thinking of installing a patsy as chair of the Publishers' Association, I wouldn't start with you."

He stood up, visibly annoyed.

"Can't you see that it's the exact opposite?" he said. "If I get you that post, which I may not be able to do, our group will have a publicity-minded brick wall at the top of the PA. That's how I see you, Schyman."

He turned toward the door.

"We mustn't delay the meeting," he said with his back to the editor.

Annika drove past the exit for Luleå airport and carried on toward Kallax. The landscape was completely devoid of color, the pine trees dark ghosts, the ground black and white, the sky lead gray. White veils of snow danced across the dark-gray asphalt, to the accompaniment of the rhythmic beat of the central road markings. The rental car's thermometer was showing 11 degrees inside the car, minus 4 outside.

She passed a topsoil pit and about three million pine trees before reaching the turning to Norrbotten Air Base.

The straight road leading to the base was endless, monotonous, the ground on both sides flat and with no sign of vegetation, the pines squat and feeble. After a gentle right-hand curve, gates and barriers suddenly came into view, with a large security block, and behind a tall fence she could make out buildings and parking lots. She was suddenly struck by the feeling that she was seeing something she shouldn't, that she was a spy, up to no good. Just inside the gate stood two military aircraft; she thought one of them was a Draken.

The road wound its way along the fence; she leaned forward to see through the windscreen better. She slowly passed the conscripts' parking lot and reached an enormous shooting range. Ten men in green camouflage, with pine twigs on their helmets, were running across the range, automatic weapons in their hands, the carbines bouncing against the recruits' chests. A road sign indicated that the road continued toward Lulnäsudden, but a NO ENTRY sign some hundred meters farther on made her stop and turn the car around. The green men were no longer visible.

She stopped by the security block, hesitating for a moment before switching off the engine and getting out of the car. She walked alongside the plain-paneled building with its reflective windows, unable to see any doors, people, or even a bell, just herself. Suddenly a loudspeaker somewhere up to her left addressed her.

"What do you want?"

Taken aback, she looked up to where the voice had come from, saw nothing but paneling and chrome.

"I'm here to see, um, Pettersson," she said to her reflection. "The press officer."

"Captain Pettersson, just a moment," said the voice, that of a young conscript.

She turned her back on the building and looked through the gates. The trees carried on inside, but between the trunks she could make out gray-green hangars and rows of military vehicles. It was hard to estimate how large the base was from the outside.

"Go through the gate and into the first door on the right," the disembodied voice said.

Annika did as she was told, like a good citizen and spy.

The officer who met her was the archetype of the successful military man: stiff-backed, gray-haired, and in good shape.

"I'm Annika Bengtzon," she said, holding out her hand. "We spoke on the phone last week. The anniversary of the attack . . ."

The man held her hand for a second too long, she evaded his open gaze and friendly smile.

"As I said on the phone, there isn't much we can say that hasn't been made public before. What we can provide are summaries of the situation as it was then, the conclusions we have previously presented, and a tour of the museum. Gustaf, who's in charge of that, is off sick today, I'm afraid, but he'll probably be up on his feet again tomorrow, if you want to come back."

"There's no chance of taking a look at the site of the attack?"

His smile grew even broader.

"I thought we cleared that up on the phone. We've never made that public."

She smiled back tentatively.

"Did you see the article by Benny Ekland in the *Norrland News* last week?"

The officer invited her to sit down at a plain table; she took off her coat and fished her notebook out of her bag.

"I've got a copy of the text here, if you'd like to . . ."

"I know the article you mean," he said, looking up at the conscript who came into the room holding a clipboard. "If you could just sign the register?"

Annika signed herself in as a visitor to the base with an illegible scrawl.

"Is there any truth in it?" she asked, declining the offer of coffee.

The press officer poured a huge cup for himself, in a mug with Bruce Springsteen on it.

"Not much," he said, and Annika's heart sank.

"There were quite a few details that were new," she said, "at least for me. Could we go through the text, statement by statement, so that I can get an idea of which bits are accurate?"

She pulled the copy of the article out of her bag.

Captain Pettersson blew on his coffee and took a cautious sip.

"The Lansen was gradually replaced by the J35 Draken in the late sixties," he said. "That much is true. The surveillance version came in '67, the fighter in the summer of '69."

Annika was reading the article closely.

"Is it true that there were sabotage attempts on the planes, with matches being stuck into various tubes?"

"Left-wing groups ran around in here a fair bit back then," the press officer said. "The fence around the base is mostly symbolic, it's fairly easy for anyone who really wants to to get over or through it. It's largely there as a marker to keep out, so it's not hard to get in if you're serious about it. The match boys presumably thought they could damage the planes by inserting matches in the pitot tubes, but I have no evidence that they were in any way responsible for the attack in '69."

Annika was taking notes.

"And the leftover fuel? Is the information about buckets being used to collect it accurate?"

"Well, yes," Pettersson said, "I suppose it is, but you can't set light to aviation fuel with a match. It's far too low octane. To set light to it, it has to be seriously warmed up, so that's incorrect. At least, that wouldn't work in Luleå in November."

He smiled nonchalantly.

"But there had been a big exercise that evening? And all the planes were outside?"

"It was a Tuesday night," the officer said. "We always fly on Tuesdays, all the bases in the country do, and have done for decades. Three sorties, the last one landing at 10:00 PM. After that the planes stand on the tarmac for an hour or so before they're towed into the hangars. The attack took place at 1:35 AM, so by then they were all indoors."

Annika swallowed, lowering the article to her lap.

"I thought we might finally be getting to the bottom of this whole business," she said, trying to smile at the press officer.

He smiled back with intense blue eyes, and she leaned forward.

"It's more than thirty years ago, now, though. Can't you at least say what caused the explosion?"

Silence spread, but she had nothing against that. The pressure was on him, not her. Unfortunately Captain Pettersson seemed completely unconcerned that she had traveled a thousand kilometers for nothing. She was obliged to drop the subject.

"Why did you come to the conclusion that the Russians were behind it?"

"By a process of elimination," he said, leaning back in his chair, tapping his pen against the mug. "The local groups were soon written off, and the security police know that there were no external activists here at the time, neither right- nor left-wing."

"How can you be so sure?"

For the first time the officer was completely serious, his pen silent.

"Local groups were put under immense pressure after the attack. A whole lot of information came out: we know, for instance, exactly who was running around with those matches, but no one said a word about the attack. Our estimation is simply that no one knew anything. If they had, we would have found out."

"Did you or the police conduct the interviews?"

He was smiling faintly again.

"Let's just say that we helped each other."

Annika turned the facts over in her mind, staring at her notes without seeing them.

"But," she said, "the degree of silence in any group is dependent on how fundamentalist they are, isn't it? How can you be sure that there wasn't a cast-iron core of fully fledged terrorists that you never caught sight of, because they simply didn't want to be seen?"

The man was silent for slightly too long, then he laughed.

"Where?" he said, standing up. "Here in Luleå? Baader-Meinhof at Mjolkudden? It was the Russians, it must have been."

"So why content themselves with one Draken?" Annika said, gathering her things. "Why not blow the whole base up?"

Captain Pettersson shook his head and sighed.

"To show that they could, probably. Get us off balance. We all wish we had the ability to look into their brains, follow their reasoning. Why did they send Polish art dealers to visit all our officers? Why beach that submarine, U-137, on the rocks outside Karlskrona? I'm sorry, but I have to give a presentation in a few minutes."

Annika zipped up her bag and stood up, pulling on her coat.

"Well, thank you," she said. "And thank Gustaf for the offer, but I'm not sure I'll have time to see the museum tomorrow. I've still got a few things to do and I'm flying home after lunch."

"Try to find the time," the press officer said, shaking her hand. "Gustaf's got it in pretty good shape."

That was completely bloody useless, she thought in the car on the way back to the main road. I can't go back to the paper and say the whole trip was a waste of time.

In restless disappointment she put her foot down on the accelerator; the car started to skid, and she eased up, horrified.

At that moment her cell phone rang: "number withheld." Before she even answered she knew it was Spike.

"Have you caught the men behind the attack then?" he asked smoothly.

She braked cautiously and indicated right, adjusting the earpiece better.

"The journalist I was supposed to meet is dead," she said. "Run down the day before yesterday in a hit-and-run."

"Ouch," Spike said. "There was a thing on one of the agencies about something like that this morning, credited to some rag up there. Was that him?"

She waited for a timber truck to pass, making her Ford shake as it sped by. Her grip on the wheel stiffened.

"Might have been," she said. "The staff on his paper were told yesterday, so it would be odd if it didn't make their own paper."

Cautiously she pulled out onto the main road.

"Have they found the driver?"

"Not as far as I know," she said, then heard herself say: "I was thinking of looking into his death a bit closer today."

"Why?" Spike said. "He was probably just driving home drunk."

"Maybe," Annika said. "But he was in the middle of a big revelation, had some seriously controversial stuff in the paper on Friday."

Which I know doesn't make sense, she thought, biting her lip.

Spike sighed loudly.

"Well, make sure it checks out, that's all," he said, and hung up.

Annika parked outside the entrance to the hotel, went up to her room and sank onto the bed. The maid had been in and made the bed, eradicating the traces of her awful night. She had slept badly, woken up in a cold sweat and with a headache. The angels had been singing to her in a chorus of rising and falling notes almost all night long: they were almost always more obstinate when she was away from home.

She plumped up the pillow behind her head, reached for the telephone on the bedside table and put it on her stomach, then called Thomas on his direct line at the Association of Local Authorities.

"He's at lunch," his secretary said sullenly.

She crept under the covers and dozed off.

Sunshine lilies sugar flowers, melancholy diamonds, oooh, oooh, dearly beloved . . .

Can't fight anymore, she thought, letting herself be swept away by the words.

* * *

She woke with a start, unsure where she was for a moment. Put her hand to her chin and discovered that it was wet, as was her neck, and realized with disgust that it was her own saliva. Her clothes were sticking unpleasantly to her body, and there was a nasty whistling sound in her left ear. She got unsteadily to her feet, went into the bathroom and peed.

When she came back into the room she realized that it was almost completely dark. In a panic, she stared at her watch, but it was only quarter past three.

She wiped her neck with a towel, checked that she had what she needed in her bag and left the room.

She picked up a map of Luleå from reception, only to find that Svartöstaden wasn't on it, but the receptionist enthusiastically added the route that would take her there.

"So you're working on a story," the young woman said.

Annika, already on her way to the door, stopped and looked at her, confused.

"Ah," the receptionist explained with a blush, "I saw that the invoice was going to the *Evening Post*."

Annika took a few steps backward, hitting her heel against the door. A moment later she was out in the wind, no parking ticket. She got into the freezing car and pulled out onto Södra Varvsleden. The steering wheel was ice cold; she fumbled for her gloves in the bag and came close to hitting a fat woman pushing a stroller. Turning the noisy ventilator on full, her heart thumping, she drove toward Malmudden.

At a red light on a viaduct over some railway tracks she checked the map again, and worked out that she was already at the bottom-right corner.

A couple of minutes later, she was at the traffic circle where Hertsövägen made way for a billboard for the Luleå Council recycling center. From now on she was reliant on road signs. She glanced up, Skurholmen left, Hertsön straight on, Svartöstaden right. She suddenly caught sight of a sign for Frasse's Hamburgers alongside her, and felt her blood sugar plummet. When the lights went green she swung off the road, parked by the gas station and went in. She bought a cheeseburger with dressing and onion and ate it ravenously as she took in the smell of frying, the painted fiberglass walls, the plastic rubber plant in the corner, the Star Wars Episode I pinball machine, the shabby wood and chrome furniture.

This is Sweden, she thought. Central Stockholm is a little nature reserve. We have no idea about what goes on out here in the real wilderness.

Feeling slightly queasy from the melted cheese and raw onion, she drove on. Dry powdery snow swirled in front of the headlights, making it hard to see even though she was alone on the road. She drove a few kilometers, until suddenly out of the haze of snow the ironworks appeared right above her. Illuminated jet-black steel skeletons that let off steam and looked almost alive. She gave a small yelp of surprise. It was beautiful! So weirdly . . . alive.

A viaduct took her across a goods yard, twenty or so rail tracks crisscrossing each other.

The final stop of Malmbanan, "the ore railway," of course. The contents of the trashed mountains in the iron field were rolled down here to the coast by those endless ore trains, she'd seen them on television when there'd been some sort of drivers' strike.

Astonished, she drove on until she reached an illuminated sign by the main entrance, and parked by what turned out to be the West Checkpoint.

The immense monster immediately above her was blast furnace number two, a growling, rumbling giant within whose innards ore became steel. Farther away were the rolling mill, the steelworks, the coke ovens, the power station. The whole site was enveloped in a rolling, rumbling sound that rose and fell, humming and singing.

What a place, she thought, feeling the cold. The angels kept quiet. It was now completely dark.

* * *

Anne Snapphane left the press conference with her knees trembling and palms sweating. She wanted to cry, or scream. The rumbling headache only increased her anger at the managing director who had taken off for the U.S. and left the whole presentation to her. She wasn't employed to stand responsible for the whole of TV Scandinavia, just the programming.

She made it to her room, dialed Annika's number and looked around desperately for a glass of wine.

"I'm standing by the ironworks in Svartöstaden," Annika yelled from Anne's home territory. "It's a real monster, absolutely amazing. How did the press conference go?"

"Crap," Anne Snapphane said in a dull voice, feeling her hands shake. "They tore me to shreds, and the boys from your lot were worst."

"Hang on," Annika said, "I have to move the car; I'm in the way of a truck. Yes! I know! I'm moving!"

This last to someone else.

The sound of a car engine; Anne looked for her headache pills in the desk drawer, but the box was empty.

"Right, tell me what happened," Annika said over the line again.

Anne forced her hands still, then put her right hand to her forehead.

"They want me to personify every supercapitalist, warmongering, American, multinational bloodsucking corporation all in one go," she said.

"The first rule of dramaturgy," Annika said. "You have to give the villain a face. Yours just happens to fit the bill. Although I think it's strange that they're so angry."

Anne carefully shut the desk drawer and put the phone down on the floor, then lay down next to it.

"Not really," she said, staring at the lights in the ceiling, breathing out and feeling the room sway. "We're challenging the established channels on the only advertising market they've not yet conquered, the global brand market. But that's not all. We're not only taking their money, we're going to take their viewers with our thoroughly commercialized shitty programs that we buy for peanuts."

"And the *Evening Post*'s proprietors will be hit hardest of all, is that right?" Annika asked.

"Because we'll be using the terrestrial digital network, yes," Anne said.

"How's your headache?"

Anne closed her eyes, seeing the strip lighting in the ceiling as blue stripes through her eyelids.

"Same as before," she said. "I've started getting pretty wobbly as well."

"Do you really think it's just stress? Couldn't you take things a bit easier?"

Annika sounded genuinely worried.

"I'm trying," Anne mumbled, letting out a deep breath.

"Have you got Miranda this weekend?"

She shook her head, a hand over her eyes.

"She's with Mehmet."

"Is that good or bad?"

"I don't know," she whispered. "I don't know if I can do this anymore."

"Course you can," Annika said. "Come around to my place tomorrow. Thomas is playing tennis, I'll get some macaroons."

Anne Snapphane let out a snort of laughter and dried her eyes.

When they had hung up Annika drove on with a nagging anxiety in her gut. For the first time she was starting to think that there was something physically wrong with Anne. Over the years her friend had seen Doctor Olsson with every symptom known to modern medicine, and up to now she had only ever needed antibiotics twice. Once she got some cough syrup as well, and when she found out it contained morphine she had phoned Annika in horror, imagining that she had become an addict.

Annika couldn't help smiling at the memory.

Slowly she swung off the road and in among the residential area of Svartöstaden.

This really was another country, or at least another town. Not Luleå, and not really Sweden. Annika let the car drift through the shanty town, astonished by its atmosphere.

The Estonian countryside, she thought, Polish suburbs.

The headlights played across shabby wooden façades of yards and outhouses and sheds, leaning roofs and ramshackle fences. The buildings were small and misshapen, could have been built out of orange boxes. The paint was peeling off most of them; the uneven handblown glass in the windows twinkled. She passed a charity shop selling clothes in aid of the struggle for freedom, although whose freedom was unclear.

She pulled up behind a recycling site on Bältesgatan, left her bag in the car, and got out. The noise from the ironworks was audible as a faint song in the distance. She took a few slow steps, looking over the fences into the yards.

"Are you looking for someone?"

A man in a woolly hat and work boots was coming toward her from one of the gingerbread houses, glancing at her rental car.

Annika smiled.

"I was just passing and had to stop," she said with her hands in her coat pockets. "What an amazing place."

The man stopped, straightening up.

"Yes," he said, "it is a bit unusual. An old workers' district from the turn of the last century. Strong sense of cohesion; there's real community spirit here. People don't often want to leave."

Annika nodded politely.

"I can understand that people end up staying."

The man pulled a cigarette from an inside pocket, lit it with a Bic lighter, then took the conversational bait and started talking.

"We've got a nursery nowadays," he said, "three classes, Villekulla, Moomin Valley, and Bullerby. We had to fight for years before the council gave in. The school takes kids up to thirteen, and there's a youth club. Broadband. We're going to have to fight to keep the old ironwork manager's house—we never seem to get out of this obsession with pulling things down."

He exhaled a hard plume of smoke, looking at her from under the rim of his hat.

"So what are you doing here?"

"I was supposed to be meeting Benny Ekland, but when I got here I found out he'd been run over."

The man shook his head, stamping his feet.

"Damn awful business," he said. "On his way home, and gets run down like that. Everyone thinks it's terrible."

"Everyone here knows everyone else?" she asked, trying hard not to sound too inquisitive.

"For good and ill," he said, "but mostly good. We take responsibility for each other; there's too little of that in the world today . . ."

"Do you know where it happened?"

"Down on Skeppargatan, on the way to the main road," he said, pointing. "Quite close to Blackis: that's the big building at the edge of the forest. The kids went up there with a flower a bit earlier. Well, I really ought to . . ."

The man headed off toward the water.

Annika stood and watched him go.

I'd like a life like that, she thought. To belong somewhere.

She got back in the car and drove in the direction the man had indicated.

The place where Benny Ekland was run down was just a couple of hundred meters from the West Checkpoint, but not visible from there. In fact it wasn't overlooked from anywhere, apart from a decrepit housing development and plate shop a hundred meters or so away. A thin row of yellow streetlights, some of them broken, spread a dusty light over the cordons, snow, and mud. To the left was an area of ragged scrub, on the right an embankment topped by a fence.

Malmvallen, she thought. The soccer field.

She switched off the engine and sat in the dark, listening.

Ekland had just written a long series of articles about terrorism. The last thing he published was about the attack on F21. After that he was run down, here, in the most desolate place in Luleå.

She didn't like coincidences.

After a few minutes a teenage boy came out of one of the blocks nearby and walked slowly up to the fluttering plastic cordon around the crime scene, bareheaded, hands in his pockets. His hair was stiff with gel, making Annika smile. Kalle had just discovered the joys of hair gel.

The boy stopped just a couple of meters from her car, staring blankly at a small heap of flowers and candles inside the cordon.

Her smile faded as it dawned on her how Benny Ekland's death had affected the people living here. They were all mourning his loss. Would any of her neighbors mourn her?

Hardly.

She started the car, intending to drive down to Malmhamnen. The moment she turned the key the boy started as though he'd been hit, and his reaction made her jump. With a cry that penetrated the car the lad rushed away, back to his house. She waited until he had disappeared behind the fence, then rolled off toward the harbor where the stolen car had been found.

The road was pitch-black and treacherous, leading to a dead end and a large gate marked LKAB, the mineral group Luossavaara-Kirunavaara Aktiebolag. Big cranes, heavy concrete quays.

She decided to drive back up to the site of the accident, creeping along at a snail's pace.

As she passed Svartöstaden Plate she looked into the block of apartments next to it. She saw the boy's spiked hair silhouetted in the bottom-left window.

"I didn't mean to scare you," she said to herself. "What made you so frightened?"

She stopped the car by the cordon and got out, taking her bag.

Looked up at furnace number 2, still impressed. Turned and looked the other way, into the wind. The road was one of the ways into the actual residential district.

Annika pulled her flashlight out of the bag and shone it behind the police cordon. The snow of recent days had covered all traces that might have been visible to a layman. The ice on the tarmac showed no signs of emergency braking, but any that had been there would have been obliterated by now.

She shone the beam on the fence some ten meters away. That was where he had been found. Inspector Suup was right: Benny Ekland's last movements had been a flight through the air.

She stood with the flashlight in her hand, listening to the distant noise of the steelworks. Turned to face the plate shop again, and saw once more the boy's head, this time in the right-hand window.

She might as well go and knock seeing as she was here.

The yard was dark, she had to use her torch to find her way. It looked like a scrap yard, and the house was ramshackle. The panels on the roof were rusty, the paint peeling.

She switched off the flashlight and put it in her bag, and went up to the plain front door. It led into a pitch-black hallway.

"What are you doing here?"

She leaped back, fumbling for the flashlight once more. The voice had come from the right, a boy whose voice was breaking.

"Is there . . . someone . . . there?" she said.

There was a click and the hall lit up. She blinked, momentarily confused. She was surrounded by dark brown paneled walls that seemed to loom over her; the ceiling felt like it was pressing down on her—she put her hands above her head and screamed.

"What on earth's the matter? Take it easy."

The boy was gangly and skinny, and was wearing thick socks. He was pressed against a door bearing the name Gustafsson, his eyes dark, watchful.

"Jesus," Annika said. "You scared me."

"I'm not the son of God," the boy said.

"What?" Annika said, and the angels suddenly started singing *summer-winter desolate longing.* "Oh, just shut up!" she yelled.

"Are you a bit nuts?" the boy said.

She gathered her thoughts, met his gaze. It was inquisitive, and slightly scared. The voices fell silent, the ceiling slid away, the walls stopped throbbing.

"Sometimes," she said, "I just get a bit dizzy."

"What are you doing creeping around here?"

"My name's Annika Bengtzon, I'm a journalist," she said. "I came to see the place my colleague died."

She held out her hand; the boy hesitated, then shook it half-heartedly.

"Did you know Benny?" he asked, pulling his slender fingers away.

Annika shook her head.

"But we wrote about the same things," she said. "I was supposed to meet him yesterday."

The hall went dark again.

"So you're not with the police?" the boy said.

"Can you turn the lights on again, please?" Annika said, hearing the note of panic in her voice.

"You are a bit nuts," the boy said, sterner now. "Unless you're just scared of the dark?"

"Nuts," Annika said. "Turn the lights on!"

The boy pressed the switch and the bulb lit up for another minute or so.

"Look," Annika said. "Could I use your toilet?"

The boy hesitated.

"I can't let crazy women into my flat," he said. "You can understand that, can't you?"

Annika couldn't help spluttering with laughter.

"Okay," she said. "I'll just pee in the hall instead."

He raised his eyebrows, opened the door with the hand that had been resting on the handle.

"But don't tell Mom," he said.

"Promise," Annika said.

The bathroom had vinyl wallpaper from the seventies, decorated with stylized sunflowers. She rinsed her face, washed her hands, ran her fingers through her hair.

"Did you know Benny?" she asked when she emerged.

The boy nodded.

"What's your name, by the way?" Annika said.

He looked at the floor.

"Linus," he said, his voice managing to perform somersaults within the space of just five letters.

"Linus," Annika said, "do you know if anyone in the building saw what happened to Benny?"

The boy's eyes opened wide, he took two steps back.

"So you are police?"

"Is there something wrong with your hearing?" Annika said. "I'm a hack, like Benny. We wrote about the same stuff. The police say that someone ran into him and fled the scene. I don't know if that's true. Do you know if anyone heard anything that night?"

"The police have already been here; they asked the same thing."

"So what did you tell them, Linus?"

His voice went into falsetto when he replied.

"That I hadn't seen anything, of course. I came home when I was supposed to. I don't know anything. You should go now."

He took a step toward her, raising his arms as though he was thinking of pushing her out of the door. Annika didn't move.

"There's a difference between talking to the press and talking to the police," she said slowly.

"I know," Linus said. "When you talk to the press you end up on the front page."

"Anyone who tells us anything can stay anonymous if they want. None of the authorities can ask whom we've spoken to, that's against the law. Freedom of expression, did Benny ever talk about that?"

The boy stood in silence, eyes wide, deeply skeptical.

"If you saw anything, Linus, or know someone who did, that person can tell me, and no one would find out that it was them who said anything."

"Would you believe them, then?"

"I don't know, that depends on what they say, of course."

"But you'd write about it in the paper?"

"Only the information, not who said it, if they didn't want me to."

She looked at the boy, knew that her intuition was right.

"You didn't come home when you were supposed to, did you, Linus?"

The boy shifted his weight from one skinny leg to the other, and gulped, making his Adam's apple jerk up and down.

"When should you have come home?"

"On the last bus; the number 1 stops at 9:36 PM."

"So what did you do instead?"

"There's a night bus as well, the 51, that goes as far as Mefos; it's for the blokes who work shifts at the steelworks . . . I get it sometimes when I'm out late."

"And then you have to walk?"

"Not far, just across the footbridge over the railway and down Skeppargatan . . ."

He looked away and padded through the hall to his bedroom. Annika followed him, and found him sitting on the bed, neatly made with a bedspread and some throw pillows. A few schoolbooks were open on the desk, an ancient computer, but everything else in the room was arranged on shelves or stacked in boxes.

"Where had you been?"

He pulled his feet up beneath him, and sat there cross-legged, looking down at his hands.

"Alex has got broadband; we were playing Teslatron on the net."

"Where are your parents . . ."

"Mom," he interrupted, looking up at her angrily. "I live on my own with Mom."

Looked down again.

"She works nights. I promised not to be out so late. The neighbors keep an eye out, so I have to sneak in if it's late."

Annika looked at the big little boy on the bed, filled for a moment with a hot and uncompromising sense of loss for her own children. Tears came to her eyes; she took several deep breaths through her mouth as she forced them back down.

That's what Kalle will be like in a few years, she thought. Sensitive, smart, cool, puppyish.

"So you took the other bus, the night bus?" she said, her voice trembling slightly.

"The half twelve from the bus station. Benny was on it as well. He knows my mom, everyone knows everyone in Svartöstaden, so I hid right at the back."

"He didn't see you?"

The boy looked at her like she was mad.

"He was pissed out of his head, wasn't he? Otherwise he'd have driven, wouldn't he?"

Of course, she thought, waiting silently for him to go on.

"He fell asleep on the bus," the boy said. "The driver had to wake him up at Mefos. I sneaked out of the back door while they were busy."

"Where did Benny live?"

"Over on Laxgatan."

He gestured vaguely in a direction that Annika couldn't make out.

"And you saw him walking home from the bus stop?"

"Yeah, but he didn't see me. I made sure I stayed behind him, and it was snowing really hard."

He fell silent. Annika was starting to feel hot in her padded jacket. Without saying anything she let it slide off her arms, picked it up and put it on the chair by the boy's desk.

"What did you see, Linus?"

The boy lowered his head even further, twisting his fingers together.

"There was a car," he said.

Annika waited.

"A car?"

He nodded frenetically.

"A Volvo V70, but I didn't know that then."

"When did you find out?"

He sniffed.

"It had reversed back onto the soccer field, you could only see the front half. The front was sticking out from behind a tree."

"So you did notice it, then?"

He didn't answer, knotting his fingers.

"How come you noticed it?"

The boy looked up, his jaw trembling.

"Someone was sitting in the car. There's a yellow streetlight at the crossing and the light was sort of shining on the car. You could see his hand on the wheel, kind of holding it, like this."

The boy held one hand up in front of him, letting it hang in the air above an imaginary steering wheel, his eyes open wide.

"So what did you do?"

"Waited. I didn't know who it was, did I?"

"But you could see it was a V70?"

He shook his head hard.

"Not to start with. Only once it had driven out. Then I could see the lights on the back."

"What about the lights on the back?"

"They went all the way up to the roof; I like the way it looks. I'm pretty sure it was a V70, gold . . ."

"And the man in the car started the engine and drove off?"

Linus nodded, shaking himself to gather his thoughts.

"He started the car and slowly pulled out, then he hit the accelerator."

Annika waited.

"Benny was drunk," the boy said, "but he still heard the car and sort of moved aside, but the car followed him, so Benny jumped the other way, but the car followed him again, and then he was sort of in the middle of the road when the car . . ."

He took a deep breath.

"What happened?"

"There were two thumps, then he flew through the air."

"Two thumps, then Benny was thrown into the air? And landed by the fence up by the soccer field?"

The boy sat in silence for a few seconds, then lowered his head. Annika had to suppress the urge to put her arms around him.

"He didn't land by the soccer field?"

Linus shook his head, wiped his nose with the back of his hand.

"In the middle of the road," he said almost inaudibly. "And the car braked so that all the lights on the back went on—that's when I saw what model Volvo it was. And he reversed slowly, and Benny was lying there, and he drove over him again, and then he sort of aimed for . . . for his head, and then he drove over his face . . ."

Annika felt her stomach turn, and opened her mouth to breathe.

"You're sure?" she whispered.

The boy nodded; she stared at the white of his scalp between the tufts of gelled hair.

"Then he got out, and dragged Benny by the feet up toward Malmvallen . . . sort of brushed him off . . . then got back in his car and turned off into Sjöfartsgatan, down toward the harbor . . ."

Annika looked at the boy with fresh eyes, through a filter of suspicion, revulsion, and sympathy. True? That's disgusting! And, poor boy.

"What did you do after that?"

The boy started to shake, first his hands, then his legs.

"I went . . . went over to Benny, he was lying up there by the fence . . . dead."

He wrapped his skinny arms around his body, gently rocking.

"Part of his head and face were like gone; the ground was wet, his whole back was bent, the wrong way, sort of . . . so I knew that . . . and I just went home, but I couldn't really sleep."

"And you haven't told any of this to the police?"

He shook his head again, wiped away the tears with a trembling hand.

"I told Mom I'd be home by quarter to ten."

Annika leaned forward, putting her hand awkwardly on his knee.

"Linus," she said, "what you've just told me is terrible. It must have been horrific. I really think you should tell another adult, because it's not good for you to go around with this sort of secret."

He pulled away from her hand, backing up against the wall.

"You promised!" he said. "You said I was anonymous."

Annika raised her hands helplessly.

"Hey," she said, "I'm not going to say anything. I'm just worried about you. This is one of the worst things I've ever heard."

She let her hands fall and stood up.

"It's really important that the police hear what you saw, but you know that. You're a smart boy. Benny's death was no accident, and you're the only one who saw it happen. Do you think the murderer should get away with it?"

The boy was staring stubbornly at his lap again.

A thought suddenly occurred to Annika.

"Did you . . . you recognized the man in the car, didn't you?"

The boy hesitated, twisting his fingers.

"Maybe," he said quietly, then suddenly looked at her and said: "What time is it?"

"Five to six," Annika said.

"Shit," he said, leaping up. "It's my turn to cook and I haven't even started."

Then he appeared in the doorway again.

"Mom'll be here any minute," he said anxiously. "You've got to go. Now!"

She pulled on her coat, took a step toward him.

"Think about what I said," she said, trying to smile.

Feeling utterly inadequate, she left the boy alone.

* * *

Thomas could feel himself getting more and more irritated as he tried one code after another on the door of the nursery. The same thing had happened only yesterday, leaving him standing here like an idiot, unable to get in.

"Do you know the code?" he asked his son.

The boy shook his head.

"Mom always does the code," he said.

A moment later the door was unlocked from inside. A woman in her forties with two snotty three-year-olds stepped onto the pavement. He muttered his thanks, held the door open for Kalle and went into the hall.

"It was fun going to the nursery," the boy said.

Thomas nodded absentmindedly, gathering his thoughts. Every time he walked into the nursery he felt like an alien; his wax jacket and briefcase and tie seemed somehow to clash with the sensible shoes and cozy sweaters of the staff. Among the tiny boots and miniature furniture he was a clumsy giant, sweaty and out of place. But mostly it was probably communication that shut him out; he had never managed to join in with the sort of contact the staff had with his children. He couldn't handle sitting and talking about the same drawing for ten minutes: the wire in his veins started tugging and itching after just a few seconds; yes, that's lovely, Ellen, is it a cat? After that he was up and away toward the next thought, the next action.

She was doing some cutting out when he arrived, and enthusiastically showed him the fish and plants she had made for her little sea.

"Shall I help you with your overalls?" he offered.

She looked at him in surprise.

"I can do that on my own," she said, putting away the scissors and paper in their respective places and going off to the cloakroom, a stern little figure with narrow legs and swinging arms.

They took the bus from Fleminggatan, but before they had even got on Thomas realized it was a mistake.

"I want to start playing hockey," Kalle said, as Thomas tried to stop a pensioner with a walker from running over Ellen.

The mere thought of driving his son through the center of the city several times a week made him shudder.

"Don't you think that might be a bit too soon?" he said, hoping to put him off.

"William's started going to Djurgården. They said he was almost too old."

Good grief, Thomas thought.

"Right, Ellen," he said, "up on the seat with you. We're almost there."

"I'm swelting," the little girl said.

"It's sweating," the boy said disdainfully. "You never learn."

"Now, now," Thomas said.

The half kilometer to their home on Hantverkargatan took fifteen minutes. Kalle fell over twice when the driver accelerated hard and then braked sharply to get over the congested junctions on Scheelegatan.

As the sweat ran down his back and the air grew thicker with carbon monoxide and coughed up virus particles Thomas swore that from now on he would ignore party politics and only vote for the party that promised a solution to the traffic in Stockholm.

"Is Mommy home?" his daughter asked once they'd finally got to the second floor of number 32.

"She's in Norrland," Kalle said. "She said so yesterday."

"Is Mommy home?" she asked again, this time turning to Thomas, in the same hopeful tone.

He saw her eyes, so completely trusting, the chubby little cheeks, the rucksack. For a moment the world spun: what have we done? What sort of responsibility is this? How on earth are we going to manage? How are the kids going to survive in this bloody world?

He swallowed hard, leaned over the child, sweeping off her damp woolly hat.

"No, darling, Mommy's working. She'll be home tomorrow. Here, hold your hat while I unlock the door."

"What are we having for tea?" his son wondered.

"Baked elk meatballs with garlic and vegetables."

"Mmh," Ellen said.

"Yummy," said Kalle.

The air in the apartment was stale and slightly pungent. The streetlights below threw quivering blue shadows over the ceiling moldings.

"Can you get the lights, Kalle?"

The children started to take off their outdoor clothes as he went into the kitchen and turned on the lamps and the oven. Annika had prepared frozen meals in plastic tubs so they could heat them in the microwave oven, but he preferred to do it the old-fashioned way.

"Can we play on the computer, Daddy?"

"If you can sort it out yourselves."

"Hooray!" Kalle said, and ran off into the library.

He settled down with the various sections of the morning paper he hadn't had time to read earlier: new terrorist attack in the Middle East, stock market falls, profit warning in the pharmaceutical industry. Suddenly he noticed that the unpleasant smell was much stronger now.

He put the paper down, got up and looked around the kitchen. When he opened the cupboard under the sink the smell practically floored him.

Fish scraps.

At once he remembered that Annika had reminded him to put the rubbish out before she left yesterday morning.

He was bent double, ready to throw up, when his cell phone rang out in the hallway. He quickly shut the cupboard door, pushing it hard to make sure, then went to take the call.

It was a colleague of his from the Association of Local Councils.

"I've got the brochures from the printers," Sophia Grenborg said. "I know you've gone home, but I'm guessing you want to see them straightaway."

It was like champagne corks going off in his brain.

"God, thanks so much for calling," Thomas said. "I'd love to see them. Can you courier a few home to me, Hantverkargatan?"

He went back to the kitchen and opened the window to air the room and get rid of the smell of fish.

"Aha," Sophia said distractedly, as though she was writing something down. "On Kungsholmen, isn't it?"

He told her the door code so the courier could get in.

"They just rang from the department," she went on. "Cramne's wondering if we can bring forward the evening meeting and do it tomorrow instead."

Thomas stopped, looking down into the backyard. He'd miss his tennis.

"Hmm," he said. "My wife's away, back tomorrow afternoon. Next Monday would be much better."

"He was pretty insistent that Monday didn't work for him," Sophia said. "Do you want us to go ahead without you?"

The thought of being left out made him speechless at first, then affronted.

"No," he said quickly, "no, that's all right. Annika should be back soon after five, so seven o'clock will be fine . . ."

"Okay, I'll pass that on. See you tomorrow evening . . ."

He sat down, still clutching the cell, the humming sound of the ventilator in the backyard filtering gently through the gap in the window.

The department, again. This new project was a real stroke of luck. After the investigation into the regional question, which had been a huge success, he had pretty much been able to take his pick among the new jobs at the Association.

It had been Annika who had suggested he look into threats to politicians. There had been other, more prestigious areas that he could have taken over, but she had seen the bigger picture.

"You want to move on," she had said in her usual unsentimental way. "Why piss about with some pretentious project at the Association if you've got a chance to make a load of good contacts in the wider world?"

So he had opted for social openness and access to politicians, and the inbuilt threat inherent in this.

There was a cold draft around his feet; he got up and closed the window.

The reason behind the project was that a survey had shown that one in four local authority heads and one in five committee chairs had suffered either violence or the threat of violence in the course of their political activity. The threats were mostly made by individuals, but threats from racist or xenophobic groups were also relatively common.

The results of the survey led to the formation of a working group to investigate threats and violence aimed at politicians. Besides the Association of Local Councils, the group included representatives from the Federation of County Councils, the National Council for Crime Prevention, the Ministry of Justice, the National Police Board, the Office of the Prosecutor-General, the security police, and several elected members of local councils.

He sat down heavily on his chair, thought about picking up the paper again but decided against it.

The project had no great status within the Association, and several eyebrows had been raised when he chose that one.

The task of the working group was to promote an open and democratic society and come up with suggestions of concrete measures for how elected representatives should behave in exposed situations. Among other things, they were supposed to develop a training course, and hold regional conferences in association with the Office for Integration and the Living History Forum.

He and Sophia from the Federation of County Councils were the conveners, and even though the project had only been running for a couple of months he knew he had made the right choice. The support they had received from the Justice ministry so far had been fantastic.

His dream of getting a government job before he was forty no longer seemed impossible.

Suddenly his cell phone started to vibrate in his hand again. He answered before it had time to ring.

"You ought to be here," Annika said. "I'm driving past the West Checkpoint of the steelworks in Svartöstaden outside Luleå, and it's so beautiful. I'm opening the window now, can you hear the noise?"

Thomas leaned back and closed his eyes, hearing nothing but the noise of a bad line established by a Swedish-American super-capitalist.

"Daddy," Kalle said. "The computer's messed up."

His son was standing in the doorway, wide-eyed and worried.

"Hang on, Annika," he said, taking the phone from his ear and turning to the boy. "I said you had to sort it out for yourselves. Press the button for twenty seconds and wait till the light goes out. Then count to ten and start it up again."

The boy ran out.

"The steelworks?" he said. "I thought you were going to the air base?"

"Yep, I've been there, but I met a young lad who . . ."

"But you'll make it okay?"

"Make what?"

He had no answer. In the silence between them he really could hear the noise in the background, some sort of low rumbling. He felt the distance between them like a deadweight.

"I miss you," he said quietly.

"What did you say?" she yelled above the noise.

He took a quick, silent breath.

"How are you, Annika?" he asked.

"Really good," she replied, too quickly and too firmly. "Have you eaten?"

"The meatballs are in the oven."

"Why don't you do them in the microwave? I put them . . ."

"I know," he interrupted. "Can I call you later? I'm in the middle of things here right now . . ."

Then he was sitting there again holding his cell phone, feeling an irrational anxiety that threatened to turn into anger.

He didn't like Annika going away, it was as simple as that. He didn't deal with it well. He was aware of that, but when he raised the subject with her she became cold and dismissive. He wanted her here beside him so he could make sure everything was all right, that she was safe and happy.

After that terrible Christmas, once the worst of the attention had died down, everything had seemed pretty good. Annika had been quiet and pale but okay. She'd spent a lot of time playing with the children, singing and dancing with them, cutting and glueing. She'd spent a lot of time on the new residents' association, and on a small extension to the kitchen that they could have done now that they'd bought the freehold on the apartment. The thought of the bargain they had got, buying the apartment for less than half the market price, made her childishly excited, but then she had always been broke. He had tried to regard the purchase more soberly, aware that money came and went. Annika never let him forget that he'd lost his last savings on Ericsson shares.

He glanced at the oven, wondering if the food was hot yet, but made no move to take it out.

When Annika started work again she seemed to slip out of reach more and more, becoming distant, unknown. She would stop in the middle of a conversation, her mouth open, eyes staring in horror. If he asked what was wrong she would look at him like she'd never seen him before. It gave him goose bumps.

"Daddy, I can't do it."

"Try one more time; then I'll come and look."

All at once he was quite powerless. He glanced one last time at the paper, realizing that another day of journalistic effort was about to go straight in the recycling.

With limbs heavy as lead he set the table, threw the children's dirty overalls in the washing machine, made a salad, and showed Kalle how to restart the computer.

Just as they were sitting down to eat, the courier arrived with the brochures they were going to discuss and evaluate the following evening.

While the children chattered and made a mess he read through the advice on how threatened politicians should behave. All the way through, and then once more.

Then he thought about Sophia.

Annika switched off the car engine outside the darkened door of the *Norrland News*, and the yellow streetlights threw oblique light on the dashboard.

The time she had spent at home had given Thomas space that he had soon annexed and made his own. In three months he had got used to total service, with the children as accessories, his evenings free for tennis and work meetings, weekends for hunting and hockey trips. Since she had started work again the same division of chores had endured. He criticized her for working, under the pretext that she needed to rest.

In fact, he just wanted to avoid heating up the meals she had prepared, she thought, surprised at how angry the idea made her.

She threw open the car door and stepped onto the snowy street. Leaned into the backseat and pulled out her bag and laptop.

"Pekkari?" she said over the intercom. "It's Bengtzon. There's something I have to talk to you about."

She was let in, and felt her way through the dark entrance hall.

The night editor met her at the top of the stairs.

"What's this about?"

She recoiled from the stale smell of alcohol on his breath, but stood as close as she could and said quietly:

"Benny may have come across something he shouldn't have."

The man's eyes opened wide, the broken veins evidence of genuine sorrow.

"F21?"

She shrugged.

"Not sure yet," she said. "I need to check with Suup."

"He always goes home at five sharp."

"He isn't dead as well, is he?" Annika said.

* * *

She was shown to the desk of the letters editor, where she unpacked her laptop once she had cleared away the neat piles of angry handwritten correspondence. She switched it on as she called the police station; Inspector Suup had indeed left at precisely 5:00 PM.

"What's his first name?" Annika asked.

The duty officer sounded surprised by his own reply.

"I don't actually know."

She heard him call: "Hey, what's Suup's name, apart from Suup?"

Muttering, the scraping of chairs.

"He's down as LG on the files."

She called 118 118 from the phone on the desk, only to find that the number was blocked. It had been the same on the *Katrineholm-Kuriren* too; a subscription to a number service had been too expensive. She pulled the plug out of the back of the phone and connected her laptop instead. Had to change the settings to get a connection, then went in on the *Evening Post*'s server.

On Telia's website she discovered there was no Suup with the initials LG in the phone book for Luleå, Piteå, Boden, Kalix, or Älvsbyn. He could hardly commute farther than that each day, she reasoned. Instead she went into the national census results, which, thank God, were now on the net.

There was a Suup, Lars-Gunnar, born 1941, on Kronvägen in Luleå.

Back to Telia again, Kronvägen in the address box, and voilà! An Aino Suup had two lines at number 19. She signed out, unplugged the lead, and put it back in the phone.

No sooner had she done that than her cell phone rang, and she put a hand to her forehead.

"I'm so fucked up," she said to Anne Snapphane. "Why on earth don't I call from this phone instead?"

"*Que?*" Anne said.

The noises behind her suggested alcohol and minimalist décor.

"Where are you?" Annika asked.

The line crackled and hissed.

"What?" Anne said. "Hello? Are you in the middle of something?"

Annika spoke slowly and clearly.

"I've uncovered the murder of a reporter. Call me at midnight if you're still awake."

She hung up and called the first of Aino Suup's numbers, but reached a fax machine. Called the second and heard the theme music of the evening news.

"So you're the sort of person who disturbs people at home?" Inspector Suup said, not sounding particularly upset.

Like Benny Ekland, Annika thought, shutting her eyes as she asked:

"That Volvo you found in Malmhamnen, was it a V70? Gold?"

The newscaster's reliable tones filled the line for a few seconds, then the volume of the television was suddenly turned down.

"Okay, you've got me really curious now," the inspector said, leaving the subject open.

"There's no leak," Annika said. "I spoke to a potential witness. Is the information correct?"

"I can't comment on that."

"Off the record?"

"Can I switch phones?"

He hung up. Annika waited for an eternity before he picked up again, this time with no television in the background.

"You might have got the duty officer to read out the details of cars stolen from Bergnäset on Saturday night," he said.

"So it's correct, then?"

His silence was all the confirmation she needed.

"Now I'd like you to tell me something," he said.

She hesitated, but only for the sake of it. Without the inspector she didn't have a story.

"I spoke to someone," she said, "who says they saw Benny Ekland get run down on Skeppargatan in Svartöstaden, between Mefos and

Sandgatan. There was a gold-colored Volvo V70 parked in the entrance to the soccer field, the front facing the road, with a man at the wheel. When Benny Ekland stumbled past the engine started, the car pulled out and drove at Ekland at full speed. My witness says Ekland tried to get out of the way, running from one side of the road to the other, but the car followed him. The collision happened more or less in the middle of the road."

"Damn it," the inspector muttered.

"It gets worse," Annika said. "Ekland hit the car twice and was thrown into the air, landing in the middle of the road. The car stopped, reversed, and drove over him again, and then over his head. After driving over his skull the driver stopped, definitely a man, got out of the car and dragged the body up the slope toward the soccer field. There he wiped down the body somehow, then drove off toward . . . what's it called . . . Sjöfartsgatan, down toward LKAB's ore terminal. What was the damage to the car?"

"Front and windscreen," Inspector Suup said without hesitation.

"You must have worked out that this was no ordinary accident: the skull was crushed and his back was broken, all the internal organs mashed up."

"Quite right, the results of the postmortem came through this afternoon. So there was someone who saw the whole thing?"

"The witness wants to stay completely anonymous."

"You can't persuade the person in question to contact us?"

"I've already done what I can, but I'm happy to try again. What do you think?"

"If the witness information is correct, which it may well be, then we'll have a premeditated murder on our hands."

Annika typed the quote directly onto her laptop.

"Can you think of anything off the top of your head that Benny wrote that could explain why someone wanted him dead?"

"Ekland wasn't afraid of controversy and unpleasantness, so it's not impossible. But I wouldn't be doing my job if I speculated like that at this point. If the witness information is correct, and I mean if, then obviously we'd be open to any possible motive."

"Are you in charge of the investigation?"

"No, I'm only the PR guy these days, but I'm the one you need to talk to. The preliminary investigation was allocated to Andersson, in the prosecutor's office, I think, but she's been in court all day so I don't imagine she knows anything about this yet."

When they had hung up Annika found her way to the newsroom. In a narrow room full of long tables and static electricity she found a group of lethargic editors, all white faces and evasive eyes.

"We have to talk," she told the night editor.

With surprising ease the fat man got up and walked ahead of her through the room, past the sports desk, and opened the door to a small space that functioned as the smoking room.

Annika stopped in the doorway; in spite of a rumbling ventilation unit in the corner of the room, the stench was awful. The man lit a cigarette and coughed violently.

"I gave up nine years ago," he said, "but yesterday morning I started again."

She took a step into the room and glanced up at the ceiling, leaving the door ajar. The walls closed in around her, she was having difficulty breathing.

"What's this about?" Pekkari said, blowing a sad little plume of smoke toward the ventilation unit.

"Benny was murdered," Annika said, her heart racing. "I have a witness who saw how he died. The police have confirmed that the witness's story matches what they know so far. Do we have to stay in here?"

The editor stared at her like he'd seen a ghost, holding his cigarette motionless, halfway to his mouth.

"Please?" Annika said, unable to wait, as she pushed the door open and staggered out.

She went over to the other corner of the almost empty sports section; one lone reporter looked up anxiously from his large computer screen.

"Hi," Annika said.

"Hi," the man said, then looked down again.

"Murdered?" Pekkari whispered in her ear. "You're kidding?"

"Not at all. I'll write the article, and you can publish it in its entirety, but you don't get to release it to the agencies. We get to do that."

"Why would you give away something like that?"

"Call it solidarity," Annika said, concentrating on getting her pulse down. "Besides, we don't exactly share the same readers. We're not competitors; we complement each other."

"I'll get our guy onto it," the editor said.

"No," Annika said. "My byline. This is my story, but you can publish it."

He looked at her in astonishment.

"That's one I owe you," he said.

"I know," Annika said, and went back to her laptop.

THURSDAY, NOVEMBER 12

Anne Snapphane woke up with a dull ache in her head and white lights in her eyes. Her mouth tasted disgusting and there was a terrible noise from under the bed. After a long sequence of missed connections, her brain finally worked out that it was the phone ringing. Her hand fumbled clumsily beside the bed and eventually caught the spiral cord of the receiver; she lifted it to her mouth with a groan.

"Have you seen the paper?" Annika said on the other end. "It's fucked. If I didn't have a mortgage I'd resign today. No, make that yesterday."

Her voice had a strange echo, like it was hitting a glass wall somewhere between Anne's ear and her brain.

"What?" Anne said, a croaking sound that bounced off the ceiling.

"*Paula from Pop Factory forced into oral sex,*" Annika read with her echoing voice.

Anne tried to sit up.

"Who?"

"I don't know if there's any point in doing this anymore," Annika said. "I've uncovered the murder of a reporter, possibly with links to terrorism, we're the only ones with the story, and what happens? Radio and television news have led all morning with Benny Ekland, giving us the credit, and what do we decide to run on the front fucking page? A fucking blow job!"

Anne gave up, slumping back onto the pillows, and laid an arm over her eyes. Her heart was thumping like a jackhammer, making her break out in a sweat everywhere all at the same time. A vague feeling of anxiety was turning her stomach.

I shouldn't have had that last one, she thought vaguely.

"Anne?"

She cleared her throat.

"What time is it?"

"Ten or so. And I've come out to that damn museum on the air base again, and do you think the bastard who runs it is back at work? Like fuck he is, so I sat out here like an idiot."

She made no effort to understand, merely accepted that she had lost it. Again.

"That's bad," she agreed.

"Are you coming this evening?"

Anne rubbed her forehead several times, trying to remember what they'd agreed. And failed.

"Can we talk later? I was just . . ."

"I'll be home after five."

She dropped the receiver on the floor, where it lay emitting a dead buzzing sound. Carefully she opened her eyes again, forced herself to look at the empty space beside her.

He wasn't there. Not anymore.

She looked up at the ceiling, then across at the window. Remembering his smell, his laughter.

The gradual realization that he would no longer be with her had left her stiff, dumb, and cold.

They had a deal. They had an agreement.

A wonderful child, a shared life, the perfect mix of freedom and responsibility. No guilt, no demands, just care and support. Separate homes, their daughter spending a week at one, then the other, with a few shared evening and weekends, Christmases, and birthdays.

She had kept her part of the bargain, never let any other bloke get too close.

But then he went and moved in with a radically monogamous woman from Swedish Television who believed in coupledom and true love.

If only the other woman had been different, Anne thought vaguely. If only she'd been nice and petite and blond and pretty and inoffensive. If only he'd picked someone for something I didn't have, but she was the same. Same sort of look, even pretty much the same job.

The sense of betrayal was somehow magnified.

It wasn't because there was anything superficially wrong with her, Anne. No, she was wrong as a person, her attitude to life was wrong, her affections and loyalties.

Tears of self-pity started to bubble up—she forced them back with sheer stubborn willpower.

He wasn't worth it.

Annika was clenching her jaw so hard it hurt.

Wasn't going to cry, not because of this, not because of the stupid priorities of the night shift. It felt like being a trainee again, only worse. Then, more than nine years ago, she had no idea of context, was able to excuse errors of judgment and getting trampled on by management by thinking she obviously hadn't understood. There must have been a higher purpose that she was unaware of, and if she could only concentrate hard enough she'd understand. She had taken pride in being open and willing to learn, not smug, ignorant, and critical like a lot of beginners.

Now she knew, and the knowledge made her paralyzed with impotence.

Sometimes she got the impression that it was just about money.

If it was just as lucrative to sell drugs, the proprietors would have done that instead.

Other days things felt better, she could see the connections in the way she had been taught: commercialism guaranteed freedom of expression and democracy; the newspaper was produced according to the wishes of the readers; and the income secured continued publication.

She eased her rigid grip on the steering wheel, forcing herself to calm down. F21 disappeared behind her as she pulled onto the long straight leading to the main road. She dialed the police station, but Inspector Suup's line was busy, and he already had calls waiting.

It doesn't matter how good I am, she thought, failing to stifle her bitterness. The thought grew and blossomed into a sentence before she could stop it: the truth isn't interesting, only the chimera that it can construct.

To stop herself wallowing in self-pity, and to stay on the line, she started asking the poor and increasingly stressed receptionist a pointless series of questions about the organization of the police station. The trick was to keep talking to the receptionist until the extension was free.

"I can put you in the queue now," the receptionist said when Suup had ended one of his calls.

She was put through to a void somewhere in digital space, but at least it was a silent void. An electronic version of "Für Elise" would have pushed her over the edge.

She had already passed the traffic circle at Bergnäset before there was a click on the line and it was her turn.

"Well, I owe you a debt of thanks," Inspector Suup said. "Linus Gustafsson's mother called us at seven this morning to say that her son is the secret witness in the *Norrland News* today. She said you'd tried to persuade the boy to talk to the police and an adult about what he'd seen; she was pleased about that. She said the boy hadn't been himself since Sunday night, not sleeping or eating properly, not wanting to go to school . . ."

She felt a tentative sense of calm.

"That's good to hear," she said. "What do you think about his story?"

"I haven't spoken to him myself, I've been stuck on the phone since half past five when you released the story to the agencies, but our officers have been at the scene with him and he seems credible."

"Quick work," Annika said, trying to sound impressed.

"They wanted to strike while it was still dark, to get the same conditions as the time of the crime, and before the media storm broke. They seem to have made it."

"And?" she said, braking at a red light just before the Bergnäs bridge.

"Let's just say that the investigation has gone from hit-and-run to premeditated murder."

"Are you going to call in the national murder unit?"

The reply was ambiguous.

"We'll have to see what we turn up after the first day or so . . ."

The traffic light turned green; she slid over the junction with Granuddsvägen.

"Benny had written a whole series of articles on terrorism in recent months," Annika said. "I'm actually on my way back from F21 right now. Do you think his death could have something to do with the article he wrote about the attack out there, or anything else he wrote?"

"I don't want to speculate. Can you hold on a moment?"

He didn't wait for her to reply; there was a dull thud in her ear as the inspector put the phone down and crossed the floor, then the sound of a door closing.

"But on the other hand," he said, back on the line again, "there is something that I've spoke to Captain Pettersson about this morning that concerns you."

She took her foot off the accelerator in sheer shock.

"I don't want to discuss it on the phone," the inspector went on. "Have you got time to come up here this afternoon?"

She shook her arm vigorously to get her watch to slide out of the sleeve of her coat.

"Not really," she said, "my plane leaves at 2:55 PM and I have to get over to the *Norrland News* before that."

"Okay, I'll see you there," he said. "We've got a team there now, and I've just promised that I'd go and talk to them about what we're looking for there."

* * *

The woman in the paper's reception was puffy from crying. Annika approached cautiously and respectfully, well aware that she was disturbing her.

"The paper's closed to visitors," the woman snapped. "Come back tomorrow."

"My name's Annika Bengtzon," Annika said gently. "I'm the one who . . ."

"Is there something wrong with your hearing?" the woman said, getting up, visibly trembling. "We're in mourning today, in mourning, one of our reporters has . . . left us. So we're closed. All day. Go away."

The red cloud over Annika's forehead forced its way into her brain and made it short-circuit.

"For God's sake," she said. "Has everyone gone mad?"

She turned her back on the woman and headed for the stairs to the newsroom.

"Hello!" the receptionist yelled. "This is a private company. Come back."

Annika kept walking, glanced over her shoulder and said, unbeatably:

"So shoot me."

After just a few steps she could hear some sort of memorial service going on upstairs. From the landing outside the main office she could see the participants, a colorless mass of gray hair, dark gray jackets, brown sweaters. Backs bent, sweaty necks, the sort of confused rage that makes people bloodless and mute. Their sighs seemed to suck up all the air, emptying the building of oxygen.

With a deep breath she slid into the back of the room, making herself invisible while simultaneously craning to see whoever was talking at the front.

"Benny had no family," the man said, a middle-aged media type in a dark suit and shiny shoes. "We were his family. He had us, and he had the *Norrland News*."

The people in the room didn't react to the words, each of them consumed by their own shocked disbelief, the impossibility of death. Fumbling hands, eyes glued to the floor or searching restlessly, each of them an island.

Reporters and several photographers stood along the walls, people from other media outlets. She could pick them out by their greedy curiosity; they didn't care. Their interest was focused on the man speaking and the mourners.

"Benny was the sort of journalist that no longer exists," the man in the polished shoes intoned. "He was a reporter who never gave up; he always had to know the truth, whatever the cost. We who had the privilege of working with Benny all these years have been given a great gift, of being able to get to know such a devoted and responsible professional. For Benny there was no such thing as overtime, because he took his work seriously . . ."

"Hmm," someone whispered in her ear, "now we're getting to the truth."

She jerked her head and saw Hans Blomberg, the archivist, standing right behind her, nodding and smiling. He leaned forward and went on in a whisper:

"Benny was popular with management because he never asked for overtime or a raise. And because he earned so little he presented them with the perfect argument: if their star earned so little, surely it was only right that the others did too?"

Annika listened, astonished.

"He broke the pay deal?" she whispered back. "Why?"

"Five weeks' paid holiday with the whores of Thailand every year, and a running tab at the City Pub. What more could a man want?"

Two older women in front of them, with matching sweaters and swollen eyes, turned around and hissed at them to be quiet.

"Where was Benny's desk?" she whispered to the archivist.

"Follow me," he said, and backed out of the room.

They left the gray, airless sea of people and went up to the next floor, up under the roof.

"He was the only one besides the publisher who had his own office," Hans Blomberg said, pointing down a short, narrow corridor.

Annika walked along it, feeling the walls pressing in on her at once, looming over her. She stopped, took a deep breath, and saw the walls as they really were.

Not moving.

The painted panels were indeed bulging slightly where they had come loose, yellow-brown, hideous.

She went up to Benny Ekland's brown-painted door and knocked loudly. To her surprise it flew open at once.

"Yes, what is it?" a plainclothesman said from a kneeling position, blowing his hair from his eyes and looking her up and down in irritation.

Behind him two other officers looked up from cupboards and drawers. Annika took a step backward, feeling herself blush.

"Sorry," she said, "I'm looking for . . . I was wondering . . ."

"This is Benny Ekland's room," the plainclothes officer said, then went on in a more friendly tone: "You're Annika Bengtzon, aren't you? The one who got stuck with the Bomber in the tunnel?"

She stared at him for a couple of seconds, contemplating running away, but nodded. She could hear the angels tuning up at the back of her mind. No! she thought. Not now.

"Suup called and said he was going to meet you here, but he's not here yet. Forsberg," he said, getting up and holding out his hand, giving her a wolfish grin beneath his mane of blond hair.

Annika looked down, bewildered, and realized that her hands were cold and sweaty.

"How's it going," she said, only to have something to say, rubbing her head lightly with one hand to get the voices to shut up.

"Suup said how you got hold of the Gustafsson boy," Forsberg said as he put a bundle of papers back on a shelf.

The policeman sighed.

"This place is a hell of a mess."

"He got quite a bit of mail today," Hans Blomberg said from behind Annika's back. "Have you been through that yet?"

The officers looked at one another, and all shook their heads.

"Where is it?" Forsberg asked.

"I put it in his pigeonhole, like I usually do. Do you want me to get it?"

Annika went with the archivist down to the mail room rather than stay and get in the way of the police.

"You don't seem to have been Benny's biggest fan," she said as Blomberg pulled out the dead man's mail.

"There's no need," the fat man puffed. "There are plenty of others fighting for that accolade. I have a more nuanced view of our star reporter."

He headed toward the stairs again. Annika followed the bobbly cardigan.

"What sort of view would that be, then?"

The man panted as he laboriously climbed the stairs.

"It didn't matter who got who a tip-off here; if there was anything worth having, then Big Ben got his hands on it. He was always the last one here in the evening, so he could go in and change a sentence or two in someone else's article and get a double byline."

"Was that his nickname, Big Ben?"

"Mind you, he was brilliant at digging up stories," Hans Blomberg conceded. "You've got to give him that."

"Annika Bengtzon?" a voice said from below.

She went back down a few steps, leaned over and looked around the corner.

"Suup," said a thin man with gray hair. "Can we have a word?"

She went down and shook the older man's hand; looked into a pair of eyes that for a moment seemed to her to belong to a child, so bright and translucent.

"I promised to talk to the staff in a little while, but this won't take long," he said. The wrinkles in his face emphasized the impression of stability and honesty.

"You're making me very curious," Annika said, going into the letters editor's room where she had written her article the previous evening.

It struck her that he wasn't bitter. He served humanity in a way that he knew was right, and in return he got respect and reassurance that confirmed that his frame of reference was the right one. He was a solid person.

She pulled out a chair for the inspector, then sat down herself on the corner of the desk.

"We appreciate the fact that you came to us with your information yesterday," the man said in a quiet voice. "And I have to say that it came as a surprise to us that you gave away your story. The *Norrland News* comes out much earlier than the *Evening Post* up here, so you weren't first, and it wasn't an exclusive."

Annika smiled, noting that the angels had gone quiet.

"You've spent a long time dealing with the press," she said, "I can tell."

"Which is why I spoke to Pettersson at F21 about some information we've had for years and have been wondering about releasing."

She felt adrenaline slowly start to spread out from the small of her back, up toward her chest.

"For years now we've had a chief suspect for the attack," he said quietly. "A young man who came to Luleå from the south at the end of the sixties, but who was originally from somewhere in the Torne Valley. He was active in a couple of left-wing groups, went under the code name Ragnwald. We've had a couple of different suggestions of his real identity, but we don't know for sure."

Annika sat in silence, staring at the inspector. The astonishing information was making her hair stand on end.

"Do you mind if I take notes?"

"Not at all."

She took out a notebook and pen and scribbled down what the inspector had told her, shaking so much that it was almost illegible.

"What makes you suspect this particular man?" she asked.

"Ragnwald disappeared," Suup said. "We believe he moved to Spain and became a member of ETA. He became a full-time terrorist, and the attack on F21 was his qualification."

There was a knock on the door frame. Inspector Forsberg looked in.

"Sorry, boss, but we've found something pretty weird."

"What?"

"An unsigned letter: bombastic, unclear content."

He cast a look at Annika and fell silent.

She was thinking furiously and trying to look unconcerned.

"Sounds like the usual sort of nutter's letter," she said. "I've got eighteen trash bags full of them."

"Read it out," Inspector Suup said.

Forsberg hesitated for just a second. Then pulled out a sheet torn from a pad of A4 paper, folded in four, which he held carefully with gloved hands.

"*There is no construction without destruction*," he read. "*Destruction means criticism and rejection, it means revolution. It involves reasoning things out, which means construction. If you concentrate on destruction first, you get construction as part of the process.*"

Annika was scribbling furiously, got half the words down. Out of the corner of her eye she saw Forsberg lower the letter.

"Does that ring any bells?" he said.

Annika saw Inspector Suup shake his head and mechanically mimicked his movement.

"We'll be upstairs," Forsberg said, and disappeared again.

"Can I go public with Ragnwald?" Annika asked.

The inspector nodded.

"And it won't mess up any investigation if I write about it?"

"Quite the reverse," Suup said.

Annika looked silently at the policeman, aware that his honesty did not mean that the ends could not justify the means. He could doubtless be pretty sly if he had to be, but that was just part of the job.

"So, why are you telling me?" she said.

The man stood up surprisingly quickly.

"The information is correct insofar as it matches our suspicions," he said. "We don't know if he actually did it, but we believe he was involved; he may even have arranged the whole thing. He must have had accomplices; you know there were footprints found at the site. There aren't many men with size 36 shoes."

This last detail was new.

He left her sitting among the readers' letters about rubbish collections and dog shit, with the distinct suspicion that she had been given more than just a scoop.

Slowly she filled in the letters she had missed in her notes.

There is no construction without destruction.

True enough, she thought.

If you concentrate on destruction first, you get construction as part of the process.

God knows.

The taxi drivers' voices by the entrance cascaded after her as she walked through the small airport, making her feel slightly hunted. Didn't they ever work? Maybe they just stood in the warm air coming out of the doors, protected against the arctic cold in their dark blue uniforms and gold buttons?

She got a seat at the back of the plane, next to a woman with two young children. The woman had one of them on her lap, while the other clambered about the cabin.

Annika felt the stress rising beyond every tolerance level: this was her only chance to get anything written.

"Excuse me," she said to the stewardess once they were in the air. "I have to work. Is it okay if I move forward a bit?"

She stood up and gestured a few rows ahead in the half-empty cabin. The toddler in its mother's lap started to scream in her ear.

"You're booked into this seat, so I'm afraid you can't move. You should have booked business class," the stewardess said curtly and turned back to her drinks trolley.

"I'm sorry," Annika said, louder this time, "but I did. Or rather my employer did. Can I move, please?"

She struggled past the mother and blocked the aisle. The stewardess squeezed past the trolley with irritated little steps.

"You heard what I said. After September 11, you can't just change seats."

Annika took a long stride closer to the stewardess, talking right in her face.

"So throw me off," she whispered, taking her laptop from the overhead locker and moving five rows forward.

With stress raging through her veins she wrote three articles before the plane touched down at Arlanda: Luleå the day after the murder announcement, the sorrow of his coworkers, and the police questioning of the witness at the crime scene. The night crew would have to put together the overview and factual boxouts. She held back the details about Ragnwald and the F21 attack—she wasn't going to let go of them that quickly.

She hurried across the slate floor of Terminal 4 and disappeared underground with her heart racing. She called Spike from the Arlanda Express and gave him an update; then he put her through to Pelle on the picture desk so they could talk about illustrations. The newly established collaboration with the *Norrland News* gave the *Evening Post* full access to the whole of their picture archive, new and old alike, which saved them having to send someone up or use a freelancer.

"Hmm, you're not going to find picture of the year among this lot," the pictures editor said, as Annika heard him clicking through the transferred material, "but they'll do for tomorrow's edition. At least some of them are decent resolution, and even in focus."

With her coat flapping, she walked from the Central Station to the place her six-year-old spent his days. The wind was damp and full of odors, soil and leaves and car fumes, the grass was still green, and half-dead leaves still clung to a few branches. The light from a million lamps overpowered the Nordic autumn evening, giving the illusion that reality could be controlled, tamed.

There are never any stars in the city, she thought.

Annika's son threw himself at her as if she had been away six months. Pressed his sticky face against hers and ran his fingers through the hair at the back of her neck.

"I missed you, Mommy," he said in her ear.

She rocked the boy in her arms, stroking the stiff little back, kissing his hair.

Hand in hand they walked off to Ellen's nursery school, until the boy pulled himself free and ran the last ten meters to the door, happily greeting Lennart and Helena who were on their way home.

Ellen was tired and reserved when she came over, didn't want to go home, didn't want a hug. Wanted to carry on cutting out pictures, Daddy would pick her up.

Annika clenched her jaw to stop herself exploding, noting that her boundaries had evaporated.

"Ellen," she said firmly, "Kalle and I are going now."

The girl stiffened, her face contorted, eyes wide open, and a desperate cry came out.

"My oversall," she screamed. "I haven't got my oversall!"

She dropped the scissors and ran over to where her outdoor clothes were hanging below a picture of her taken that summer at her grandparents' country cottage on Gällnö, and searched frantically through the clothes, trying to pull on the overall.

Annika could sense the disapproving stares of two other mothers farther down the corridor.

"Well, come on now," she said, going over to her daughter. "I'll help you, but you've got to stop being cross."

"It's called an overall," Kalle said.

On the way home Ellen let out occasional little sobs.

"We go on the bus with Daddy," the boy said as they stood huddled on a traffic island at the traffic lights on Kungsholmsgatan.

"It's too crowded and hot on the bus," Annika said, feeling suffocated by the very thought of it.

She had to carry Ellen from Bergsgatan. Once they were home, she quickly lit a fire in the stove to force the cold back from the drafty windows, and ran down to the yard with the stinking bag of rubbish, her hands and legs moving without her active participation. Then she put the rice on as she fished her laptop out of her bag and turned it on, switching the cable from the phone in the kitchen, and putting a pack of cod into the microwave to defrost.

"Can we play on the computer, Mommy?"

"It's Daddy's computer."

"But Daddy lets us. I know how to start it."

"Watch *Bolibompa* instead; it'll soon be on," she said, connecting to the paper's server.

The boy went off, shoulders drooping. She cut the cod into slices as her laptop signed in, turned the slices in salt and flour, then put them in a heavy pan with a bit of melted butter in the bottom. She listened to the frying sound as she sent over the three articles, then splashed some lemon juice over the fish, dug out some frozen dill and scattered that over the top, then poured in some cream, warm water, fish stock, and a handful of frozen prawns.

"What are we having for dinner, Mommy," Ellen said, looking up at her from under her fringe.

"Darling," Annika said, leaning over to pick her daughter up. "Come here, come and sit up here."

Her daughter cuddled into her lap, put her arms around her neck.

"Oh, sweetie," Annika said, rocking her, breathing into her hair. "Are you hungry?"

The girl nodded hesitantly.

"We're having fish in cream sauce with rice and prawns; you like that, don't you?"

She nodded again.

"Do you want to help me make the salad?"

A third nod.

"Okay," Annika said, putting her on the floor and pulling a chair over to the countertop next to the stove. "Have you washed your hands?"

The girl ran into the bathroom; there was the sound of running water, and Annika suddenly felt giddy.

She took out an apron and a fruit knife, tied the strings behind Ellen's back, showed her how to hold the knife. She let her cut some cucumber while she dealt with the lettuce and a handful of tomatoes. Poured over some olive oil, balsamic vinegar, and some Italian salad herbs, and let Ellen toss the salad.

"Brilliant!" she said, putting the bowl on the table. "Can you lay the table? You know how it goes, don't you?"

"You're missing Björne," Kalle yelled from the television room, and the girl dropped the cutlery and ran off. Annika noted how filthy her socks were as she ran out.

Then came the sound of the front door being unlocked; she heard the children's jubilant cries and the noise of Thomas's briefcase being dropped on the bench in the hall.

"Hello," he said as he came into the kitchen and kissed her on the forehead. "Who have you been talking to?"

She reached up on tiptoe to kiss him on the lips, wrapping her arms around his neck and holding him close. For some reason the image of Forsberg, the police officer, popped into her head.

"I haven't been talking to anyone," she said to her husband's neck.

"You've been engaged for half an hour."

She let go of him abruptly.

"Shit," she said. "I'm still online."

Hurried to the laptop, pulled out all the wires, and plugged the phone back in.

"We can eat straightaway," she said.

"I don't want anything," Thomas said. "We've got a meeting with the department this evening so I'll be eating with the working group."

Annika stopped, the pan of fish in her hand.

"I thought you were playing tennis tonight," she said, bewildered.

She was burning her fingers in spite of the oven gloves, and quickly put the pan down on the trivet.

"The bloke from Justice wants a quick run-through over a bite to eat."

"You could have a bite with us first," Annika said, pulling out a chair for Ellen.

She looked up at her husband, saw him sigh soundlessly, and put the rice on the table.

"Kalle," she called toward the television room. "It's ready!"

"But I want to watch this," the boy shouted back.

She spooned out rice and fish for Ellen, and put the salad next to her.

"Ellen made the salad," she announced to the room in general. "You can help yourself, can't you?"

Then went into the television room and switched off the set, making her son howl with annoyance.

"Stop that," Annika said. "Food before television, you know that. Go and sit down."

"What are we having?"

"Fish stew with rice and prawns."

The boy made a face.

"Prawns, yuk."

"You can pick them out. Hurry up, before it gets cold."

Thomas was eating contentedly when she went back into the kitchen.

"How is it?" she asked, sitting down opposite him.

"The prawns are a bit tough," he said. "You always put them in too early."

She said nothing, merely helped herself to the food, realizing that she wouldn't be able to eat a single mouthful now.

Thomas pulled his woolly hat down over his ears as he left the building, and took a deep breath of the cold air. He was full to the point of bursting, a feeling he had come to appreciate more and more.

The good life, he thought vaguely. Pleasure and love, on every level.

He stretched his limbs, confident, calm.

It was good to have Annika back. Everything was so nice and comfortable when she was home, and she was so much better with the kids.

They had it pretty good.

He stopped outside the door with his briefcase, not sure if he should take the car. They were meeting on Södermalm, at a bar on Hornsgatan where they could get a separate room. They'd probably have wine, and he'd either have to stay sober or take a chance on driving home. On the other hand, it was Thursday, the night the street was cleaned, so he'd have to move it anyway.

He turned left, then left again into Agnegatan.

Hope the bastard starts, he thought, opening the door of the Toyota with a rough tug.

He was so pissed off with the car. It was already old when he met Annika, but she refused to take a loan out against the apartment so they could buy a new one.

"I take public transport," she said. "That's good enough for you as well. Only idiots insist on driving in this city."

She was quite right about that, though that wasn't the fault of drivers, but the politicians.

He drove along Hornsgatan. The street was supposed to be closed to cars, but he did it anyway.

Naturally, the streets around Zinkensdamm were due to be cleaned that night as well. With a sinking heart and a rising pulse he drove around trying to find a street that wasn't going to be cleaned that had any parking spaces left. Nothing.

He stopped right outside the bar. Annika would go mad if she found the parking fine charged to their shared account, so he'd have to remember to pay it in cash.

He stood for a moment, checking out the bar.

A dive, he thought. Just a cheap lousy bar.

He sighed, pulled off his hat and stuffed it in his coat pocket, took out his briefcase and went in.

The bar was smoky and noisy, with some sort of generic mainstream rock on the speakers and dartboards on the walls. Old ads for various beers were evidently meant to strike a cultural note. A jukebox glowered silently from one corner.

"Thomas, over here!"

Sophia Grenborg was sitting in a booth to the right of the bar, and he headed gratefully toward her. Greeted his colleague warmly, feeling only a small pang of guilt. Three years ago they had applied for the same job. He had got it, even though she was better qualified. Whenever they had met over the years since then he always felt slightly guilty, which made him act more than usually friendly.

"Where's Cramne?" he asked, pulling off his wax jacket.

"He's not here yet," Sophia said, moving to make space on the bench. "I wonder what was going through his mind when he arranged to meet in a place like this."

He burst out laughing; he'd been thinking exactly the same thing. He settled down next to her, noting that she was drinking beer. She followed his gaze, shrugged, and smiled.

"Seemed to make sense here," she said.

He raised a hand and stopped a young waiter and ordered a large glass of beer.

"What do you think of the brochure?" she said.

Thomas pulled up and opened his briefcase and put a pile of papers on the table, the leaflet at the top.

"It's pretty much okay," he said, putting the briefcase back down. "There are a few things that got a bit woolly in the last version, though. We have to spell out exactly what politicians should do if they're threatened, not to frighten them, just so they take it seriously and think about it. Maybe give a few statistics on how they usually behave, and some figures from the National Council for Crime Prevention."

This was basically what Annika had said when she looked

through the brochure just before he set out. Sophia blinked, seemed quite impressed. He puffed out his chest.

"That makes a lot of sense," she said. "Can I note that down?"

He gave a short nod, looking around for the man from the department, then turned his attention to his beer.

"Something else I was thinking," Sophia went on, as she wrote in her notebook. "What do you think of doing a more general survey? Find out what the public think about violence against their democratically elected representatives?"

He looked at her, aware that he hadn't been listening.

She put her pen and notebook in her bag.

"I mean," she said, "what values do we apply to attempts to silence politicians? Shouldn't we find out?"

Thomas frowned, hiding his enthusiasm.

"You mean we should look at how people relate to the phenomenon?"

"Yes," she said, leaning forward, "and at the same time see how we can change those opinions by an awareness campaign."

He nodded slowly.

"Maybe we could get some support in the press," he said. "Get a debate going, influence people's opinions the old-fashioned way."

"Yes!" she said with enthusiasm. "Get the PR department involved, speed up press releases."

"A series of articles about our new heroes," Thomas said, seeing the headline in his mind. "The local politician battling right-wing extremists and anarchists in his small town."

"But without exaggerating the threat and scaring off the people starting out in politics," Sophia said.

"Are you the ones having the meeting about democracy?" the young waiter said as he put the glass of beer down on Thomas's papers.

Quick as a flash Thomas lifted the glass, but he was too slow to stop a ring of bubbles soaking into the proposal for clearer guidelines.

"Cramne rang," the waiter continued, "he asked me to tell you he can't make it tonight. That'll be thirty-two kronor."

He stood there expectantly, waiting to be paid for the beer.

Thomas felt himself getting angry for several reasons at once, bubbling over like the head on the beer that was dripping onto his hands and trousers.

"What the fuck?" he said. "What is this?"

Sophia straightened up and leaned toward the waiter.

"Did Cramne say why?"

The young man shrugged, shifting impatiently as he waited to be paid.

"Just that he couldn't make it, and that I should tell you. And he said you were welcome to go down and eat, and he'll pay the bill next time he comes in."

Thomas and Sophia looked at each other.

"Per Cramne lives upstairs," the waiter said, pointing with his pen. "Fifth floor. And he's in here about as many times a week. We have a table reserved in the restaurant, down the narrow staircase behind the toilets."

Thomas took out exactly thirty-two kronor from his wallet, then put it and all his papers back in his briefcase.

"I don't have time for this," he said, getting ready to stand up.

The waiter disappeared.

"We could go through what this sort of survey might look like," Sophia said. "Seeing as we're already here. And see if we could simplify the advice about threats. That's the most important thing, after all. That politicians feel more secure in their posts, and know how to deal with threats and violence."

"I canceled my tennis for this," Thomas heard himself say, sounding like a disappointed child.

"And I canceled my salsa class. We could at least let the government pay for dinner to make up for it."

He relaxed and smiled back at her.

* * *

Anne Snapphane was breathing hard in the stairwell, looking up at its curved shape, slowly calmed by the gentle curves of the wall. It was so far to the second floor, and she felt very unsteady.

She stopped on the next landing, peering out through the tinted glass at the courtyard. There was a light in Annika's old window in the little house down there.

Picturesque, and yet so cramped. She couldn't put up with living in the city again, she realized, just as she realized that this hangover really wasn't any fun.

The doors of Annika's apartment were tall as church doors, heavy as stone. She knocked cautiously, conscious that the children had only just gone to bed.

"Come in," Annika said quietly, backing into the hall. "I've just got to say good night to Kalle, then I'll be with you."

Anne sank onto the bench in the hall and pulled the too-tight shoes off her feet. She could hear Annika laugh and the boy giggle, and sat there with her outdoor clothes on until her forehead began to itch under her hat.

Then she went into the living room with all the ornate plaster detailing, slumped onto the sofa, and leaned her head back.

"Do you want coffee?" Annika said as she came into the room with a plate of macaroons.

The thought was enough to make Anne's stomach churn.

"Have you got any wine?"

Annika put the plate down.

"Thomas has," she said, "but he's so fussy about it. Don't take any of the fancy stuff, it's . . ."

She gestured toward the glass cabinet.

All of a sudden it was easy to stand up; Anne's feet scarcely touched the floor as she glided toward the wine rack. Turned the bottles, read the labels.

"Villa Puccini," she said. "That costs eighty-two kronor a bottle and is completely wonderful. Can we have that?"

"Why not?" Annika said from the hall.

With a practised hand Anne soon had the foil off and pulled the cork out so hard that she splashed her top. Her hands trembled slightly as she took a crystal glass from the shelf below and poured out the dark-red liquid. The taste was divine, full-bodied and round and healthy all at the same time; she took several large gulps. Filled the glass again, then stood the bottle back in the cupboard. Then she settled into one corner of the sofa, pulling out one of the occasional tables for her glass. Suddenly life seemed much simpler.

Annika walked into the living room, breathing out. Once the children were in bed it always felt as though a huge weight had lifted. She no longer had to rush around like a mad thing, but slowing down meant that everything caught up with her. Her thoughts came back; she started to feel empty again. The apartment became a desert to wander aimlessly across, a stuccoed and ornately paneled prison.

She sank into the other corner of the sofa, her body light and head empty, aware that she was cold. She pulled her knees up, forming a tight ball, and looked at her friend. She could see that Anne was a bundle of nervous anxiety, from her drawn features, and the fevered search for something that could put the world in its place again. She knew that Anne wouldn't find it. In contrast, Annika had learned the trick of abstaining, of shutting off, of waiting for things to balance out again.

Anne was working her way through Thomas's wine in deep gulps.

"I can understand your frustration," she said, glancing at Annika as she put her glass down. "Even I don't remember Paula from Pop Factory."

Annika pointed at the cookies, pushed a few stray crumbs around with her finger, wondering if she could manage a bite. She gave up, leaned back into the sofa, and closed her eyes.

"I have to choose my battles," she said, "otherwise I run out of energy. Going and making a fuss in front of Schyman would be shooting myself in the foot. No, thanks, not this time."

"Trust me, you really wouldn't want my job," Anne said. "I can promise you that much."

They sat listening to the background sounds for a moment. Through the noise of the number 3 bus on the street below, dark shadows crept across the corners, rising and falling.

"I just need to check the news," Annika said, reaching for the remote. The shadows withdrew with a hiss.

The television flickered into life, and Anne stiffened.

"Mehmet's new monogamous fuck is a news editor there," she said.

Annika nodded without taking her eyes from the screen.

"So you said," she said. "Hang on a moment."

She turned up the volume. Over the beat of the theme music the newscaster read out the headlines in verbless sound bites: "Suspected murder of a journalist in Luleå, 4,000 laid off at Ericsson, new library proposals from the ministry of culture, good evening, but first the Middle East, where a suicide bomber has this evening killed nine young people outside a café in Tel Aviv . . ."

Annika lowered the volume to a murmur.

"Do you think it's serious, then, Mehmet and this one?"

Anne took a gulp of wine, swallowing audibly.

"She's started picking Miranda up from nursery," she said, her voice flat and peculiar.

Annika thought for a moment, trying to imagine how that would feel.

"I couldn't handle that," she said, "another woman looking after my children."

Anne pulled a face.

"I haven't got much choice, have I?"

"Do you want more children?"

Annika heard the loaded subtext of her question, as if she had been steeling herself to ask it. Anne looked up in surprise, and shook her head.

"I want to be an individual," she said. "Not a function."

Annika raised her eyebrows.

"That's the whole point," she said. "Becoming part of something that's bigger than your usual human inadequacies, something more important. Voluntarily giving up your freedom for someone else, that never happens anywhere else in our culture."

"I've never thought of it like that," Anne said, taking another drink. "But when you put it like that, that was one of the reasons why I didn't want to live with Mehmet. Being alone with my thoughts is vital, otherwise I'd go mad."

Annika knew that Anne thought she had never understood the way she and Mehmet had lived, never realized how well it worked until it suddenly collapsed.

"But being an egotist doesn't necessarily make you any truer to yourself," Annika said, then realized how harsh her words sounded. "I mean, we have to deal with any number of things every day. Not just kids, but jobs, sports, anything. How many people get to go around being individuals in their jobs, how much could I be Annika Bengtzon if I was in the national ice hockey team?"

"I knew there was a reason why I hate sports journalists," Anne muttered.

"But seriously," Annika said, leaning forward. "Being part of a context is vital, having a function that's bigger than us individually. Why else would people be attracted to sects and other groups of nutters if there wasn't something really appealing about it?"

"I don't like sects either," Anne said, taking another gulp of wine.

The conversation faded. The low buzz from the television made Annika's scalp itch. She leaned back in the sofa again, their silence making the air cold.

"What was the response to the press conference?" she asked, to break the chill.

Anne put the glass down on the table and rubbed her temples with her fingers.

"The bosses in New York don't give a damn about local criticism, as they call it, so I've decided not to care either. People can bark at us all they like, but they can't make us shut up."

An image of Svartöstaden filled the screen behind the newscaster, and Annika turned the sound up again.

"Police have confirmed that the death of journalist Benny Ekland is being treated as suspected murder, and that he was killed by a stolen Volvo V70."

"They haven't come up with anything new," Annika said, lowering the volume again.

"He was murdered by a Volvo?" Anne asked, putting her hands down again.

"Didn't you read my article?"

Anne smiled briefly.

"There's been so much . . ."

"I can't understand why everyone's so worked up about your channel," Annika said. "Why can't the others just use the same digital network?"

"Well," Anne said, picking up her empty glass, "they can, but they've invested billions in satellites and their own cable networks. We're a damned big threat to the whole of their income. They'll do whatever they can to crush us."

Annika shook her head, stood up and went out toward the kitchen.

"Do you want some water?"

"No, I'd like some more wine," Anne called after her.

The passageway to the kitchen was dark and full of silent sound. In the kitchen the subdued lighting of the exhaust fan looked like a camp fire from a distance. The water sloshed in the dishwasher, sending cascades up against its stainless-steel walls.

She poured two large glasses of water, even though Anne didn't want any.

When she came back her friend was still sitting in the sofa with her empty wineglass in her hand. The alcohol had made her face relax.

"I think you're wrong," Annika said, putting the glasses on the table between them. "The owners of the *Evening Post* are renowned for protecting freedom of speech, and they've been dealing with this sort of public-interest issue for a century now."

"Out of the goodness of their hearts?" Anne Snapphane said, slurring her words slightly. "It's made them rich, hasn't it? And there are more of them with every passing year. They need the income from their TV investments, believe me."

"But they've got so many other businesses," Annika said. "What makes you think they care so much about the television channels?"

"Look at their publishing interests," Anne said. "They publish thousands of books each year and never get to the top of the charts. All their newspapers apart from the *Evening Post* are hemorrhaging money. And they're selling or shutting down their radio stations."

Her eyes were drawn to the silent television, and Annika followed her gaze and suddenly saw the broad, dark figure of the minister of culture fill the screen. She turned up the sound.

"From July 1, every council district will be obliged to have at least one public library," Karina Björnlund, the minister of culture, announced, her gaze fluttering about. "This new libraries law is a great step toward equality."

She nodded emphatically on the screen, and the unseen reporter was evidently expecting her to go on. Karina Björnlund cleared her throat, leaned toward the microphone and said: "For knowledge. Equality. Potential. For knowledge."

The reporter withdrew the microphone with his gloved hand and said: "Doesn't this initiative tread on the toes of local accountability?"

The microphone came back in the shot, as Karina Björnlund bit her lip.

"Well," she said, "this is an issue that has been debated over many years, but we are proposing new state subsidies of 25 million kronor for the purchase of books for public and school libraries."

"God, she's mad, isn't she?" Annika said, turning the volume down again.

Anne raised her eyebrows, seemingly unconcerned.

"I don't understand why you're so against it," she said. "That proposal she's talking about is what's making my channel possible."

"She should never have been made a minister," Annika said. "Something went wrong after the whole Studio Six business. She was only the trade minister's press secretary back then—Christer Lundgren, you remember him . . . ?"

Anne frowned, thinking hard.

". . . and she didn't make a very good press secretary either, and then she gets to be minister of culture after the election."

"Aah," Anne said, "Christer Lundgren, the minister everyone thought killed that stripper."

"Josefin Liljeberg, exactly. Even though he didn't do it."

They sat in silence again, watching Karina Björnlund talk soundlessly. Annika had an idea of why the press secretary had become a minister, and suspected that she herself, entirely innocently, had been a contributing factor to her appointment.

"Do you mind if I turn it off?" she asked.

Anne shrugged. Annika considered getting up and fetching something else, anything else, to eat or drink or look at, something to consume, but she stopped herself, gathered her thoughts, allowed the gray anxiety to wash over her, and hopefully go away.

"I got a load of really sensitive information from a policeman in Luleå today," she said. "About a bloke from the Torne Valley who probably blew up that plane at F21 and went on to become an international terrorist. What would make anyone leak that after thirty years?"

Anne let the words sink in.

"Depends on what the policeman said," she replied. "I don't suppose he was stupid, so there's a reason behind the leak. What do you think he was after?"

Annika played with her glass of water, waiting for the grayness to pass.

"I've been wondering that all day," she said. "I think the terrorist has come back, and the police want him to know that they know."

Anne frowned, then her gaze cleared, intoxication fading.

"Isn't that a bit of a long shot?" she said. "Maybe they want to scare someone who knows him. His old friends. Warn political groups, left and right alike, against God knows what. You can't possibly know what the police's motives are."

Annika took a sip of water, swallowed with difficulty, then put the glass down. Decided to break up the shadows herself.

"The officer said he's checked with the press officer at the air base, which means the military have discussed it, so this is something they've been planning for a while. But why now, and why me?"

"Well, I don't know why now," Anne said, "but why you is pretty obvious, isn't it? How many famous crime reporters are there on Swedish papers?"

Annika thought in silence for a few seconds, as an emergency vehicle drove past outside.

"But what if this has something to do with the murder of that journalist. It all fits too neatly."

"Well, it's not impossible," Anne said. "Are you going to run the story?"

Annika sighed, echoing the fire engine.

"I suppose so," she said, "although it's up to Schyman to decide. I think he's starting to get tired of me."

"Maybe you're just getting tired of him," Anne said, taking a macaroon.

Annika's face was impassive; she pulled her knees up to her chin and wrapped her arms around her legs.

"I just want to be left to get on with my job."

The young waiter put two gins and tonic on the table and removed the coffee cups and cognac glasses, replaced an almost finished candle and emptied the ashtray.

"The kitchen closes at ten, but the bar is open till one, so just say if you'd like anything else."

Then vanished silently up the thickly carpeted staircase.

"Who knew that this was here!" Sophia smiled, throwing her arms out.

Thomas couldn't help laughing. The atmosphere in the cellar of the bar was almost surreally oriental, the walls and floor covered in layer upon layer of thick, dusty carpets, gleaming bronze dishes piled in the corners, oil lamps on low stone tables. They were alone, facing one another across a large oak table on heavy leather chairs. The ceiling consisted of vaulted brickwork that appeared to be seventeenth century.

"These old brick buildings hold a lot of secrets," Thomas said, embarrassed that he was slurring his words.

"You live on Kungsholmen?" Sophia asked, looking at him over the rim of the gin glass.

He nodded, sipping his drink.

"Old stove," he said, "lots of ornate plasterwork, creaking parquet floors, the lot."

"Your own?"

"These days. We bought out the tenancy a year ago. What about you?"

Sophia lit a menthol cigarette, sucking in the nicotine, and blew the smoke out in small rings.

"Östermalm," she said. "My family own a building there."

He raised his eyebrows, impressed, but she lowered her eyes and smiled.

"We've had it for generations," she said. "Mine's small, only three rooms; there are other members of the family who need the fancy rooms more than me."

He took a handful of the peanuts that had been on the table since they started.

"You live alone?"

"With Socks, my cat. Named after the Clintons' cat, if you remember . . ."

He laughed, of course. Socks in the White House.

"And you've got a family?" she said, putting her cigarette out.

Thomas pushed his chair back a bit.

"Yep," he said happily, crossing his hands on his stomach. "Wife, two kids. No cat, though . . ."

They laughed.

"Does your wife work?" Sophia asked, sipping her drink.

He let out a deep sigh.

"Far too much."

She smiled, and lit another cigarette. The silence between them grew like a soft deciduous tree full of promise, trembling leaves, and sunlight. Summer, all warmth and peace, was alive and well in their oriental cellar.

"She spent a while at home last winter," he said, more somber now. "That was great. It suited the children, it suited me. It even suited the apartment, we renovated the kitchen and even managed to keep it clean."

Sophia had leaned back in her chair and folded her arms. He could see the look in her eyes, and realized the effect his words had had.

"I mean," he said, swallowing more gin, "I don't mean women should be housewives and just stand by the stove and have babies, nothing like that; of course, women should have the same opportunities for education and careers as men, but there are loads of nice jobs in journalism. I don't see why she insists on writing about violence and death for a tabloid."

All of a sudden he could hear his mother's voice in his head, words she had never said but he knew she was thinking:

"Because that's what she is. A tabloid person who attracts trouble. You're too good for her, Thomas, you could have found a good woman."

"She's a good woman," he said out loud. "Intelligent, but not very intellectual."

Sophia looked at him, her head to one side.

"The two don't have to go together," she said. "You can be talented without being well read."

"Exactly," Thomas said, taking a large gulp of gin. "That's exactly it. Annika's incredibly smart. The problem is that she's so damn unpolished. Sometimes she goes about things like a bulldozer."

Sophia covered her mouth with her hands and giggled; he looked at her in surprise, then started laughing as well.

"But it's true!" he said, then got serious again. "She is pretty unusual, in all sorts of ways. Never lets go once she's decided to do something."

Sophia had stopped laughing and was looking at him sympathetically.

"It must be hard to live with that sort of stubbornness," she said.

Thomas shook his head slowly, emptying his glass.

"My mother can't stand her," he said, putting the glass down. "She thinks I married beneath me, that I should have stayed with Eleonor."

Sophia looked quizzically at him.

"My first wife," he said. "She was a bank director. Is a bank director. She's remarried now, with the only IT guru who landed on his feet. Last I heard, they'd bought their own island outside Vaxholm."

The tree of silence spread its boughs above them, mature, calm. They sat in silence and looked at each other as her cigarette burned away in the ashtray.

"We may as well share a taxi," Sophia said. "We're more or less going in the same direction."

The boy stopped in the door of the bus and swallowed hard. He leaned forward to look at the road, the wind blowing sharp ice crystals into his face. There was a smell of fumes and iron.

"Are you getting off or what?"

He looked sheepishly at the bus driver, took a quick breath, jumped the two steps and landed on the pavement. The door closed behind him with a hiss, the bus glided away with a muffled noise caused by cold and snow.

It disappeared into Laxgatan, the sound drowning behind

heaps of snow and fencing. He stood there on the pavement, looking carefully around him, listening hard. He couldn't even hear the ironworks.

He forced himself to breathe out, calm down. There was no reason to be frightened.

He spat in the snow.

Shit, soon he'd be as nervous as that reporter from Stockholm. She was really jumpy. They'd read her article in the *Norrland News*, and he'd shown Alex how she behaved in the hallway.

"It's her," Alex had said. "The one who was held hostage by the Bomber, you know. Probably left her a bit funny in the head afterward."

He hadn't been much good at the game tonight, not really on form. He was actually really good at it, much better than Alex, but this evening he'd been zapped to ash by several other players. He was annoyed that he'd blown his stats; he kicked away a lump of ice so hard it made his foot hurt. Might be just as well to start again with a new character. Cruel Devil would never be a Teslatron God with useless results like this to make up for. Ninja Master, maybe, but he was aiming for the top.

He slowly walked out of the yellow circle of the streetlight, heading for the house. There were lights on in Andersson's flat, blue light seeping into the darkness, the old man was probably watching the sports news.

Suddenly a shadow fell over the façade of the building, a flashing demon that gasped and disappeared. The boy struggled for breath, so hard that it froze his throat. He felt his muscles tense, his legs ready for flight. Eyes and ears open to the darkness, absorbing every trembling nuance.

Still not a sound. Blue light from Andersson's window. Icy chill from the ground that was slowly working its way through the soles of his shoes.

Nothing. Someone went past a window somewhere.

He forced his shoulders down again, realizing that he hadn't breathed for a minute or so. Started panting in a loud rattle, feeling the tears rise.

Fucking shit, the boy thought, fucking damn shit.

Without thinking anymore, he gave in to his fear and raced blindly toward the door. It was just as dark as usual in the yard, but he knew where Andersson left his scrap and crossed the hazardous path with ease.

He yanked open the outer door and hit the button to light up the hall with damp gloves. His whole body was shaking as he dug for the door key in his jacket pocket.

The door fell open just as he realized he was about to wet himself. Letting out a small whine, he rushed into the bathroom and yanked up the toilet lid.

He shut his eyes and sobbed as the warm urine landed more or less in the toilet. Afterward he just pulled up his pants and sat down on the toilet, leaving his trousers and long johns in a puddle around his feet. The sunflowers smiled down at him from the wallpaper.

Why had he got so scared, like a little kid? He snorted at his own behavior, he'd never been scared of the dark before.

Slowly he stood up, flushed, washed his hands and rinsed his mouth. He couldn't be bothered to brush his teeth tonight. He kicked off his trousers, gathered up his clothes, and went into his room.

There was someone sitting on his bed.

The thought came from nowhere and he didn't believe it, even though he could see for himself.

There was a shadow sitting on his bed.

His arms fell, his clothes landing in a heap on the floor. He tried to cry out, but probably made no sound because the shadow was moving very slowly, got up, came toward him, filling the room, right up to the ceiling.

A howl emerged, echoing off the walls; the boy turned and tried to run, then all sound was switched off, color vanished, the picture went fuzzy. He switched his eyes to the blinding light in the hall, saw his own hand fly past his face, felt his weight shift from one foot to the other, got no air, the doorway came closer, then slid sideways, a clammy glove against his forehead, another on his left arm. A flashing reflection of the hall light in something shiny.

Chaos, a howling sound in his brain, warm liquid on his chest.

Then a thought, a final, radiant, clear thought:

Mom.

FRIDAY, NOVEMBER 13

The train rumbled hypnotically through the night, rattling feverishly, singing monotonously. The man lay in his first-class compartment staring out of the window, trying to make out the line of treetops against the dark starry sky. The pain was pushing through the morphine, making him gasp.

With an effort he took out another tablet from the case under the pillow, swallowing it without water. He felt its effects before it had even hit his stomach, soothing him to peace at last.

He suddenly found himself at one of the vast meetings of his youth, in a huge campsite outside Pajala, thousands of people on hard wooden benches, the smell of damp wool and sawdust. The men up on the platform made speeches, first one in Finnish, then the other translating into Swedish, the endlessness of their voices, rolling, rising, falling.

With a jerk the train pulled in to a station. He looked out along the platform. Långsele.

Långsele?

Panic hit him hard and mercilessly, good grief, he was going in the wrong direction! His arms flew up, his head rising from the synthetic pillow, his breath panting.

Dans quelle direction est Långsele?

South, he thought. It's south, just above Ånge.

He sank back onto the pillow, trying to ignore his own smell, checking that the duffel bag was still at the end of the bed, coughed weakly. He heard a door slam, and a jolt as the train got ready to leave. He looked at his watch. 5:16 AM.

There was no reason to worry. Everything was going as planned. He was on his way, invisible, untouchable, like a flickering shadow. Free to travel in his own thoughts in an unfree world, free to return or disappear.

And he chose to return to the meeting at the campsite, to conjure up images that had lain dusty and rusty, faded with age, but still clear.

One pair of speakers followed the other, the strictly arranged presentation that always began with a reading from the Bible, half in Finnish, then Swedish, then the interpretations, variations, analysis, and occasionally the personal confession: I was in trouble, searching throughout my youth, something was lacking in my life and I found my way to Sin, and I found women and drink and stole a watch from a friend, but then I met a fellow believer during my national service and Jesus Christ brought light into my life, because my brother sowed a seed in my heart.

Lying in his compartment, he smiled, listening to the stories, full of pain and angst, jubilant and grateful.

But they never really took off, he interrupted himself. There was never any shouting, never any raised voices. Never any ecstasy.

He recalled the boredom of youth.

Often he had let the voices fade away and drift out of the tent together with the thoughts, hopes, and restlessness. The city of tents and trailers on the meadow outside was more appealing, an ocean of possibilities concealed behind horse carts and Volvos. His sideways glances at unknown girls on the bench in front, in their head scarves and long skirts, his awareness of their warmth, the sheen of any stray locks of hair.

The awareness that his thoughts and hard penis were sinful.

He was rocked to sleep with the smell of horse manure in his nostrils.

Annika was walking through Kronoberg Park, breathlessly, with crunching steps. It was cold, high pressure threatening to bring arctic weather. The tarmac was slippery with ice, the trees smothered in blankets of frost. The grass, yesterday damp and green, was now frozen stiff and swept in silver. The wind didn't reach her through the trees, leaving the traffic fumes hanging as gray veils along the paths.

This was as light as it was going to get. The daylight was thin and shadowless; she lifted her head and squinted up at the sky. It was made of pastel-colored porcelain, shades of blue fading to gray, white, slightly pink clumps of cloud, driven by the north wind high above.

She hurried along behind the dog-rest area, the blades of grass crackling as they were crushed beneath her feet. She approached the Jewish cemetery from the back, near the place where Josefin had been found. She stopped by the black iron railing, her glove stroking its curves and stars, frost dusting her shoes like icing sugar.

The cemetery had been renovated a couple of years ago. Fallen, eroded lumps of sandstone had been replaced on their plinths; the wild shrubbery had been cut back, the trees trimmed. And somehow the magic had vanished; the sense of experiencing a gap in time that Annika had always felt there. The sounds of the city encroached in a way that they never did before, the spirits that had owned the place had gone.

Only Josefin's was left.

She sank to her knees and looked through the railing in the same way she had done that time so many summers before, that hot summer when the number of wasps broke all records and the election campaign just went on and on. Josefin had been lying there, mouth open in a soundless scream, eyes dull and matte, the young girl with all her dead dreams. There was a rustle in a frozen branch, a siren bounced off the buildings on Hantverkargatan.

He got his comeuppance in the end, Annika thought. Not for what he did to you, but at least he didn't get away with it.

And Karina Björnlund gathered enough ammunition to get a ministerial post.

She stretched her legs, looked at the time, then left Josefin with a gentle stroke of the railing. She hurried across Fridhemsplan, the wind hitting her face in Rålambshov Park so that she was fiery cheeked by the time she reached the entrance of the *Evening Post* office.

She made it to her aquarium without triggering any trip wires, and threw her outdoor clothing in a heap in the corner.

Ragnwald, she thought as the computer whirred into life, putting the past behind her and overcoming her restlessness by forcing herself to concentrate on the present.

What does it mean? Who are you?

Once Explorer had started up she googled the name, only getting a limited number of results.

A summary of details about a Folke Ragnwald, died 1963, a genealogical site based in Malta, a Christian Democrat candidate, no indication for which constituency.

She read quickly, checked a few more results.

A French genealogical site, a German site about royalty, a newsletter about a Danish pop star.

She checked ragnwald.com, and got a mass of amateur pictures from an IT fair full of Jolt Cola.

She shut down the browser and rang Suup in Luleå instead.

"We're a bit tied up at the moment," the inspector said, sounding very upset.

"What's happened?"

Annika picked up a pen out of reflex, immediately feeling guilty about whatever it was.

"We don't know yet," the policeman said. "Can you call back after lunch, we should know more then?"

His voice struck a chord inside Annika, making her clench all the muscles in her face.

"It's Ragnwald," she said. "It's something to do with the terrorist."

The rejection of this sounded so surprised that she accepted it at once.

"Not at all," Suup said. "Call back after two PM. You'll get nothing out of me until then."

She looked at her watch, realizing there was no point in pressing him right now, eighteen hours before her deadline. She thanked him, hung up, and laid her notes from their last meeting on the desk in front of her. She needed another cup of coffee before she got going.

She went through the corridors with her head down, to the coffee machine behind the sports desk, evading people's gazes, and got two coffees at once. She sat down at the keyboard with the two plastic cups and arranged her material, trying to piece together an image of her terrorist.

The young man from the Torne Valley who traveled south, but eventually came back to Luleå.

She let her hands fall, drank some coffee.

Why would a young man travel south in the sixties?

Work or college, she thought.

Why would he come back?

Because whatever had happened was over and done with.

Why Luleå?

If the place you come from feels too restrictive, but you still want to go home, you'd pick one of the larger towns in the area.

But why the biggest?

He must have lived in a big city. Maybe one with a university. Stockholm, Uppsala, Gothenburg, or Lund.

She typed the cities into her computer, then realized her mistake.

The young man need not have stayed in Sweden; he could have worked or studied anywhere.

Although this was long before the EU, she reminded herself.

Let that thread fall, and picked up the next.

Where did he go after that?

ETA? Spain? Why?

Political conviction, she thought, but there was a filter of doubt in front of her computer screen.

The Basque separatists were, of course, one of the few terrorist groups that had actually succeeded in achieving some of their goals, including democracy and extensive political autonomy for the Basque Country. If ETA hadn't blown up Franco's successor in December 1973, Spain's transition to democracy would have been more difficult, and as far as she knew, the Basque Country today had its own police and its own tax system, and was well on its way to becoming a tax haven for international business.

But ETA had also, perhaps more than any other group, been afflicted with the self-perpetuating nature of terrorism. After the free elections of 1977 there was a whole generation of middle-aged Basques who had done nothing throughout their adult lives but conducted terrorist activities against the Spanish state. Peaceful daily life became too dull, so they decided the democratic state was as bad as the dictatorship and set about killing again. And the Spanish state took its revenge by creating GAL, the antiterrorist liberation group . . .

She needed to read more about ETA, but she knew they were among the least approachable terrorist groups in the world, killers for the sake of killing. As self-appointed representatives for a homeland that had never existed they demanded compensation for injustices that had never been committed.

She wrote "read more Björn Kumm" as a reminder, then went on.

Why Ragnwald? Did the code name have any deeper meaning? Did it symbolize something she ought to know?

She looked the name up in the *National Encyclopaedia* and found out that it was a combination of Old Icelandic *ragn,* divine power, and *vald,* ruler.

The ruler with divine power, not a bad alias. Did it actually mean anything, other than delusions of grandeur?

But then what was terrorism, if not that?

She sighed, fighting against a wave of tiredness sweeping her eyes. The coffee was cold and tasted disgusting. She went out and poured the contents of the almost full cups down the toilet, stretched her back, blinded by the neon lights.

Looked over at Berit's desk, but she hadn't arrived yet.

She shut the door of her aquarium carefully behind her and continued.

What about the shoes? The footprints had been common knowledge for years, one of the few pieces of evidence the perpetrators had left, but their size had never been made public.

Thirty-six. That couldn't be anyone but a small woman, or a very young man, actually a boy. But what was most likely? That a twelve-year-old blew up a plane, or that an adult woman did it?

So he probably had a woman with him, she noted.

But who would want to do something like that? Suup hadn't said anything about a woman. She wrote the question on her notes, but if she had to speculate?

Historically, which women had become terrorists?

Gudrun Ensslin had been Andreas Baader's partner. Ulrika Meinhof became world-famous when she freed Baader. Francesca Mambro was convicted of blowing up the railway station in Bologna together with her boyfriend Valerio Fioravanti.

Ragnwald's girlfriend, she wrote, and summarized:

The young man from the Torne Valley went away and worked or studied in a large town down south, then came back to Norrbotten, joined a left-wing group under the name Ragnwald, the ruler with divine power, which suggested a certain megalomania. He got a girlfriend whom he persuaded to blow up a fighter jet. Then he fled the country and carried on as a killer with ETA.

She sighed and read through her notes.

If she was going to get any of this in the paper it had to be considerably more articulate and factual. She looked at the time; it would soon be time to call Suup again.

Miranda rang the doorbell with her usual insistence. Anne Snapphane hurried down the stairs so that the old bastard downstairs wouldn't go mad, one hand clutching the towel around her, the other holding a towel around her hair.

The door jammed; it always did when it was below freezing.

The girl ran to her without a word, and she leaned over and held her tight. From the corner of her eye she saw Mehmet approach from the car with their daughter's bag, neutral but contained.

"There are muffins in the kitchen," Anne whispered in the girl's ear, and the child let out a little cry and ran upstairs.

In a moment of defiance and pride she stood up without wrapping the towel around her, not caring if the neighbors saw her. Completely naked, apart from the towel around her hair, she looked Mehmet in the eye and took the little bag. He lowered his gaze.

"Anne," he said, "you don't have to . . ."

"You wanted to talk to me," she said, forcing her voice to sound calm. "I presume it's about Miranda."

She turned her back on him, her buttocks dancing in front of his face as she climbed the stairs. She went into the bathroom and pulled on a dressing gown, stopping in front of the mirror, trying to see herself through his eyes.

"Do you want coffee?" she called, staring into her own eyes.

"Thanks," he said, "I'm fine. I have to get to work."

She swallowed, realizing that this was going to be unpleasant. He wanted a quick line of retreat, not a scalding mug of coffee to empty in hurried embarrassment.

"I'm going to have one anyway," she said, pulling the towel from her head. Running her fingers through her wet hair she made her way to the kitchen and poured herself a large mug.

He was standing at the living room window, looking out at the neighbor's garden.

"What is it?" she said, as she sat on the sofa.

"We're getting married," Mehmet said, turning around.

She felt the arrow hit her without trying to stop it.

"Nothing to do with me or Miranda," she said, blowing on her coffee.

He sat down opposite her, legs wide apart, leaning forward with his elbows on his knees.

"We're expecting a child," he said. "Miranda's going to have a little brother or sister."

Her head started to spin, and against her instinct she looked down at the floor.

"I see," she said, clutching the mug tightly. "Congratulations."

He sighed.

"Anne," he said. "I know how hard this must be for you . . ."

She looked up, took a deep breath.

"No," she said. "I don't want your sympathy. What will it mean, in purely practical terms, for Miranda?"

Mehmet pressed his lips together in that way she knew so well, and she was overcome by a hot, intense longing for the man before her; her heart and groin ached. To her own irritation she let out a little sob.

He reached out a hand to her cheek; she closed her eyes and let him stroke her.

"I'd like her to live with us," Mehmet said. "Full time. But I won't fight for it if you don't want that."

She forced herself to laugh.

"You can take most things from me," she said, "but not my child. Get out."

"Anne . . ."

"Get out!"

Her voice was cracking with rage.

Their daughter appeared in the doorway, looking from one to the other in surprise.

"Are you angry?" she said, a half-eaten muffin in her hand.

Mehmet stood up, strong and lithe as a hunter, went over to the child and kissed her hair.

"See you next Friday, darling."

"Why is Mommy sad? Have you been horrid to her?"

Anne shut her eyes and heard his steps disappear down the

stairs. She waited until the front door had closed before running to the window to watch him go.

He walked to the car without looking up, taking out his cell phone from his inside pocket and dialing a number.

To her, Anne knew. He was calling his fiancée to tell her what had happened, that it was done, that it had been unpleasant, that she had got upset and aggressive. I don't think she'll let Miranda go without a fight.

Berit Hamrin knocked on her glass door, opening it a crack and sticking her head in.

"Hungry?"

Annika let her hands drop from the keyboard, and thought for a moment out of duty.

"Not really."

Berit opened the door wide and came into the room.

"You need to eat," she said firmly. "God, the state in here, how can you work in this mess?"

"What?" Annika said in surprise, gazing around with a look that was sheepish before she even started. "What's wrong with it?"

"You do have somewhere to hang your clothes, you know," Berit said, hanging up Annika's outdoor clothes. "There, that's better. It's lasagne in the cafeteria today; I've already asked for two portions."

Annika logged out of the system so that no one got the idea of reading her notes or sending false emails from her account.

"What are you up to today?" she asked, to distract her colleague from the chaos she had surrounded herself with.

Berit was on temporary transfer from the crime section to the political team ahead of the impending EU elections.

"Oh, writing up the latest pissing contest," she said with a sigh. "Nothing's happening, but people are taking up positions, talking across party boundaries, looking for differences of opinion where there aren't any."

Annika laughed, following Berit out into the main office.

"I can see the headline: The secret EU game, and a low-resolution shot of lights in the window of a government building."

"You've been working here too long," Berit said.

Annika shut the door behind her and headed off toward the canteen. As she followed Berit, the world seemed manageable, safe, the floor stable, no need for any doubts.

The cafeteria was half empty, the lighting subdued. A little sun spilled from the row of windows at the far end of the room. No faces were visible, just dark silhouettes against the murky half light from the porcelain sky.

They sat at a table overlooking the parking lot with their steaming plates of microwaved lasagne.

"What are you working on?" Berit said, once she'd got to the bottom of the plastic dish.

Annika sliced suspiciously at the layers of pasta.

"That journalist's murder," she said, "and the attack on a plane at F21. The police have a suspect, have had for years."

Berit raised her eyebrows, catching a piece of meat that was trying to escape from the corner of her mouth, and waved her fork in the air encouragingly.

"His name's Ragnwald, someone who fled the Torne Valley for the south, came back and became a terrorist, then went to Spain and joined ETA."

Berit looked skeptical.

"And when is this supposed to have happened?"

Annika leaned back and folded her arms.

"End of the sixties, early seventies."

"Hmm," Berit said. "The delightful age of revolution. There were a lot of people who thought they could liberate the masses through terrorism, and just not in our circle."

"Which one was your circle?"

"*The Vietnam Bulletin*," Berit said, scraping at the oil at the bottom of the dish. "That's how I got started as a journalist, I must have told you?"

Annika checked quickly in her all too fallible memory.

"Which circles wanted terrorism, then?"

Berit was staring at Annika's half-eaten dish.

"Are you done with that?"

Annika nodded, Berit sighed, put her knife and fork down.

"I'll get coffee," she said, and stood up.

Annika stayed where she was, watching her colleague queue up for coffee, her short hair sticking out at the back, radiating patience. She smiled as Berit came gliding back with two cups of coffee and some cookies.

"Now you're spoiling me," Annika said.

"Tell me about your terrorist," Berit said.

"Tell me about the sixties," Annika countered.

Berit put the cups carefully on the table and looked sharply at Annika.

"Okay," she said as she sat down and stirred two lumps of sugar into her coffee. "It was like this. In 1963 came the official break between the Communist Party of the Soviet Union and the Chinese Communist Party. The split affected every communist movement around the world, including us. The Swedish Communist Party split into three groups."

She waved her left index finger.

"The right-wing group," she said, "led by C.-H. Hermansson. They distanced themselves from both the Stalinists and the Maoists, and ended up with a sort of old-fashioned revisionism that we may as well call Social Democracy. They're today's Left Party, with almost ten percent of our parliamentary seats."

Berit took a sip of coffee, then raised her long finger.

"Then there was the center," she said, "led by the chief editor of *Norrskensflamman,* Alf Löwenborg, who lined up on the Soviet side."

She changed finger.

"And then there was the left-wing group, led by Nils Holberg, which favored China."

"When did all this happen?" Annika asked.

"The Swedish Communist Party broke up after its twenty-first party congress, in May 1967," Berit said. "The party changed its name to the Left Party Communists, and the left-wing group broke away to form the Communist Association of Marxist-Leninists. After that things developed quickly. The Vietnam movement, Clarté, the Rs—the revolutionaries—all popped up. In the spring of 1968 it culminated with the occupation of the student union and the rebel movement in Uppsala. They were actually worst of all, the Uppsala rebels. They spent the whole of that spring making threats against us."

She held her right hand up to her ear like a phone.

"'If you don't attend the revolutionary mass meeting to listen to the grievances of the masses, some comrades will come and fetch you.'"

"Sounds nice," Annika said. "And they were Maoists?"

"Well, the real Maoists were no problem. They always asked: what would the Master himself do? Would he personally have committed these acts in the name of the revolution? If the answer was no, they didn't do it. It was the hangers-on who were worst, the ones out for kicks, with their mass psychosis and sect behavior."

She looked at the time.

"I have to go," she said. "The Green Party have promised a statement about Baltic fishing quotas at one o'clock."

Annika gave a theatrical yawn.

"Ha ha," Berit said, standing up and picking up the sticky plastic tray to take over to the trash. "It's all right for you, writing about your dead journalists. Over in my corner we're dealing with the really important stuff, like all those murdered cod . . ."

Annika laughed, then silence fell coldly around her. A whiff of old lasagne wafted up at her, sticky and fatty, and she pushed it away. She became conscious of the colleagues around her, some of them talking quietly, but most of them on their own, bent over newspapers as they clutched their plastic cutlery. Somewhere behind the counter a microwave pinged, and two men from sports were buying eight pastries.

She drank her coffee slowly, one of the many dark silhouettes outlined against the cold light, one of the workers at the newspaper factory.

A function. Not an individual.

Thomas never really liked meetings in the offices of the Federation of County Councils. Even if he was broadly in favor of looking into how far the two associations should be merged, he always felt slightly at a disadvantage when they met on Sophia Grenborg's home territory. It was mostly small things, like not knowing his way around, using the wrong elevator, not knowing the names of the other staff.

Mind you, he didn't know their names at the Association of Local Councils either, he realized.

He took a deep breath and pushed open the door out onto Hornsgatan, feeling the cold bite at his ears immediately. Over the years his ears had become extremely sensitive, the result of too many outdoor ice-hockey matches in the biting cold when he was young. But the Federation of County Councils was only across the street, so it would be pretty stupid to put on a woolly hat just to cross the road.

He found his way through the labyrinth on the fifth floor, feeling slightly stressed. Sophia came toward him, her blond page cut swaying, shiny and straight, as she walked, her jacket unbuttoned, her heels clicking on the wooden floor.

"Welcome," she said, taking his hand in hers, small and soft, warm and dry. "The others are already here."

He started to shrug off his coat, immediately anxious that they had been waiting for him.

She took a step closer, he could smell her perfume. Light, fresh, sporty.

"You're not late," she whispered. "They're drinking coffee in the conference room."

He breathed out, smiled, surprised that she had realized what he was thinking.

"Good," he whispered back, looking into her eyes. They were a strikingly bright blue.

"How do you feel today?" she whispered back. "A bit hungover?"

He grinned.

"One thing is sure," he said quietly. "You can't be hungover. You look absolutely great."

She lowered her eyes; he could have sworn she was blushing, then heard his own words as an echo, realizing their meaning, and started to blush himself.

"I mean . . . ," he said, stepping back.

She looked up, took a step forward to keep pace with him, and put her arm on his coat.

"It's fine, Thomas," she whispered, so close that he could feel her breath.

He looked into her eyes for a few seconds, then turned away, pulling off his scarf and putting his briefcase on a bench, opening it and putting the scarf inside. Wondered if his ears were still bright red.

"I've handed out the brochures," she said. "I hope that was okay."

He stiffened slightly, looking down at the pack of brochures he had planned to hand out. Now the whole initiative, which was partly his responsibility, looked like it had come from Sophia and the Federation of County Councils.

He shut his briefcase.

"Of course," he said shortly, feeling his smile stiffen. "You can tell your webmaster to get in touch with ours, because we've got the content online, and it would make sense if you did too."

She twisted her fingers nervously and showed him to the conference room.

"Yes," she said, "I know."

Per Cramne, the representative from the ministry of justice, stood up as he entered the room, and hurried over to greet him.

"I really must apologize about yesterday," he said. "It's these damn EU elections . . ."

Thomas put his briefcase on the table and raised both hands.

"No problem," he said. "We had other things to discuss anyway. The Association of Local Councils and the Federation of County Councils have a congress in the spring; we're discussing a possible merger, and I'm in the planning group, so . . ."

He realized his mistake too late; Cramne had already glazed over, couldn't care less about any merger.

"Is everyone here?" Cramne said, turning away. "Let's get going then. It is Friday, after all."

Thomas took out his documents, refusing to look around to see if anyone else had seen the embarrassing incident.

Cramne began, of course; the ministry of justice was always top of the hierarchy. The representatives from the National Police Board, the Public Prosecutor's Office, and the security police declined to speak. Instead Thomas took the initiative and presented the folder they had prepared, specifying the arguments why unknown threats against elected representatives were a real danger to democracy, outlining proposed changes, and the direction of the work to come. He told them about his contact with the National Council for Crime Prevention that morning, nodding to the council's delegate, and describing the proposal they had sketched out.

"I believe we need to investigate public opinion," he concluded. "This is a problem that concerns everyone. Not just every politician, but every citizen. We have to make it clear that this is a broader issue. How does society regard threats and violence against our democratically elected representatives? What values do we apply to attempts to silence politicians? And can we change those values with a public information campaign?"

He turned over a sheet of paper, aware that he had the complete attention of the group.

"I think we should try to instigate a debate in the press," he said, "try to influence public opinion the old-fashioned way. Articles that show local politicians as heroes for our time, examples of people battling right-wing extremists and anarchists in small towns, but without exaggerating the threat and scaring off people just starting out in politics . . ."

The decision to set up a research group to look into this, under Thomas's leadership, was swiftly taken. Press material would be developed to accompany the release of the findings of the working group from the press department of the Federation of County Councils.

Thomas concluded the meeting with an anecdote about a councillor from Jämtland that always got a laugh, then they packed up; the meeting was dissolved, and within a minute the others had all vanished.

It was, after all, Friday afternoon.

He was left standing with his papers, sorting his notes as Sophia collected the material the delegates had left behind. He wasn't sure how to handle the fact that he had ridden roughshod over her, taking the credit for the whole initiative. The folder was just as much her work as his, as was the discussion of a survey.

"Well, I have to say," Sophia said, standing next to him, "that you were really fantastic today."

He looked up in surprise, aware that beads of sweat were breaking out on his forehead.

She didn't seem annoyed, in fact quite the reverse. Her eyes were beaming.

"Thanks," he said.

"You really know how to present things and get the right decisions taken," she said, moving another step toward him. "You got everyone to go along with it, even Justice."

He looked down in embarrassment.

"It's an important project."

"I know," she said, "and it shows that you think so. You really believe in what you're doing, and it feels so right to work with you on this . . ."

He took a deep breath, giddy with her perfume.

"Have a good weekend," he said, picking up his briefcase and heading for the door.

Annika dialed Inspector Suup's direct line, after nagging the receptionist to let her have the number, with a sense of foreboding in her stomach. The more she thought about it, the stranger he had seemed during their conversation that morning. Was he regretting letting her have the information about Ragnwald? Had he thought it would be in the next day's paper? Was he disappointed?

Her hands were damp with sweat as she listened to the phone ring.

"What's happened?" she asked him when he had picked up.

"Something really bad," he said. "Linus Gustafsson is dead."

Her first reaction was relief, the name meant nothing to her.

"Who?" she said.

"The witness," Suup said, and the shutters went up in her brain, letting blinding chalk-white laser light into her synapses, crashing through walls and defenses like a tornado, guilt establishing itself as the winner over the rest of her turbulent thoughts. She heard herself gasp.

"How?"

"His throat was cut, at home in his bedroom. His mom found him in a pool of blood when she got home this morning."

She was shaking her head violently.

"No, it can't be true," she whispered.

"We believe that the killings are somehow connected, but we don't know how yet. The only common denominator so far is that the boy was a witness to the first murder. The methods are completely different."

Annika sat, her right hand over her eyes, feeling the deadweight in her chest pounding, making it hard to breathe.

"Is this my fault?" she managed to say.

"What did you say?"

She cleared her throat.

"Linus told me that he thought he recognized the killer, but then he cut off our conversation," she said. "Did he tell you who he thought it was?"

The inspector was no good at pretending; his surprise was genuine, and extreme.

"That's news to me," he said. "Are you sure?"

She forced herself to think logically and take her responsibility as a journalist.

"I promised him complete anonymity," she mused out loud. "Does that apply now that he's dead?"

"It doesn't matter anymore; he came to us of his own accord, which releases you from your responsibility," the police officer said, and Annika knew he was right. She breathed out.

"When I spoke to him he said that he might have recognized the murderer, but I didn't put that in my article. I didn't think it made sense to highlight that, especially since we hadn't finished talking."

"You were right not to," the policeman said. "It's a shame it wasn't enough."

"Do you think he could have told anyone else?"

"We haven't asked, but I'll get on to it."

The silence was oppressive, Annika felt the weight of her own responsibility blocking their communication.

"I feel responsible," she said.

"I can understand that," the inspector said, "but you shouldn't. Someone else is responsible for this, and we're going to get him. You can be sure of that."

She rubbed her eyes, thinking hard.

"So what are you doing? Going door to door? Looking for fingerprints? Checking for footprints, cars, mopeds?"

"All that, and a whole lot more."

"Talking to friends, teachers, neighbors?"

"To start with."

Annika made some notes, her whole body shaking.

"Have you found anything?"

"We're going to be very careful with any information we get."

Silence again.

"A leak," Annika said. "You think you've got a leak that revealed the boy's identity."

A deep sigh at the other end.

"There are a few people who might have said something, including the boy himself. He never spoke to the mass media, but at least two of his friends knew he was the witness. His mom told her boss at work. Or what about you?"

"I haven't told anyone," she said. "I'm absolutely certain of that."

There was silence again, a doubtful silence: she was an outsider; he didn't know much about her, what she was all about; a big city journalist whom he might never meet again—could she be responsible?

"You can trust me," she said quietly. "Just so you know. How much of this can I write about?"

"Don't mention the cause of death; we haven't released that. You can quote me saying that the murder was extremely violent and that the Luleå police are shocked at its brutality."

"Can I mention his mother? The fact that she found him?"

"Well, that's logical, so you can say that, but don't try to contact her. She probably isn't home anyway, I think my team took her off to the hospital suffering from shock. She had no one apart from the boy. The dad seems to have been a tragic case, one of the gang that sit and drink outside the shopping center and terrorize the shopkeepers along the main street."

"It couldn't have been him?"

"He was in a cell, drunk, from 5:00 PM yesterday, was taken off to dry out in Boden at seven this morning."

"That's what I call an alibi," Annika said. "Is there any way I can help? Are you looking for anything in particular that we could draw people's attention to in the paper?"

"The last person we know who definitely saw the boy was the

driver of the last bus out to Svartöstaden last night, and that reached the final stop just after ten. The preliminary report says the boy died shortly after that, so if anyone saw him around that time we'd like to hear from them."

"You've checked out the bus driver?"

Suup gave a deep sigh.

"And all the passengers," he said. "We're going to get this bastard."

A thought occurred to her from out of nowhere.

"In his bedroom, you said? How did the killer get into the flat?"

"No signs of a break-in."

Annika thought, forcing herself to outpace the guilt until the burden was out of reach, gone forever, and she knew she was running needlessly. She was well aware of what little effect adrenaline and willpower have on a guilty conscience.

"So he might have let him in himself," she said. "It could have been someone he knew."

"Or else the killer went in without knocking, or was waiting for him in the dark. The lock on the flat was pretty hopeless: one good pull and it comes open."

She forced herself to think clearly and sensibly, getting lost in the familiarity of the inspector's tone.

"What can I write?" she asked once more. "Can I mention this?"

The policeman suddenly sounded very tired.

"Write whatever you want," he said and hung up.

And Annika was left holding the phone, staring at the list of questions she had written about Ragnwald in her notebook.

She had hardly replaced the receiver in its cradle before it rang again, an internal call that made her jump.

"Can you come and see me?" Anders Schyman asked.

She didn't move, paralyzed, and tried to get a grip on reality again. She let her eyes roam over the mess on her desk, the pens and notepads and newspapers and printouts and a mass of other stuff, tools for constructing the truth, tools for building stability. Don't let the guilt catch you, twist, turn, get away. She took hold of the edge of the desk and squeezed it hard.

It was her fault, oh God—she had persuaded the boy to talk.

She was at least partially responsible for this; her ambition had been decisive in determining the boy's fate.

I'm so sorry, she thought. Please, forgive me.

And gradually it eased: the pressure on her lungs grew lighter; the cramp in her hands stopped; she could feel her fingers aching.

I have to talk to Mom. Not now, but later.

There was a future, tomorrow was a new day, and there would be others after that, if she only allowed there to be.

If you sit by the river long enough, you will see the bodies of your enemies float by.

She let out a sob, smiling at the Chinese proverb Anne Snapphane often quoted.

You're not dying, she thought. It just feels like it.

She gathered together her papers.

The editor in chief was standing by the window with a printout in his hand, staring down at the Russian embassy. Annika glanced at the conference table, but he had at least rolled up his sales graphs and diagrams today.

"Sit down," he said, looking back at the room and indicating a chair.

She sat down, feeling extremely uncomfortable.

"I've read your outline about Ragnwald," Anders Schyman said, "and I see what you mean when you said it wasn't an article, just an idea."

Annika crossed her arms and legs and realized she was adopting an extremely defensive position, relaxed and straightened her arms and legs instead.

"And I'm not convinced by the article you wrote about Benny Ekland. It was speculative to an extent that felt rather unfortunate."

She could no longer resist the temptation to fold her arms.

"How do you mean?"

Schyman leaned back, his shirt coming loose above his navel.

"I think you're applying the term 'terrorism' with pretty broad strokes these days," he said. "Not all criminals are terrorists, and not all violence is terrorism. We have to keep a bit of distance and relevance in our journalism, not give in to inflation and always use the most powerful words. We'll have to use those words for real events, probably sooner than we imagine . . ."

She heard herself let out a deep, ironic sigh, and threw her arms out.

"Oh, please," she said. "Don't preach to me about press ethics."

He clenched his jaw so hard that a vein started to throb in his neck.

"I'm not preaching, I just want to point out . . ."

Annika leaned forward, feeling the blood rush to her head.

"I thought you supported me in my role as an independent reporter," she said, "that you trusted my judgment about what's important."

"Annika, believe me, I do, but . . ."

"There's something here, I can feel it; this guy had stumbled across something he shouldn't have."

". . . if you'll just let me finish, I'd like to stress that I support you completely in your role, but in spite of that I am also legally responsible for what gets published, so I take the decisions about whether or not we should identify people as terrorists, and that's why I'm explaining my position to you, to save you making a load of trips and doing a load of work for nothing."

Annika had stopped in the middle of a gesture, almost standing, leaning across the editor in chief's desk, mouth open, her face livid. In the silence left by his words the thoughts were racing through her head, trying to find solutions and explanations.

"It's Spike," she said. "Has Spike said something about my trips?"

Schyman sighed and stood up.

"Not at all. I'm just pointing out that this business with terrorism and terrorists has started to take up a great deal of your time at work."

"Well, perhaps they've been fairly important subjects in recent years."

Annika sat down, and the editor walked around her chair and over to the conference table.

"I'd just like you to consider whether there might be some other reason why you should be particularly interested in these things."

"What do you mean?"

Schyman sighed again, running his fingers over the tubes containing the graphs.

"That I'm identifying myself with the terrorists, is that what you mean? That I've killed someone myself, and that makes my brain conjure up compulsive killers where there aren't any? Or do you mean the tunnel, the dynamite the Bomber hooked me up to? Has that made me so crazy that I'm seeing Bombers behind every bush, is that what you mean?"

Anders raised both hands in a placatory, soothing way.

"Annika," he said, "I don't know, all I can say is that this story is really peculiar, I can't run a story about a Ragnwald who might be dead and buried, or a gardener in Moscow, or a diver for the coast guard, or whatever the hell he might be, because this is serious stuff, serious allegations."

"Ragnwald is his code name, he isn't identified anywhere."

"Maybe he's better known as Ragnwald than his real name, because we just don't know, do we?"

She didn't answer, feeling her teeth grind as she stared into the curtains that hid the embassy compound.

"Besides," he said, "common sense suggests that the idea behind your article isn't very sensible. The Swedish countryside isn't exactly famous for producing full-blown terrorists, is it?"

She looked at him in astonishment.

"Are you kidding?" she said. "Or are you just ignorant? The letter bomb was invented by a man from Toreboda, and the first one blew up in the hands of Director Lundin on Hamngatan in August 1904."

"Look," he said, his tone still suggesting that he wanted to placate her. "Things are going really well for the paper right now. We can't put ourselves in a position where we risk the credibility we've built up with our readers with some vague accusations of terrorism."

She leaped up, adrenaline pumping.

"Credibility? You mean you think people buy the paper for our serious and cutting-edge journalism?"

She let out a short burst of laughter.

"Anna Nicole Smith on the front page three days in a row last week," she said. "A boy who masturbated on a reality show on Saturday. The crown princess kissing her boyfriend on Sunday. What is this? Can't you see what you've done to this paper? Or are you kidding yourself as well?"

She could see he wanted to explode but was choosing not to.

"I thought you were happy about the progress the paper's been making," he said, in a slightly strained voice.

"Working with sale signals on the front cover and billboards, isn't that what you call it? Do you know what I call it? Focusing on crap and shit."

"We're a second paper. We have to push tabloid stories harder than a first paper. Or don't you want us to get ahead?"

"Not at any cost. I think it's a tragedy that you've dropped all quality control on this paper."

She was surprised at how angry he seemed.

"That's not true," he said in a very controlled tone of voice. "We are still running damned serious investigative journalism inside the paper, you know that perfectly well. I think you need slightly more perspective than our more vulgar critics, if I might put it like that. Be fair."

"That doesn't stop me from regretting the way journalism is

going. The boundaries between reality and fiction are being erased. Along with the other tabloids we're writing about reality television as if it was the most important and relevant thing happening. Now that can't be right, can it?"

"You're forgetting Cain and Abel," Schyman said, trying to smile.

"What about them?"

Annika folded her arms on her chest, waiting.

"Being seen, the most important thing for human beings, didn't you once say that? About television, actually? Being in a reality show that's being filmed and shown on the net twenty-four hours a day is like being seen by God, all the time."

"So who's God?" Annika said. "The camera lens?"

"Nope," Schyman said. "The viewing public. When did any of us last have the chance to be God?"

"You get to be God every day, at least on the paper," Annika said. "Just as omnipotent, unjust, and full of poor judgments as the real God was with Cain and Abel."

Now it was Schyman's turn to be speechless; Annika could hear her accusations echo in the silence, and wished she'd bitten her tongue.

"I'm just extremely damned upset that my story about the murdered journalist was thrown off the first page," she said, in an effort to excuse her remarks.

He snorted, shook his head, and walked over to the window.

"Your journalist wasn't a name," Schyman said, toward the glass of the window. "And besides, the link to terrorism was extremely vague."

"And how much of a name is Paula Pop Factory?"

"Paula came second in the competition last spring and released a single that got to number seven in the charts. She's reported the incident to the police and is prepared to have her name and picture published, even in tears," Schyman said, without sounding the slightest bit ashamed.

Annika took two steps toward his back.

"And why does she do that? Because she's fallen out of the charts. Surely we ought to think for a moment before we start doing the bidding of two-bit celebrities like her? Who's she accusing, anyway?"

"If we applied your principles about not covering reality shows, you'd never find out," he said, turning around, his expression suggesting an attempt at humor.

"I just wondered if we ought to identify the man by name and picture too?" she said, noticing that her voice was starting to tremble. "I'm just intrigued to know how low we've sunk."

The editor in chief's face collapsed in the twilight.

"*Highlander* on TV Plus is systematically sexually exploiting applicants to reality shows," he said in a neutral tone. "We haven't written about that, not yet, but we're working on it."

He put his hands over his eyes.

"Do you know, Annika," he said, "I can't be bothered to argue with you about this. I don't need to justify to you the priorities that are actually responsible for saving this paper from closure."

"So why are you doing it, then?"

"What?"

She gathered her papers, tears bubbling under the surface.

"I'm going to carry on," she said, "if you've no objection. But I realize that you have to prioritize. If Ozzy Osbourne throws another T-bone steak into his neighbor's garden, I realize that I'm fucked."

She walked out before he could see her tears of rage.

They were sitting in front of the television, two glasses of wine in front of them. Annika was staring at the flickering picture without registering it. The children were asleep, the dishwasher was rattling away in the kitchen, the vacuum cleaner was waiting for her out in the hall. She felt completely paralyzed, staring at a man walking to and fro in the foyer of a hotel, as the day, the week, hammered against the inside of her skull, heavy pressure weighing on her chest.

The boy, Linus, who had been so sweet with his spiky hair, so sensitive and hesitant; she remembered his eyes, intelligent, watchful. Schyman's dry voice echoed through her head; your journalist wasn't a name, I don't need to justify myself to you.

Thomas suddenly laughed out loud, making Annika jump.

"What is it?"

"He's so fucking brilliant."

"Who?"

Her husband stared at her as though she was a bit slow.

"John Cleese, of course," he said, waving his hand toward the television. "*Fawlty Towers.*"

He looked away from her, concentrating on the television again, leaning forward and taking a sip of wine, smacking his lips appreciatively.

"By the way," he said, "did you drink up my Villa Puccini?"

She shut her eyes for a moment, then glanced at him.

"What do you mean, your?"

He looked at her in surprise.

"What's up with you? I just asked if you'd drunk my wine, I was thinking of opening it tomorrow."

She got up.

"I'm going to bed."

"But what is it now?"

He threw out his arms as he sat in the sofa, she turned her back on him and sailed out toward the hall.

"Anki, for God's sake. Come here. I love you. Come and sit with me."

She stopped in the doorway, he got up, walked over to her, wrapped his arms around her shoulders. She felt his heavy arms on her and around her, one hand on each breast.

"Annika," he whispered, "come on. You haven't touched your wine."

She couldn't help letting out a tearful sob.

"Do you want to know what I did at work today?" he said enthusiastically, pulling her back to the sofa again, pressing her down and sitting beside her, holding her to him. She ended up with her nose in his armpit, it smelled of deodorant and detergent.

"What?" she muttered into his ribs.

"I gave a damned good presentation of the project for the whole working group."

She sat still, waiting, expecting him to go on.

"What about you?" he said eventually.

"Nothing special," she whispered.

SATURDAY, NOVEMBER 14

The man was walking hesitantly and breathlessly up Linnégatan toward the Fyris River. He was clutching his left hand against his stomach, and holding the right one up to protect his ear, grimacing slightly, not at the pain but rather at the memories the train journey had released. He was defenseless; they flooded over him, thundering through him, crashing like a tidal wave right into his brain and stirring up the sludge that had been lying on the bottom so long that he had forgotten it existed. Now it had all come back, the images and smells and sounds that had never done any harm as long as they were hidden untouched among the other forgotten nonsense, but now they were singing, chanting, and proclaiming so loudly that he couldn't hear himself think.

He found himself staring up at a window on the second floor of the Fjellstedska student hostel, one with an advent star and a little plant on the windowsill. They were there again, the girls he had had in there behind that barred window three and a half decades ago, his first women; he could feel their beery breath and blushed at his own clumsy shyness.

He had been so amazed; the world had seemed so strange. His naïve astonishment at its size and opportunities. His bitter disappointment when its limitations slammed in his face like iron gates.

The howl of the sounds became lonely; he could feel the draft from the floor, the rat that stared at him from the windowsill that ice-cold morning, the same windowsill; he saw it in another light, the frost on the inside of the glass, the rag rug he had taken with him to remind him of Mother, the nice one where she had woven in his childhood smock and her worn-out petticoat.

"It came from Kexholm," she said, letting him feel the fabric, linen so fine that it could have been velvet, because linen from Karelia was the finest in the world, and the fabric crackled beneath his child's fingers and he appreciated the power of the old country, Mother's childhood home, and understood her terrible sense of loss.

He gave a snort; this was too difficult—however would he manage?

The task. He had never failed yet, and he wasn't about to start now where his family was concerned; they were all he had left.

He turned his back on the student hostel, keeping the window in the corner of his eye as long as he could, letting it slide away. He would never see it again.

He took a few stumbling steps along Svartbäcksgatan, feeling the noise subside, and it was easier to breathe. Slowly everything around him settled down; he had no particular memories of this place of imminent Christmas commerce; it must have looked completely different at the end of the sixties. He straightened his back, letting the hand fall from his ear, absorbing reality in all its deceitfulness, thus laying his senses bare to another cacophony, the false notes of the shrieking plate-glass windows. They begged and enticed—half-naked plastic mannequins without heads; noisy battery-driven toys made in China; flashing strings of lights running across dressing gowns and silk ties; cordless electric tools to charge and use, charge and use.

He raised his head to escape the windows and his eyes fixed on an artificial pine garland in green plastic that was stretched across the whole street. He turned off to the right, across the river, up to the university, with the castle to his left and the Carolina Rediviva library up ahead of him, with its priceless treasure, the Codex Argenteus, the "Silver Bible."

He stopped to catch his breath, hearing the howling monster of consumption like a waterfall behind him.

The cold was particularly harsh today, he could hardly remember ground this frozen. He was amazed at how the stillness of air from the arctic could emphasize colors and light, sharpening and clarifying sensory perceptions. He stared up at the cathedral's twin towers as they struggled, heavy and full of shadows, to reach the translucent sky. He closed his eyes—it was long ago, so long ago, he had almost forgotten what it felt like to breathe in the glass-clear air that could only be found in Uppsala. He could feel how the glass was taking possession of his insides, freezing his airways and the soles of his feet to ice. His teeth started to chatter in an alien, unconscious way.

He struggled on and stopped outside the ornate main building of the university, brick and limestone, looking up the long flights of steps and studying the four statues above the entrance, the four faculties of the university when it was founded: theology, law, medicine, and philosophy. His gaze wandered back to the first of these, the woman with the cross, his faculty.

You betrayed me, he thought. You should have been my life's work, but you turned into a lifetime of denial.

He walked up the steps, his eyes fixed on the three heavy oak doors, the huge iron handles. Well-oiled hinges swung the door open surprisingly easily, and he walked cautiously into the entrance hall. The cathedral-like space opened up above him with its three enormous glass domes. His steps echoed against the mosaic floor and smooth granite pillars, the stucco detailing, the paintings on the ceiling, bouncing off the staircase up to the auditorium as it curved past the wise, gilded words of the great humanist, Thorild: *To think freely is great, but to think correctly is greater.*

Freedom, he thought, the tyranny of our age. The betrayal of medieval human beings, living in innocence, in their unchanging and uncontested places in society, a life of determined content that never needed nor led to any doubt. People who set the salvation of the soul above all else: economic gain, personal freedom, the questioning of social structures.

He turned his back on the room—the awakening of the Renaissance almost made him weep with rage: Eve's betrayal of Adam, the whore who tricked humanity into biting into the fruit of the tree of knowledge, its innocence raped. The blinding dawn of avarice that went on and on for centuries, poisoning people's relationships with ambitions of profit and glory, until Luther arrived, the fallen angel, the jailer who forged the last link of the rattling leg iron of the working class. Slavery, humanity, shall be your lot, through capital and pleasure and freedom.

And he hurried out of the heavy academic atmosphere and the burned color scheme, turning right outside the door and finding himself facing a strangely familiar building on Övre Slottsgatan, all strict angles and faded metal, and all of a sudden he was back again, back when the building was new; he had never seen such a modern building, the student union hall.

That was where he felt he belonged, his spiritual home, where he had discovered an antidote to the things he had found inadequate and evasive in the great tented meetings and grinding services of Læstadianism. This was where he encountered the Master's words for the first time: *People of the world, unite and defeat the American aggressors and all their lackeys. People of the world, be courageous, and dare to fight, defy difficulties, and advance wave upon wave. Then the whole world will belong to the people. Monsters of all kinds shall be destroyed.*

He shut his eyes and it was suddenly dark around him and within him; it was late at night again, as it had been before, windswept and cold, he was a lone island in the night sea, standing between ecstasy and the applause rolling out through one of the modern building's misted windows. Mao's words were like fireflies in the darkness, recited by trembling young voices and received euphorically, without any trace of doubt: *The Chinese and Japanese peoples should unite, the people of various Asian nations should unite, all oppressed people and nations of the world should unite, all peace-loving countries should unite, all countries and individuals subject to U.S. imperial aggression, control, intervention, or bullying should unite and form a broad united front against U.S. imperialism to frustrate its plans for aggression and war and to defend world peace.*

Soon afterward they came out, sweaty, pumped up, happy, satisfied, and he went up to them and they saw him, people saw him; they asked him if he was a true revolutionary and he said yes, people of the world, unite and defeat the American aggressors and all their lackeys. And they slapped him on the back and said, Tomorrow, comrade, laboremus, seven o'clock, and he nodded and was left standing there with a new fire in his soul. The landing strip of life suddenly lit up beneath him and he knew it was time to go down.

He sighed and opened his eyes. It had gotten dark, and he was tired. He would soon have to take his medicine again. It was quite a way to the motel he had booked into, and he had to find the right bus again. Anonymous rooms in a large establishment, never taxis.

He walked back toward the central station again, one hand on his stomach and the other hanging by his side.

Aware that he was an almost invisible man.

MONDAY, NOVEMBER 16

The clouds had gathered overnight. Annika stepped out of the door with a child in each hand, crouching beneath a sky that lay heavy as lead above the rooftops. She shuddered involuntarily, hunching her shoulders against the cold.

"Do we have to walk, Mommy? Can't we get the bus? We always get the bus with Daddy."

They took bus number 40 the two stops from Scheelegatan to Fleminggatan. After a painless drop-off she emerged back onto the street again, her heart and mind empty. She had planned to walk to the paper, but all the air had gone out of her and she couldn't be bothered to splash through the miserable slush all the way to Marieberg. So she took the number 1, one of the new bendy buses that were such a mistake, seeing as traffic in the inner city moved slower than seven kilometers an hour and it was always quicker to walk, but she got a seat at the back by the window, streaked with brown-gray rain, as the bus rattled like a medieval donkey cart off toward the newspaper factory.

She got her usual two mugs of coffee before going into her room, closing the door carefully behind her, and drawing the curtains as best she could, then discovered that the machine must be broken; the drinks were no more than lukewarm. The bitter taste on her lips became a warped personal insult, making her cheeks flush. She couldn't be bothered to go and throw the coffee away, and let it stand on a corner of the desk in anticipation of mold and decay.

Without any fuss she wrote a focused and straightforward article about the attack on the F21, using previously known facts, the new information from the police about the suspect, the potential terrorist who went under the name Ragnwald, and his little comrade.

She read the text grumpily, the lack of caffeine throbbing dully in her head. It was thin, but that couldn't be helped. Schyman wanted hard facts, not a poetic description of a time that had once existed and a man who may well have done the same.

With leaden limbs she got up to see if she could find any coffee anywhere when her phone rang. The screen told her it was Thomas. She stopped where she was, hesitating as it buzzed at her.

"I'm going to be late tonight," he said, the familiar words that she knew he was going to say, but they sounded strained, not as nonchalant as they usually did.

"Why?" she asked, looked out at the room without seeing.

"A meeting of the working group," he said, following the familiar track. "Well, the key members anyway. I know it's my turn to pick up the kids, but could you?"

She sat down and put her feet up on the desk, peering through the gaps in the curtains at the dull floor of the newsroom, the endless day rolling ahead of her, until her eyes reached the caretaker's booth.

"Fine," she said, "I'll get them. Has anything happened?"

His reply came a bit too late and a bit too loud.

"No, nothing," he said. "What made you think that?"

She listened to the silence after his words.

"Tell me what's happened," she said quietly.

When he spoke his voice sounded harassed.

"A woman rang about an hour ago," he said. "She and her husband filled in my questionnaire back in the spring. They were both councillors for the Center Party, and now her husband has died. I've been on the phone ever since, trying to get the group together . . ."

Annika listened quietly, hearing her husband's slightly strained breathing forming pulses on the line.

"Why did she phone you to say that?"

"The project," he said. "They'd kept the papers we sent out about threats to politicians, and I was listed as the contact. She thinks her husband was murdered."

Annika dropped her feet to the floor.

"Why does she think that?"

Thomas gave a deep sigh.

"Annika," he said. "I don't know if I can do this."

"Just tell me what happened," she said, in the voice she used when the children were hysterical.

He searched for words, hesitating.

"I don't know if I can," he said.

"If something really has happened I'll find out anyway."

Another sigh.

"Okay. Her husband was shot in the head with his civil defense rifle, sitting in an armchair, and that's what the problem is, according to his wife, because it was her armchair. He never sat in it. If he was going to shoot himself, he would have done it in his own chair."

Annika searched for a pen.

"Where does she live?"

"Do you think he could have been murdered? What do you think they'll do to the project? Are they likely to shut us down? If they think we contributed in any way . . ."

"Where does the woman live?"

He fell silent; a surprised sullenness hit her ear.

"Huh?"

She bit her pen, hesitated, and rattled it against her teeth.

"That sounds a bit immature," she said. "A man is dead and you're worrying about your job."

His reply came quick as a flash.

"And what do you do whenever there's a murder? All you do is moan about your bosses and your miserable colleagues."

She held the pen still, then put it down on the desk, and there was a faint click in her left ear. She almost thought he had hung up on her.

"Outside Östhammar," he said, "a little village in northern Uppland. They're farmers. I don't know how late I'm going to be, it depends on what we decide, and naturally on what the police say."

She left his sense of grievance well alone.

"Have you spoken to the police?"

"To begin with they thought it was suicide, but after the wife objected they're looking into it more closely."

Annika put her feet back up on the desk.

"Even if the man was killed," she said, "it doesn't necessarily mean he was shot because he was a politician, if you get what I mean. He may have had debts, addictions, rejected children, mad neighbors, anything."

"I know," Thomas said curtly. "Don't wait up."

"By the way," Annika said to the curtains, "what's her name?"

A short, buzzing silence.

"Who?"

"The woman, of course, the wife who called you."

"I don't want you getting involved with this."

They faced each other's antagonism for an indeterminate length of time, until Annika capitulated.

"Your job isn't on the line," she said. "If he was murdered, then your project only becomes more important. If anyone's going to end up in the shit it's the politicians, because they should have started your work much earlier. With a bit of luck you can stop this sort of thing happening again."

"You reckon?"

"You're not the bad guys this time, trust me. Mind you, it might be helpful if it was me who wrote the article."

Thomas was silent for several seconds, Annika could hear him breathing.

"Gunnel Sandström," he said eventually. "The husband's name was Kurt."

Thomas hung up, beads of sweat on his brow. He had been on the point of giving himself away.

When Annika had asked "her" name, he had Sophia Grenborg's

name on the tip of his tongue, her shiny hair and smiling eyes, the sound of her heels clicking in his ears, her perfume in the room with him.

That was close, he thought in a muddled way without really realizing what had been close, merely aware that something had gone up in flames; something had happened, a process had started which he didn't know if he could handle, but he still couldn't stop it.

Sophia Grenborg, with her apartment on Östermalm, in her family's building.

His mother would like her, the thought ran through his head. She was actually not dissimilar to Eleonor. Not in appearance, Eleonor was tall and sinewy, Sophia was short and petite, but they had something else in common, an attitude, a seriousness, something deeply attractive that Annika didn't have.

The sort of person you don't mind having in your home, was how Annika had once described Eleonor over the phone in his hearing, and there was something in that: Eleonor and Sophia moved effortlessly through office corridors and meeting rooms, glamorous salons, and international hotel bars. Annika just got clumsy in situations like that, her clothes more disheveled than usual, looking incredibly uncomfortable in her own skin. Whenever they went anywhere she just wanted to talk to the locals and eat in the bars where the locals ate, and wasn't remotely interested in culture or the exclusive hotel pool.

He cleared his throat a couple of times, then picked up the phone and dialed Sophia's direct line at the Federation of County Councils.

"It's fine," he said. "I'd love to come to the jazz club after the meeting."

Annika picked one of the paper's cars that had studded tires; it might be icy on the narrow lanes of northern Uppland. The radio was tuned to one of the commercial stations, but she left it on as long as they weren't playing ads.

In a quarter of an hour she had crept seven hundred meters along the jam-packed Essinge superhighway, and angrily turned off the adrenaline-thumping pop music and retuned to Radio P2. The news in Serbo-Croat turned into news in Arabic, then something she guessed might have been Somali. She listened to the rhythm of the foreign languages, searching for words she recognized, picking up the names of places, countries, a president.

After the Järva Junction the traffic started to move, and once she had passed Arlanda Airport it thinned out considerably. She put her foot down all the way to Uppsala, then turned off right toward Östhammar.

The agricultural landscape of Roslagen spread out around her, dark brown soil in frostbitten furrows, islands of buildings, rust-red–painted farmhouses and white-plastered barns. Communities she didn't even know existed flew by, places with schools and supermarkets and health centers, where people lived out their lives without her having any idea, hot-dog kiosks boasting curtains with abstract designs from IKEA, the occasional Christmas garland. The gray light erased the sharpness of her surroundings, and she switched on the windscreen wipers.

The road was gradually becoming narrower and more twisted the farther north she got. She got trapped behind a local bus that stuck to sixty kilometers an hour, at best, for more than ten kilometers before she had a chance to overtake, and had to force herself not to get stressed. Half the point of this trip was to get her out of the office. She had pulled the directions Gunnel Sandström had given her out of her bag while she was behind the bus.

Over the traffic circle, toward Gävle, seven kilometers north, then a red farmhouse on the right with an old wagon in the drive and a garden gnome on the veranda. Perfectly straightforward, but she still almost missed the turning and had to brake sharply, realizing that the roads really were slippery. She pulled in behind the wagon, leaving the engine on for a few moments as she looked up at the farmhouse.

The large main house on the right, with new siding, but the window frames needed painting. A fairly new stained wood veranda, a little white china lamp, and four small African violets in the kitchen window. On the left an office and silo, stables and workshops, a heap of manure and some pieces of agricultural machinery that evidently hadn't been used for some time.

A proper old farm, she thought, efficiently but not pedantically run, traditional but not sentimental.

She switched off the engine and caught a glimpse of the woman as a shadow in the kitchen. Taking her bag, she walked up to the house.

"Come in," Gunnel Sandström said in a thin voice. Puffy eyes. Annika took her dry little hand.

She was about fifty, short, and fairly plump, radiating that sort of vanity-free self-confidence. Short gray hair, a wine-red belted cardigan.

"I'm so sorry for your loss," Annika said, thinking the words sounded clumsy and feeble, but the woman's shoulders drooped slightly, so the words seemed to have hit their mark.

"Please, take your coat off. Can I offer you some coffee?"

Annika could still feel the gastric effects of the cold coffee from the machine in her mouth, but said yes anyway. She hung up her coat and pulled off her outdoor shoes; the woman was acting on reflex, following patterns of behavior ingrained over decades. In this house visitors were offered coffee, no matter what. Gunnel went to the stove and turned on the fast plate, measured four cups of water into the pot, then four spoons of roasted ground coffee from the green-and-pink tin next to the spice rack, then rested her right hand on the handle, ready to pull the pot off the heat when it came to a boil.

Annika sat down at the kitchen table, her bag beside her, and surreptitiously studied Gunnel Sandström's mechanical movements, trying to estimate the woman's mental state. She could smell bread, coffee, manure, and something that might have been mold. She let her eyes wander across the open hearth, the varnished pine cupboards, the beams in the roof, the green patterned linoleum floor.

"I don't read the *Evening Post* very often," Gunnel Sandström said once the coffee had come to the boil and she was stirring it. "There's so much nonsense in it these days. Nothing to do with anyone's real life. Nothing that means anything to people who live like we do."

She put the pot on a mat on the table, then sat down and seemed to collapse.

"Thomas, my husband," Annika said, "told me that both you and Kurt were active in local politics."

Gunnel Sandström was looking out of the window; Annika followed her gaze and saw a bird table surrounded by flapping wings and scattering birdseed.

"Kurt was on the council," she said. "I'm chair of the women's group, and a co-opted member."

"For which party?" Annika asked.

"The Center, of course. We care about the countryside. Kurt has always been interested in politics, from when we first met."

Annika smiled and nodded, then stood up.

"Shall I get some cups?" she asked, walking toward the draining board.

Gunnel Sandström flew up.

"Oh, I'm sorry, how silly of me; sit down, please."

She fussed about a bit longer, with cups and saucers and spoons and sugar and milk and half-frozen cinnamon buns dusted with ground almonds.

"How did you meet? In the Center Party's youth group?" Annika asked when Gunnel Sandström had sat down again and was pouring the coffee.

"No, oh no," the woman said. "Kurt was a radical in his youth; lots of our generation were in those days. He was part of the move to the countryside out here; he joined a collective in the early seventies. We met for the first time at a meeting of the road owners' association. Kurt thought the payment system should be fairer. It caused a huge fuss around here."

Annika took out her pen and notepad from her bag, noting down the details.

"So he's not from here?"

"From Nyland, outside Kramfors. He studied biology in Uppsala, and after his finals he and a few friends moved out here to start a chemical-free farm. It wasn't called organic in those days . . ."

The woman looked out at the birds, disappearing into the past. Annika waited for her to begin again.

"It didn't go very well," she went on after a while. "The members of the collective fell out. Kurt wanted to invest in a silo and a tractor; the others wanted to buy a horse and learn to turn hay. We were already seeing each other by then, so Kurt came to work here on the farm instead."

"You must have been very young," Annika said.

The woman looked at her.

"I grew up here," she said. "Kurt and I took over when we got married, in the autumn of '75. My mother's still alive, lives in a home in Östhammar."

Annika nodded, suddenly aware of the monotonous ticking of the kitchen clock, and got the impression that the same clock had made the same noise against the same wall for generation after generation, and for one giddy moment she could hear all those seconds ticking through the years, a cacophony reflecting a fragment of eternity.

"Belonging," Annika heard herself say. "I can't imagine belonging somewhere like that."

"Kurt belonged here too," Gunnel Sandström said. "He loved his life. There's no way he would have contemplated suicide even for a second—I swear to that."

She looked at Annika and her eyes were flashing, transformed into two blazing torches, and Annika could sense the woman's utter conviction, knowing at once and without any doubt that she was right.

"Where did he die?"

"In the living room," she said, getting up and walking over to the double doors beside the fireplace.

Annika walked into the large room. It was cooler than the kitchen, and it had a damp, enclosed feeling, with a scratchy blue-green fitted carpet covered with rag rugs. There was an old tiled stove in one corner, a television in another, two sofas facing each other at the far end of the room, a swiveling brown leather armchair beneath a standard lamp, with a small table alongside.

Gunnel Sandström pointed, her finger trembling.

"That's where Kurt sits," she said. "Always. My chair is normally on the other side of that little table. After dinner we always sit here and read: council papers, the local newspaper, journals, paperwork from the farm. We do everything in our armchairs."

"Where's your chair now?" Annika asked, although she had a good idea.

The woman turned to her, her eyes full of tears.

"They took it away," she said quietly. "The police, to examine it. He was sitting in it when he died, holding the rifle in his right hand."

"Did you find him?"

The woman stared into the space left by her armchair, images chasing through her head so vividly that Annika could almost see them. Then she nodded.

"I was at the scouts' autumn bazaar on Saturday afternoon," she said, still staring at the empty space on the carpet. "Our daughter runs the cubs, so I stayed behind to help her tidy up afterward. When I got home . . . he was sitting there . . . in my chair."

She turned away, the tears overflowing, and stumbled, hunched over, back toward the kitchen table. Annika followed her, rejecting an impulse to put her arm around the woman's shoulders.

"Where was he shot?" Annika asked softly, sitting down beside her.

"In the eye," Gunnel Sandström whispered, her voice echoing faintly between the walls like a rattling wind; the clock ticked, salt tears ran down the woman's face, no sobbing or any other movement. Suddenly something happened to the temperature in the kitchen—Annika could now feel the dead man in the next room, present in the form of a cold breath, a faint note from the angelic choir pressing into her consciousness.

The woman was sitting quite still, but she raised her eyes to look into Annika's.

"If you were going to shoot yourself," she breathed, "why would you aim for your eye? Why would you stare down the barrel when you pull the trigger, what would you expect to see?"

She closed her eyes.

"It doesn't make sense," she said in a louder voice. "He would never have done that, and certainly not in my chair. He's never sat in it, not once. He was sending me a signal that someone was forcing him to do it. It was something about that phone call."

She opened her eyes; Annika saw her pupils suddenly widen, only to contract again.

"We had a call on Friday evening," she said. "Late, after 9:30. We had just watched the news, and were about to go to bed, we have to be up early for the cows, but Kurt went out, he didn't say who it was, just got dressed and went out, and was gone for a long time, I lay awake waiting and he didn't get back until eleven o'clock, and of course I asked who he'd been to see, but he said he'd tell me later because he was tired; but after the cows something else came up and we never got a chance to talk about it properly, so I went off to the scouts and when I got back he was . . ."

She slumped, putting her hands in front of her face, Annika didn't hesitate this time but put an arm across the woman's shoulders.

"Did you say this to the police?"

She collected herself at once, stretched for a napkin and wiped her nose, then nodded. Annika let her arm drop.

"I don't know if they were interested," she said, "but they wrote it down anyway. On Saturday I was so upset I didn't think to say anything, but I called them yesterday and then they came and collected the armchair and looked for fingerprints on the doors and furniture."

"And the gun?"

"They took that on Saturday, said it was standard procedure."

"Kurt was in the civil defense?"

Gunnel Sandström nodded.

"All these years," she said. "He did the officer's course at the Home Guard Combat School in Vellinge."

"Where did he keep the rifle?"

"In the gun cabinet. Kurt was always meticulous about keeping it locked. Even I don't know where he kept the key."

"So he must have taken it out himself?"

Another nod.

"Have you ever been threatened?"

She shook her head this time, slumping a little farther.

"No strange phone calls before the one on Friday, no odd letters?"

The woman stiffened, tilting her head slightly.

"There was a strange letter in today's post," she said. "Complete nonsense, I threw it in the trash."

"A letter? Today? Who from?"

"Don't know, it didn't say."

"Have you emptied the trash?"

Gunnel Sandström thought for a moment.

"I don't think so," she said, getting up and going over to the cupboard under the sink, where she pulled out the garbage can and rummaged through the crusts and potato peelings.

She looked up at Annika.

"It's not here," she said. "I must have emptied it after all."

"You wouldn't have thrown it somewhere else?" Annika asked.

The woman put the garbage can back in the cupboard.

"Why do you think it's important?" she asked.

"I don't know if it is important," Annika said. "What did it say?"

"Something about the peasants' movement, I don't really

know. I thought it was something about the Federation of Swedish Farmers."

"A brochure, a leaflet?"

"No, nothing like that. Handwritten."

"Think for a moment. Is there anywhere else you might have put it?"

"In the fireplace, I suppose," she said, pointing.

In two strides Annika was at the hearth; there were several crumpled balls of paper in there, at least two of them colored flyers from local shops. She took a length of wood out of the wood basket and prodded them.

The woman came over to her, holding out her hand for them.

"Yes, it might be here; I do throw paper on here sometimes. It's good for getting the fire started."

"Hang on," Annika said. "Have you got any gloves?"

Gunnel Sandström stopped and looked up at her in surprise, then disappeared into the hall. Annika leaned forward to look at the balls of paper. Three were glossy ads, one green with black text, and the fifth was a sheet of lined A4 paper.

"Get that one," Annika said when the woman came back wearing a pair of leather gloves, pointing at the lined paper.

Gunnel leaned over, and with a little groan managed to get hold of it. She straightened up and smoothed it out.

"Yes," she said. "This is it."

Annika moved to stand beside her as she slowly read out the anonymous text.

"*The present upsurge of the peasant movement is a colossal event,*" Gunnel read in a tone of blank suspicion. "*In China's central, southern, and northern provinces, several hundred million peasants will rise like a mighty storm, like a hurricane, a force so swift and violent that no power, however great, will be able to hold it back.*"

She lowered the letter.

"What does that mean?"

Annika shook her head.

"I don't know," she said. "Have you still got the envelope?"

They found it beneath the ads, a simple little envelope with the "Sverige" brand, and an ice hockey player on the stamp, addressed to the Sandström family and postmarked in Uppsala the previous day.

"Can you lay it out on the table so I can copy it?"

Dark fear swept across Gunnel's face.

"Why? Do you think it's something serious?"

Annika looked at the woman, her gray hair, her knitted cardigan, soft cheeks, and bent back, and was overwhelmed by a sympathy that took her breath away.

"No," she said, trying to smile. "I don't think so. But I still think you should tell the police about the letter."

Annika copied the text on the kitchen table. The letters were even, soft, and round, the words symmetrically placed on the page, every other line left blank to make it easier to read. She noted the torn edge, which showed that the sheet had been ripped from a pad of lined paper, and wondered if she ought to feel the quality of the paper in one corner, but decided against it.

"Are you going to write anything in the paper about Kurt?" Gunnel Sandström asked when she had stood up and pushed in her chair.

"I don't know," Annika said. "Maybe. If I do, I'll call you first to let you know."

She took the woman's hand.

"Have you got anyone to look after you?" she asked.

Gunnel nodded.

"We've got a son and two daughters; they're coming this afternoon with their families."

Annika felt the room spin again; there was something here, a sense of belonging that ran through the generations, a love that had lived here for centuries.

Maybe people shouldn't leave their roots, she thought. Maybe our longing for progress ruins the natural force that makes us capable of love.

"You'll be okay," she said, surprised that she was so certain.

Gunnel looked at her with eyes that Annika could see were devoid of something vital.

"I'm going to get justice as well," she said.

Then she suddenly turned and went out into the hall, then up a creaking staircase to the floor above.

Annika quickly pulled on her outdoor clothes, and hesitated at the foot of the stairs.

"Well, thank you," she shouted cautiously.

No reply.

Berit Hamrin bumped into Annika at the caretaker's booth by the elevators.

"Are you coming for something to eat?" she asked.

Annika put the car keys on the counter and looked at the time.

"Not today," she said. "I've got loads to check, and I have to get the kids. Are you faint with hunger, or have you got time to look at something?"

Berit pondered this theatrically.

"Faint with hunger," she said. "What is it?"

"Follow me," Annika said, and sailed off toward her office, careless of what she left in her wake. She tossed her outdoor clothes in the usual corner and emptied the contents of her bag on the desk, picking out her notebook. She leafed through to the last page, then rushed around the desk and tugged open the second drawer, pulling out another pad.

"Read this," she told Berit, holding up two pages of notes.

Her colleague took the first pad and read the opening line.

"*The present upsurge of the peasant movement is a colossal event,*" she said out loud, then put the pad down. "But this is a classic text."

"In what way?" Annika said, like a coiled spring, and without looking away from Annika, Berit intoned loudly and clearly from memory:

"*In China's central, southern, and northern provinces, several hundred million peasants will rise like a mighty storm, like a hurri-*

cane, a force so swift and violent that no power, however great, will be able to hold it back."

Annika felt her jaw drop, and stared speechless at her colleague.

"Report on an investigation of the peasant movement in Hunan," Berit said. "Written in 1949, if I remember rightly. One of Mao Zedong's most famous works. We all knew it by heart."

Annika searched through a box and pulled out a couple more notebooks, and leafed through them until she found what she was looking for.

"What about this?"

She gave Berit the notes she had taken up in Luleå.

"*There is no construction without destruction*," Berit read. "*Destruction means criticism and rejection, it means revolution. It involves reasoning things out, which means construction. If you concentrate on destruction first, you get construction as part of the process.*"

"And?" Annika said.

"Another Mao quote. Why have you written them down?"

Annika had to sit down.

"They're letters," she said. "Anonymous letters to murder victims. The destruction one was sent to Benny Ekland's workplace a couple of days after the first murder, the peasants' movement was sent to a local councillor in Östhammar the day after his presumed suicide."

Berit sat down on Annika's desk, her face pale.

"What the . . . ?"

Anna shook her head, pressing her hands to her forehead.

"I have to speak to Linus Gustafsson's mother," she said.

The phone rang out into echoing, frozen space a thousand kilometers north. Her hand was sweating as she pressed the phone to her ear.

"Should I go?" Berit mimed, pointing first at herself, then at the sliding door.

Annika shook her head, closed her eyes.

In the middle of a ring the phone was picked up, the voice that answered sounded newly woken, confused.

"My name's Annika Bengtzon, I'm calling from the *Evening Post* in Stockholm," Annika said in the slow, clear tone of voice she had learned to use in her years as a night editor, the shift when most phone calls reached people who were fast asleep.

"Who?" the woman on the phone said.

"I was the one who wrote about Linus in the paper," Annika said, suddenly feeling tears welling up. "I just wanted to call to say how very sorry I am."

Suddenly the boy was in front of her, his spiked hair and watchful eyes, his defensive body language and uncertain voice—she couldn't help a sudden and audible sob.

"Sorry," she said, "I . . ."

She put her hand over her mouth to cover her sobs, ashamed that Berit, who was now sitting down in one of the chairs, should see her like this.

"It wasn't your fault," the woman said, awake now.

"Are you his mom?"

"I'm Viveka."

She stressed the "e."

"I feel horribly guilty," Annika said, realizing that the phone call wasn't turning out as she had imagined. "I shouldn't have written about Linus. Then he might still be alive today."

"We'll never know," the woman said flatly. "But I thought it was a good thing that you got it out of him. I couldn't work out what was wrong with him. He was a different person after it happened, and he refused to tell me what it was."

"Well," Annika said, "but what if . . ."

The woman interrupted her, rather sharply.

"Do you believe in God, Annika Bengtzon?"

Annika hesitated as the tears dried up.

"Not directly," she managed to say.

"Well, I do," the woman said slowly, and with slightly forced emphasis. "It's helped me through many trials over the years. The Lord called Linus to Him, and I don't understand why, but I accept it."

Sorrow lay like an ice-cold wind on the line from Luleå, making Annika shiver, a vacuum of something hideously jet-black stretching out toward her, the destructive power of human loss, where God's love might provide the flickering flame that prevented the definitive final chill.

"My grandmother died," Annika said. "Seven years ago. I think of her every day. I can't even begin to imagine your loss."

"I have to continue my time on earth without Linus," his mother said, "even if I can't see right now how I'm going to manage. But I'm firm in my faith that God the Father is doing what is best for me, that his hand rests above me."

The woman fell silent, Annika could hear her weeping. She waited, not sure if she should try to end the conversation and hang up.

"In time I may come to understand why," the woman went on suddenly, in a clear, lucid voice. "And I shall meet Linus again, of course. In the House of Our Lord. I know this to be true. It gives me the strength to carry on living."

"I wish I had your God," Annika said.

"He is there for you too," the woman said. "He is there, if only you want to take him to you."

The silence that followed could have been difficult, but to her surprise Annika found it warm and red.

"There was something else I wanted to ask," she said. "Have you had anything strange in the post since Linus died?"

Viveka Gustafsson thought for a few seconds before she replied.

"You mean that thing about youth?"

Annika looked over at Berit.

"Youth?"

"An anonymous letter arrived, no signature or anything, I thought it was a note of sympathy from one of the neighbors who didn't want to disturb me by knocking."

"Have you still got the letter?"

The woman let out a deep sigh that stemmed from the hopelessness of having to do anything connected with the living, the sort of daily life that had brought light and warmth and solidarity for decades, but had now suddenly lost all meaning.

"I think I put it in the pile with the newspapers; hang on, I'll go and get it . . ."

A sharp noise hit Annika's ear as the other phone was put down on a wooden table somewhere in Svartöstaden. There was the sound of rustling on the line, of footsteps coming and going?

"Sorry to take so long," the woman said tiredly, "I've got it. It says: *How should we judge whether a youth is revolutionary? How to discern this? There is only one criteria: if he is disposed to stand, and stands in practice, with the great worker and peasant masses. He is revolutionary if he wants to do so and does it; otherwise he is nonrevolutionary or counterrevolutionary.*"

Annika stared wide-eyed at Berit and grabbed a pen.

"Can you repeat that slowly, please? I'd like to write it down. *How should we judge whether a youth is revolutionary?*"

"*How to discern this? There is only one criteria: if he is disposed to stand, and stands in practice, with the great worker and peasant masses. He is revolutionary if he wants to do so and does it; otherwise he is nonrevolutionary or counterrevolutionary.*"

"*How to discern this? There is only one criteria . . .*"

Berit nodded, mimed "Mao." Viveka Gustafsson continued reading down the line.

"*. . . if he is disposed to stand, and stands in practice, with the great worker and peasant masses. He is revolutionary if he wants to do so and does it; otherwise he is nonrevolutionary or counterrevolutionary.*"

"Have you mentioned this to the police?"

"No," the woman said, and for the first time life filtered in, a surprise which one day would lead to curiosity, and finally to actual joy in being alive. "Should I have?"

"What does the letter look like?"

"Well," the woman said, "what can I say? It looks like an ordinary sheet torn out of a pad."

"A4? Lined?"

"Blue lines. Is that important?"

"Have you still got the envelope?"

"Yes, it's here."

"What does it look like?"

"Look like? An ordinary little white envelope, like when you fold a sheet of paper in four. Addressed to us, the Gustafsson family. Normal stamp, postmark . . . what does it say? Luleå, but I can't see the date."

"What sort of stamp?"

A few seconds' silence.

"Someone playing hockey."

Annika screwed her eyes tight shut, forcing her pulse to slow down.

"I think you should call the police and tell them that you've received this letter. I might mention the fact that you got it in the newspaper—is that okay with you?"

The woman's surprise had turned to confusion.

"But," she said, "why would you do that?"

Annika hesitated, unable to be entirely honest with Viveka Gustafsson.

"I don't really know if it means anything or not," she said. "It would be wrong of me to speculate about something I don't know."

The woman reflected on this, and it sounded almost as if she was nodding.

"When you don't know, you shouldn't say," she said. "I'll speak to the inspector."

"Call me if there's anything I can do for you," Annika said, empty words that echoed into the gaping black mouth of sorrow.

"What a weird conversation," Berit said. "For a while I thought the boy was actually here in the room."

Annika pressed her hands against her cheeks, noticing that they were trembling.

"It's the same killer," she said. "It can't mean anything else."

"Which police districts?"

"Two cases in Luleå, one in Uppsala."

"It would make sense to talk to the national murder commission at once. If it hasn't already reached their desks, it'll soon be there after that call."

"You're sure?" Annika said. "All three are quotations from Mao?"

Berit stood up, drying her eyes, and walked toward the door.

"Now you're insulting an old revolutionary," she said. "Well, I'm finally going to get some food. Or else I'll be a dead revolutionary."

She closed the door behind her.

Annika stayed where she was, listening to her own heartbeat.

Was there any other explanation? Could different people, unknown to each other, send quotations from Mao to people whose relatives had just met a violent death, on similar paper, with the same sort of stamp on the envelope?

She stood up and walked over to the glass wall that separated her world from the newsroom, looking across the people out there, and trying to glimpse the real world through the window beyond the sports desk. From the fourth floor she could only make out a faint gray horizon, and some single flakes of snow drifting gently down toward the top of a tall birch tree.

We live in a desperate country, she thought. Whatever made people want to settle here? And why are we still here? What makes us put up with it?

She closed her eyes hard, and she knew the answer. We live where those close to us live, we live for those we love, for our children.

And then someone comes along and kills them, destroying the meaning of our lives.

Unforgivable.

She hurried back to her desk and dialed Q's cell phone.

The metallic voice of his cell explained that he was busy in meetings for the rest of the day, that messages couldn't be left: try again tomorrow.

She dialed his direct line at the national crime unit, a secretary answered after various clicks indicating that the call was being transferred.

"He's in a meeting," she said. "And he has another meeting straight after that."

"Yes, I know," Annika said, shaking her arm to look at her watch, 3:32 PM. "We agreed to see each other briefly between his meetings, and I'm supposed to show up just before four."

The secretary was suspicious.

"He hasn't mentioned that."

"He knows it won't take long."

"But he has to be in the ministry of justice at 4 PM, the car's picking him up at a quarter to."

Annika jotted that down, writing "Rosenbad 4" on her notepad, Justice occupied the fourth and fifth floor of the main government building, with the Cabinet Office directly above.

Not that the whole department was there: all the committees were spread around various locations.

"Of course," she said. "It was that committee, wasn't it . . . ?"

The sound of the secretary leafing through some papers.

"JU 2002:13, the new correctional treatment act," she said.

Annika scribbled out "Rosenbad 4" and wrote "Regeringsgatan" instead.

"I must have misunderstood," she said. "I'll try to catch him tomorrow."

She stuffed her notes in her bag, grabbed her hat, gloves, and scarf, searched for her cell phone in the mess on her desk but failed to find it, and assumed it must be somewhere in her bag, then yanked open the sliding door and headed for the news desk.

Jansson had only just arrived, and was sitting there bleary-eyed and unkempt with a plastic cup, reading the local papers.

"There's something wrong with the machine," he said to Annika, pointing at the cup.

"Isn't it time for a smoke?" she said, and Jansson immediately took out his cigarette packet.

Annika stepped inside the empty glass smoking cubicle, which stood in isolated majesty in the middle of the newsroom floor.

"I may have found a serial killer," she said as Jansson lit his twentieth cigarette of the day.

He exhaled a plume of smoke and stared up at the extractor fan.

"May?"

"I don't know if, or what, the police know," she said. "I'm hoping to grab Q on his way to a departmental committee in quarter of an hour."

"So what have you got?"

"Three deaths," she said. "A journalist killed in a hit-and-run and a murdered boy in Luleå, and a local councillor shot in Östhammar. The relatives all received anonymous letters the day after the deaths, handwritten Mao quotations on lined A4, posted in 'Sverige' envelopes with ice-hockey players on the stamps."

Jansson fixed his glazed eyes on her, exhausted by eighteen years on the night shift, a fourth wife, and a fifth baby.

"Sounds like you're home and dry," he said. "The police just have to confirm it."

"With a bit of luck they'll have more information."

The editor looked at his watch.

"Get downstairs straightaway," he said, putting out the half-smoked cigarette in the chrome ashtray. "I'll get a car."

She left the smoking room, spun to her right and raced, with tunnel vision, toward the elevator. She ran down the stairs because both elevators were busy.

A taxi was waiting outside the main entrance.

"Name?" the driver said.

"Torstensson," Annika said, and sank into the backseat.

An old trick of the trade from the previous editor's time. Annika, Jansson, and a few of the others got into the habit of always booking taxis in the editor in chief's name, because it was usually quicker to jump into another taxi than the one you yourself had booked. Occasionally the booked taxi driver who had been left waiting angrily for "Torstensson" would go in and shout his name in the newsroom, which never failed to be funny. Even though Torstensson had been elbowed out by Schyman in conjunction with the death of Michelle Carlsson, the old tradition lived on.

Sleet was whipping at the windows of the car, making Annika blink and flinch. The traffic was solid; a traffic light up ahead turned red, then green, then red without the line of cars moving at all.

Annika could feel adrenaline making her fingers itch.

"I'm in one hell of a hurry," she said. "Is there any other way of getting there?"

The driver looked at her over his shoulder with a scornful expression.

"You called for a taxi," he said. "Not a tank."

She checked the time, trying to tell herself that the traffic would be just as bad for Q.

"After these lights there's a bus lane," the taxi driver said encouragingly.

At three minutes to four he pulled up on Hamngatan, at the corner of Regeringsgatan. She scrawled her name on the receipt for the invoice, leaped out of the taxi with her bag hanging from one arm and stress hammering inside her chest.

The traffic was roaring around her, splashing water and mud up her trousers. The banks and shops had all put in their Christmas windows already, the yellow and red lighting flashing in her eyes. She peered through the sleet.

Was she too late? Had he already gone in?

A dark blue Volvo with tinted windows pulled up outside Regeringsgatan 30–32; she noticed it because it was far too unobtrusive. Before her brain had even worked out why, she knew he was inside. She rushed over and positioned herself by the doorway, so he would have to pass her on his way in.

"My secretary said you called and were fishing," he said as he slammed the back door of the Volvo. The car glided away quickly and noiselessly into the traffic, swallowed up by the snow, totally neutral.

"I want to know if you know about the serial killer," she said, staring at him, icy water trickling down her temples.

"Which one?" he said.

"Very funny," she said, feeling the sleet run down the back of her neck. "The one sending Mao quotes to his victims."

Q stared at her for several seconds; she saw the snow settle on his hair and slowly slide down toward his eyebrows. The shoulders of his flame-colored raincoat were soon soaked. The bare hand clutching his briefcase imperceptibly gripped the handle tighter.

"I'm not with you," he said, and she felt a chill come from inside out rather than the other way around.

"The journalist in Luleå," she said. "The boy who witnessed his death. A Center Party councillor in Östhammar. There must be something that connects them."

He took a couple of paces toward her, his eyes darkly watchful, and tried to get past her.

"I can't talk now," he said from the corner of his mouth.

She moved quickly to the right, blocking his path.

"It's Ragnwald," she said in a low voice when he was right in front of her. "He's back, isn't he?"

The commissioner looked at her for several long seconds, their white breaths mingling as they were blown away by the wind.

"One fine day you're going to be too smart for your own good," he said.

"Have been, all my life," she said.

"I'll call you this evening," he said, and she let him walk around her, hearing him speak into the entry phone, and the click as the lock opened.

Anne Snapphane was walking straight into the wind, no matter which direction she faced. Every time she changed direction, the sleet changed as well. As usual she cursed the fact that she had been so amenable when Mehmet had suggested that Miranda go to a nursery in his block rather than near her. He was firmly settled in his home, and she wasn't, so it had made sense at the time.

But not anymore, four years and eighteen thousand hours of traveling back and forth later.

The nursery really was in an idyllic setting, in an inner courtyard off one of the quietest and smartest streets on Östermalm. Almost all Miranda's friends there had names with "von" or "af," or some ornate nouveau riche construct like Silfverbielke.

Okay, so there was a pair of twins called Andersson, but they were the daughters of Sweden's most popular film actress.

She turned the last corner and was met with a storm of icy shards, making her gasp, ready to admit defeat. She stopped to catch her breath, squinted and could just make out the entrance farther down the street, as she leaned against the building at her side.

It wasn't the wind or sleet that was getting to her, she was well aware of that. And it wasn't some hideous disease that would end up being named after her either.

It was her job, or rather it was the boiling cauldron of power struggles that the owners of the company had ignited when they set up TV Scandinavia.

Today the family that owned the biggest film distribution company in Scandinavia, and which also happened to own Annika's damn tabloid, had sabotaged all the negotiations they had conducted with both foreign and Swedish film companies. The oral agreements that formed the very foundation of TV Scandinavia had been broken, one by one, starting at half past eight that morning. The family had been busy over the weekend, scaring the life, not to mention the profit, out of every single independent film company north of the equator.

I wonder what's going to happen, Anne thought, closing her eyes against the darkness. Is this television company built on solid ground, or quicksand?

She was desperate to get home, and desperate for a drink, a damn large glass of vodka with lemon and ice, cotton wool for the brain, and a chance for her body to relax.

Not in front of Miranda, she thought; she could see Annika's face in front of her when she had told her about her father's drinking, how he had made such a fool of himself, falling over and shouting, until he was eventually found dead in a snowdrift a few hundred meters from the works in Hälleforsnäs.

Can't let that happen, she thought, bracing herself against the wind and setting off again toward the nursery.

A strong smell of small children and wet raincoats hit her as she opened the door. The porch was a sea of brown mud, with the cheery command "Hello! All shoes off!" on a colorful sign above the shoe rack.

Anne wiped her feet halfheartedly: the state of the doormat suggested that it wasn't going to do any good. Then she tiptoed into the hall where all the little blue shelves, an alcove for every child, were full to overflowing with children's clothes, stuffed toys, drawings, photographs of holidays, birthdays, Christmases.

She took a deep breath, about to call to her daughter, when she caught sight of the woman in the door to the kitchen.

Tall, thin, with long, strawberry blond hair in soft curls over one shoulder. A Palestinian shawl.

Anne blinked.

So ridiculously medieval, wearing a Palestinian shawl.

The woman stiffened when she saw Anne, her eyes taking on a look of slight panic.

"I . . . ," she said, collecting herself. "My name's Sylvia, I'm Sylvia."

She took a few steps forward, and held out her hand.

Anne Snapphane stared at the woman, a nauseous feeling growing like a tornado in her stomach, unable to lift her hand or return the greeting.

"What are you doing here?" she said, sounding brittle and echoey in her own ears.

Mehmet's new woman, his fiancée, his future wife, the woman who was carrying his new child; she was standing in front of her looking confused and pretty terrified.

"I . . . was going to pick Miranda up, but she said that you . . ."

"It's my week," Anne said, unable to understand why her voice was coming from so far away. "Why are you here?"

Sylvia Pregnant Fiancée ran her tongue over her lips and Anne noticed they were sensual—she was beautiful, Sylvia was much more beautiful than she was, jealousy and spite pricking her eyes like knives, warping her sight. She was beside herself with spite and humiliation and realized at that very moment that she had lost, and if she allowed herself to look destroyed then she would be. She would have to construct some self-respect for herself.

"I must have got it wrong," Sylvia said. "I thought I was supposed to be collecting her today. I thought it was my day."

"Do you start all your sentences with 'I'?" Anne said, suddenly able to move again, her legs maneuvering past Sylvia Beautiful Pregnant Fiancée and into the kitchen and a yell of "Mommy!"

Miranda flew into her arms holding an apple core in one hand and buried her sticky mouth in her hair.

"Darling," Anne whispered. "I bet you almost blew away today!"

The girl leaned back and looked at the ceiling.

"They had to tie me down," she said. "Then I flew like a kite all the way to Lidingö."

Anne laughed, the girl wriggled loose and ran past Sylvia Beautiful without taking any notice of her stepmother. She called over her shoulder:

"Can we have pancakes for tea? Can I break the eggs?"

Anne walked up to Sylvia, who was in her way by the door.

"Still here?" she said dully.

"I feel so sick," Sylvia said, tears welling up in her eyes. "I don't understand how I could get it so wrong. Sorry. It's just . . . I feel so ill the whole time. I spend all my time being sick."

"Get an abortion, then," Anne said.

Beautiful Sylvia flinched as though she'd been slapped, her face turning bright red.

"What?" she said.

Anne took a step closer, breathing right into the other woman's face.

"The worst thing I know," Anne said, "is spoiled bitches whining. You really expect my sympathy?"

Pregnant Lovely Sylvia took a step back and hit her head on the door frame, mouth and eyes wide-open.

Anne walked past her, feeling her face blazing, went over to her clever little daughter who was putting her clothes on and chattering about different sorts of pancake batter. She took her hand and left the nursery, Sylvia's offended muteness at her back.

Annika was frying fish sticks and making mashed potatoes from powder, something she never did when Thomas was home. Thomas was used to well-made, proper food; his mother had always placed great importance on having good ingredients, but then it could hardly have been that hard. The family had owned a grocery store, after all. It wasn't as if her beloved mother-in-law suffered from the strain of working in the shop itself. She just went down and picked out what she wanted without paying, and looked after the accounts, so of course she had time to cook.

Thomas had never peeled a potato for himself. Ready-made food had been a complete mystery to him when Annika turned up with her tins of ravioli.

His children, on the other hand, seemed perfectly happy to eat reshaped fish and powdered mashed potatoes.

"Do we have to eat the red stuff?" Kalle asked.

She had dutifully cut up a red pepper on their plates, which they were now both picking out.

She was itching to get going; she knew she had at least four hours' work ahead of her.

"No," she said. "You can watch a film if you like. Which one would you like?"

"Yay!" Ellen said, throwing her arms out and knocking her plate to the floor.

Annika got up and picked up the plate, which had survived, and the food, which hadn't.

"*Beauty and the Beast*!" Kalle said, jumping down from his chair.

"No!" Annika said, noticing that she was shouting. "Not that one!"

The children stared at her, wide-eyed.

"But we got it from Grandma," Kalle said. "Don't you like *Beauty*?"

She swallowed her stress and knelt down by the children.

"*Beauty and the Beast* is a really bad film," she said. "It lies to us. The Beast takes Beauty and her father prisoner; he torments both of them, kidnaps them and locks them up. That isn't nice, is it?"

Both children shook their heads in silence.

"Exactly," Annika said. "But Beauty still has to love the Beast, because if she loves him enough then she'll be able to save him."

"But that's good, isn't it?" Kalle said. "That she saves him."

"But why would she do that?" Annika said. "Why would she save the Beast, when he's only been horrid to her?"

She could see the boy's confusion, and Ellen's uncomprehending eyes, and put her arms around Kalle.

"You're a good boy," she whispered to him. "You don't know how horrid people can sometimes be. But there are horrid people, and you can't cure them with love."

She stroked his hair and kissed him on the cheek.

"Why don't you watch *Mio, My Mio*?"

"That's so scary," Ellen said. "Only if you watch it with us."

"What about *Pippi*, then?"

"Yay!"

Thirty seconds after she had started the film, there was a buzzing sound from the depths of her bag. She ran into the bedroom with the bag, shut the door, and emptied the contents on the unmade bed. The cord of her cell phone had got tangled up with the spiral binding of one of her notebooks.

It was Q.

"I've checked the quotes you mentioned."

She pulled out the right notebook and a pen.

"And?" she said, sinking to the floor with her back against the bed.

"Bloody weird coincidence," he said. "A bit too weird to have happened by accident."

"Do you have anything else that connects the three deaths?"

He sighed deeply at the other end.

"We don't know yet, but there are no similarities in the way they were killed. The deaths are very different. We've found fibers on the victims, but nothing that matches. No fingerprints."

"Just the letters?"

"Just the letters."

"So what conclusions are you prepared to draw?"

Another sigh.

"The man from Östhammar was murdered, we know that much now. He was shot from a distance of at least one meter, and it's difficult to hold an AK-4 that far away and still pull the trigger. Of course there's a connection between the boy and the journalist, but so far we haven't found any link to the local councillor. The boy saw the hack get run down, so that's a fairly standard motive. Maybe he could have identified the killer."

"Or else he knew the killer," Annika said.

There was a moment of surprised silence from the commissioner.

"What makes you say that?"

She shook her head, looking at the wallpaper.

"He pretty much said so," she said. "Then he got very scared, made me leave."

"I've read the report of his questioning by the police in Luleå. There's nothing in there about him being scared."

"Of course there isn't," Annika said. "He was protecting himself."

The silence on the line was suspicious.

"You don't think the boy knew him at all," Annika said, "because you think it was Ragnwald."

The door flew open and Ellen came into the bedroom.

"Mommy, he's got the remote control, he says I can't have it."

"Hang on," she said, putting the cell phone down, getting up and going back to the television with Ellen.

Kalle was curled up in a corner of the sofa, clutching the remotes for the television and the video to his chest.

"Kalle," Annika said, "let Ellen have one of them."

"No," the boy said, "she keeps pressing buttons and messing it up."

"Okay," Annika said, "then I'll take them both."

"No!" Ellen howled. "I want one!"

"That's enough!" Annika shouted. "Give me the damn remotes and sit and watch quietly, or you'll have to go to bed!"

She grabbed the remotes and walked back into the bedroom with Kalle's cries ringing in her ears.

She shut the door and picked up the phone again.

"Ragnwald," Q said.

"Suup leaked some information to me, to let Ragnwald know that you know that he's back," Annika said. "Were you involved in that decision?"

He snorted.

"I haven't seen any article so far."

"It'll be in tomorrow's paper, although it's a pretty thin story, I have to say. Suup didn't give me much. I think you've got a lot more than that."

The commissioner didn't respond.

"How much do you know?" Annika asked. "Have you got an ID?"

"A couple of things first," Q said. "You can use the anonymous letters, but not the fact that they contain Mao quotations."

Annika was taking notes.

"And Ragnwald?"

"We're sure he's back."

"Why? To kill these individuals?"

"He's been gone for more than thirty years, so he must have a damn good reason for coming back. But what that is, we don't yet know."

"Is he the Mao murderer?"

"Nice headline, shame you can't use it. I don't know if it's him. It might be, but I wouldn't swear to it."

"But he was the one who blew up the plane at F21?"

"He was involved somehow, but we don't know if he was there for the explosion itself."

"What's his name? His real name?"

Commissioner Q hesitated.

"You got a serial killer out of me," Annika said. "Surely I can get a terrorist out of you?"

"You can't use it," Q said. "We've kept his details quiet for thirty years, and it has to stay that way for a bit longer. This is only for your own personal records. No notes on the computer, no stray notes in the office."

Annika swallowed hard, her pen poised, her pulse throbbing in her neck. She drew breath to ask about the level of secrecy when the door suddenly flew open and Kalle rushed in.

"Mommy, she's got Tiger! Make her give him back!"

A short circuit in Annika's brain meant that she breathed enough air for a primal scream. She felt the color in her face rise, and looked at Kalle with crazed eyes.

"Out!" she whispered. "Now!"

The boy looked at her in horror, then turned and ran, leaving the door wide open behind him.

"Mommy says you have to give Tiger to me," she heard him shout. "Now!"

"Nilsson," Q said. "His name's Göran Nilsson. Son of a Læstadian minister from Sattajärvi in Norrbotten, born October 1948.

Moved to Uppsala to study theology autumn 1967, back in Luleå a year or so later, worked in cathedral administration, vanished November 18, 1969, and hasn't been seen under his true identity since then."

Annika was writing so hard that her wrist hurt, hoping she could later decipher her scribbles.

"Læstadian?"

"Læstadianism is a religious movement in Norrbotten, some aspects of which are incredibly strict. No curtains, no television, no birth control."

"Do you know why he's called Ragnwald?"

"That was his code name in the Maoist groups in Luleå in the late sixties. He kept it as his stage name when he became a professional killer, but his ETA identity is probably French. He's most likely been living in a village in the Pyrenees, on the French side, and moving across the border pretty much at will."

Annika could hear the children fighting it out in the television room.

"So he really did become a real, professional killer? Someone like Léon?"

"No, people like that don't exist outside Luc Besson films, but we know he was involved in a few assassinations for money. I have to go, and it sounds like you need to sort things out there."

"They're fighting over a stuffed tiger," Annika said.

"O man, your legacy shall be violence," Q said, and hung up.

She watched the end of *Pippi* with the children, one on each knee, then brushed their teeth and read two chapters from the Bullerby books out loud to them. They sang three songs from the *Swedish Songbook* together, then they went out like lights. She was dizzy with tiredness when she finally sat down to write. The letters floated like islands on the screen; she couldn't seem to tie them down, and was struck by an intense sense of falling, a short second of complete impotence.

She fled from the screen into the bathroom and splashed cold water in her face, then went into the kitchen and boiled some water; measured four spoons of coffee into the French press, pouring the water on as it boiled, and forcing the metal filter down hard. She took the coffee and a mug from the Federation of Local Councils and sat down at the computer again.

Empty. She had nothing left.

She picked up the phone and called Jansson.

"I can't pull it together," she said. "It isn't working."

"You can do it," Jansson said, his voice alive with the adrenaline of the news torrent. "I need you now. We can help each other out here. Where have you got stuck?"

"Before I've even started."

"Take it from scratch. One. There's a serial killer on the loose, that's the angle for the front page. Start with the summary, describe the deaths in Norrland, the quotes in the letters."

"I'm not allowed to," she said, and typed "serial killer, describe Luleå."

"Well, just balance the information as best you can. Two. You bring in the murder of the Östhammar politician, that's new and we've got an exclusive on that. The wife's story, police work. Was it murder?"

"Yep."

"Good. Three. You link Östhammar to Luleå and describe the police's desperate search for the killer. You've got the front page, six, seven, eight, nine, and the centerfold for your old terrorist, we've already put him in."

She made no response, just sat there in silence listening to the noises behind the editor's voice, a newscaster's voice on the television, a phone ringing, the tapping of a keyboard, a symphony of efficiency and cynicism that was supposed to represent one of the mainstays of democracy.

She could see Gunnel Sandström in front of her, her wine-colored cardigan and soft cheeks, and suddenly felt a huge, infinite sense of powerlessness.

"Okay," she whispered.

"Don't worry about pictures," Jansson said. "We'll fix that here. There was a bit of fuss about the fact that you went to Östhammar without a photographer, but I explained that you went on a hunch and had no idea you were going to get a hole in one. We've sorted pictures of the farm; the old girl didn't want to be in them, but we've got the boy's mother and the editor in chief of the *Norrland News* as next of kin; that reporter wasn't much of a family man, if I've got that right?"

"That's right," Annika said quietly.

"Any chance of a shot of the letters?"

"Tonight? Difficult. But it wouldn't be too hard to mock something up; you've got all the details."

"Pelle!" Jansson yelled in the direction of the picture desk. "Studio shot of some letters, right away."

"Ordinary 'Sverige' envelopes," Annika said, "stamps with a hockey player on. The contents are just ordinary lined A4 from a pad, with slightly ragged edges like when you can't be bothered to use the perforations, text written in ballpoint, every other line, filling up about half the page."

"Anything else?"

"For God's sake, make sure you say that the picture's a mock-up."

"Yeah, yeah. When do we get your stuff?"

She looked at the time, on solid ground again.

"When do you want it?"

Thomas emerged from the pitch-black interior of the jazz club onto the illuminated street, his legs soft with beer and his brain vibrating with music. He wasn't really into jazz, was more of a Beatles man, but the band tonight were good, talented, tuneful, had real feeling in their music.

Behind him he heard Sophia's ringing laughter, her response to something the guy at the coat check had said. She knew everyone there, was a real regular, which is how they got the best table. He let the door swing shut, buttoned his coat and turned his back to the wind as he waited for her. The noise of the city had no rhythm: it sounded out of tune after the soft jazz. He looked up at the neon signs above him, feeling his skin reflecting pink and green and blue, fumes in his hair.

She was so at ease with life, so happy, her laughter ran like a silvery spring stream over the dark floor of the club, over the heavy conference table; she was ambitious and dutiful and quietly spoken and grateful for what life gave her. With her he felt happy, satisfied. She respected him, listened to him, took him seriously. He never had to justify who he was; she never moaned or nagged; she seemed genuinely interested when he talked about his parents and childhood in Vaxholm. And she sailed as well, her family had a place on Möja.

He heard her behind him and turned around to see her step out of the darkness and take a few tentative moves down the steps in her neat little boots and tight skirt.

"There's going to be a jam on Friday," Sophia said. "That gets massive sometimes. Once I was here until half past six the next morning; it was just brilliant."

He smiled into her warm eyes, sucked into the sheer blueness of them. She stood in front of him and pulled up her shoulders, put her feet close together, and burrowed her hands deep into her coat pockets, smiling up at his face.

"Are you cold?" he asked, noticing that his mouth was completely dry.

She carried on smiling as she shook her head.

"Not at all," she said. "I'm perfectly warm."

He gave in and pulled her to him. Her head was just under his nose; she was taller than Annika, her hair smelled of apples. She wrapped her arms around him, holding him tight. A violent jolt went through his body, so hot and rigid that it took his breath away, making him gasp.

"Thomas," she whispered against his chest, "if only you knew how much I've been longing for this."

He gulped and closed his eyes, holding her even tighter, absorbing her smell, apples and perfume and the wool of her coat, then relaxed and saw her turn her face to his. He was breathing through his mouth as he stared into her eyes, saw the pupils contract, noticing that she was panting.

If I do this there's no way back, he thought.

If I give in now, I'm lost.

And he leaned forward and kissed her, endlessly slowly and carefully; her lips were cold and tasted of gin and menthol cigarettes. Shivers ran up and down his spine. Then she took a little step toward him, almost imperceptible, but their teeth met and the warmth from her mouth entered his and a moment later he thought he was going to explode; good grief—he had to have this woman, he had to have her now.

"Do you want to come home with me?" she whispered against his neck.

He could only nod.

She let go of him and beckoned to a taxi, with her usual success. They stepped apart; she adopted a look that said sensible Federation of County Councils representative, adjusted her hair, and simultaneously sent him a radiant glance across the roof of the car. They climbed in their respective back doors, she gave the driver the address of her apartment on Östermalm. Then they sat in their corners of the backseat with their hands clasped hard together beneath her handbag as the taxi rattled them through the city center and up toward Karlaplan.

He paid with his business account, signing with trembling fingers.

She lived at the top of a magnificent building from 1898. The marble staircase was discreetly lit by soft brass lamps; a thick carpet swallowed their steps as she quickly pulled him toward the elevator. They closed the ornamental gate and she pressed the button for the sixth floor, then pulled off his coat. He let it fall to the floor, not caring if it got dirty, and took off her coat and jacket and blouse, filling his hands with her breasts. She moaned gently against his shoulder, both of her hands massaging his groin. Then she found the zipper, opened it, and pulled his erection out of his underwear. He couldn't help closing his eyes and leaning back, afraid he was going to faint.

Then the elevator stopped with a jolt; she kissed him and laughed into his mouth.

"Well, project leader, come on. We're nearly there."

They gathered their clothes and bags and briefcases and tumbled out of the elevator. She hunted for the keys in her handbag, and he ran his tongue over the back of her neck as she unlocked the door.

"I have to turn the alarm off," she whispered.

After a few bleeping sounds they were in her hallway, his hands caressing her naked waist. They moved upward and found her breasts, she pressed her behind against him before turning around and pulling him with her onto the floor of the hall.

Her eyes were radiant, her breathing light and urgent, and as he pushed into her she held his gaze and he was lost, drowning, wanted to carry on drowning until he died; then he died and everything went black for a moment when he came.

All of a sudden he was conscious of his own panting. He was lying with his knee in one of her shoes, and realized that they hadn't even closed the door; a cold draft was making his sweaty skin shiver.

"We can't stay like this," he said, sliding out of her.

"Oh, Thomas," Sophia said. "I think I'm in love with you."

He looked at her lying beneath him with her blond hair spread over the parquet floor, lipstick smeared on her cheek, her mascara under her eyes. A sense of incredible awkwardness suddenly came over him, and he looked away and stood up. The room swayed a little; he must have drunk more than he thought. From the corner of his eye he saw her get up beside him, still wearing her bra, her skirt awry.

"That was wonderful, wasn't it, Thomas?"

He gulped and forced himself to look at her, slender, slightly fragile out of her clothes, defenseless and breathless as a small child. He forced himself to smile at her; she was so sweet.

"You're wonderful," he said, and she stroked her hand quickly against his cheek.

"Do you want coffee?" she asked, closing the front door and unzipping the back of her skirt, letting it fall to the ground along with her bra.

"Please," he said as she walked naked through the apartment. "Thanks."

A moment later she was back, wrapped in an ivory dressing gown, and holding another one, wine red.

"Here," she said. "The shower's on the left at the end."

He took the dressing gown and considered the shower for a moment. Even if Annika was asleep when he got home, it wasn't worth taking the risk.

Sophia had disappeared off to the right somewhere; he thought he could hear the hiss of an espresso machine. Cautiously he stepped into the room in front of him, and found himself in a studio with an eight-meter-high ceiling and huge windows facing the dull city sky. The walls were brick, the floor the same oiled oak as in the hall.

He couldn't help being impressed. This was what an apartment should really look like.

"Sugar?" Sophia called from the kitchen.

"Please," he said, and hurried toward the bathroom.

He showered quickly and thoroughly, using the most neutrally scented soap he could find, scrubbing his crotch and washing around his cock with a sponge. Took care not to get his hair wet.

She was sitting at a table of smoked glass in the designer kitchen when he came in wrapped in his wine red dressing gown, she was smoking one of her menthol cigarettes.

"You have to go home?" she said, framing it as a question.

He nodded, sat down, wondered what he was feeling. Mostly he felt pleased. He smiled at her, touching her hand.

"Right away?"

He sat for a moment, then nodded. She put the cigarette out, pulled her hands away and put them in her lap.

"Do you love your wife?" she asked, staring at the table.

He swallowed, didn't know what to say, didn't actually know whether he did or not.

"Yes," he said, "I think so."

He let his subconscious conjure up images of Annika, and his response to her.

Once, when he was still living with Eleonor, he had dreamed about her, and in the dream she had had burning hair. Her head had been covered with flames, singing and dancing around her face, and she was quite unconcerned about it; fire was her natural element: it ran like silk along her back and shoulders.

After that night he had often imagined her like that, as someone who dwelled in fire.

"She's boundless, somehow," he said. "Has none of the barriers normal people have, can put herself through pretty much anything if she's set her mind to it."

"Sounds a bit uncomfortable," Sophia said.

He nodded slowly.

"And fascinating," he said. "I've never met anyone like her."

Sophia smiled at him, a careful, friendly smile.

"I'm glad you came."

He smiled back.

"So am I."

"Shall I call a taxi?"

He nodded again, then looked down at his hands, waiting quietly as she went out to the phone.

"Five minutes," she said.

He drank up his coffee, it was too strong and too sweet, then stood up and put the cup on the draining board. He went out into the hall and quickly gathered together his clothes, pulling them on with concise, efficient movements.

Once he had pulled on his coat and found his briefcase she slid up behind him, a light shadow of perfume and apple scent. She wound her arms around his waist, lay her cheek against his back.

"Thanks for this evening," she whispered.

He blinked a few times, turned around and kissed her gently.

"Thank *you*," he whispered.

She locked the door behind him, and he could feel her watching through the peephole in the door until the elevator carried him down with it.

Out in the street it had started to snow. The taxi wasn't there yet, he stood and leaned his head back, staring up through the flakes.

I wonder how long it will be before one of them hits my eye, he thought.

Kurt Sandström had been shot in the eye.

The group's first murdered politician.

The meeting of the project group this evening had been good, short and constructive. They had quickly agreed that there was no immediate threat to the project in terms of the media, but rather the opposite. They couldn't have stopped the murder, but they could work in a more constructive way from now on to prevent any recurrence, precisely because of what had happened. Tomorrow their discussion would continue up in the department on Regeringsgatan.

The car glided up soundlessly through the thickening snow, he jumped in when he suddenly noticed it. From the backseat he told the taxi driver his address, Hantverkargatan 32.

He must have dozed off, because the next moment they were there. He fumbled for his business account card and paid, gathered his things with some difficulty, pushed the door shut and stopped to look up at the house.

The lights in the apartment were still on; he glimpsed a shadow moving inside.

Annika was still up, even though she was always so tired in the evening, after all those years on the night shift.

Why wasn't she asleep? What was she doing, wandering from room to room?

There were only two reasons.

Either she was still working, or else she suspected something, and once these thoughts had formulated themselves in his head the result was inevitable.

Guilt and regret hit him in the guts like the kick of a horse, the utterly fundamental paralysis that comes from unwelcome awareness. He couldn't breathe; his diaphragm contracted and made him collapse.

Oh, good God, what had he done?

What if she found out.

What if she understood.

What if she already knew.

Had someone seen something? Had someone called? Maybe someone had tipped off the paper?

He was breathing raggedly and with some difficulty, forcing himself to be sensible.

Tipped off the paper? Why the hell would anyone tip off the paper?

He was on the verge of losing his grip.

Slowly he straightened up, and looked up at the windows again.

The living-room light was out now, she was on her way to bed.

Maybe she knows I'm coming, he thought. Maybe she's trying to fool me into thinking she doesn't know, even though she knows everything. Maybe she'll pretend to be asleep when I go in and then kill me in my sleep.

And he saw her in front of him with fire for hair, clutching an iron bar with both hands, poised to strike.

He felt like crying as he unlocked the front door, unable to think how he could bear to look at her. He walked up the two flights of stairs with silent steps and stopped outside the door—their door, the big double doors with the stained glass that Annika thought was so beautiful.

And he stood there with the keys in his hand, shaking, a vibration in his stomach like a jamming jazz band, looking at the doors with strange eyes until his breathing was calmer, something like normal, and he could move again.

The hall was dark.

He crept in and closed the heavy door quietly behind him.

"Thomasch?"

Annika popped her head out of the bathroom, and took the toothbrush out of her mouth.

"How did it go?"

He collapsed on the hall bench, feeling utterly empty.

"It was a devil of a meeting," he said. "Everyone's in shock."

She vanished into the bathroom again; he heard water running, the sound of spitting. The sounds rolled into the hall and were amplified, growing until he had to put his hands over his ears.

She came out of the bathroom, black tanga briefs forming a triangle over her genitals, her large breasts swinging.

"It may have been a devil of a meeting," she said, settling down next to him and putting her hand on the back of his neck, "but I don't think this death has anything to do with the devil's political views. I'm pretty sure you can all relax."

He looked up at her, feeling her breast against his arm; realized he had tears in his eyes.

"How can you know that?"

"No one really knows anything at all yet," she said, "but there's something bigger behind this than just the local council in Östhammar."

She kissed him on the cheek, stroked the arm of his coat, and stood up.

"I'm speeding like an idiot tonight," she said. "I've drunk two hundred liters of coffee this evening."

He let out a deep sigh.

"Me too," he said.

"You smell of smoke and drink as well," she said over her shoulder as she went into the bedroom.

"I hope so," he said, "because the taxpayer was paying."

She gave a flat little laugh.

"Are you coming?" she called.

I can do this, he thought.

I'm going to be able to do this.

TUESDAY, NOVEMBER 17

The billboards shrieked out their bright yellow message about serial killers and police hunts all the way along Fleminggatan, standing out like sunflowers against an iron gray lawn in the morning light. Annika saw them flash past from the window of the bus and felt the same strange effect as usual, a fascination at having put something into the world that goes on and lives its own life, that her articles could reach hundreds of thousands of people whom she would never meet, that her words would generate emotions and reactions that she would never know.

The journey to work passed quickly, accompanied by the screaming sunflowers.

In the newspaper's lobby, where a whole wall was papered each morning with that day's newsbill, they formed an entire enthusiastic choir.

Up in the newsroom she noted the change in temperature as she sailed out across the sea. Her lowered head was met with reassuringly warm glances where she usually encountered blocks of ice. She dominated that day's paper and was back on track; someone to reckon with, all the old stuff forgotten because things were happening again, nineteen hours to deadline, and she had the picture byline on page six.

She turned her back on the ingratiating glances and slid the glass door of her room shut behind her with a bang.

Göran Nilsson, she thought, throwing off her outdoor clothes, frowning with tiredness. Born 1948 in Sattajärvi, emigrated professional killer since 1969.

No point looking him up on national databases, she realized. He would have been erased from the National Population Address Register decades ago.

She drummed her fingers in irritation as a million slow programs started up on her computer, then googled Göran Nilsson and got several hundred results.

There were so many Göran Nilssons in the world, a university professor of construction technology, a psychology researcher, a manufacturer of wooden fish, a Moderate councillor from Karlstad, an organic farmer in Halland, a chef for the council in Norrköping, none of these was her Göran Nilsson, because her Göran Nilsson had opted out. Of all the choices a human being could make in their lives, her Göran Nilsson had decided to work full time at bringing death to other people.

She searched through the results.

In the forties and fifties "Göran" must have been popular as part of a double-barreled name, because there were Stig-Görans and Lars-Görans and Ulf-Görans and Sven-Görans, and a whole load of other combinations.

She turned instead to the yellow pages website to see how common the name really was, trying different districts at random.

There were 73 in Blekinge alone, 55 in Borås, 205 in Stockholm, and 46 in Norrbotten.

Several thousand in the whole country, in other words.

She had to narrow the search somehow, add another word to the terms.

göran nilsson sattajärvi.

No results.

The letters, she thought. Maoism or left-wing groups.

Bingo. Masses of hits like Kristina *Nilsson*, *Mao* Zedong, *Göran* Andersson, all in the same result.

Tried to find pictures instead: göran nilsson mao.

Four results, small squares on the screen that she squinted at, leaning forward.

Two were logos for something she didn't investigate further, one cultural revolutionary portrait of the Master himself on someone's home page, and finally a black-and-white picture of some young people in dated outfits. She looked closer, reading the description: 022.jpg, 501 x 400 pixels—41k, homepage/usebell/rebellhistory035 .htm. She clicked on the link and reached a home page that someone had set up about their youth in Uppsala, and found a caption that put the picture in context.

After the establishment of the fundamental April 9 Declaration, Mats Andersson, Fredrik Svensson, Hans Larsson, and Göran Nilsson were prepared to bravely mobilize the masses in the name of the Master.

She read the text twice, surprised at the slightly ridiculous religiosity it suggested. Then stared at the young man on the far right, his shoulder hidden behind the man next to him, short hair, nondescript features, evidently not that tall. Dark eyes that were staring at a point to the left of the photographer.

She clicked back to the front page of the site and discovered that there were more photographs from Uppsala on the server, several from various demonstrations, but mostly from parties of one sort or another. She looked through all of them, but the dark young man named Göran Nilsson didn't appear on any of the others.

Could it be him? Could he really have been an identifiable activist in the sixties, in which case he might well appear in various media from those days?

Archives like that were never available digitally. There, it was all envelopes of pictures and cuttings.

Her newspaper had the largest archive in the country. She grabbed the phone and asked the archivists to check if they had anything on a Göran Nilsson in Maoist groups at the end of the sixties.

The woman who took her call showed little enthusiasm.

"When do you need it?"

"Yesterday," Annika said. "It's urgent."

"When isn't it?"

"I'm sitting here waiting and can't do anything until I hear from you."

An almost inaudible sigh on the line.

"I'll do a quick check and see if I can find him in his own right. Reading through everything that was published on Maoism would take several weeks."

Annika stood and looked out over the newsroom until she got an answer.

"Sorry. No Göran Nilsson described as a Maoist. We've got a couple of hundred others though."

"Thanks for checking so quickly," Annika said.

What other archives were there from that period, in the places where Maoists were active?

The university cities, she thought. *The Competitor* existed then, but there was no point in calling them. *Upsala Nya Tidning*? She had no contact there. Was there a newspaper in Lund?

She scratched her head in irritation.

What about Luleå?

She had picked up the phone and dialed the *Norrland News* reception before even realizing she was doing it.

"Hasse Blomberg was off sick yesterday. I don't know if he'll be in today," the receptionist said, ready to disconnect her.

Annika suddenly felt an immediate and inexplicable fear; good God, surely nothing could have happened to him?

"Why? Is it serious?"

The receptionist sighed, as if she were dealing with someone who was a bit slow.

"Burned out, like everyone else. Personally I think they're just lazy."

Annika started.

"You're not serious?" she said

"Have you thought that all these people started getting burned out when we joined the EU? All the shit coming over our borders comes from the EU, people, toxins, burnout. And to think I voted yes. Fooled, that's what we were."

"Is Hans often ill?"

"He only works part-time now; got a disability pension a while back, and he's not often here even on the days he's meant to be."

Annika bit her lip, she had to get into the *Norrland News* archive as soon as possible.

"Can you ask him to call me when he comes in?"

She left her name and number.

"If he comes in," the receptionist said.

Göran Nilsson, she thought as she hung up and stared at the young man on her computer screen.

Is that you, Göran?

The coffee machine had been repaired and the drinks were hotter than ever. She took her two mugs into her office, letting the caffeine warm her brain.

Her eyes were stinging from lack of sleep: she hadn't slept well last night. She had lain there with her eyes closed for hours while Thomas twisted and turned, moaning and scratching. The death of the local councillor had really shaken him.

She shook off her tiredness and carried on searching, typing in "Sattajärvi," and reached a site about a building project at the end of the nineties, she was visitor number 16,781. There was a map; she leaned toward the screen to find the village and could just make out the tiny letters spelling out the names in the surrounding area: Routuvaara, Ohtanajärvi, Kompeluslehto.

Not just another language, she thought. Another country, frozen solid, stretching up across the tundra above the Arctic Circle.

She leaned back.

What was it like growing up north of the Arctic Circle in the fifties, in a family where the father was a religious leader in a strict and weird belief system?

Annika knew the Swiss psychoanalyst Alice Miller had found that a striking number of West German terrorists were the children of Protestant ministers. Miller saw a connection—the terrorists' violence was a rebellion against a strict religious upbringing.

The same could easily be true of Sweden and Læstadianism, Annika thought, rubbing her eyes.

At that moment she caught sight of Berit hurrying past behind the dusty curtains, forced her mind to clear, and pulled herself up out of her chair.

"Have you got a minute?" she called from her door.

Berit took off her hat and gloves and folded her scarf.

"I'm thinking of going to lunch early today; do you want to come?"

Annika logged out of the system, fished her purse out of her bag, and discovered she was out of lunch vouchers.

"Do we have to go down to the canteen?" she said, looking around, suspicious of the newfound warmth.

Berit hung up her coat on a hanger, brushing the garment's shoulders with her hand.

"We could go out if you like, but I did go past the Seven Rats, and it looked pretty empty. They've got stir-fried chicken with cashew nuts."

Annika bit the nail of her left index finger, considering the offer, then nodded.

"What have you been out doing?" she asked as they went down the stairs.

"Rumors about a government reshuffle," Berit said, puffing her hair where it had been squashed by her hat. "The prime minister hasn't got long before the EU elections, and if he's going to rearrange his ministers he has to do it now."

They came out in the foyer, Annika sticking close behind Berit, and they went into the canteen.

"And?" Annika said, picking up an orange plastic tray.

Berit shook her head.

"You know what it's like. Not a squeak in advance."

"Which ones are likely to go this time?" Annika wondered, trying not to look at the endless sea of easy-clean tables.

"Well, Björnlund, for a start," Berit said. "She's the worst culture minister we've ever had. She hasn't come up with a single proposal in nine years. The business minister's wife is ill and he wants to look after her, so he's going at his own request. The housing minister hasn't been the success the party was hoping she would be, so she'll probably go and the post will be abolished."

Berit had vouchers and paid for Annika too.

"So who comes in in their place?"

They sat down facing each other in a corner of the canteen.

"There are rumors that Christer Lundgren is on his way back from exile at Swedish Steel in Luleå," Berit said, opening her bottle of low-alcohol beer.

Annika got a cashew nut stuck in her throat and burst into a hysterical coughing fit.

"Are you okay? Do you want me to thump you on the back or something?"

Annika shook her head and held up a hand.

"It's okay," she said, with tears in her eyes. "Is that true?"

Berit took a large forkful of stir-fried chicken.

"Well, he never left the management committee, so a ministerial post was probably always in the pipeline. Are you sure you're okay?"

Annika nodded, breathing slowly with her hand on her chest.

"It's evidently time to bring him in from the cold now," Berit went on. "He's clearly done a decent job up there. New business minister would be my guess, but you never know. It depends on whether the Swedish people have forgotten about the stripper he was supposed to have killed."

"Josefin," Annika said. "Liljeberg. Well, he didn't kill her."

"You and I know that, but . . ."

Annika felt the food swelling in her mouth; the tasteless chicken was too much for her. She pushed the plate away.

Several years ago she had told Berit her thoughts about Christer Lundgren's resignation, showing her the documents and travel receipts that proved that the trade minister hadn't even been in Stockholm the night Josefin Liljeberg was killed. He had been meeting someone in Tallinn in Estonia, a meeting that was so controversial that he would rather accept a murder charge than reveal whom he had met.

There was only one explanation, Annika and Berit had agreed. Lundgren was sacrificing himself for his party. Whom he met in Tallinn and what they discussed could never be revealed.

The fact that the government had been forced into the meeting because of a threat that the truth about the IB affair might be revealed could never be proved. Nor could the fact that it was about the illegal export of weapons from Sweden to one of the former republics of the Soviet Union. But Annika was still convinced.

And she had told Karina Björnlund.

She had made the mistake of trying to get a comment from Christer Lundgren by telling the whole story to his press secretary. She never got a reply.

All that had happened was that Björnlund suddenly became a cabinet minister.

"My stupid question paved the way for our minister of culture," Annika said.

"Probably," Berit said.

"Which means that it's really my fault that Sweden's got such useless cultural policies, doesn't it?"

"Quite right," Berit said, standing up. "Do you want anything? Salad? More water?"

Annika shook her head, and watched her colleague as she opened a bottle of Ramlösa and poured it into a glass.

"What did you really want to see me about?" Berit said as she came back and settled into her seat again.

"I'm after your past," Annika said. "What was the April 9 Declaration?"

Berit chewed a mouthful of food, a thoughtful look in her eyes, then shook her head.

"Nope, no idea," she said. "Why do you ask?"

Annika drank the last of her water.

"I saw it in the caption to a picture on the net—some lads in the sixties who were going to mobilize the masses in the name of Chairman Mao."

Berit stopped chewing and stared at her.

"Sounds like the Uppsala Rebels," she said.

She put her knife and fork down, ran her tongue over her teeth, and nodded to herself.

"Yes, that fits," she said. "They made some sort of declaration in the spring of sixty-eight. I can't swear that it was April 9, but they were certainly extremely active that spring."

She laughed and shook her head, then picked up her knife and fork again and went on eating.

"What?" Annika said. "Tell me!"

Berit sighed and smiled.

"I told you how they would phone and make threats to us at the *Vietnam Bulletin*?" she said. "The Uppsala Rebels were proper little idiots. Every day they held marathon meetings, in various locations; they usually started at one o'clock in the afternoon and carried on till long after midnight. A friend of mine who went along once said there was very little politics involved; he described it as more of a hallelujah orgy."

"A revivalist meeting?"

Berit took another mouthful, some water, and swallowed.

"That's what they reminded some people of, yes. Everyone who attended was a firmly committed Maoist; they stood up one by one and gave witness about how Mao's thoughts had been like a spiritual atom bomb for them. After every speaker there was wild applause. Every now and then there'd be a break, and they'd have sandwiches and beer; then they'd carry on with a new round of personal witness statements."

"Like what?" Annika said. "What did they say?"

"They quoted the Master. Anyone trying to formulate their own phrases was immediately accused of bourgeois use of language. The only exception was 'Death to the fascists in the Communist Association of Marxist-Leninists.'"

Annika leaned back in her chair, picking out a cashew nut from under a lettuce leaf and popping it in her mouth, chewing thoughtfully.

"But," she said, "surely they were communists as well?"

"Oh yes," Berit said, wiping herself with the napkin. "But nothing upset the rebels more than those who *almost* thought like them. Torbjörn Säfve, who wrote a brilliant book about the rebel movement, called it 'paranoid discontent.' The sort of posters people put up on their walls was a big deal for them. If anyone had a poster of Lenin that was bigger than the picture of Mao, that was regarded as counterrevolutionary. If the top edge of a picture of Mao was lower than the top edge of a picture of Lenin or Marx, that was enough for someone to be accused of a lack of conviction."

"I don't suppose you knew an active rebel by the name of Göran Nilsson?" Annika asked, looking expectantly at Berit.

Her colleague reached for a toothpick and pulled off the plastic, frowning.

"Not that I can recall," Berit said. "Should I?"

Annika sighed and shook her head.

"Have you tried the archive?" Berit asked.

"Nothing."

Berit frowned in concentration.

"The first of May that year, the rebels marched through Uppsala in a big, organized demonstration. As far I remember, all the big papers covered it. Maybe he was involved?"

Annika got up, her tray in one hand and her purse in the other.

"I'll check at once," she said. "Are you coming?"

"Why not?" Berit said.

They went out of the canteen's back door and took the emergency staircase to the second floor, then went through a narrow corridor to the huge text and picture archive. Everything ever printed in the *Evening Post* and *Fine Morning News* in the past hundred and fifty years was stored here.

"The files are at the back on the left," Berit said.

They found the morning papers from May 1968 after a minute or so. Annika pulled down the bound bundle from the top shelf, covering herself in dust and dirt. She coughed and pulled a face.

On May 2, 1968, the front page was full of the rebels' demonstration through Uppsala the day before. Annika frowned and looked more closely.

"Are these your revolutionary rebels?" she said in disbelief. "They look like any other middle-class kids, the whole lot of them."

Berit ran her hand over the yellowing newspaper, a rustling sound beneath her dry fingertip, her middle finger stopping on the cropped head of the leader of the march.

"That was a conscious decision," she said, her voice distant. "They were supposed to look like ordinary people as much as possible; they tried to agree on a prototype for the highly industrialized worker, but I don't think that ever happened. But they did agree on a smart jacket and white shirt. They were really weird in Uppsala."

She leaned back against the bookcase, folded her arms and looked blankly up at the ceiling.

"The first week of May 1968 a general strike broke out all over France," Berit said. "One million demonstrated in Paris against the capitalist state. The rebels wanted to show solidarity with their French comrades and organized a revolutionary meeting on the Castle Hill in Uppsala one Friday evening. A gang of us from the *Bulletin* went along, it was really awful."

She shook her head and looked down at the floor.

"There were a lot of people there, at least three hundred, and the rebels made the mistake of carrying on like they usually did at their own séances, with readings from their holy scriptures. Most of the audience were just ordinary people, and they reacted as you'd imagine, started booing and laughing."

Annika was absorbed in the story and took a step closer.

"What scriptures?"

Berit looked up.

"Readings from Mao, of course," she said, "Lin Biao's pamphlet,

Long Live the Victory of the People's War!, the Chinese Communist Party's Sixteen Points for cultural revolution . . . The rebels lost all their inhibitions at that meeting, and when the masses failed to support them they fell back on their usual tactics, savage, rabid diatribes."

She shook her head at the memory.

"One direct consequence of that meeting was that ordinary left-wing organizations were no longer allowed to sell the *Spark* and the *Vietnam Bulletin* in workplaces. Can you see your Göran?"

"I'm going to stay and read for a while," Annika said, pulling over a rickety chair.

"Well, you know where I am if you need me," Berit said, and left her among the paper and dust.

Anne Snapphane was floating across the laminated floor of the corridor, over the rectangles of light from the doors, past photocopiers and flattened packing cases, adrenaline pulsing in her fingertips.

She had won! The three big independent film companies had agreed to keep the oral agreements they had already given to sell their films to TV Scandinavia.

A man from the largest of them had also revealed the pressure applied by the family that owned the main competition to get them to pull out: apart from a complete boycott of the company's products, in both distribution and funding, they should prepare for a thorough investigation of all their activities from the family's media group. All the company's dealings would be examined and criticized regardless; actors who worked for the company would be the subjects of intense media gossip; and columnists would step up the pressure and demand the resignation of the directors.

"I react really badly to mafia behavior," the company boss said: he had actually been born in Sicily, and didn't exactly scare easily.

You really bit the dust this time, you bastards, Anne thought, hearing champagne corks popping inside her.

She sat down on her chair and put her feet up on her desk.

TV Scandinavia was going to work. Sweden wasn't a banana republic. One single family didn't have the power to dictate over freedom of speech, and couldn't ban other media because they threatened its own economic interests: that wasn't how democracy worked.

She opened the bottom drawer of her desk and pulled out an unopened bottle of whisky, weighing it in her hand and fingering the seal. Humming an old song, she wondered if she didn't deserve a little celebration?

The telephone rang, making her start. She quickly pushed the bottle back in the drawer and locked it before she picked up the receiver.

"What did you do to Sylvia yesterday?"

Mehmet's voice was treacherously smooth, but Anne knew him; knew there was lava and sulfur bubbling beneath the calm surface.

"Surely the real question is, what the hell was she doing at my daughter's nursery?" Anne said, as the world shattered into tiny pieces. Anger and despair turned the sky outside black.

"Can't we at least behave like adults?" Mehmet said, the temperature of his voice rising.

"And which particular adult plan had you worked out yesterday? That I'd get to the nursery and find that Miranda had disappeared? What was I supposed to think? That Miranda had left me because she'd rather be with Sylvia? That she'd been kidnapped?"

"Now you're just being ridiculous," Mehmet said, his voice no longer able to conceal the infernal heat.

"Ridiculous?" Anne screamed down the phone, standing up. "Ridiculous?! What the hell are you up to with your cozy fucking nuclear family? First you come around and say you and your new fuck want custody of my daughter; then she tries to steal her from the nursery—what the hell are you up to? Are you trying to terrorize me?"

"Calm down," Mehmet said, and the phone went ice cold, the heat exchanged for hatred, the chill striking her ear, making her stiffen.

"Go to hell," she said, and hung up.

She stood there, staring at the phone. It rang after the number of seconds it took to press the redial button.

"So now Miranda's yours alone? What happened to all your fine ideals about mutual responsibility? Your high-flown theories about shared parenting: that the child should belong to the collective and not the individual?"

Anne sank onto her chair again, feeling that she was being sucked into a morass that she never imagined she would end up in, a stinking swamp of bitterness and ill will and envy, the place where all below-the-belt blows come from, and she couldn't help it; she was there already: the quicksand had her, and if she struggled she would only sink to the bottom even faster.

"Oh, come on," she said. "Who betrayed who? Who left who? Who's trying to mess things up? It damn well isn't me."

"Sylvia spent the whole evening crying; she was inconsolable," Mehmet said, his voice sounding thick and tearful in a way that made Anne furious.

"Good grief," she shouted. "It's hardly my fault she's got bad nerves!"

Mehmet paused for breath, gathering his larynx for a full-frontal assault.

"Sylvia said that you had destroyed her, and there's something you need to know, Anne Snapphane: if you ruin things for my family, I won't be responsible for my actions."

Anne felt the air being squeezed out of her lungs, all the oxygen disappearing from her brain.

"Are you threatening me?" she said. "Are you mad? Have you really sunk that low? Has she given you brain damage?"

The distance on the line grew, rolling around and around the swamp, and when he came back on the line he was light-years away.

"Okay," he said, "if that's how you want it."

And then it was silent, gone, the dialogue broken, and all around her everything was bubbling and frothing, and Anne leaned over her desk and wept.

* * *

Annika was getting more and more restless as she climbed the stairs back to the newsroom. Her search through old editions had given her nothing but dirty hands and dusty jeans. The sixties and the political currents of the time had not been consciously addressed in the contemporary media; every day was just a new headline, then as now, with ads to sell and headlines to write and police reports to check.

The layout and print quality of newspapers in the sixties were terrible, scratchy fonts and badly pixelated pictures; she was glad she hadn't been working then.

But every age has its own ideals, she thought as she headed toward her glass room. You live in an age just as much as you do in a place, and the sixties wouldn't have suited her.

Did the twenty-first century, though?

She heard the phone start to ring and lengthened her strides.

"I heard you were trying to get hold of me," said Hans Blomberg, the archivist of the *Norrland News*.

"Oh, I'm glad you called," Annika said, pulling the door shut behind her. "How are you?"

A brief moment of surprise.

"Why do you ask?"

She sat down on her chair, surprised that he sounded so nonplussed.

"The receptionist said you were ill; I was worried."

"Ah, yes, the tenderness of women," Hans Blomberg said, sounding as Annika remembered him, and she had to smile, picturing him sitting there in his cardigan next to his battered desk with the bulletin board above it, the child's drawing, the sign telling him to hold out until retirement.

"Nothing serious, I hope?" Annika said, stretching back in her chair.

"No, no," the archivist said. "Just the usual. I'm past my sell-by date, but I'm probably okay in the fridge for a few more days before they throw me out, but no one uses me; I just get older and sourer, taking up space for fresher produce, but it'll sort itself out; it's like this for everyone these days."

Her smile faded as he spoke; the tone was cheerful but his frustration obvious.

"Ha," Annika said brightly, choosing to ignore the bitterness. "To me you're like a vintage wine."

"Oh, it takes a Stockholm girl to appreciate a real man. What can I help you with, young lady?"

"A general question of an even older vintage," she said. "I'm trying to find information about a young man from Sattajärvi who lived in Luleå at the end of the sixties, probably worked for the church. His name's Göran Nilsson."

"Is he dead?" Hans said, his pen scratching in the background.

"I don't think so," Annika said.

"So we'll leave the dear departed alone, then. What do you want to know?"

"Anything. If he won a jitterbug competition, demonstrated against imperialism, robbed a bank, got married."

"Göran Nilsson, you said? You couldn't have picked a more common name, then?"

"I've looked everywhere but haven't come up with anything," Annika said.

The archivist groaned loudly; Annika could see him gripping the desk and heaving himself out of his chair.

"This might take a few minutes," he said, and that was the understatement of the day.

Annika had time to look through hemnet.se and read about all the detached houses for sale in the Stockholm region, and fell for a fantastic, newly built house on Vinterviksvägen in Djursholm, for a measly 6.9 million. She went to get some coffee and spoke to Berit, then tried to ring Thomas's cell and left a message for Anne Snapphane before there was a noise on the line again.

"Well, I've looked for easier things," he said with a deep sigh.

"Have you any idea how many Göran Nilssons there are in the archive?"

"Seventy-two and a half," Annika said.

"Exactly right," Hans said. "And the only one from Sattajärvi I could find was in the wedding announcements."

Annika raised her eyebrows, feeling her mood slump.

"The wedding announcements? What, the kind of thing ministers did in church when people got married back in the 1800s?"

"Well," Hans said, "it was actually obligatory until 1973, but you're right about the church connection. The banns had to be read in church for three Sundays in a row before a wedding, to keep everyone happy."

"So why did they put it in the paper?"

Hans thought for a moment.

"That's just how it was in those days, there was a special column. The cutting is from September 29, 1969, do you want me to read it out loud?"

"Yes, please," Annika said.

"Parish assistant Göran Nilsson, born in Sattajärvi, now of Luleå, and student Karina Björnlund, born and living in Karlsvik. The wedding will take place in Luleå City Hall, Friday, November 20, at 2:00 PM."

Her pen raced across the notepad as she tried to keep up with him, feeling the goose bumps prickle, and had difficulty breathing. Good God, bloody hell, this was impossible.

She forced herself not to get even more excited, not yet, she couldn't be sure until she checked.

"Well, goodness," Annika said hoarsely. "Thanks, thanks a lot. You're a vintage champagne."

"Whenever, my dear, just give me a call."

They hung up and Annika had to stand up. Yes! Her mind was racing, the rush of blood pumping in her ears. She ran out into the newsroom with her heart pounding, but gathered her senses somewhere near the sports desk and realized that she actually didn't have anything yet. She got a cup of coffee from the machine and hurried over to Berit.

"Where's the minister of culture from?" she asked.

Berit looked up from her screen, glasses on the tip of her nose.

"Norrbotten," she said. "Luleå, I think."

"Not from somewhere called Karlsvik?"

Berit took off her glasses and lowered her hands to her lap.

"Don't know," she said. "Why do you ask?"

"Where does she live now?"

"A suburb, north of the city somewhere."

"Married?"

"Living with someone," Berit said, "no children. What are you after?"

Annika rocked back and forth on her heels, shaking the noise from her head.

"Just information," she said, "an old wedding announcement I need to check."

"A wedding announcement?" Berit said as Annika walked off without explaining, heading back to her room with a glazed expression and shutting the door. She sat down at her screen as her pulse slowed. Then she raised her hands and let them slowly uncover the truth.

She started with www.regeringen.se, the government site, and downloaded a PDF file about the head of the ministry of culture. It had a picture of Karina Björnlund giving a crooked smile, and information about her areas of responsibility: cultural heritage, art, the printed word, radio and television, faith communities.

In the personal section of the file it said that she was born in 1951 and raised in Luleå, and now lived in Knivsta with her partner.

Nothing about Karlsvik, Annika thought, and clicked on to Infotorg, the big information website.

She looked up Karina Björnlund Knivsta on the census and found one match, a woman born in 1951. She clicked on background information and got the name of the parish she was born in.

Lower Luleå.

She bit the inside of her cheek, her palms were itching, she needed to look deeper. She left Infotorg and went onto Google again, and did a general search for "karlsvik" and "lower luleå," and got nineteen results. The top one was the history of a saw fitter, an Olof Falck from Hälleström (1758–1830) in what was now the parish of Norrfjärden in the Piteå council district. Annika did a search within that page and discovered that one of the saw fitter's descendants, a Beda Markström, born 1885, had settled in Karlsvik in the parish of Lower Luleå.

Searched for a map and found it.

Karlsvik was a small community just outside Luleå, on the other side of the river.

She leaned back, letting the information sink in. It was making her scalp itch, her mouth dry, her fingers twitch.

She jotted the main points in her notebook, then dialed the editor in chief's internal number.

"Have you got a few minutes?"

The air in the conference room on the seventh floor of the Federation of County Councils was sour with stale oxygen. Coffee fumes and old nicotine breath mixed with the sweat of middle-aged men in wool jackets. Thomas wiped his brow. Unconsciously he slid a finger under the knot of his tie and pulled it open to let in more air.

This was the conference group's first official meeting, which meant that the hierarchies and structures had not settled in yet. The mood of backslapping had slid into territorial scent marking the longer the meeting went on. Thomas realized that it would take at least one more marathon meeting until they could get anything sensible done.

The congress of the Federation of County Councils and the Association of Local Councils at Norrköping in June was due to consider one very large and very serious question. The two groups would each hold their own individual conference but with several common sessions. The main question was whether they should merge. The common and overriding theme of the congress was "the citizen and the future."

Thomas opened his eyes wide, staring at the congress timetable.

He couldn't escape. Sophia was with him everywhere. Now she was there between the lines of the committee's proposals for long-term programs, her heels clicking through the documentation about collaboration and the congressional information sent out to members of the Federation of County Councils.

Thomas leaned back, listening to the director of communication give a long list of directives, and let his eyes roam across the participants.

Sophia in a pin-striped suit and silk blouse with sparkling teeth and apple hair over by the window.

Sophia in her lacy bra and parted lips leaning against the flip chart.

Sophia with no underwear on riding the overhead projector.

He cleared his throat and shook his head, forcing his brain back to reality.

At the far end of the designer table sat the information director, who was also chair of the project group, and one of those responsible for factual content. The pair responsible for organization and administration poured more coffee and picked at the rapidly hardening pastries. The other participants had gathered near the window, where they sat with their jackets pressed hard into the backs of their chairs, trying to look as though they weren't about to yawn.

His reality. Sophia's reality.

What was Annika doing right now? What did he know about her reality?

Without him understanding how it happened, or what had been said, the meeting broke up to the scrape of chairs and relieved voices. He pulled himself together, and, without looking up, gathered his documents.

"Samuelsson," said a voice above him, and he looked up quickly.

"How's the collaboration with the Federation of County Councils going?"

Thomas stood up and shook the information director by the hand, feeling his brain solidify and his words dry up—what the hell was he supposed to say to that?

"Oh," he said, gulping audibly, "it's going pretty well."

"No real areas of conflict?"

He pulled his hand away to hide the fact that he was breaking into a sweat.

"As long as we're working toward the same goal, and have a good number of independent players in the project, it's working fairly well," he said, wondering exactly what he meant by that.

"That Sophia Grenborg, what's she like?"

The question forced the last oxygen from his lungs; he opened his mouth but was unable to breathe.

"Oh," he heard himself say. "You know, fine. A bit dull. Upper class, has never had any real setbacks in life . . ."

The information director looked at him in surprise.

"I meant what's she like to work with. Is she pressing the Federation's interests at our expense?"

To his embarrassment, Thomas could feel himself blushing, what a stupid mistake.

"It's okay as long as we don't let our guard down," he said. "We can't let them get the upper hand, so there's a certain amount of positioning going on in advance of the congress, if I can put it like that . . ."

The information director nodded in concentration.

"I understand," he said. "Listen, could you summarize your experiences, partly within your current area of focus, but particularly with regard to the regional issue, as soon as possible?"

"Of course," Thomas said, straightening his tie. "Just tell me what you want and I'll get down to it."

The information director boxed Thomas lightly on his left shoulder.

"That's what I like to hear," he said, and glided out of the room.

The room emptied of people, leaving Thomas closing his briefcase. One of the secretaries had opened a window wide to let in some breathable air again, a cold draft swept around his legs and beneath his jacket.

How was the collaboration with the Federation of County Councils going? Sophia Grenborg, what was she really like?

Thomas turned his back on the thought, picked up his briefcase and headed sternly toward the elevators. Some of the group members were standing there chatting as they waited, he gave them a quick smile and headed down the stairs.

The corridor outside his room was silent and gloomy, the structural pattern of the walls emphasized and warped by the lamps spreading light in fountain-shaped shadows. He hurried into his room, shut the door, and sank down at the desk.

He couldn't carry on like this. Why had he let things get this far? Everything he had struggled for for years was at risk of ruin: the relationships he had built up with his family and his employers would be worthless if he was discovered sharing a bed with the Federation of County Councils. His eyes fixed on the picture of Annika and the children that he had put in a silver frame on the desk, a photograph he had taken last summer at his aunt's seventieth birthday party. The picture didn't do them justice. The children were dressed up and slightly stiff, Annika was in a knee-length dress that flowed and softened her sharp-edged body; she had plaited her hair so that it hung quiet and controlled, like a whip down her back.

"That says a lot about how you'd like other people to see us," Annika had said when she saw which picture he had chosen to frame.

He hadn't responded, had actively chosen not to engage in yet another discussion that would never lead anywhere.

It was important to him how he was perceived by other people, that was true. Ignoring the impression you made was both irresponsible and stupid, that was his confirmed opinion. Annika thought the exact opposite.

"You can't be loved by everyone," she would say. "It's better to take a stand for what you believe than trying to please everyone."

He ran a finger over the hard, dull metal frame, his nail lingering over Annika's curved breasts.

An insistent internal call made him jump.

"You have a visitor in reception, Sophia Grenborg from the Federation of County Councils. Do you want to come down and fetch her?"

He felt the sweat break out on his brow and under his arms.

"No," he said. "She knows the way. You can let her come up."

He put down the receiver, got up from his chair and crossed the floor, opening the door slightly and looking around the room as if he had never seen it before. He decided to lean against the desk, and crossed his arms and legs as he listened hard for noises out on the stairs. He could only hear his own heart thumping, and struggled to identify his feelings but found only bottomless confusion.

He didn't know. He was expectant, but he was ashamed. He felt longing, and he felt hatred.

He heard footsteps making the noise that only hers made; the steps echoed through the silence of the corridor, light and happy.

She pushed the door open and stepped into his office, and her eyes were shining; there was a shyness and hesitancy in them that couldn't be submerged by the great wave of goodwill pouring out of them.

He walked toward her, turned off the main light, and pulled her to him as he pushed the door shut. He kissed her hard and senselessly; her mouth was bitter and warm; he took her breasts in his hands, as her hands reached inside the back of his trousers.

They panted into each other's mouths and pulled off their clothes and lay down on the desk; the mug of pens hit him in the back and he swept it aside along with everything else behind him; she climbed on top of him, her eyes capturing his, her lips swollen and trembling. He slid inside her as if she were warm butter, and leaned his head back and shut his eyes as she slowly began to ride him. The slow waves made his body take flight. As his orgasm approached he opened his eyes wide and happened to stare straight into Annika's, as she tried to hide her resigned tolerance of the family party she had not been able to avoid.

He couldn't help the cry he let out at the same time as his sperm.

In the silence afterward he could hear the monotonous whir of the air-conditioning, the singing of the wires in the elevator shaft, an abandoned phone on another floor that rang and rang and rang.

"We're mad," Sophia whispered in his ear, and he couldn't help laughing; yes, they really were mad, and he kissed her and stood up. She tumbled off him and fluid ran out of her and down onto one of the project papers.

They hastily adjusted their clothes, giggling and fumbling. Then stood close together, their arms around each other's waist, smiling into each other's eyes.

"Thanks for today," Sophia said, and kissed him on the chin.

He caught her mouth, eating her tongue.

"Thank *you*," he breathed.

She pulled on her coat, picked up her briefcase, and was about to leave when she suddenly stopped.

"Oh," she said. "I almost forgot what I came for."

He was sitting on his chair, leaning back, feeling the sleepiness that always followed ejaculation. Sophia put her briefcase on his desk, opened and took out a folder of papers bearing the logo of the ministry of justice.

"I spent some time with Cramne this afternoon, we went through the outline for the action plan," she said and smiled at him with an almost bovine look on her face.

He felt his face close up, the need for sleep vanish.

"What?" he said. "I thought I was supposed to do that?"

"Cramne called me; he couldn't get hold of you because you were in some meeting or other. You can read it through this evening and call me early tomorrow morning, can't you?"

He looked at his watch.

"I have to pick up the kids," he said. "I don't know if I'll have time tonight."

Sophia blinked, something pale falling across her nose.

"Okay," she said, her voice suddenly smaller and sharper. "Call me when you can."

And she turned and left the room, shutting the door behind her. Thomas stayed in his chair, suddenly aware of the stickiness around his cock.

How was the collaboration with the Federation of County Councils going? Sophia Grenborg, what was she really like?

He lunged forward, crumpled up the project document and threw it in the trash. Left Sophia's discussions with the department next to the mug of pens and hurried off to the nursery.

Annika's legs had almost gone to sleep on the uncomfortable chairs outside Anders Schyman's room when the editor in chief finally opened the door and let her in.

"I've got ten minutes," he said, turning his back on her before she replied.

She stood up, trying to shake some life into her legs, and feeling strangely ill at ease. She followed Schyman's broad back into the room, taking nervous steps on the swaying floor. She was unnerved by his attempt to hurry her along, and sank into one of his visitors' chairs, putting her notes on top of some sort of diagram on his desk.

The editor in chief went slowly back behind his desk, sank into his creaking chair, and leaned back.

"You're not letting go of this terrorist angle, then," he stated, clasping his hands together over his gut.

"I've uncovered information that's extremely controversial," Annika said, staring down at her notebook, realizing it was open on the wrong page. She quickly pulled the notes over to her and searched feverishly for the summary she had put together. Schyman sighed.

"Just tell me instead," he said, and Annika put the book down in her lap. She was fighting against a stubborn sense of falling, which was making the floor sway like mad.

"The terrorist's name is Göran Nilsson," she said. "Born in Sattajärvi in the Torne Valley in 1948, the son of a Læstadian preacher."

She picked up her notes and leafed through them.

"He moved to Uppsala to study theology at the age of nineteen, joined the Rebel movement in the spring of 1968 and became a Maoist. Abandoned his studies and moved back to Norrbotten where he worked for the church. He joined Maoist groups in Luleå under the code name Ragnwald, and seems to have lost his faith, because he arranged a civil marriage ceremony. One way or another he was involved in the attack on F21, even if the police don't believe that he actually carried it out. He disappeared from Sweden on November 18, 1969, and hasn't been seen since then. The wedding, which was supposed to take place on November 20, in Luleå City Hall, just two days after the attack, was canceled."

Schyman nodded slowly.

"Then he went to Spain and became a professional killer for ETA," he filled in, glancing at the newspaper spread out on one of the side tables.

Annika raised her hand, putting her feet down hard to find solid ground.

"It's F21, that's the interesting bit," she said.

"I thought you said the police had discounted him, that he wasn't the one who carried out the attack?"

She swallowed silently, nodded.

"So who blew up the plane?" Anders said in a neutral tone of voice, his hands still.

She was silent for a few moments before she replied.

"Karina Björnlund," she said. "The minister of culture."

The editor in chief didn't move a muscle. His hands remained clasped above his shirt buttons, his back stayed at the same angle, his eyes didn't move—but the air in the room had suddenly turned gray, difficult to breathe in.

"I presume," Schyman said after a silence of indeterminate length, "that you have a bloody good conclusion to this accusation."

Annika tried to laugh; the noise came out as a dry snigger.

"Not really," she said, "but the minister really is the most likely culprit."

Schyman leaned forward quickly, heaving himself out of the chair with the help of the desk, and walked across the floor, not looking at Annika.

"I don't know that I want to listen to this," he said.

Annika was halfway out of her chair to follow him, but felt the whole room lurch and sank back and picked up her notes.

"The footprints found at the scene were size thirty-six," she said. "They must have been made by either a child or a small woman, and of those two alternatives an adult woman with small feet is most likely. Women hardly ever turn to terrorism unless it's together with their men. Ragnwald planned the attack; his fiancée carried it out."

Schyman interrupted his restless wandering across the floor and turned to face her, hands by his sides.

"Fiancée?"

"They were due to get married, parish assistant Göran Nilsson from Sattajärvi and Karina Björnlund from Karlsvik in the parish of Lower Luleå. I've checked all the Göran Nilssons and Karina Björnlunds with their backgrounds against the historical information in the National Population Address Register, and they're the only two."

"The terrorist and the culture minister?"

"The terrorist and the culture minister."

"They were getting married two days after the attack?"

Annika nodded, watching her boss's unfeigned astonishment, and felt the ground slowly solidify beneath her again.

"How do you know that?"

"A wedding announcement in the *Norrland News* published less than four weeks before the attack."

Anders folded his arms, rocked back on his heels and looked out of the large, dark window toward the Russian embassy.

"You're quite sure that Karina Björnlund, in the autumn of 1969, was planning to marry a man who ended up becoming a professional killer?"

She cleared her throat and nodded, and Schyman continued his reasoning.

"And our minister of culture would have destroyed the property of the state, murdered one conscript, and wounded another, all for the sake of love?"

"I don't know that, but it seems logical," Annika said.

The editor in chief went back to his chair and sat down carefully.

"How old was she?"

"Nineteen."

"Was she living with this bloke?"

"She was still registered at her parents' address in Karlsvik."

"What was her job?"

"In the wedding announcement it said she was a student."

Anders picked up a pen and wrote something on the corner of a diagram.

"Do you know," he said, looking up at Annika, "this is the biggest load of crap I've ever heard."

He let the pen fall; the small sound of plastic on paper grew and echoed in the silence, the floor opened up beneath her and she was falling.

"I'm glad," he said, "that you came to me with this information, and not anyone else. I hope you haven't mentioned this nonsense elsewhere?"

Annika felt the heat rising in her face, and her head was starting to spin.

"No," she whispered.

"Not to Berit? Not Jansson? Not your grandmother?"

"My grandmother's dead."

He studied her closely for a few seconds, then straightened his back.

"Good," he said, turning away. "From now on you won't be covering terrorism at all. You will not spend a minute more on Karina

Björnlund or this damn Ragnwald or any explosions in Luleå or anywhere else, is that understood?"

She jerked back against her chair, away from his breath, which had come extremely close again.

"But," she said, "isn't it at least worth carrying on and checking?"

Anders looked at her with such incredulous astonishment that she felt her throat burning.

"That Sweden's most sought-after terrorist for more than three decades happens to be a teenage schoolgirl from a village in Norrbotten who lived with her mom and went on to become a minister in a Social Democratic government?"

Annika was breathing fast through her mouth.

"I haven't even spoken to the police . . ."

"So much the fucking better."

". . . They must have questioned her, maybe there's an entirely innocent explanation . . ."

An angry signal from the intercom silenced her.

"Herman Wennergren is here now," his secretary said over the crackling speaker.

The editor in chief took three long strides to the intercom and pressed the button.

"Ask him to come in."

He released the button and looked over at Annika; she felt his look condemn her to the underworld.

"I don't want to hear another word about this," he said. "Get out."

Annika stood up, surprised that she hadn't collapsed completely, grabbed her notebook with hands that seemed alien to her, and aimed for the door at the end of a long tunnel.

Fumbled her way through it.

Schyman watched the door close behind Annika Bengtzon, disappointment burning in his gut.

So incredibly sad. Annika was so thorough, so ambitious. Now she had evidently lost her grip completely. Lost touch with reality and fled into some sort of fantasy world with terrorists in government and professional killers involved with local politicians in Östhammar.

He had to sit down, and turned his chair so that he ended up looking at his own reflection in the dark glass, trying to make out the contours of the concrete buildings spread out below the Russian flag.

What were his responsibilities as her boss in a position like this? Should he tell occupational health? Was Annika Bengtzon a danger to herself or anyone else?

He saw himself gulp as he sat there in his office chair.

He hadn't noticed any suicidal tendencies or signs of violence. The only thing he knew for sure was that her articles were no longer reliable, and that was something he was paid to deal with. Bengtzon needed to be managed much more strictly than before, both by him and the other editors.

Sad, he thought again. There had been a time when she was very good at digging up stories.

The door flew open and Wennergren strode into his room without knocking, as usual.

"It's a good idea to pick wars you can win," the chairman of the board said through clenched teeth, dropping his briefcase on the sofa. "Can I have some coffee?"

Schyman leaned forward, pressed the button on the intercom and asked his secretary to bring two cups. Then he got up and walked slowly, back straight, toward the sofas where Wennergren had sat down, still wearing his coat, unsure what this unannounced visit meant.

"A bad day on the battlefield?" he said, settling down on the other side of the table.

The chairman of the board fingered the lock of his briefcase, his nails clicking against the metal in an unconscious and irritating way.

"You win some, you lose some," he said. "I can give you good news that I appear to be winning on your flank. I've just come from a meeting of the Newspaper Publishers' Association, where I proposed you as new chair after the new year. The last chap hasn't worked at all, so we all agree we need a change, and my suggestion met surprisingly little resistance. No one had any objections, neither publishers nor directors."

Wennergren seemed genuinely surprised.

"Maybe they were just shocked," Schyman said, as his secretary brought in a coffee tray full of cups and cookies.

"I don't think so," the chairman said, grabbing a ginger cookie before the tray had reached the table. "The managing director called you a collective capitalist—what do you think he meant by that?"

"Depends if the tone was positive or negative, and what values you attach to the description," Schyman said, sliding over the question.

Wennergren took a careful sip from the china cup with pouting lips and his little finger sticking out.

"It's possible that the other groups are gathering their forces," he said, after swallowing a small mouthful. "We shouldn't crack open the victory champagne just yet, but I think I can get you through as chair. And once you're there, at the board's first meeting I want you to raise a particular question that's of the utmost importance to our proprietors."

Schyman leaned back in his chair and concentrated on keeping his expression completely neutral, as the true nature of his elevation dawned on him with crystal-clear transparency:

He was expected to be the proprietors' weapon on the ostensibly unbiased and apolitical forum that the Newspaper Publishers' Association purported to be.

"I see," Schyman said blankly. "What question would that be?"

Wennergren was chewing a caramel slice.

"TV Scandinavia," he said, brushing some crumbs from the corners of his mouth. "Are we really going to allow American capital onto our airwaves without any real debate?"

The second front, Schyman thought. The one being lost. The old boy really is worried.

"I thought it was being debated everywhere," he said, not sure if he should be annoyed at the attempt to direct him as a lobbyist, or if he should pretend it was bad news.

"Of course," Wennergren said, wiping his fingers on a napkin. "How many articles have we had about it in the *Evening Post*?"

Schyman stood up rather than raise his voice and went over to sit at his desk.

Never before had the family that owned the paper exerted any pressure on him to write on issues where they had economic interests. He realized immediately what a large and sensitive issue the launch of the American channel must be for them.

"A precondition of my enjoying any sort of respect in the publishing community is that I maintain a critical and independent line toward our proprietors in all circumstances," he said, picking up a pen without using it.

"Naturally," Wennergren said, also getting up, and picking up his briefcase and buttoning his coat. "An independent line, of course, to anyone looking on. But you're not stupid, Schyman. You know whom you work for, don't you?"

"Journalism," Schyman said, feeling his temper fraying. "Truth and democracy."

Wennergren gave a tired sigh.

"Yes, yes," he said. "But of course you appreciate what's at stake. How the hell are we going to get rid of TV Scandinavia?"

"Make sure they don't get a broadcasting license," Schyman said at once.

Wennergren sighed louder.

"Obviously," he said. "But how? We've tried everything. The government is completely unshakable. This American consortium fulfills all the criteria for access to the digital broadcast network. The proposal is up in parliament next Tuesday, and the ministry of culture isn't going to change its conditions just because we want it to."

"As soon as that?" Schyman said. "So it must be done and dusted already then?"

"All the committee stages and consultation were finished long ago, but you know what Minister Björnlund is like. She has trouble getting anything done, let alone on time. We've checked with the parliamentary print office, and they haven't received the text yet."

Schyman looked down at his desk, and in one corner of the latest balance sheet were the words he had scribbled down as he had considered how hard he should be on Annika.

Karina Björnlund engaged terrorist Ragnwald, blew up plane F21????

He stared at the words, feeling the pressure rise.

What did he want the media landscape in Sweden to look like in the future?

Did he want the Swedish media to be in the custody of responsible and seriously engaged proprietors with a long tradition of pursuing issues like democracy and freedom of expression? Or could he let them be stifled by a global, dollar-rich entertainment giant? Could he deliberately risk the *Evening Post*, the *Morning News*, the publishing companies, radio and television channels, purely because he insisted on maintaining his form of mute and stereotypical ethics? Ethics that no one would ever know that he followed, nor at what cost?

And ultimately: was he prepared to sacrifice his own career?

Anders picked up the balance sheet containing the notes and looked at the chairman of the board.

"There is something," he said. "Something that Karina Björnlund really doesn't want made public."

Wennergren raised his eyebrows, intrigued.

The winter sleet hit Annika in the face with mocking nonchalance, making her gasp for breath. The doors slid shut behind her, the sucking sound mixed with the crunch of ice caught in the mechanism. She put her hand over her eyes to block the light of the paper's illuminated logo above her head. In front of her the street and the world stretched out, vast and impenetrable, her center of gravity sank, through her stomach, past her knees. How could she possibly take another step? How was she going to get home?

This is the biggest load of crap I've ever heard. I hope you haven't mentioned this nonsense to anyone else?

At the back of her head the angels were tuning up their mournful voices, no words, just notes, reaching her through eternities of emptiness.

From now on you won't be covering terrorism at all. You will not spend a minute more on Karina Björnlund or this damn Ragnwald.

How could she have been so wrong? Was she really going mad? What had happened to her head? Was it because of the tunnel? Was something up there broken beyond repair?

She put her hands over her ears, closing her eyes tight to shut the angels out, but instead she kept them in; they started up seriously inside her brain, moving into her consciousness and formulating their meaningless plaints.

Summer greeting sugar heat eternal tiredness.

No. I don't want this.

Her cell phone started buzzing from the bottom of her bag; she shut her eyes and felt the vibrations filter through her notebook, chewing gum, the bag of sanitary napkins, the padding of her coat, hitting her in the waist, spreading warmth in her stomach. She stood and waited until it had stopped.

I don't want to hear another word about this.

Stockholm stopped in the silence around her; the noise of traffic on the expressway disappeared; damp ghosts gathered around streetlights and neon signs; her feet floated free of the ground; she took off and slowly floated above the pavement outside the entrance, down toward the garage, over the frozen grass lawn, past the concrete traffic island.

"Annika!"

She fell to earth with a bump, gasping for breath, and found herself standing right outside the crunching, sliding doors, the wind tugging at her hair again, spitting and snarling.

"Hurry up, you're getting soaked."

Thomas's old green Toyota had pulled up alongside the entrance down to the garage; she looked at it in surprise—what was it doing here?

Then she saw him wave from the open driver's door, his blond hair wet and sticking to his forehead, his coat stained with sleet; she ran toward him, right into his smiling eyes, flying over the tarmac and patches of ice, drowning in his endless embrace.

"Good thing you got my message," he said, leading her around to the passenger side, carrying on talking as he opened the door and helped her in. "I tried to call your cell phone but there was no answer so I told the caretaker that I'd come past and pick you up; I had to move the car anyway so it's not really any trouble, I've picked up some goodies and I thought we could maybe . . ."

Annika was panting slightly through her half-open mouth.

"I think I'm coming down with something," she whispered.

"Right, let's get you home and tucked up properly in bed, isn't that right, kids?"

She turned around and saw the children sitting on their safety seats in the backseat; she smiled weakly.

"Hello, darlings. I love you."

WEDNESDAY, NOVEMBER 18

The man walked with floating steps past the campsite reception, his body fluid, his mind razor sharp. He felt sturdy, strong. His legs had the spring he remembered, muscles tensing and relaxing. He filled his lungs, hardly noticing the stab in his stomach as his diaphragm expanded. The air was so strangely and distantly familiar up here, like a song you used to sing as a child and had forgotten, then suddenly hear again from a distance on a crackling radio.

Sharp, he thought, and stopped. Cold and watchful.

He turned his gaze upward and squinted at the sky; one or two battered flakes were struggling to reach the ground, jerkily sailing through the layers of air.

He had come here in order to come home, to be reunited with his family. He hadn't had any expectations of the country or the landscape, all too aware of how the mills of capitalism ground down culture and infrastructure. Which was why his joy at seeing it all again was so unexpected, the huddled houses and snow-covered roads, the closeness of the sky and the desolate, closed pine trees. Even the changes felt safe; he had known that the occupation would make progress during his absence.

He walked toward the road where the girl had once lived, the ramshackle row of workers' housing with single cold taps and outdoor toilets; he wondered if he was in the right place. It was hard to tell. Karlsvik had changed in the way he had feared but couldn't imagine. On the heath outside the town, where the blueberries grew in thick carpets in the summer of 1969, where he had rolled around with Karina until they bumped into an anthill, there was a striped, paneled monstrosity in white and pale blue that boasted that it was the largest indoor arena for football and commercial exhibitions in northern Europe. He didn't need convincing.

By the river, where they had chased each other around the ruins of the old harbor and timber yard, they had built a four-star campsite with a collection of little wooden cottages: he had booked into one of them.

In the harsh winter air he could suddenly smell bubbling water on its way out to the Gulf of Bothnia, and could see the city in front of him far off on the far shore, remembering all the old remnants of the sawmill days, the fragments of wood and other rubbish that lined the edge of the river. He wondered if there was still anything left, if the pines had finally fallen into the water from the steep sandbanks by the shore.

He walked straight on, light and steady, along carefully scraped winter streets covered with a thin layer of ice, gravel, and pine needles. The paths left by the snowplows were straight and regular, the surrounding houses unrecognizable to him.

The area had been renovated, with the picturesque ambition reserved for the cultural elite and senior civil servants. The many rows of workers' housing had had their rust-red or ocher-yellow color restored, but in a shiny plastic version. Wooden carvings shone white in the lead-gray twilight, ramrod-straight window frames spoke of expensive replacements made with the best timber. With its playground's colorful swings, the recycling bins' neat lids, and the carefully swept front steps, the place presented a dishonest and decadent excess.

It was empty and dead. He could hear a dog bark; a cat jumped up onto a heap of snow in the distance, but Karlsvik was not alive: it was merely a mirror, intended to reflect the people who lived there and perceived themselves to be happy.

He stopped in the middle of that thought, remembering that the lives of common people always rested in the hands of the great capitalists, then as now.

He came out onto Disponentvägen and immediately recognized her house, the façade red and enticing like the moist lips of a whore, his gaze drawn automatically to her window on the second floor. Green window bars, an aerial on the roof like a giant insect.

His girl, his own Red Wolf.

Women had always thought him shy and reserved, a gentle and careful lover. Only with Karina had he been truly great. Only with her had lovemaking taken him beyond eroticism, and made love appear as the miracle it actually was. With her and her friends he had created his own family, and all through the racing years and seconds they had always been with him.

She hadn't wanted to talk to him.

When he looked her up she had rejected him. The betrayal burned in his face—she had been their glittering star. She had been given her proud name because they wanted to stress the group's Nordic background; they were communists from the Realm of the Wolf. Even if they believed themselves to be part of the Chinese people, there was nothing to stop them from stressing the transgression of national boundaries in the fight for freedom.

But she had allowed herself to be intoxicated by the terrible sweetness of power, had turned her back on him. Now he turned his back on her childhood home and left the houses behind him. He walked jauntily on toward the heritage trail alongside the campsite, stopped by a heap of plowed snow and looked into the thin pine trees.

The remains of Norrbotten's first ironworks could just about be glimpsed as gray foundations. He saw the spiky fragments sticking out of the snow, twisted wreckage from mankind's vain desire to govern its own fate.

The history of the ironworks was short and violent. Several hundred people worked here just before the turn of the last century, working to purify the iron ore found in the area; they made what use they could of the raw materials in their own district, and that could only ever end one way.

Southern Swedish ironmasters bought the factory after the First World War, stripped it of machines and equipment, sold the workers' housing, and quite literally blew the ironworks up.

Some people are allowed to blow things up. Not everyone, though.

Suddenly there was another jolt of pain in his diaphragm, and he realized he was freezing. The medicine was wearing off; he ought to get back to the cabin. He was suddenly aware of his smell again; it had got much worse in recent days. His mood sank when he thought about the dry nutritional powder he was forced to live off; this was no decent life.

Today was exactly three months since the diagnosis.

He shook off the thought and carried on walking, toward the pulp mill.

All that was left now was the warehouses, the shameful great buildings that were lent to the Germans during the war to store munitions and supplies. Weapons, grain, tins of food: the Nazis could store them here and collect them for their troops in Norway or the Soviet Union. Thirty men from the town had worked here, Karina's father among them. She had always claimed that it was working for the Germans that drove her father to drink.

Excuses, he thought. Man has his own free will. He can choose to do or not do anything, except death.

And he had chosen, and his choice was to fight against imperialism with death as his means of expression, death as a tool against people who in turn had chosen to impose oppression and captivity upon his brothers and sisters.

Brothers and sisters, he thought.

He grew up a single child, but eventually he acquired a family anyway. Created his own flock, the only one he had ever taken responsibility for, and the only one he had betrayed.

The pain settled into his stomach; his lack of responsibility afflicted his body and made it heavy. He turned back toward the campsite, and walked with painful steps back toward reception.

What sort of father was he? He had left his flock to fend for themselves, had fled as soon as things started to heat up around him.

The Black Panther, he thought, stopping beside the snow-covered mini–golf course to catch his breath, letting his lost children come to him. His heir and eldest son, the most impatient and restless of them, the most uncompromising—the Panther had taken his name from the freedom fighters in the U.S.A. There had been some discussion about that in the group, someone had claimed that calling yourself something American was counterrevolutionary. The Panther himself claimed the opposite, said that taking the name of America's own critics supported the fight against the lackeys of capitalism.

Personally he had remained on the sidelines, watching the others argue. When they couldn't agree he cast the deciding vote and sided with the Panther.

His chest grew thick and tight when he thought about how the young revolutionary had changed. Without his leader the Black Panther had become a mere shadow instead of a force to be reckoned with.

The other children had gone their separate ways and ended up far from their ideals. Worst of all was the White Tiger. The middle-aged Tiger was so different from the skinny boy he remembered that he almost suspected they had switched him for someone else.

He walked slowly toward his cabin, the smallest one, called a Rälsen. The White Tiger had walked with him here that summer, and suddenly he was beside him once more, the boy who had chosen his name because the color symbolized purity, clarity, and the animal for its stealth and strength.

He had been pure of heart, the man thought, and today his heart is as black as the steelworks he runs.

Behind curtains and around corners he caught glimpses of people busy with inconsequential human activities. Drinking coffee, writing shopping lists, hatching mean plots against their competitors, and dreaming of sexual fulfillment. The cluster of cabins was almost fully occupied, visitors to one of the fairs in the huge monstrosity, which suited him fine. No one had spoken to him since he had checked in after his trip to Uppland.

He stopped outside his cabin, aware that he was swaying, that his powers would soon be gone. His two last children came to him.

The Lion of Freedom had been given his name, because it was agreed that someone in the group ought to symbolize their solidarity with Africa, and the Lion himself had been incapable of any truly great thoughts. There was nothing wrong with the lad's convictions, but he needed a strong leader to help him find the right path. Together they had decided to make the roar of the Lion of Freedom echo across the whole of the oppressed black continent and liberate the masses.

The Lion of Freedom was the one who probably needed him most, so was also the one for whom things had turned out worst.

I'll take care of you, my son, he thought, and went into his little cabin.

He sat on the chair by the door and struggled to take off his shoes. His diaphragm was really hurting now, and bending down made him feel sick.

He groaned and leaned back against the chair, shutting his eyes for a moment.

His other daughter, Barking Dog, had been noisy and difficult in the sixties, but so much could have happened. It would be interesting to meet her. Maybe she was one of the ones who really deserved her inheritance.

He went over to the wardrobe to check that the duffel bag was still there.

THURSDAY, NOVEMBER 19

The front door clicked shut with a bang and silence spread its padded feet through the apartment. Annika was alone again. She lay in bed with her head burrowed into the pillow and her knees drawn up to her chin, the duvet cover damp with anxiety. The angels were humming in the background, monotonous and powerless.

She had to get up today, at least to pick up the children. She was never usually ill; Thomas wasn't used to being responsible for them, both dropping them off and picking them up and preparing food and reading to them and putting them to bed. It made him grouchy and irritable and gave her a guilty conscience.

She snuggled deeper under the covers.

Things could be worse, she thought.

If the children got sick. If Thomas left her. If the paper was shut down. If war broke out in Iraq, all of that would be worse. This is nothing.

But it was something. It was like a big hole where the foundation of her professional confidence had been.

She had trusted Schyman. Trusted his judgment.

Something had happened, either to him or to her. Maybe to both of them. Maybe it was because of the story, maybe it was too big for them.

Or else she really had gone mad in the tunnel.

She realized that this was a definite possibility.

Had she lost the ability to judge relevance and probability? Was she on the verge of losing her grip on reality?

She pulled the covers over her head and let the thought creep up on her. It stopped beside her, settling down on her pillow, and as she looked at it realized that it really wasn't dangerous.

The story was what it was, and she was right.

There was something there.

Schyman might have been right before, but he was wrong this time.

She threw off the duvet and gasped for air. She hurried naked into the bathroom, peed, brushed her teeth, and showered, in rapid succession.

The apartment echoed desolately without Thomas and the children; she stopped in the doorway to the kitchen and looked at the mess they had left behind them from breakfast, without really seeing it. Instead she listened to the sound of silence, sounds she never appreciated when they were all home and she had another function apart from just being an individual. When she became part of something bigger than herself, the little, insignificant nuances didn't get through to her. In her role as Universally Responsible for Life, she flew high above both whispers and cries. Only shrieks and demands of life-maintaining action, like Food and Scotch Tape and Where's Tiger, managed to reach her then.

Now she was just her own self, off sick, holed below the water line and declared lobotomized, a used-up reporter who had passed her sell-by date, and the nuances submerged her, making her listen in mute astonishment.

The fridge was rumbling, deep and steady, a half-tone lower than the ventilation unit on the roof of the next building. The smell of frying was creeping in from somewhere, a restaurant in the block heating up pans and griddles and preparing Lunch of the Day. The buses at the stop down on Hantverkargatan sighed and groaned; sirens from the fire engines stationed by Kronoberg Park were on their way in or out, rising or falling.

Suddenly the panic struck.

I can't bear it.

All the muscles in her body strained, sound and breathing vanished.

There's nothing wrong, she thought. It just feels like it. I'm not suffocating, but the opposite; I'm hyperventilating, it'll pass, just wait, calm down.

The floor came closer and pressed against her thighs and elbow. She ended up staring under the dishwasher.

He completely invalidated me as a person, she thought, a moment of clarity that brought back sound and color. Schyman wasn't just seeing me as a reporter; he took away my honor and value as a person. He's never done that before. He must be under serious pressure from an unlikely desire to be accepted. I'm not accepted. He can't go into battle on my side right now, because it would cost too much.

She got up, noticing that she had banged her knee. Her arms and feet ached, a sign that she had absorbed too much oxygen.

Her panic attacks had disappeared for several years. She hadn't had any since the children were born, until the Bomber got her. Now they came at irregular intervals, with the same violence and terror as they had before.

I wonder if I need happy pills, she thought.

She knew that Anne Snapphane had got hold of a large bottle that was hidden in her bathroom cabinet out on Lidingö.

But it's all imagination, she thought. I'm scared of my own fear. They're just mental projections; drag them into the light and they'll vanish, let them out and look at them and they'll just disappear.

She stood there with her hand on the dishwasher, feeling the gases in her blood stabilize.

She knew she was right. There was a link between Ragnwald, the minister of culture, the attack on F21, and the death of the boy, the journalist, and the councillor.

She had also clearly understood that she was not allowed to look into the case anymore, under any circumstances.

I don't want to hear another word about this.

At work, no, she thought. But if I make a few calls when I'm off sick at home, then it doesn't count.

So she went into the bedroom and got dressed, then went back into the kitchen and made coffee, without clearing the mess left by Thomas and the children; just pushed all the dirty crockery into a corner of the table and sat down with her mug of coffee, her pad of paper, and a ballpoint pen from the Association of Local Authorities.

She needed to know more about both the terrorist and the minister in order to see the bigger picture. She had the internet at home, but only via an old modem. Thomas had wanted to get broadband but she had refused, because he spent too much time on the computer already.

Check the church records, she wrote, backgrounds, and parents.

Ask for the minister's public records, start with the mail, then journeys, representations, declarations, property register, company register, and so on.

Read more about ETA and Læstadianism.

She looked at the short list.

That's enough for today.

She picked up the phone and asked directory inquiries to put her through to the parish office in Sattajärvi. And discovered that there wasn't one. She asked for the numbers of all parish offices covered by the local code for Pajala, and, apart from Pajala itself, was given numbers for Junesuando and Tärendö.

Sattajärvi was covered by Pajala.

Göran Nilsson was born October 2, 1948, the only son of Toivo and Elina Nilsson. His mother was registered January 18, 1945, birthplace given as Kexholm. The couple married May 17, 1946. Father died 1977, mother 1989.

She wrote all of this down and thanked them.

Kexholm?

She would have to go on the net after all.

Käkisalmi, also known as Kexholm, turned out to be at the mouth of the Vuoksen River, where it flowed into Lake Ladoga on the Karelian Isthmus, not far from the old Swedish city of Viborg.

In other words, now in Russia.

She found a site through the county council in Luleå, with a lot of information about the history of the area.

In the autumn of 1944 Karelia was invaded by the Soviet Union and the whole district was emptied of its original inhabitants. Four hundred thousand people fled deeper into Finland, and some of them carried on to Sweden.

She stared at the screen.

Ethnic cleansing, she thought. An old concept, only the terminology is new.

Did that mean anything? Was it important that the terrorist's mother had been driven from her home by Russian soldiers?

Not sure. Maybe.

She logged out and called the parish office in Lower Luleå. It was always easier to do this sort of research over the phone, when no one could see her nosy great snout.

Karina Björnlund was born September 9, 1951, second child of three to the marriage of Hilma and Helge Björnlund. The couple divorced in 1968, the mother remarried and now lives on Storgatan in Luleå. Father dead. Brothers Per and Alf.

So what did that tell her?

Nothing.

She thanked the parish secretary and got up, restless, and walked around the apartment before picking up the phone again and calling the *Norrland News*.

"Hans Blomberg is off today," the sour receptionist said.

"Put me through to the archive anyway," Annika said quickly before she got another rant about the EU.

A young woman answered.

"I know the powers that be have decided that we should cooperate with the *Evening Post*, but no one ever asks us if we have enough time to do it," she said, sounding stressed. "You can have the password, then you can log in direct and check the archive over the net."

She needs to calm down before she ends up like Hans, Annika thought.

"What I'm looking for probably isn't on the net," she said. "I'm after the earliest cuttings you have for Karina Björnlund."

"Who? The minister of culture? We've got kilometers worth of columns about her."

"The very earliest ones. Can you fax them to me?"

She gave her home number, making a mental note to remember to turn the fax machine on.

"How many? The first hundred?"

Annika thought for a moment.

"The first five will do."

The sound of air being exhaled, a long sigh.

"Okay, but not before lunch."

They hung up and Annika went out into the kitchen and cleared the breakfast things, checked what was in the freezer and worked out that she could do chicken fillets in coconut milk for dinner.

Then she tied on her shoes and pulled on her jacket.

Have to get out, have to breathe.

She picked up a microwaved pasta dish with mushrooms and bacon from the 7-Eleven on Fleminggatan, and ate it slowly with a plastic spoon as she crossed Kungsbron into the city center.

She threw the paper tray in a bin by the junction of Vasagatan and Kungsgatan, then walked quickly toward Hötorget, only to slow down on Drottninggatan, Stockholm's only truly continental pedestrian street, with its mix of heaven and hell, street vendors, performers, whores, and the frozen tramps who filled the gaps between the retail palaces and strings of lights and roads crossing the street. She was pushed forward in the crush, strangely full of tenderness; she was jostled along by people, and felt something oddly melancholic as she took them in, the mothers with clenched teeth and squeaking, swaying buggies; groups of beautiful young women from immigrant suburbs with high heels and clear voices, finally out of sight of home, with their hair dancing above unbuttoned jackets and tight tops; important men with their universal uniforms of briefcases and stress; slick Östermalm kids with Canada

Goose jackets and posh nasal "i" sounds; tourists; hot-dog sellers; couriers; idiots and drug dealers; she let herself be swept along with them, drawn in among them, maybe even find a home at the bottom of their big, forgiving, common well.

"Isn't that the Blaster? That's her, isn't it? Look! In the tunnel, she was on telly . . ."

She didn't turn around, knew that the whispering would pass, *if you sit by the river long enough, you will see the bodies of your enemies float by;* soon no one would remember the Bomber in the tunnel anymore and she would be just one among all the others in the well, a gray-black flake slowly drifting down toward the sludge at the bottom, ignored by everyone.

She stopped before the glass door to number 16, one of the government's discreet departmental entrances. The window frames were all polished copper, and behind large empty glass windows and well-tended potted palms was a reception desk with bulletproof glass and a uniformed guard.

Annika pushed open the two doors, the grit on the soles of her shoes scraping against the marble floor, and went up to the guard, her skin creeping with the feeling that she was a shameless infiltrator. She tapped on the microphone in front of the closed screen.

"It works," the elderly man behind the glass said; she saw his lips move and heard the words to her left, through a hidden speaker.

"Oh, good," Annika said, trying to smile and leaning toward the microphone. "I'd like to check Karina Björnlund's post."

It was done: the spy is here, about to go through the bins and the mail box.

The man picked up a phone and pressed some buttons.

"Take a seat and I'll call the registrar."

She went over to the waiting area, three curved brick-red sofas, one EU flag and one Swedish flag, a designer rack holding a mass of magazines, a metal statue possibly supposed to be a small child. Maybe a girl.

She stopped and looked at the statue, was it bronze?

She took a step closer. Who was she? How many inquisitive spies had she watched come and go?

"Hello? Was it you that wanted to look through the minister's register?"

She looked up and found herself face to face with a middle-aged man with a ponytail and sideburns.

"Yes," Annika said. "That's me."

She held out her hand, not mentioning her name. According to the freedom of information laws, you could check public documents without having to prove your identity, a law she was happy to safeguard as often as she had the chance. At least it saved her from having to feel the slightest shame, because they didn't know who she was.

"This way."

They passed two locked doors and a passageway painted in diagonal stripes, and took the elevator up to the sixth floor.

"To your right," the man said.

The marble floor was replaced by linoleum.

"Down the steps."

Worn oak tiles.

"This is my room. So, what did you want to see?"

"Everything," Annika said, taking off her jacket and deciding to get as much spying done as possible. She put her coat and bag on a chair in the corner.

"Okay," the man said, starting up a program on the computer. "Karina has had 668 official items since she started as a minister almost ten years ago. I've got the whole list on here."

"Can I have a printout?"

"This year?"

"Everything."

The registrar's expression didn't change; he just started his printer.

She glanced down the first page of the printout: registration date, item number, in date, documentation date. Then the name of the person who had been in charge of the item, the person who had sent it in, name and address, a description of the item in question, and finally what it led to.

Decision, she read, ad acta.

"What does 'ad acta' mean?" she asked.

"No reply," the man with the ponytail said, turning to face her. "Archived without action. Could be an encouraging note, or rambling letters from our more regular correspondents."

She went through the descriptions of the items: an invitation to the Cannes Film Festival, a request for a signed photograph, a plea to save a publishing company from closure, five questions from class 8B in Sigtuna, an invitation to the Nobel dinner in Stockholm City Hall on December 10.

"Where are all these letters and emails physically stored?"

"The items you're reading through now are still current, so they're with secretaries."

She took the second page and her eye was caught by the first item.

Statement from the Newspaper Publishers' Association regarding changes to broadcast rights for digital television.

Anne Snapphane's channel, she thought.

"Could I look at this one?"

The registrar stretched his back, looked at the printout she was holding out, and adjusted his glasses.

"You'll have to contact the person dealing with that," he said and pointed at the name below the document date.

She moved on; there were periods of heavy correspondence regarding proposed legislation.

She reached a printout of items received very recently.

Registration date: November 18.

Sender: Herman Wennergren.

Regarding: Request for meeting to discuss a matter of urgency.

"What's this?" Annika asked, handing the man the sheet.

He read silently for a moment.

"An email," he said. "Received Tuesday evening, registered yesterday."

"I want to know what was in that email," she said.

He shrugged.

"I can't help with that; it's with the person who's dealing with it. Anything else?"

She turned away, continued to look through the list, oddly agitated.

Why would the *Evening Post*'s chairman suddenly decide that he had to meet the minister of culture on Tuesday afternoon?

She forced her worries to one side.

Sender: Anonymous.

Regarding: Drawing of yellow dragon.

Decision: Ad acta.

Read the entry again.

"What's this?" she said, leaning forward and pointing, waiting for the man to put on his glasses and look.

"An anonymous letter," he said. "We get quite a few of those. Mostly newspaper cuttings or slightly muddled opinions."

"Many yellow dragons?"

He laughed.

"Not too many."

"Where are the anonymous letters?"

"I collect those here; they have their own box."

The registrar took off his glasses and reached for a brown file labeled Government Offices: Anonymous Post. He opened it and took out the letter at the top.

"We keep them in boxes arranged by year, five years up here and then they go into the central archive. Every envelope is stamped on the back."

He held out the little envelope, letting her read it.

Stamped October 31 that year.

"What's in it?"

"I think this one's the dragon."

He pulled out a sheet of A4 paper folded in four, smoothed it out and handed it to Annika.

"I don't know why they sent it here," he said, "but maybe it counts as culture."

It really was a little dragon in the middle of the sheet of white paper, drawn with a rather shaky hand and colored with yellow ink.

Something clicked inside Annika's head: she felt it physically.

She had seen a dragon almost exactly the same as this recently, but where?

"Can I have a copy of this?" she asked.

While the man went out into the corridor to get a photocopy, Annika picked up the envelope the dragon had arrived inside. Addressed to Minister of Culture Karina Björnlund, Stockholm, La Suède.

She looked closer at the stamp.

Postmarked in Paris, *le 28 Octobre.*

Ragnwald had probably lived in the French part of the Pyrenees for the past thirty years. There could be a connection, but where had she seen the drawing before?

She closed her eyes tight and searched her memory, catching a glimpse of something in a temporary file somewhere in her frontal lobe.

She opened her eyes wide, listening for the registrar.

She could hear him talking to someone down the corridor.

She looked around the room and discovered a little Post-it note stuck to the bottom of his computer screen.

She crept over to the computer and leaned down to read the note.

Karina direct, then a number through the departmental exchange, then the word *cell* followed by a GSM number.

She stared at the number: 666 66 60.

Twice the number of the beast, and then a zero.

Was that just coincidence, or did it say something about Karina Björnlund?

"Anything else I can help you with?"

Annika jumped and straightened up, turned around and smiled disarmingly.

"Maybe another time," Annika said and picked up the sheaf of printouts, ten years of incoming mail to the minister of culture.

She headed for the elevators with relief.

Mehmet filled the whole of Anne Snapphane's office doorway, angry energy radiating from his head. Anne's reflex reaction at the sight of him was pure, unalloyed joy, a blinding white jubilation that shot up from her stomach all the way to her scalp.

"We've got to sort this out," he said. "Now, before it gets so infected that we can never get to grips with it."

Her happiness didn't want to go; it clung on as a fading hymn of praise: He came! He came here to me! I'm important to him.

Anne saw him lean against the door frame with all the elegant nonchalance that she loved so much, her handsome man, the man she longed for so much at night that she woke from the orgasms. She pushed her swivel chair back from the desk and slowly stood up.

"I want that too," she said, holding out her hand to him.

He pretended not to see it, staring down at the floor.

"Sylvia's been off sick all week," he said, quietly and angrily.

Her jubilation shattered, she could hear the splinters hitting the plastic mat.

"I haven't betrayed anyone," she said, the sharp edges cutting her voice.

He raised both hands in a calming gesture.

"We've got to get past that bit," he said. "It's no one's fault; the guilt belongs to everyone and no one. It wasn't working between us, surely we can at least agree on that?"

Defiance was forcing tears into Anne's eyes; she gasped for breath far too audibly before replying.

"I thought it was working," she said.

"But I didn't," he said. "So it couldn't go on. If two people are going to live their lives together they have to agree about that, don't they?"

She closed her eyes for a few seconds, then raised her head and tried to smile.

"Serfdom has been abolished, you mean?"

He took a couple of steps into the room.

"Anne," he said in a pleading tone that made her smile fade. "If we can't sort out normal communication, now, then we'll be sitting with a payment plan that'll last forever. And Miranda will be the one it costs most. We can't mess up like this."

She pressed her fingertips against the desk, looking down at her shoes.

A flash of insight worked its way up from her feet, through her gut, rushing up to her head; she suddenly saw the world from his point of view, realized what was important for him.

Miranda, his daughter. His new woman and new child. She was no longer in his consciousness in that way, all tenderness was exhausted and gone; now she was a necessary evil, someone he once shared a child and a bed with, a by-product from a past life that he would always have to deal with.

Self-pity threatened to suffocate her, a feeble embarrassing sound escaped her throat. She took several silent breaths.

"But I love you," she said, without looking at him.

He went over to her and hugged her; she wrapped her arms hard around his waist and leaned her head against his neck and wept.

"I love you so bloody much," she whispered.

He rocked her gently, stroking her hair, and kissed her on the forehead.

"I know," he said softly. "I understand that it hurts, and I'm sorry. Forgive me."

Anne opened her eyes to his polo sweater, feeling a tear run down her nose and hang there.

"There's no point in clinging onto pride anymore," he said quietly. "Will you be okay?"

She wiped her nose with the back of her hand.

"I don't know," she whispered.

* * *

There were five sheets in the fax machine when Annika got home. Her outdoor clothes fell in a shapeless heap on the hall floor again, she was going to have to go out to pick up the children later anyway.

She settled onto the wooden chair by the hall table, surrounded by piles of bills, and looked quickly through the documents the woman at the *Norrland News* archive had faxed through, in the order they had been published in.

The first cutting indicated that Karina Björnlund had been a promising athlete as a teenager. The article was a report from the NC, which Annika presumed meant either Norrland Championship or Norrbotten Championship. The picture was grainy, with too much contrast, Annika had to screw up her eyes to make out the skinny young girl with a ponytail and the number 18 on her chest, waving a bunch of flowers jubilantly toward the photographer. There was something ecstatic about the picture that was still almost tangible, thirty-five years after it had been taken. Karina Björnlund was a success; she won all the sprint distances at the championship and was predicted a glorious future.

For some reason it made the register detailing the minister's post feel even more shameful.

Annika put the picture of the athlete at the bottom of the pile and went on.

The second cutting was an article about the Working Dogs' Club in Karlsvik, and showed Bamse the golden retriever and his owner, Karina Björnlund, along with five other dogs and owners, getting ready for a display in the sports hall that weekend. The picture was smaller than the last one, the black heavier, and she could only really make out the minister's white teeth and the dog's dark tongue.

The third was stamped June 6, 1974, and showed a group of new graduates from the medical secretarial course at Umeå University. Karina Björnlund was third from the left in the top row.

Annika glanced across the homogenous group in the picture, no men, no immigrants, most of them with their hair in a page cut, one side curled to form a wing over one eyebrow.

The fourth cutting was the smallest, a note from 1978 under the heading Names & News, in which the Norrbotten County Council announced that Karina Björnlund had been appointed as secretary to the commissioner of the council.

The fifth was a report of what had evidently been a turbulent public meeting in the county council offices in the autumn of 1980. The picture showed four men discussing the coordination of health care in the district, with expansive gestures and presumably raised voices. In the background stood a woman in a flowery skirt, with watchful eyes and folded arms.

Annika looked at the sheet more closely and read the small print of the caption.

Council Commissioner Christer Lundgren defended the position of politicians on the issue of a new central hospital for Norrbotten in discussions with the Medical Council and the pressure group Protect Our Health. His secretary Karina Björnlund listens.

Okay, Annika thought, letting the paper drop. So that's how she did it. She got a job with Christer Lundgren, who eventually became trade minister, clung on to his coattails and followed him all the way into government.

She looked at the cutting again, and saw it had been published on page twenty-two, a long way back for a local paper, and read the start of the article, which was about some technicality in the political decision-making process. She skimmed the rest of the piece until her eye caught the picture byline at the bottom right corner.

Hans Blomberg, council reporter.

She blinked, looked again.

Yes, it was definitely him, a much younger and thinner version of the archivist at the *Norrland News*.

She let out a snort, suddenly picturing the archivist's background as clearly as the messy table in front of her. There were people like him on every paper: conscientious but unimaginative reporters who covered Important Things, political decisions and social developments, the sort of person who wrote dull texts and defended the fact with reference to the seriousness of the subject, looking down derisively on journalists who wrote engaging, committed articles. He had probably been union representative at some point, fighting for all the hopeless cases, but never for people like her, because they could look after themselves.

And now he was sitting in the archive and counting the days until his misery was finally over.

Little Hans, she thought, twisting her arm to check the time.

Time to pick up the rug rats.

Ellen rushed toward her, arms open wide, Tiger dangling from her left hand. The joy that welled up within Annika was so hot that something melted—the sight of tights and pigtails and the red dress with a checkered heart on it made something hard and sharp give way and disappear.

She caught her daughter as she jumped at her, astonished at the child's utter trust, and stroked her straight little legs and arms, her soft shoulders and stiff back, inhaling the divine softness of her hair.

"I made a candy machine," Ellen said, struggling to get down, and taking Annika by the finger and pulling her over to the craft corner.

Out of cardboard and tape, Ellen had built a machine where you put candy in one end and it rolled through various channels and holes into a little bowl on the other side. Annika had an old piece of chewing gum in her bag, so they used that to see if the machine worked, and it did, almost, the gum rolled too badly to go all the way through, but they agreed that it was a wonderful invention that needed to be tested with real candy on Saturday.

"We'll show Daddy," the child said, about to pick up her cardboard creation, as the top swayed disconcertingly and Annika leaped forward.

"We can't really bring it with us today," she said, taking hold of the cardboard, "because we have to go into town and buy new shoes for Kalle. We'd better leave the candy machine here so it won't get broken."

She put the contraption back on the worktop; the girl's mouth fell open, her eyes welled up with tears, her lip starting to quiver.

"But," she said, "that means Daddy won't get to see it."

"Yes, he will," Annika said, crouching down beside her. "The machine's safe here, and we can get it tomorrow instead. Maybe you could paint it?"

Ellen looked down at her feet, shaking her head and making her pigtails dance.

"What lovely pigtails you've got," Annika said, taking hold of one of them and tickling her daughter's ear. "Who did those for you?"

"Lennart!" Ellen said, giggling and shrugging to escape the tickling. "He helped me with the candy machine."

"Come on, let's go and get your brother," Annika said, and the battle was over. Ellen put on her overalls, hat, and gloves, and even remembered to take Tiger home with her.

Kalle's school was on Pipersgatan, two blocks away. Annika held Ellen's warm little hand in hers as they carefully negotiated the puddles and sang "Little Ida's Summer Song," a gentle plea for better weather.

Kalle was sitting in the reading corner concentrating on a book about Peter-No-Tail. He didn't look up until Annika crouched down next to him and kissed the top of his head.

"Mommy," he said, "where's Uppsala?"

"Just north of Stockholm," she said. "Why?"

"Can we go and see Peter and the other cats one day?"

"Definitely," Annika said, remembering that there were special cat walks where you could follow in the author Gösta Knutsson's footsteps around the churches, castle, and university.

"I think she's prettiest," he said, pointing to a white cat and slowly spelling out "Ma-ry Cream-nose."

Annika blinked.

"Can you read?" she said, astonished. "Who taught you to do that?"

He shrugged.

"On the computer," he said. "Otherwise you can't play."

He stood up, closed the book and put it back on the shelf. Then looked sternly down at her sitting on the red cushion.

"Boots," he said. "You promised. My old ones have got a hole in."

She smiled, caught hold of one trouser leg and pulled him to her; he laughed and struggled, and she blew on his neck.

"We'll get the bus to the Gallery," she said. "Go and get your clothes on. Ellen's waiting for us."

The number 1 pulled up just as they reached the bus stop, and the three of them found seats right at the back.

"Army green," Kalle said. "I don't want blue again; only babies have blue boots."

"I'm not a baby," Ellen said.

"Of course you can have green," Annika said. "As long as they've got some."

They got off at Kungsträdgården and hurried across the street between the showers of slush thrown up by the cars driving past. They tugged off their hats and gloves and scarves when they were inside the shopping center, stuffing them into Annika's capacious bag. In a shoe store on the upper floor they found a pair of army green, lined rubber boots in the right size, tall enough and with reflective patches. The boy refused to take them off; Annika paid and they took the old ones home in a bag.

They got out in the nick of time, Ellen had got too hot and was starting to whine, but she fell silent again once they were out in the cold and darkness of Hamngatan, quietly walking along with her hand in Annika's. She took Kalle's hand as well as they went to cross the road by the department store NK, concentrating on fending off the cascades of dirty water from the cars, when the silhouette of a person on his way out of the shop across the street caught her eye.

That's Thomas, she thought without realizing she was thinking it. What's he doing here?

No, she thought, it isn't him.

The man took a couple of steps forward, his breath lit up by a streetlight, yes, it was him!

Her face broke into a broad smile, the warm joy that melted things came back; he was out buying Christmas presents! Already!

She laughed; he was such a Christmas freak. Last year he started buying presents in September; she remembered how angry he got when she found them at the bottom of his wardrobe and had wondered what those parcels were and what they were doing there.

A violent spray of slush hit them and Ellen yelped. Annika pulled the children back from the curb and yelled angrily at the taxi. When she looked up again Thomas was gone; she searched the crowd for him, and saw him again. He was turning to face someone. A woman with blond hair and a long coat went up to him and he put his arm around her. Thomas pulled the other woman to him and kissed her, and there was complete silence and everyone else vanished, Annika was staring down a long tunnel and at the other end her husband was kissing a blond woman with a passion that made her insides freeze and shatter.

"Mommy, it's green!"

But she didn't move, and people jostled her; she saw their faces talking to her but their voices were mute, she saw Thomas go off, vanishing with his arm around the blond woman's shoulders, the woman's hand around his waist; they walked slowly away with their backs to her, enclosed in their coupledom, swallowed up by the sea of people.

"Why aren't we going, Mommy? Now it's red again."

She looked down at her children, their faces looking up at her, eyes clear and questioning, and realized that her mouth was wide open. She swallowed a scream, snapped her mouth shut, looked at the traffic.

"Soon," she said, in a voice that came from deep underground. "We'll go next time."

And the lights turned green and the bus came and they had to stand all the way to Kungsholmstorg.

The children started singing as they climbed the stairs; the tune was familiar but she couldn't place it, she couldn't find the right door key and had to try several times. Kalle asked if he could keep his boots on and she let him, but he had to wipe them properly on the mat first, and he did, clever boy.

She went into the kitchen and picked up the phone, dialed his cell phone number but got the message service. He had turned it off—he was walking with his arm around a blond woman somewhere in Stockholm, not answering when she called.

So she called his office, and Arnold, his tennis partner, and no one anywhere answered.

"What are we having for tea?"

Kalle was standing in the door in his shiny new boots.

"Coconut chicken with rice."

"With broccoli?"

She shook her head, feeling a panic attack bubbling up, and clutched the sink, looking into her son's eyes and deciding not to drown.

"No," she said. "Water chestnuts and bamboo shoots and baby sweet corn."

His face relaxed, he smiled and came a step closer.

"Do you know what, Mommy?" he said. "I've got a wobbly tooth. Feel!"

And she reached out her hand, saw that it was trembling; she felt his left front tooth and, yes, it was definitely loose.

"That'll come out soon."

"Then I get a gold coin from the tooth fairy," Kalle said.

"Then you get a gold coin from the tooth fairy," Annika said, turning away, she had to sit down.

Her innards had solidified into a grotesque lump of razor blades and shards of ice, cutting her when she breathed. The kitchen table was swaying slowly from side to side in a desolate sea: *there's no point*, it sang, *there's no point*. And the angels tuned up in the background: *winter beautiful summer love honey blossom . . .*

Suddenly she felt that she was about to be sick. She dashed into the bathroom behind the kitchen and her stomach turned inside out, half-digested pasta from 7-Eleven tore at her throat, making her tears overflow.

Afterward she hung across the toilet, the stench making her brain revolt.

Beyond the sun eternal love, the angels sang at full volume.

"Shut up!" she yelled, slamming the toilet lid.

She walked angrily into the kitchen, pulling out all the ingredients for dinner; burned herself on the flame when she put the rice on; cut herself when she sliced the onion and prepared the chicken, shaking as she opened the tins of coconut milk and baby sweet corn and Asian chestnuts.

Was she wrong? It wasn't impossible. Thomas looked like a lot of other Swedish men, tall and fair and broad-shouldered, with the beginnings of a stomach, and it had been dark and they were quite a long way away; maybe it wasn't him standing there with the blond woman at all.

She gripped the stove, closed her eyes and took four deep breaths.

Maybe it wasn't him. Maybe she'd seen wrong.

She straightened up, relaxed her shoulders, opened her eyes, and heard the door open.

"Daddy!"

The children's cries of joy and sturdy welcoming hugs, his deep voice expressing a mixture of happiness and cautious fending-off; she fixed her gaze on the extractor fan and wondered if it showed, if there was something in his face that would give her the answer.

"Hello," he said from behind her, kissing her on the back of her head. "How are you feeling? Better?"

She breathed in and out before turning around and setting her eyes on him.

He looked the same as usual.

He looked exactly like he usually did.

Dark gray jacket, dark blue jeans, light gray shirt, shimmering silk tie.

His eyes were the same; they were a bit tired and slightly disillusioned, his hair thick and brushlike above his bushy eyebrows.

She noticed she was holding her breath and took a deep, greedy gulp of air.

"Oh," she said, "a bit better."

"Are you going to work tomorrow?"

She turned around to stir the chicken, hesitating.

"No," she said. "I've just been sick."

"As long as you don't give us all this winter vomiting bug," Thomas said, sitting down at the kitchen table.

It couldn't have been him. It must have been someone else.

"How was work today?" she said, putting the saucepan on a trivet from DesignTorget.

He sighed, holding the morning paper out in front of him, preventing her from seeing his eyes.

"Cramne at Justice is difficult to deal with. A load of talk and not much action. The girl from the Federation of County Councils and I are having to do most of the work, and he gets the credit."

Annika stood still, the pan of rice in her hand, and stared at the headline on the front page of the paper, something to do with a leak about the culture proposal that was due next week.

"The Federation of County Councils," she said. "What was her name again?"

Thomas inadvertently let one corner of the paper fold back; she met his eyes for an instant before he shook the paper to make it stand up again.

"Sophia," he said. "Sophia Grenborg."

Annika started at the picture of the minister of culture illustrating the article.

"What's she like?"

Thomas carried on reading, hesitating a few moments before replying.

"Ambitious," he said, "pretty good. Often tries to lobby for the Federation at our expense. She can be damned annoying."

He folded the paper, got up and tossed it onto the windowsill.

"Right," he said. "I'll get the kids. I don't want to miss tennis this week."

And he came back into the kitchen with a squealing child under each arm, put them on their chairs, felt the loose tooth and admired the new boots, flicked the pigtails and listened to tales of candy machines and promises to visit Peter-No-Tail in Uppsala.

I'm imagining things, she thought. I must have seen wrong.

She tried to laugh, but couldn't thaw out the sharp stone in her chest.

It wasn't him. It was someone else. We're his family and he loves us. He'd never let the children down.

They ate quickly, didn't want to miss Bolibompa.

"That was great, thanks," Thomas said, giving her a peck on the cheek.

They cleared up together, their hands occasionally touching, their eyes meeting for brief moments.

He would never leave me.

She poured detergent into the dishwasher and switched it on. He took her face in his hands, studying it with a frown.

"It's good you're going to have another day at home," he said. "You look really pale."

She looked down, took his hands away.

"I feel a bit washed out," she said, and walked out of the kitchen.

"Don't wait up," he said to the back of her head. "I promised Arnold I'd finally go for a beer afterward."

She turned to ice in the doorway, the razor-sharp stone rotating in her chest. She stood still, feeling her heart thud.

"Okay," she said, and got control of her muscles again, moving one foot in front of the other, out into the hall, into the bedroom, onto the bed. She heard him take his sports bag and tennis racket out of the hall cupboard. He called good-bye to her and the children; she heard their distracted reply and her own silence.

Had he noticed anything odd about her?

Had he reacted in a particular way?

She took a deep breath and let it out slowly.

To be honest, she had been a bit strange this past year. He wasn't just reacting to this evening.

She got up, walked around the bed to use the phone on her little table.

"Thomas said you were ill," Arnold said, the only one of Thomas's old friends who had ever really accepted her. "Are you feeling any better?"

Annika swallowed and muttered.

"Well, I can quite see why he can't play tonight when you're this bad, but this is the second week in a row."

Annika fell. The floor beneath her became a black hole and she was sailing off through space.

"I'll have to find another partner if he keeps canceling."

"Can't you give it a bit longer?" Annika said, sinking into the bed. "He appreciates your matches so much."

Arnold sighed, irritated.

"Okay," he said, "but Thomas is a real damn pest. He can never make a decision and stick to it. If you book a fixed time on court for the whole autumn, you can't just decide not to use it."

Annika put a hand over her eyes, her heart racing.

"Well, I'll tell him," she said, and hung up.

Some time must have passed, because suddenly the children were with her in bed, one on each side of her. They were singing something she vaguely recognized and she hummed along, and in the background the angels sang a harmony.

These are my children, she thought. He'll never take my children away from me.

"Right," she said, "it's time for bed now."

And she got them into bed by reading them a story, without any awareness of what she was reading; she tucked them in and kissed them and went around turning out the lights. She huddled into the alcove by the living-room window and rested her temple against the ice-cold glass. She could feel the draft from the ill-fitting frame against her thighs, and listened to the wind as it tried to creep around the hinges. Her insides were mute and calm, weighed down by the rumbling stone.

The apartment lay in darkness behind her. The swinging streetlight outside cast yellow shadows across the room; from the outside her windows were nothing but black holes.

She listened, trying to detect the children's breathing, but could only hear her own. She held her breath, but her hearing was blocked by her heartbeat, the blood rushing and racing and bubbling in her head.

Unfaithful, she thought. Sven was always unfaithful.

She had refused to see it for all those years, and the only time she protested, he had hit her in the head with a pair of pliers. Without realizing it, she fingered the small scar on her forehead; it was almost invisible now, she hardly ever thought about it.

She was used to men being unfaithful.

She could see him in front of her, her first love, her childhood friend, her fiancé, the sports star. Sven Mattsson who loved her more than anything else in the world, Sven who worshipped her so much that no one else could get close to her but him, couldn't even talk to her, and she wasn't allowed to think about anyone else but him, actually, nothing else but him. Anything else would be punished, and he punished her, he punished her and punished her until the day he stood before her by the furnace in the Hälleforsnäs works with his hunting knife in his hand.

She turned away from the image, stood up and shook it off, shrugging it off the same way she shrugged off her nightmares: the familiar nightmares that came back after that night in the tunnel, the men from Studio Six who were discussing what to do with her, Sven with his bloody knife, her cat flying through the air with its guts hanging out.

And now Thomas was unfaithful.

Right now he was probably in bed together with blond Sophia Grenborg, maybe he was entering her right now, maybe they were licking each other's genitals or relaxing in each other's sweat.

She stared at the yellow shadows, planted her feet firmly on the wooden floor, the newly sanded floor that she had varnished three times, folded her arms over her chest and forced herself to breathe slowly. The apartment responded to her with gentle caution.

How much was she prepared to sacrifice to hold her life together?

She had a choice. It was just a matter of making a decision.

The realization made her shoulders relax, and it was suddenly easier to breathe; she went over to her computer and logged onto the net. In the darkness she went onto InfoTorg and looked up Sophia Grenborg in Stockholm in the census results, getting a load of hits.

The woman she had seen with Thomas outside NK was in her thirties, or slightly younger. Certainly not over thirty-five.

Annika narrowed the search.

As the representative of the Federation of County Councils in a research project looking into threats to politicians, she couldn't be younger than twenty-five.

She removed anyone born after 1980.

Still too many.

She logged out and went into the Federation's own website, and looked among the employees.

She spelled her name with "ph."

So incredibly damnedly anally retentively absurdly goddamn pretentious.

Back to InfoTorg and the name search.

Sophia Grenborg. Just the one. Twenty-nine. Lived in Upper Östermalm, born in Engelbrekt parish, oh how terribly, terribly, damned smart.

She printed out the page through the fax machine and logged out. With the printout in her hand she rang the duty desk of the National Police Board and asked for a copy of the passport belonging to the person with Sophia Grenborg's personal identity number.

"Ten minutes," the officer said tiredly.

Without making a sound she checked that the children were asleep, then crept out into the Stockholm night.

It had started to snow. Wet flakes materialized against the dirty gray sky, falling onto her face when she looked up. All sounds descended half an octave, striking her eardrums with doubt and deception.

She hurried through the snow, leaving damp tracks behind her on the pavement.

The entrance to the Stockholm Police Headquarters was on Bergsgatan, two hundred meters from her door. She stopped at the big electric gates, pressed the pedestrian intercom, and was let into the oblong cage that led to the door itself.

The copy hadn't arrived yet, so she was told to take a seat for a few minutes.

She sat down on one of the chairs along the wall, swallowed, and refused to feel bad.

All passport photos in Sweden were still public documents and could be requested at any time. There had been discussions about restricting access, but so far no decision had been taken.

I don't need to explain myself, she thought. I don't need an excuse.

When she was given the envelope she couldn't wait to see if she was right, and turned away from the reception desk and pulled out the Polaroid picture.

It was her.

No doubt at all.

Sophia Grenborg.

Her husband was walking around Stockholm kissing Sophia Grenborg.

She returned the photograph to its envelope and went back to her children.

Margit Axelsson had believed in the innate power of human beings all her life. She was convinced that every individual had the power to influence events; it was just a matter of willpower and engagement.

As a young woman she had believed in global revolution, that the masses would be freed and cast off the yoke of imperialism as the world rang out with hymns of praise.

She stretched her back and looked out over the room.

Today she knew that you could act on a large scale, or on a small scale. She knew that she was making a contribution, day by day, in her work with the children at the nursery, the collective future, everyone's responsibility, but also in her work here, in the ceramics room of Pitholm's People's Hall.

The Workers' Educational Association had always believed that those who had received the fewest of society's resources should be compensated through education, cultural activities, and opportunities. She regarded it as justice applied in the educational and cultural sphere.

Study groups were a lesson in democracy. They took as their starting point the belief that every individual has the capacity and desire to develop themselves—to exert influence and take responsibility, that every individual is a resource.

And she saw how the members grew, young and old alike. When they learned to handle the clay and the glazes their self-confidence grew, their understanding of the opinions of others, and, with that, their ability to actively influence what went on in the society around them.

She had to remind herself of this as she stood beside her sculpture.

She had had to live with the mistakes of her youth all her life. Not one day had passed without her peace of mind being disrupted by the thought of the consequences of her actions. For long periods the impact was small, superficial; life and work functioned as a bandage on her guilt. But other days she could hardly get out of bed, paralyzed with rage at her own inadequacy.

Those days had got fewer over the years. Nonetheless, she knew they took their toll, had always known that the guilt she carried would kill her. She wasn't just thinking about how overweight she was, how the comfort eating helped her through the bad patches, but about the gnawing away of her own psyche, her inability to fend off anxiety. She was often ill, had an unusually poor immune system.

And now he was back.

All those years she had had nightmares about him, turning around quickly in dark alleyways and imagining him behind her, and now he was really here.

Her reaction hadn't been as violent as she had imagined.

She didn't scream, didn't faint, just noticed her heartbeat quicken, and felt slightly dizzy. She sank onto a chair in the hall with the yellow dragon in her hand, his unpleasant, childish signal that they should go to their old meeting place.

She knew he would seek her out. He wanted something more than just a group meeting like they used to have. The yellow dragon was just a reminder, a way of bringing the Beasts back to life. He had already contacted the Black Panther; she knew that because the Panther had called her for the first time in thirty years to tell her, asking what she thought about the Dragon coming home.

She had merely hung up. Hadn't said a word, just hung up and pulled the cord out of the socket.

But you never escape, she thought, looking at the sculpture that she never managed to finish, the child and the goat and the profound communication between them, beyond words and visions, based on understanding and intuitive sensitivity. She could never quite manage to express that, and she wasn't going to get any further tonight.

Her back ached; she moved heavily over to the damp blanket that stopped the piece from drying out and cracking. She wrapped it up the usual way, and tied it in place. She took off her apron, hanging it up with the others and going off to check the kiln and wash her hands. Then she went around and looked at her students' creations, making sure they had covered their work correctly, that the finished pieces weren't drying too quickly, gathering up some stray tools. She filled the kiln ready for firing the following day, leaving some space for the Friday group at the top.

She stopped in the door, listening to the silence. As usual on Thursdays, she was the last one out. Both the watercolor group and the shipping exam class had usually shut up shop and turned off the lights by half past nine.

She changed her shoes, pulled on her outdoor clothes, shut the door behind her and locked it with a jangling key ring.

The corridor ahead of her was weakly lit and full of dark shadows.

She didn't like the dark. Before the events at the air base it had never bothered her, but since then the screams and flames pursued her in a way that made night prickly and threatening.

She started walking, past the pottery room, the woodwork shop, and the model railway. She reached the end of the corridor and carefully went down the creaking stairs, past the cafeteria and library. She checked the doors, shutting and locking them.

The front door stuck in the cold; it always did. She managed to force it shut with a groan, and locked it with a tangible feeling of relief. She took several deep breaths before embarking on the slippery journey down to the street. At every committee meeting she requested that the steps be gritted, the decision was always taken, and the caretaker always informed.

She clung on to the metal handrail, moving her considerable bulk down toward the street with her breath pluming from her mouth like a flaming torch. She was weak at the knees when she finally reached the pavement.

Snow was falling, thin and sharp, falling silently and gently in the still air. It had got considerably colder during the evening, the temperature continuing to plummet as the snowflakes stopped.

The new snow crunched under the rubber soles of her boots. She took her sled and pushed it ahead of her on squeaking runners down toward the main road.

I ought to walk more, she thought.

Snow had settled on the porch, but her legs were frozen and she decided to leave it for Thord. She scraped her boots on the coir brush, unlocked the door, and stepped into the hall.

She was so hungry she felt faint.

Pulling off her boots, she hung up her coat, went into the kitchen without turning on the light, and opened the fridge door.

She had prepared a starter of prawns and eggs before she left, and took it over to the table, wolfing it down so fast that she got mayonnaise on her nose. Afterward she sat there panting, feeling empty inside, and stared at the sink, realizing how tired she was.

She had to be up to open the nursery early next morning; she would have to be up at half past five to get there in time.

I should go to bed, she thought, without moving.

She sat there in the dark kitchen until the phone rang.

"Are you still up? You know you should be in bed."

She smiled at her husband's voice.

"I was just going," she lied.

"Did you have a good evening?"

She sighed gently.

"That youngster can never get enough attention; she needs constant reassurance."

"And the sculpture?"

"Nothing."

A short silence.

"You haven't heard anything?" Thord asked.

"Heard anything?"

"From them?"

She shook her head.

"No."

"I'll be home at two. Don't you lie there waiting, though."

She smiled again.

"I was just . . ."

They hung up and she climbed slowly up the stairs. The twiggy shadow of a snow-covered birch swept across the walls as a car drove past, headlights on full.

In spite of everything, she was lucky. The girls had grown into healthy, motivated individuals, good people with the right basic values that society needed. And Thord, her jackpot in life.

She ran a finger over the wedding photo that occupied pride of place on the landing.

She washed her face and brushed her teeth, peed and flushed, undressed and went onto the landing again. She folded her clothes and put them on a chair next to the linen cupboard.

She had just pulled on her nightgown when the man stepped out of the closet. He looked just as she remembered him, except a little heavier and grayer.

"Is that you!" she said in surprise. "What are you doing here?"

She wasn't frightened. Not even when he raised his gloved hands and put them around her neck.

Panic only hit when her airway was blocked and the adrenaline shock reached her brain. The room tilted, she saw the ceiling arching over her and his face coming closer, his hands rigid as steel around her neck.

No thoughts, no feelings.

Only the muscles of her bowels relaxing and the unexpected warmth in her underwear.

FRIDAY, NOVEMBER 20

Thomas walked into the apartment like a stranger. He had been far away for a long time, didn't know if he could find his way back. The attic apartment on Grev Turegatan in Östermalm was many light-years off, but now he was home. He felt it in his whole body; it was an immense relief to him.

Home, where he lived.

The apartment sounded like it usually did, with the gentle murmur of people sleeping and poor ventilation; the air was cool from the badly fitting windows and smelled of cooking, as usual. He hung up his coat, put his tennis racket and sports bag down on the hall floor, pulled off his shoes. He saw the reality of his deception in front of him, the unused sports kit, the dry towel.

He gulped and shrugged off the guilt from his consciousness. He padded in to the children in his socks, leaned over them, their wide-open mouths and pajamas and stuffed toys.

This was reality. The attic apartment in Östermalm was cold and calculated, the furniture studied and ingratiating. Sophia Grenborg's apartment was blue and stripped back; his home was warm and yellow with sleeping children and swinging streetlights.

Then he went toward the bedroom, walking slowly on feet that grew ever heavier. Stood in the doorway and looked at his wife.

She had fallen asleep lying across the bed with her tights and top and underwear on, her mouth open just like the children's. Her eyelashes cast long shadows across her cheeks; she was breathing deeply and evenly.

His eyes roamed across her hard body, edgy and muscular and powerful.

Sophia Grenborg was so white and soft, she whimpered all the while they made love.

Suddenly he was overcome with an unexpected feeling of complete and utter shame. It made him feel sick; he backed out of the room, leaving her there, lying across the bed without a cover.

She knows, he thought. Someone's told her.

He sat at the kitchen table, resting his elbows on his knees, and ran his fingers through his hair.

That's impossible, he thought. She wouldn't be sleeping so soundly if she knew.

He sighed deeply, unable to escape.

He knew he would have to lie next to her, unable to sleep, listening to her breathing and longing for apple hair and the traces of menthol cigarettes.

He stood up in the dark, confused, knocking his hip against the sink. Surely he wasn't longing to get away?

Or was he?

A sticky little hand patted Annika on the cheek.

"Mommy, bye bye, Mommy."

She blinked at the light, not sure for a moment where she was. She realized a second or so later that she had fallen asleep with half her clothes on, looked up and saw Ellen leaning over her with limp pigtails and peanut butter around her mouth.

A broad grin broke out inside her.

"Hello, darling."

"I'm going to stay at home today."

Annika stroked her daughter's cheek, cleared her throat and smiled.

"I don't think so, I'll pick you up after lunch," she said, struggling up by straining her stomach muscles and kissing the girl on the mouth, licking at the peanut butter.

"Before lunch."

"It's Friday, so there'll be ice cream today."

The girl pondered this.

"After," she said, and ran out.

Thomas looked in through the door, his usual, normal face with its tired morning eyes and hair sticking out.

"How are you feeling?"

She smiled at him and shut her eyes, and stretched like a cat.

"Okay, I think."

"We're off now."

When she opened her eyes he was gone.

Today she didn't wait for the silence; she was in the shower before the front door had closed behind them. She washed her hair, put on a face mask, trimmed her split ends and massaged her legs with cream. She put mascara on her eyelashes and filed her nails smooth, and picked out a clean bra. She made coffee and a sandwich that she knew she would have trouble eating.

Then she sat at the kitchen table and felt the anxiety rush toward her, rolling out of the corners like dark clouds of smoke and poison gas, and she fled; she left the coffee and sandwich and an unopened yogurt on the table and fumbled with the door.

Outside the snow had stopped, but the sky was still solid gray. Hard shards of ice were being blown about in the wind, along the streets and pavements, catching on her face and hair. She couldn't make out any colors, the world had turned black and white, the sharp stone twisting in her chest.

Sophia Grenborg. Grev Turegatan.

She knew where that was. Christina Furhage used to live there.

Without thinking, she started walking.

The façade was honey yellow and heavy with plaster embellishments, icicles hanging from the extremities. The bay windows hung in bunches on the walls, the glass shimmering unevenly and hand-blown, the door dark brown, carved.

Her feet and ears were freezing; she stamped the ground and adjusted her scarf better.

Wealthy middle class, she thought, going up to the door.

The intercom was the modern sort that didn't give away where in the building people lived. She leaned back and looked up at the façade, as though she'd be able to work out where Sophia's apartment was; the snow blew into her eyes, making them water.

She crossed the street and stood in the doorway opposite, pulled out her cell and dialed 118 118, then asked for Sophia Grenborg's number, Grev Turegatan, and was put through. If Sophia had a caller-display phone, then her number wouldn't show, only the number for directory inquiries.

The phone rang. Annika stared at the building; somewhere in there it was ringing and ringing, a telephone beside a bed where her husband had been last night.

After the fifth ring an answering machine clicked in. Annika held her breath, listening to the woman's happy, breezy voice.

"Hello, you've reached Sophia, I can't take your call right now, but . . ."

Annika hung up, the breezy voice ringing in her ears, the stone in her chest starting to glow and spit.

She went back to the door, pressed one name after another until an old lady finally answered.

"Electricity," Annika said. "We need to read the meter in the basement. Can you let us in?"

The lock buzzed and she pushed the door open on well-oiled hinges.

The stairwell was all gold-and-black marble, wooden panels of heavily polished oak reflecting the light from bronze lamps. A thick dark blue carpet swallowed all sound.

Annika ran a finger along the beautiful grain of the dado rail as she walked toward the list of occupants beside the elevator.

Sophia's name was listed in splendid isolation for the sixth floor.

Slowly she started to climb the stairs all the way up to the attic floor, soundlessly, slightly giddy.

Sophia's front door was more modern than the others in the building. A white security door in the middle of a brick wall that was several meters high.

Annika stood and stared at the brushed bronze nameplate, her feet wide apart, anchored to the marble. Her chest rose and sank, the stone tore and pulled. Then she took out her cell phone again and dialed directory inquiries again, this time asking for the number of the Federation of County Councils.

"Sophia Grenborg, please," she said.

The voice that answered sounded just as breezy as it had on the answering machine.

"My name's Sara, and I'm calling from the journal *County Council World*," Annika said, staring at the nameplate. "I'm calling a few people before Christmas like this to see if I could just ask one quick question."

Sophia laughed, a light, tinkling sound.

"Well," she said, "I suppose so . . ."

"What would you like for Christmas?" Annika said, running the palm of her hand over Sophia's front door.

The woman at the other end laughed again.

"A kiss from my beloved," she said, "although some bath salts would be good too."

Everything went black before Annika's eyes, a dark sheet drifting past through her brain.

"Beloved?" she said in a flat voice. "Would that be your husband?"

More laughter.

"He's a bit of a secret at the moment. *County Council World*, you said? That's a decent magazine; you cover the things that matter in our field really well. Which issue will this be in?"

Annika closed her eyes and ran a hand over her forehead; the stairwell was starting to tilt, a sucking wave shifting from wall to wall.

"Sorry, what?"

"The questionnaire! Will it be out before Christmas?"

She was forced to crouch down, leaning her back against the door.

"We don't quite know how much space we've got, it depends a bit on ads."

Did *County Council World* have ads? She had no idea.

The line fell silent. Annika could hear Sophia breathing, listening to the other woman's rhythmic intake of air.

"Well," Sophia said, "if there wasn't anything else . . ."

"My surname's Grenborg too," Annika said. "Do you think we could be related?"

The laughter was less hearty this time.

"Hmm, what did you say your name was?"

"Sara," Annika said. "Sara Grenborg."

"Which branch of the family?"

Was she imagining things, or had Sophia's "i"s got a bit longer, a bit posher?

"Södermanland," Annika said.

"We're from Österbotten, from the Väse manor house. Are you descended from Carl Johan?"

"No," Annika said. "From Sofia Katarina."

All of a sudden she could no longer be bothered to listen to Sophia La-di-da damned Grenborg. She hung up in the middle of a word.

She sat in silence and waited for her pulse to stop racing, resting a hand against Sophia Grenborg's front door, gradually absorbing the woman into her bloodstream.

Closed her eyes and concentrated on the cold staircase, listened to her voice, saw her sitting doing her lovely work in her lovely Federation, just loving the articles in *County Council World*. A woman so bloodless and well-behaved and appreciated that her own husband had chosen to kiss her outside NK, a woman who was everything she would never be.

She left the building without looking back.

* * *

The man woke up with the pink duvet cover tickling his nose. He snorted, then groaned as the pain from his stomach reached his brain. The wooden panels in the ceiling swayed slowly to and fro; he looked away and stared into the boarded walls, shocked at how bad his breath smelled. The smell was taking him over.

La mort est dans cette ville, he thought, panting for breath.

He could see the doctor's face floating above him, as it had the day he woke up from the anesthetic, his friend's clenched jaw and evasive gaze; he had already been informed about the consequences and alternatives and understood immediately.

Inoperable, untreatable. Three to six months from the diagnosis. The remaining time would entail a lot of pain, sickness, digestive trouble, weight loss, severe nausea, extreme tiredness, low blood pressure. Treatment consisted of antisickness medicine, painkillers, and nutritional supplements.

He knew he would fade, almost rot, away. The smell would become more intrusive; his friend the doctor had advised him not to try to hide it with scent or aftershave. It wouldn't help.

He looked around the room, over the kitchen area in the corner and the panels on the walls and the colorful rag rugs on the plastic floor, trying to find something that wasn't moving. He stopped at the window; through the gap between the heavy curtains he could see blue daylight, cold, crisp. Gradually the world stopped swaying and he was able to breathe a bit better, and soon slid into his dreamlike borderland where the limitations of reality were gradually wiped away.

"I'm from Bojen Sailing Club, and I'd like to book a seminar room from 7:00 PM on Tuesday," he heard himself say with a peculiar echo in the background; in front of him the librarian on Namnlösa Gatan, big ledgers open on the desk, and he knew she no longer believed him, because he couldn't possibly be both sailor and fly fisherman and butterfly collector and genealogist.

Everyone who came to the meeting had a code name, regular names like Greger or Torsten or Mats. When he chose Ragnwald he was met with frowns; you shouldn't give yourself airs, but he was better than them and they knew that, if not then, then in Melderstein.

He laughed quietly and chuckled in his in-between world and returned to the old works that fever-hot night in early summer 1969, when the world was on the brink of the great revolution and they were ready; they had practiced in advance for armed struggle and had guards patrolling the camp day and night. The company carved cudgels by the campfire; they discussed guerrilla warfare and practiced self-defense.

In Norway the antagonism between left-wing activists and the others had been much greater than in Sweden. A radical bookshop had been bombed, they were convinced that it would soon be their turn, and they weren't about to let themselves be led like lambs to the slaughter.

The fact that they were doing their training in Melderstein was particularly amusing, because the regime at the old works was religious. But because he had booked it as a parish assistant in Luleå no one had questioned his motivation, and now they had held thundering Maoist meetings in the little works church.

He was filled with the complete sense of harmony he had experienced in those few days, reliving once again how his capacity to remember all the quotations had given him a central position in the leadership even though the delegates had come from all over the country. They practiced battle skills and survival all through the night, and it was there that he met Red Wolf.

He smiled at the ceiling, drifting off on the waves, seeing before him her soft face and thin little body.

She was so young and so wide-eyed and she saw him as a Master. No one else had his experience of the Rebel movement and the Student Union occupation; he was secure on his throne, and even though little Red Wolf had come only to keep her friend company at the summer camp without realizing what it was about, she was swept up in it; she became a Servant of the Revolution quicker than he had dared hope, and she did it for his sake.

For his sake.

Karina who kissed him behind Melderstein Church; he could still recall the taste of her chewing gum.

He turned over in the bed.

In Bojen Sailing Club they had formed cells where they decided where people would live and work. An apartment in Örnnäset and the night shift at the ironworks. A small cottage in Svartöstaden and work with the local council. They had organized strikes, worked through tenants' associations, unions, according to Mao's political theory about the people's front, the people's movements, but it was all going too slowly: they spent too long discussing things. The Fly Fishing Club was full of false authorities who loved the sound of their own voice. The movement's popularity brought with it a load of pretend revolutionaries who only came for the girls and the beer. After Melderstein the mood became rancorous. Two comrades challenged him for the leadership, with the support of others, so he took his family and left. He left bourgeois small-town communism to die its slow, natural death, and formed his own group to plan how to get hold of real power.

The knife in his stomach twisted again. Ventricular cancer, stomach cancer, apparently rare in Europe these days, strikes without warning. Operation to see if it's treatable or not. Symptoms similar to those of a gastric ulcer, and a gastroscopy discovers an ugly running sore and a suspected tumor, later identified under a microscope. And the patient is opened up, the surrounding organs are found to be full of cancer, and they close up the stomach again. Metastases on the lungs, bones, and brain, gradual death from general organ failure from too great a burden of tumors.

Three to six months.

Suddenly his father was standing beside his bed and he was panting hard, bouncing off the walls. I accuse you. I hold you responsible for the fall of Adam and Eve.

And the whip was raised and hit him in the diaphragm, a violent convulsion that made him throw up the nutritional powder onto his pillow. His father's voice grew louder, filling the room like a symphony of dissonance.

"You must start your life again, devilish child, evil art thou, mean and filled with Satan."

He tried to protest, beg for mercy; the same song he had sung throughout his childhood, Father, please Father, have mercy, but the whip fell, striking him on the mouth. The pain made him stop breathing for a moment.

"The Devil shall be driven from thy heart and thy eternal soul shall be saved for the Kingdom of Heaven."

The whip was raised yet again and he looked up at the man who floated beneath the ceiling in his threadbare preacher's outfit, and he knew that his salvation would soon be over.

"Father," he whispered, feeling the vomit and blood running through his nose. "Mother never had any more children. Do you know why?"

The noise in the room died away as his father fell silent, the fevered look in his eyes vanished and the whip stopped.

"I remained alone," he whispered to his father, "and you never knew why. God knows that you did your duty to populate the earth, but there were never any more children. And you never realized why?"

His father floated hesitantly under the roof with bloodless lips.

"She aborted them with the Sami woman in Vittangi," he panted, "my brothers and sisters, she got the Sami woman to take them out of her belly rather than let you get your hands on them and beat the sin out of them."

And the whip came to life again and hit him in the head and the world was empty.

Annika threw her clothes in their usual heap on the floor in the hall, swept away her uneaten breakfast, and put her laptop on the kitchen table. She logged into www.lf.se and looked at the organization of the Federation of County Councils, and on the back of the morning paper she jotted down the departmental titles Democracy & Health Policy, Economics & Devolution, and the Department of International Finance.

She was thinking hard, her hand over her mouth.

That ought to be enough. Three different sections that probably didn't have the best internal communication. Three stressed middle managers on the same level.

She took a few deep breaths and called the number of the Federation's reception. Started by asking for the head of Democracy & Health Policy.

"Hello," Annika said, clearing her throat, "my name's Annika Bengtzon and I'm calling from the *Evening Post* . . ."

The overworked manager interrupted her abruptly.

"I'll have to refer you to our press office; we have public relations people there who can answer any questions you may have."

She could hear her thudding heartbeat and hoped it couldn't be heard at the other end.

"I know," she said, "I understand that, but my call isn't really about the sort of thing I can talk to the press office about. Sorry."

Silence.

"What?" the man said. "What do you mean?"

Annika closed her eyes and said in a steady voice:

"I should begin by saying that I'm not going to quote you; I'm not actually writing an article yet. I just want to sort out and clarify some details that emerged when we looked into various aspects of your operations."

Stress had given way to surprise and suspicion when the man responded.

"What do you mean? What aspects?"

"It's about overcharging on one of your projects."

It sounded like the man was sitting down.

"Overcharg . . . ? I don't understand . . ."

Annika stared at the ventilation unit.

"As I said, I won't quote you at all at this stage. I just want to check a few things out, and I'd appreciate it if this conversation stayed between us. I shall never mention that I spoke to you, and you don't have to say that you spoke to me."

Silence.

"What's this about?"

She could physically feel the tug on the line as he took the bait.

"Overcharging from the account connected to the project looking into threats against politicians," Annika said. "The one you're conducting together with the Association of Local Councils and the Department of Justice."

"Threats against politicians?"

"The working group trying to prevent violence and threats against politicians, yes. I have to point out that we think the project is incredibly important, and as far as we can tell the work has been very productive, but the problem is in your accounts."

"I don't actually know what you're talking about."

Annika waited, let the silence do the talking: her surprise carried off down the line, muddying the manager's senses.

"I see," she said slowly, "I was under the impression that you wanted to get to the bottom of this . . ."

Now the man started to get angry.

"What do you mean? The bottom of what? Who says there's anything irregular going on here?"

Annika sharpened her voice when she answered.

"I hope you're not trying to find out my sources. As I'm sure you're aware, that's a criminal offense. I shall ignore that last question."

Silence fell again, growing, pulsating.

"Can't you tell me?" the Federation manager eventually said. "What's all this about?"

Annika took a deep, audible breath, then spoke with a low, confidential tone of voice.

"According to my source there has been overcharging from the account containing the funds for the working group investigating threats to democratic representatives. One member of the group is said to have inflated the joint costs in order to conceal private expenditure."

"Sophia Grenborg?" the man said, astonished. "Is she supposed to have committed fraud?"

"I can't answer that," Annika said apologetically, "I was just wondering if you could keep me informed of the result of your investigation. Not that you should make public any costs that don't concern me, but please, just tell me if, or when, you decide to involve the police."

The manager cleared his throat.

"Well, anything like that is a long way away at this point," he said. "Naturally, we shall have to begin by conducting a thorough internal investigation. We'll be contacting our auditors at once."

Annika closed her eyes and swallowed.

She wished the manager the best of luck and hung up.

Then sat in silence wondering how long she ought to wait before the next call.

Not at all, she decided.

So she called the head of Economics & Devolution and started with hesitant questions about the Federation's policy regarding the involvement of employees in nonoperating sham companies. When the man got angry and was on the point of hanging up she asked if they had investigated why Sophia Grenborg, one of their employees, had only been assessed for an income of 269,900 kronor for the previous calendar year.

The man had been thoroughly taken aback.

She concluded with the question:

"The Federation of County Councils is funded by the taxpayers. Do you think it's acceptable for the Federation's employees to attempt to get out of paying tax?"

Naturally, he could only reply one way:

"Of course not."

She promised to get back to him to find out how the internal investigation was getting on.

After that she got up, finding that the muscles in her legs were completely stiff, and she had a cramp in the back of her thigh. The lump in her chest twisted and tore at her, its metallic sharpness had spread through her body and was threatening to paralyze her.

She slapped her legs with her fists until they obeyed her again, then heated up a mug of coffee in the microwave and made the third call, to the head of International Finance. She asked what the Federation thought of right-wing extremism among its employees. She had received information that one of their employees had previously been active in an extremist group, and that the employee's cousin had been convicted of incitement to racial hatred, and she was wondering how appropriate it was that this person was now involved in the project looking into threats, among them threats from the extreme right, against our political representatives?

The head of International Finance was unfortunately unable to comment on that at the moment, but he promised that the matter would be investigated and if she called him on Monday or Tuesday she could probably get some sort of comment.

Afterward she slumped on the kitchen chair, feeling the floor sway, her head and limbs numb.

She had jumped.

Now she just had to land on her feet.

SUNDAY, NOVEMBER 22

Thomas reached for the coffeepot and found it was empty. He felt himself getting annoyed, his jaw clenching, he sighed inaudibly and glanced at his wife on the other side of the kitchen table. She was onto her fourth mug, had drunk the whole pot, which he had made, herself, before he had managed to get a single cup. She didn't notice his frustration, was deeply immersed in an essay by a professor of Islamic studies on the question of exactly who could be regarded as an Iraqi. She had pulled her hair into a messy knot on top of her head, idly brushing aside a stray lock that had fallen in front of her eyes. Her dressing gown was loosely tied; he could see her smooth skin beneath the toweling.

He looked away and stood up.

"Do you want more coffee?" he said sarcastically.

"No, not for me, thanks."

She didn't look up, paid him no attention.

I may as well be part of the furniture, he thought. A means of her living comfortably and writing whatever damn articles she feels like.

He composed himself and filled the little pan with more water. At home in Vaxholm they had always had an electric kettle, both at his parents' and during his marriage to Eleonor, but Annika thought that was unnecessary.

"Just another machine. We've got so little space as it is. Besides, it's quicker to boil water on the gas stove than in a kettle."

She was right about that, but that wasn't the point.

The point was that his space was shrinking. She took up so much damn space. The more she took, the less there was left over for him.

Before the business with the Bomber he hadn't seen it so clearly. Back then, everything happened slowly: his space was stolen a piece at a time without him noticing, the children arrived and she got the editing job and of course he did his bit, but then everything got back to normal again while she was at home and could look after the apartment and the kids, and now he was suddenly expected to retreat to his little corner and hand over his life to her.

He looked at his wife as the pan of water began to bubble. Sharp and edgy, slight, with soft breasts. Vulnerable and fragile and hard as nails.

She must have felt him looking at her, because she looked up at him, confused.

"What?" she said.

He turned away.

"Nothing."

"Right," she said, picking up the paper and leaving the kitchen.

"Hang on," he called after her. "Mom rang and asked us to Sunday lunch; I said yes. Hope that's okay?"

Why am I asking? he thought. Why am I apologizing for accepting an invitation to visit my own parents?

"What did you say?"

She walked sternly back into the kitchen; he turned and looked at her, standing there with the newspaper dragging on the floor.

"Twelve o'clock," he said. "Lunch in Vaxholm."

She shook her head, steaming with disbelief.

"How can you say yes to something like that without even asking me?"

He turned back to the stove again, pouring water into the French press.

"You were on your cell phone again; I didn't want to disturb you."

"This is disturbing me more, if I can put it like that. Well, I'm not going."

He was seized by an overwhelming and unreasonable impulse

to shake her until the knot of hair on the top of her head came loose and her teeth shook and the dressing gown slid from her shoulders.

Instead he closed his eyes and tried to control his breathing, addressing his reply to the ventilation unit.

"I'm not going to end up with the same crap relationship with my parents that you've got with yours."

He heard from the rustling of the newspaper that she'd left the kitchen.

"Okay," she said expressionlessly from the hall. "Take the children, but I'm not going."

"Of course you're coming," he said, still to the ventilation unit.

She came back into the kitchen—he looked at her over his shoulder. Was naked apart from her socks.

"And if I don't?" she said. "Are you going to hit me over the head and drag me there by my hair?"

"Sounds good," he said.

"I'm going to have a shower," she said.

His eyes were drawn to her buttocks as she walked back down the hall. Sophia was much more curvy, and her skin was pink. Annika's had a green tint; in the sun she quickly went a deep olive color.

She's an alien, Thomas thought. A little green woman from another planet, scratchy and shapeless and unreasonable.

Was it possible to live with an alien?

He shook off the thought with a gulp.

Why was he making everything so damned hard for himself?

There was a way out: he had a choice. He could get back the life he missed, living with a soft and pink woman with humanity and apple hair who would welcome him into her attic apartment.

Good grief, he thought, what am I going to do?

The next second the phone rang.

No, he thought. It's her. What's she ringing here for? I said she could never call here.

A second ring.

"Are you going to get that?" Annika called from the shower.

A third.

He grabbed the phone with throbbing temples, trying to find some saliva in his mouth.

"Thomas and Annika," he heard himself say with a dry mouth.

"I have to talk to Annika."

It was Anne Snapphane. She sounded like she was suffocating, and he felt such a huge sense of relief that he could feel it in his balls.

"Of course," he said, breathing out. "I'll get her."

Annika climbed out of the bathtub, grabbed a towel, and left a trail of wet footprints behind her as she walked to the phone. The sharp stone twisted and turned in her chest, the angels humming anxiously in the background. She avoided looking at Thomas as she passed him and picked up the phone; his coolness made her keep her distance from his back.

"Have you read the paper this morning?" Anne said, her voice hoarse and tight.

"Have you got a hangover?" Annika said, pushing the cheese away to make space on the kitchen table. Thomas sighed loudly and moved two millimeters to make space for her.

"Like a bitch, but that doesn't matter. Björnlund has shut down the channel."

Annika pushed the bread away to make more room.

"What are you talking about?" she said.

"The minister of culture has just made me redundant. Says so in the paper."

Thomas demonstratively turned ninety degrees away from her, his shoulders screaming out that he was actively distancing himself.

"What? I've just read it."

"Top of the first page."

Annika leaned forward and took hold of the first part of the paper as Thomas was reading it to peer at the front page; he snatched it away in irritation.

"Hang on," Annika said, "can I just take a quick look? '*Björnlund changes terms for digital broadcast rights.*' And?"

"The board were told last night, they got the last plane from New York and landed half an hour ago. They've already announced that the launch is being postponed. There's an official board meeting at two thirty, and all our planning's going to be stopped and TV Scandinavia wound down. I'm going to end up as the arts reporter for Radio Sjuhärad."

"But," Annika said, hitting Thomas on the knee to get more room, "we shouldn't think the worst. Why can't you become a satellite channel, or a cable channel?"

Anne started crying and the seriousness of the situation hit Annika, as well as guilt.

"Hang on, I'm going to change phones," she said.

She put the receiver down and accidentally knocked Thomas as she jumped from the table.

"Damn it," he said, crumpling the paper in his lap.

"Just carry on, I'm moving," Annika said and skipped down the hall and into the bedroom with her towel around her, then dropped it on the floor.

She crept under the covers and picked up the phone by the bed.

"There's got to be a solution somewhere" was the first thing she said. "What's the problem?"

Anne pulled herself together.

"I told you before," she said grouchily, and Annika interrupted her.

"I know I haven't been a good listener. To me it's always seemed a bit technical, like if I started telling you about print timings and plate changes. Tell me."

She sat up among the pillows and Anne took a deep breath.

"The whole point of TV Scandinavia is, or was, to reach the whole of Scandinavia. That's twenty-five million potential viewers, roughly a tenth of the population of the U.S.A. And to reach that many people you need to be available in every household in Sweden, and that means broadcasting from Teracom's transmitters. Advertisers in the American market aren't interested in target groups smaller than that."

"Teracom?"

"The national broadcast network; it used to be part of the old nationalized Televerket but got turned into a profit-making public company instead, along with everything else."

The angels were silent, completely beaten by Anne Snapphane's despair. Annika realized that the stone wasn't doing anything, just lying heavy and cold beneath her ribs.

"And there are no other masts; you're not allowed to put up your own?"

"Are you joking? Teracom is heading for bankruptcy even though all the masts already exist."

Annika relaxed and tried to think of a solution, happily grasping the opportunity Anne had provided, and leaving Thomas and Sophia and the children and Vaxholm behind.

"But there's hardly anyone who can watch digital television," she said, "you have to have one of those boxes, don't you? Is it really such a big deal?"

"In a couple of years digital television is all we'll have. In the U.S.A. the analogue network is due to be switched off in 2007, and we're only a year or so behind them. The government proposition is the big deal. When the terrestrial digital network works with the same criteria as the rest of the business—in other words the world of satellite and cable—then the market will explode."

Ellen's excited yell penetrated the bedroom door a couple of seconds before the girl herself ran in, Kalle only a meter or so behind, growling in a deep voice and making claws with his fingers.

"Mommy, help! The Tiger's after me!"

"No," Annika said, and tried to calm them down with her hand, which was pointless; the children tumbled over her on the bed, laughing hysterically. "But I don't get it," she said into the phone. "How can the government proposal shut down the channel?"

"Up to now the government has decided who would have access to the state's television masts, both analogue and digital broadcasting. There are only three analogue channels, of course, and those are clearly the result of a purely political decision: channels one, two, and four."

"Ellen," Annika said, "Kalle, go and get dressed. You're going to go and see Grandma and Grandad."

"Digital transmissions take up much less frequency space," Anne said, "so when the three analogue channels stop broadcasting there'll be enough space for twenty-five new digital channels. In this proposal the government is finally acknowledging that they shouldn't be controlling who broadcasts what, so they're delegating such decisions to the Radio and Television Authority."

"Do we have to, that's no fun," Kalle said, acting as spokesman for them both. "We aren't allowed to run indoors there."

"Come on," Annika said. "Brush your teeth and make sure you put on clean underwear."

"None of this is really new," Anne said. "The proposal spent over a year in committee and out for consultation. That's why the Americans decided to make this investment, but today's paper says there's a new clause in the directive to the Radio and Television Authority that wasn't there before."

Annika sent the children out, screwed her eyes shut and tried to concentrate.

"And?"

"During the consultation there was a framework of ten points that television companies had to meet, according to paragraphs one, two, and four of the third chapter of the 1996 Radio and Television Act. Now there are suddenly eleven points."

Annika sank back into the pillows.

"So Karina Björnlund has squeezed in an extra condition at the very last minute."

"Exactly, with only days to go. Point number eleven says: 'Applicants with primarily foreign ownership broadcasting to more than one country in Scandinavia but not to other EU states do not have the right to broadcast via the terrestrial digital network.'"

"And that means . . . ?"

She could hear Thomas shouting something to the children out in the kitchen.

"That everyone who meets those conditions can broadcast, but not us."

"A law specifically aimed at TV Scandinavia," Annika said. "She'll never get that through parliament."

"Yes, she will, the Greens are in favor."

"But for heaven's sake, why?"

"The government's been retreating on road tolls. But from next year there'll be pollution limits on all the roads around Stockholm, just so that Karina Björnlund can put a stop to TV Scandinavia."

Annika could hear the skepticism in her own voice as she said:

"But that's completely unreasonable. Why the hell would she do that?"

"That," Anne said, "is a damned good question."

Then she quietly started to cry. Thomas yelled something out in the hall and Ellen started to howl.

And as the children screamed and the echo of despair came down the line from Lidingö, the angels suddenly started up again, the words tumbling into each other, and she saw the entry in the minister's correspondence register in front of her like a mirage.

Request for meeting to discuss a matter of urgency.

"Have you drunk anything today?" Annika asked, loudly enough to drown out her internal voices.

Anne collected herself for a moment before answering.

"No," she sniffed. "But I've thought about it. I poured some gin, but flushed it down the toilet. Enough now, you know?"

Her despair seemed to have run its course, ebbing into single sniffs, and the children stopped screaming out in the kitchen.

"First Mehmet and then this. I can't go on."

"Yes, you can," Annika said. "Get some clothes on and come over here, leave the car."

"I don't know if I can."

"Yes, you can. Thomas and the kids are going to Vaxholm, and I've got nothing to do all day. Promise you'll come."

"I can't stay out here, I can't bear it . . ."

A new attack of sobbing bubbled up.

"That miserable old bastard downstairs always snooping, and Miranda going to and fro between us, and all the snow to clear every winter . . ."

"Come here and we'll look on the net for a new house. It's about time you moved into town like everyone with any sense."

Anne fell silent, breathing down the line, first quickly, then slower.

"I need to think things over first."

"You know where I am."

Kalle came up to Annika at the front door, wearing his new green boots with the reflective patches. His cheeks were glowing from the heat inside his overalls, his eyes large and shiny.

"Why is Daddy cross with us?"

Annika kneeled down next to him and stroked him on the cheek.

"Daddy's tired," she said. "He's been working hard. It'll be better soon."

She smiled into his eyes, conveying calm and security that she didn't feel.

"I want to stay at home with you," Ellen said.

Annika turned to her daughter, who was sweating from having to wait.

"Anne's coming to see me, she's a bit sad and I'm going to help her with something."

"Grown-ups can be sad too," Kalle said.

Annika had to look away to hold herself together; the stone in her chest was about to burst—my gorgeous children, my darling darlings.

"See you soon," she said, getting up and adjusting the belt of her dressing gown.

Thomas came flying out into the hall with his hair in a mess and a little black cloud hanging over his head.

"What are you looking for?" Annika said, keeping her voice steady.

"My cell phone. Have you seen it?"

"Do you have to take it with you?"

He looked at her as if she was an idiot.

"Have you tried calling it?" Annika said.

His expression changed from derision to surprise. She swallowed and floated over to the phone and dialed his cell phone number. His coat pocket rang.

"Drive carefully," she said as he nudged the children through the door ahead of him.

A dark, wounded look back over his shoulder.

The door closed and she stood there with ice-cold feet in the draft that crept in from the stairwell. She had no floor below her; she was in free fall; the sky rushed around her, the angelic choir thundering. She knew the seeds she had sown were sprouting and growing in the heads of the Federation's middle managers.

Sophia Grenborg, she thought, Sophia Grenborg, you miserable bitch, and the angels started shrieking, with an intensity she had never suffered before; they screamed their indignation on an entirely indecent scale.

Sophia fia lia mia beyond beyond salvation!!!

She clapped her hands over her ears, clenched her jaw and fled, away from the door, away from the draft, back into bed, and pulled the covers over her head.

Salvation's summer meadows fia lia fine Sophia.

Took deep breaths and concentrated on not hyperventilating and cramping.

Ragnwald, she thought. The ruler with divine power. The plane at F21. An explosion. A young man burning. Love for a young athlete, active in the working dogs club. Theology studies in Uppsala, awakening courtesy of Chairman Mao. Death as a profession.

Benny Ekland, questionable star reporter. Linus Gustafsson, watchful boy with hair gel. Kurt Sandström, farmer politician with a firm grip on life.

She threw off the duvet, reached for the phone, and dialed Q's direct line.

If he answers, it's a sign, she thought, and forced the thought away at once, because what would happen if he didn't answer—what demons would she have let loose then?

But he did answer, and he sounded tired. She sat up in bed and the angels withdrew immediately.

"Has something happened?" she asked nervously.

"Are you thinking of anything in particular?"

She shut her eyes, relieved to hear his voice.

"I don't mean whether or not you've been fucked."

"Okay," Q said. "And what would you know about things like that?"

She tried to smile toward the phone.

"Our friend Ragnwald. Have you found him?"

He pretended to yawn.

"Seriously," she said, yanking the phone cord. "You must have made some sort of progress. Kurt Sandström, what's happened with him?"

"He died. Definitely died."

She leaned back hard against the pillows, feeling the stone settle down, and almost relaxed.

"Göran Nilsson from Sattajärvi," she said. "How can someone vanish for thirty years without you or Interpol or the CIA or Mossad or anyone else getting hold of him? How is that possible?"

Q was silent for several long seconds.

"We haven't exactly been dragging our feet, whatever you might think."

"No?"

She looked up at the ceiling.

"You knew he lived in France, how hard can it be? Surely it's just a question of getting out the vacuum cleaner and pressing the on button?"

"The French police have big vacuum cleaners that suck up almost every sort of particle. This one kept getting through the filter, for all those years."

Reality clarified and her free fall stopped; she was floating weightless and secure, calm.

"How could he do that? If he's as dangerous as you think, if he really was an international killer who took on assassinations for loads of money, how could he possibly get away with it? Why didn't anyone catch him?"

"We don't know how much money was involved, or if there was any money at all. Maybe he killed out of pure, unadulterated conviction."

"But how do you know it's him?"

"There are a number of cases where we're convinced, and several more where we're pretty sure, and a whole heap of bodies where we've got nothing but our suspicions."

She was safe now, stable in her heaven.

"But why Ragnwald? Did he leave fingerprints? Little napkins with lipstick kisses at the crime scenes?"

"Undercover agents," Q said. "The security apparatus."

"Ah," Annika said. "You mean rumors and speculation."

"Now you're just being silly."

They were silent for a few moments; her chest felt warm, as did the stone.

"But there's something I don't understand," Annika said when the silence had grown so large that she suddenly feared that she was alone on the line. "Someone must have had some way of communicating with him, because otherwise how would he contact his employers?"

"How do you mean?"

"Someone must have hired him for all those messy jobs. How did they get hold of him?"

The commissioner was quiet for a moment.

"Off the record," he said, and she swiveled her head. "Through ETA. For years the Spanish police have suspected a doctor in Bilbao of being his go-between, but they've never had enough evidence to charge him. This is sensitive stuff in the Basque Country. If their colleagues start openly harassing and accusing decent members of the civilian population, the whole region could ignite. The doctor in question is an unimpeachable family man, a professional with his own practice specializing in internal medicine."

"Couldn't you have hired Ragnwald for something yourselves?" Annika asked. "Lured him into a trap?"

A moment of hesitation.

"Attempts may have been made, but I know nothing about that."

So that's where the boundary of his openness was. She decided not to press him, and rubbed her feet together, feeling the circulation coming back again.

"But if he wasn't in France, where was he?"

"He most likely spent a lot of time in France," Q said, back on solid ground again, "but he didn't live there. We don't think he settled anywhere."

"So he's spent thirty years camping?"

A short, weary sigh.

"We believe he pretended to be from north Africa," Q said, "as part of the group of illegal immigrants who drift around the countryside looking for seasonal work."

"A farm laborer?" Annika said.

"They move from place to place, from country to country, wherever the crops are ready to harvest. Living in barracks or camps for short periods, tens of thousands of people who split into smaller groups when the work is done, moving on somewhere else, always on the way somewhere, never getting there."

Annika nodded unconsciously, seeing them before her like in that Lasse Hallström film, whatever it was called?

"And no one says anything about anyone else," she said.

"Total loyalty," Q said. "No one cares if someone disappears for a few weeks, or a few months, or forever."

"And aren't surprised if you turn up again," Annika filled in.

"No questions," Q said.

"Cash in hand at the end of the day."

"No bank accounts," Q said.

"No rent to pay, no family to provide for."

"A lot of the seasonal laborers have families," Q said. "Some of them provide for their extended family as well, but not our Ragnwald."

"He picks grapes and oranges and shoots politicians in his spare time."

"When he's not working in the docks or mines or somewhere else where he can be invisible and, in practical terms, unpaid."

They were silent for a while.

"But why haven't you got him if he's back in Sweden now?"

Q gave a deep sigh.

"It's not as easy as you seem to think," he said. "Killers who kill with no apparent motive are the hardest to catch. Take the Laser Man: he shot ten randomly chosen people in Stockholm over the course of a year and a half before he was caught, and he lived in the middle of the city, had his own car, said hello to his neighbors on the stairs; in other words he was a rank amateur. The man we're dealing with now has killed four people that we know of. There's nothing to connect them, apart from the boy witnessing the first murder. The methods are completely different—Ekland was run over, the boy's throat was cut, Sandström was shot. No fingerprints, the fibers we found don't match from one crime scene to the next."

"That could just mean he changed his clothes and wore gloves."

"Exactly," Q said.

"No witnesses?"

"The best witness, the boy, is dead. Nobody else has contributed anything significant at all."

Annika listened back to these latest comments in her mind.

"Four," she said. "You said four."

Q was blank.

"What?"

"There's been another murder," she said, sitting up in bed without thinking. "He's done it again. What? Who?"

"You must have misheard me. I said three."

"Rubbish," Annika said. "Someone's been killed in the last couple of days and another Mao quote has been sent to the relatives. Either you tell me exactly what's happened or I start ringing around."

He laughed.

"An empty threat. If someone's been killed the media would already be circling like vultures over the story."

She responded to his laughter with a snort.

"That's crap," she said. "Not if it's a woman who's been killed. Her husband has probably already been arrested, and it would surprise me if even the local paper gave it their standard couple of lines."

"Standard?"

"*Family quarrel ends in tragedy.* Not nice, not interesting, and impossible to write about. Tell me what you know and we can come to an arrangement."

The silence was thick with thought for several seconds.

"I've said it before," he said eventually. "You're slightly creepy. How the hell could you know that?"

Annika leaned back on the pillows again, a fleeting smile crossing her face.

"And she's got no connection to the other three?"

"Nothing we've found yet. Margit Axelsson, a nursery teacher in Piteå, married, two adult daughters, strangled on the landing of her home. Her husband was working shifts and found her when he got home."

"And was immediately suspected of the murder?"

"Wrong. The time of death was before midnight, and he was in the liaison office at F21 with his colleagues until one thirty when he finished his shift."

Annika felt the adrenaline reach her brain and automatically stretch her legs out, forcing her to sit up straight.

"F21? He works at F21? Then there is a connection, then. The explosion of the Draken."

"We've already checked. He did his national service at I19 in Boden; wasn't attached to the air base until 1974. The fact that a murder victim's husband's employer happens to coincide with a crime scene which may have a connection to Ragnwald isn't enough to get my pulse racing, unlike you, apparently."

"The quote," she said. "What does it say?"

"Hang on a moment . . ."

He put the phone down, opened a drawer, looked through some papers, cleared his throat, and came back on the line.

"*People of the world, unite and defeat the American aggressors and all their lackeys. People of the world, be courageous, and dare to fight, defy difficulties and advance wave upon wave. Then the whole world will belong to the people. Monsters of all kinds shall be destroyed.*"

They thought in silence for a while; the swaying stopped.

"Monsters of all kinds shall be destroyed," Annika said. "Monsters. Of all kinds. Including nursery school teachers."

"She taught for the Workers' Educational Association as well. Ran courses in napkin folding and ceramics. We're not paying too much attention to the quotation, I don't think you should either. The woman putting the profile together thinks he uses them as messages, like your lipstick kisses."

"Have you got someone in from the FBI?" Annika asked, swinging her legs off the side of the bed, warm feet against cold wood floor.

"That was in the seventies," Q said. "We've been doing our own profiles of suspects for ten years."

"Sorry," Annika said. "What's she come up with?"

"You can pretty much guess. Male, older rather than younger, driven by hatred of a society that he has a partially warped view of, compensating for humiliations he's suffered. Single, few friends, poor self-image, strong need for validation, restless, has difficulties holding down a job, fairly intelligent with good physical strength. More or less."

Annika shut her eyes and tried to memorize the details, aware that he wasn't telling her everything.

"So why the quotes?" she said. "Why that sort of scent marking?"

"On some level he wants us to know. He's so incredibly superior to us that he can afford to leave these reminders of himself."

"Our Ragnwald," she said. "It feels almost like I know him. Imagine how it could have been: if that plane hadn't blown up he might have been on his way to the Nobel dinner in the city hall in three week's time."

She realized from the surprised silence that Q hadn't followed her train of thought.

"Karina Björnlund," she said. "Minister of culture. She's going to the Nobel dinner this year, or has at least been invited, and if Ragnwald hadn't had to disappear, they would have been married."

"What are you talking about?" Q said.

"Of course, there's no way of knowing if the marriage would have lasted, but if it had . . ."

"Listen," Q said. "Where the hell did you get that from?"

Annika twisted the phone cord.

"The banns were published," she said. "They were due to have a civil wedding in Luleå City Hall at 2:00 PM on the Friday after the attack."

"Not a chance," Q said. "If that was true we'd know about it."

"Marriages had to be announced in those days; they had a note in the paper."

"And where was this note published?"

"The *Norrland News.* I've got a bundle of cuttings from there about Karina Björnlund. Do you really mean to tell me you didn't know they were together?"

"A teenage fling," Q said. "Nothing more. Besides, she ended it."

"Retrospective adjustment," Annika said. "Karina Björnlund would do anything to save her own skin."

"I see," Q said. "Little Miss Amateur Profiler has spoken."

Annika was thinking about Herman Wennergren's email, "*Request for meeting to discuss a matter of urgency,*" and then the minister of culture's last-minute amendment of the government proposal, so that the law on the deregulation of digital broadcasters would exclude TV Scandinavia—just like Herman Wennergren wanted—and the only remaining question was what arguments her paper's proprietors had applied to make her change her opinion.

In her mind Annika could hear her own voice asking the trade minister's press secretary to convey her request for a comment on the IB affair, and heard herself revealing the Social Democrats' biggest secrets to Karina Björnlund. And just a few weeks later Björnlund was made a minister, in one of the most unforeseen promotions ever.

"Trust me," Annika said. "I know more about her than you do."

"I've got to go," Q said, and she had nothing to add because the angels were gone now; they had withdrawn to their hiding place.

She put the phone down and hurried over to her laptop, switching it on and pulling on a pair of socks as the programs loaded, then typed in the new details from the conversation until the backs of her knees started to sweat and her ankles began to freeze.

The door rang. Annika opened it cautiously, not sure what she would find out there. The angels started humming anxiously, but calmed down when she saw Anne Snapphane standing there breathless on the landing, lips white, eyes red.

"Come in," Annika said, backing into the apartment.

Anne didn't answer, just walked in, hunched and self-contained, through the double doors.

"Are you dying?" Annika asked, and Anne nodded, slumped onto the hall bench, and pulled off her headband.

"It feels like it," she said, "but you know what they say in *Runaway Train*."

"Anything that doesn't kill you makes you stronger," Annika said, sitting down beside her.

As the central heating clicked, a toilet somewhere in the building flushed, and a bus pulled up at a bus stop and set off again down below. They sat there staring at the cupboard with the carved pineapples that Annika had bought from a flea market in Stocktorp.

"There are always noises in town," Anne eventually said.

Annika let some air out from her lungs in a dull sigh.

"At least you're never alone," she said, getting up. "Do you want anything? Coffee? Wine?"

Anne Snapphane didn't move.

"I've stopped drinking," she said.

"Oh, it's one of those days, is it?" Annika said, standing and looking beyond the balcony at the courtyard below. Someone had forgotten to close the door to the room containing the wastebaskets; it swung back and forth in the violent winds playing around the building.

"It feels like I've been thrown in a bottomless pit and I'm just falling and falling," Anne said. "It started with Mehmet and his new fuck, then the talk about Miranda living with them, and now that my job has gone there's nothing I can hold on to anymore. Drinking on top of all that would be like pressing the fast-forward button."

"I see what you mean," Annika said, putting her hand on the door handle to help her stay upright.

"When I walk around town everything seems so strange. I don't remember it ever looking like this. It's hard to breathe; somehow, everything's so fucking gray. People look like ghosts, I get the idea that half of them are already dead. I don't know if I'm alive. Can anyone live like that?"

Annika nodded and swallowed audibly; the door to the trash room crashed twice, bang, bang.

"Welcome to the darkness," she said. "I'm sorry you've come to keep me company."

It took a few moments for Anne to appreciate the seriousness of her words.

"What's happened?" she said, getting up, taking off her coat and scarf and hanging them up, then going over to Annika to join her looking down at the trash room.

"It's a whole load of things," Annika said. "My position at work is pretty shaky, Schyman has forbidden me to write about terrorism. He thinks the Bomber made me a bit crazy."

"Huh," Anne said, folding her arms.

"And Thomas is having an affair," she went on, almost in a whisper, the words rolling around the walls, growing larger and larger until they got caught on the ceiling.

Anne looked skeptically at her.

"Whatever makes you think that?"

Annika's throat contracted, the sticky little words wouldn't come out. She looked down at her hands and cleared her throat, then looked up.

"I saw them. Outside NK. He kissed her."

Anne's mouth had fallen half open, skepticism and disbelief dancing across her face.

"Are you sure? You couldn't be mistaken?"

Annika shook her head, looked down at her hands again.

"Her name's Sophia Grenborg; she works for the Federation of County Councils. She's on the same group as Thomas, you know, the one looking into threats to politicians . . ."

"Shit," Anne said. "Shit. What a bastard. What's he say? Does he deny it?"

Annika closed her eyes and put a hand to her forehead.

"I haven't said anything," she said. "I'm going to deal with this my own way."

"What?" Anne said. "Rubbish. Of course you've got to talk to him."

Annika looked up.

"I know he's thinking about leaving me and the children. He's started lying to me as well. And he has been unfaithful before."

Anne looked astonished.

"Who with?"

Annika tried to laugh and felt the stone forcing tears into her eyes.

"With me," she finally said.

Anne sighed heavily and looked at her with eyes of black glass.

"You've got to talk to him."

"And I hear angels," Annika said, taking a deep breath. "They sing to me, and sometimes they talk to me. As soon as I get stressed they start up."

And she shut her eyes and hummed their melancholy song: *summer winds longing hearts gold rain lilies . . .*

Anne took hold of her shoulders and pulled her around to face her with a stern, dark expression on her face.

"You've got to get help," she said. "Do you hear me, Annika? For God's sake, you can't go around with a load of fairies in your head."

She took a step closer, shaking Annika until her teeth rattled.

"You mustn't let go, Anki, listen to me."

Annika pulled free of her friend's grasp.

"It's okay," she said quietly. "They go away when I have something to think about. When I'm working, doing things. Do you want coffee, then?"

"Green tea," Anne said. "If you've got any."

Annika went into the kitchen with a peculiar bounce in her step, feeling the angels' astonishment right down to her stomach; she had given them away. They didn't think she'd do that; they were sure they'd be able to sing and console her and terrorize her forever without anyone ever finding out.

She poured water in the little copper pan, lit the stove with the lighter that only just managed to muster enough of a spark to ignite the blue flames.

Consoling longing, they were singing now, their voices weak, isolated: *little daughter sunshine darling . . .*

She gasped for breath and slapped the side of her head with one hand to make them shut up.

Anne came into the kitchen in her stockinged feet, she had got some color back in her face, an inquisitive look in her eyes.

Annika tried to smile.

"I think they're mostly trying to comfort me," she said. "They only sing nice things."

She walked over to the pantry and felt in the half darkness inside for any kind of tea that could be thought of as green.

Anne sat down at the kitchen table; Annika could feel her eyes on her back.

"But it's you doing it," Anne said. "Don't you get it? You're consoling yourself; you're looking after the little child somewhere in there. Did anyone used to sing you songs like that when you were little?"

Annika blew away a mean comment about amateur psychology and actually managed to find some Japanese tea, which was claimed to speed up your metabolism, that she'd been given by someone at work.

"Are you serious about moving?" she said, returning to the now boiling water. "I can recommend Kungsholmen. We islanders are a bit better than everyone else."

Anne picked up a few stray crumbs from breakfast between her thumb and forefinger and thought for a moment before replying.

"Somehow I suppose I thought Mehmet would move out to us, or that we'd just carry on like we were forever, if that makes any sense? He sort of . . . belonged, and without him it's . . . wrong. It's miserable and a long way away and the old bastard downstairs is always trying to sneak a look under my dressing gown when I go down to get the paper."

"So what's most important?" Annika said, pouring tea through the strainer into the cup.

"Miranda," Anne said without thinking. "Although I realize I can't be a martyr and give up everything important for her sake, but the house on Lidingö has never been that important to me. Of course I like modernism, but I can probably survive without the right sort of interior design."

"Maybe you could put up with a bit of art nouveau if you had to?" Annika said, carrying the mugs over.

"Even a bit of national romanticism. Cheers."

Annika sat down facing Anne and watched her blow on the hot drink.

"Östermalm, you mean?"

Anne nodded, grimacing as she burned her tongue.

"As close as possible, so she can walk between us."

"How big?"

"How expensive, you mean? I can't add anything in cash."

They drank their tea in silence, listening to the door of the trash room bang at irregular intervals down in the courtyard. The kitchen swayed gently in the weak winter light, the angels hummed uncertainly, the stone twisted and scratched.

"Hemnet.se?" Annika said, and stood up, unable to sit there any longer.

Anne slurped her tea and followed her to the computer.

Annika sat down and concentrated on icons and keys, the Internet started up and the modem signed in with little clicks and crackles.

"Let's start with the ultimate," she said. "Three rooms, balcony, and open fire on Artillerigatan?"

Anne sighed.

There was one like that for sale, 115 square meters, three floors up, in excellent condition, new kitchen, fully tiled bathroom with bathtub and sink, viewing Sunday at 4:00 PM.

"Four million?" Anne guessed, peering at the screen.

"Three point eight," Annika said, "but it'll probably go up when they start getting offers."

"That's absurd," Anne Snapphane said. "I can't afford that. What would the monthly payments on a 4-million mortgage be?"

Annika shut her eyes and did the math in her head.

"Twenty thousand, plus fees, but minus tax deductions."

"What about something smaller?"

They found a two-room apartment on the ground floor on the wrong side of Valhallavägen for 1.5 million.

"Unemployed," Anne said, sitting down heavily on the arm of

Annika's chair. "Abandoned by my daughter's father, halfway to alcoholic, and with a two-room apartment on the ground floor. Can I sink any lower?"

"Reporter for Radio Sjuhärad," Annika reminded her.

"You know what I mean," Anne said, and stood up. "I'll go and look at Artillerigatan. Did they give the door code?"

Annika printed out the details with the code and agent's number.

"Are you coming?"

Annika shook her head, and sat and listened as Anne went into the hall and pulled on her boots and coat, headband and scarf.

"I'll call and tell you all about it," she said from the front door, and the angels sang a little farewell song, *bye bye Anne homely heart.*

Annika quickly performed a new search and the voices faded away, as she looked at the newly built house on Vinterviksvägen in Djursholm, which was still for sale, for just six point nine million.

Oak flooring in every room, open-plan kitchen and dining room, Mediterranean blue mosaic in both bathrooms, a level, child-friendly garden with newly planted fruit trees, for more pictures click *here*.

And she clicked and waited as the pictures loaded, pictures from someone else's life, staring at a double bed in a cream-white bedroom with en suite bathroom.

A family lives here, she thought, and they've decided to move. They got hold of a real estate agent who did a valuation, took his digital camera and put together a stupid sales pitch, put it all on the net and now anyone can stare at their bedroom, judge their taste, study the way they've filled the space.

Homey-lomey! the angels sang. *Stay at homey!*

She got up quickly and went over to the phone, dialed 118 118 with trembling fingers. When a woman answered, she asked for the number of Margit Axelsson in Piteå.

"I've got a Thord and Margit Axelsson in Pitholm," the operator said slowly. "He's listed as an engineer, and her as a nursery school teacher—could that be right?"

She asked to be put through and waited with bated breath as the phone rang. The angels kept quiet.

An old-fashioned answering machine took the call, her head was filled with a woman's cheery voice against the slightly distorted background noise of a tape that's been played too many times.

"Hello, you've reached the home of the Axelsson family."

Of course, the home of: we live here.

"Thord and Margit aren't in at the moment and the girls are at university, so leave a message after the beep. Bye for now."

Annika cleared her throat as the machine clicked and whirred.

"Hello," she said weakly after the signal on a tape somewhere outside Piteå. "My name's Annika Bengtzon and I'm a reporter on the *Evening Post*. I'd like to apologize for intruding at this time like this, but I'm phoning about something particular. I know about the Mao quotation."

She hesitated for a moment, not sure if the woman's relatives knew that there were three letters with similar content.

"I'm trying to contact Thord," she said. "I know you didn't do it."

She fell silent again, listening to the gentle hiss of the tape, wondering how long she could stay quiet before the call was cut off.

"Over the last few weeks I've been investigating the explosion of a Draken plane at F21 in November 1969," she said. "I know about Ragnwald; I know that he was together with Karina Björnlund . . ."

The receiver was picked up at the other end, and the change in background noise made her jump.

"The explosion?" a rough male voice said. "What do you know about that?"

Annika gulped.

"Is that Thord?"

"What do you know about F21?"

The man's voice was curt, subdued.

"Quite a bit," Annika said, and waited.

"You can't put anything in the paper unless you know," the man said. "You can't do that."

"I'm not going to," Annika said. "'*People of the world, unite and defeat the American aggressors and all their lackeys. People of the world, be courageous, and dare to fight, defy difficulties and advance wave upon wave. Then the whole world will belong to the people. Monsters of all kinds shall be destroyed.*' What does that mean?"

The man didn't answer for a long time. If it wasn't for the sound of a television in the background she would have thought he'd hung up.

"Have any other journalists called?" she asked eventually.

She heard the man swallow, an uneven sigh into the mouthpiece that made her move the receiver away from her ear.

"Nope," he said. "Up here they know what they think."

He paused, maybe he was crying; she waited in silence.

"They wrote that I was taken in for questioning but released due to lack of evidence."

Annika nodded mutely; no one calls a murderer.

"But it wasn't you," she said. "The police are certain about that."

The man gave a deep sigh, his voice trembling when he spoke.

"That doesn't matter up here," he said. "The neighbors saw me get taken away in a police car. From now on I shall be known as Margit's murderer to people around here."

"Not if they catch the culprit," Annika said, hearing the man start to sob. "Not if they get hold of Göran Nilsson."

"Göran Nilsson," he said, blowing his nose. "Who's that?"

She paused, biting her tongue, not sure of how much the man knew.

"He's also known under his alias," she said. "Ragnwald."

"You mean . . . Ragnwald?" the man said, spitting the name out. "The Yellow Dragon?"

Annika started.

"Sorry, what did you say?"

"I know of him," Thord Axelsson said warmly. "The mad Maoist who ran around Luleå as a revolutionary in the late sixties; I know he's back. I know what he's done."

Annika grabbed a pen and a sheet of paper.

"I've never heard the code name Yellow Dragon used for him before," she said. "Ragnwald was the name he used in the Maoist groups that used to meet in the basement of the library."

"Before the Wild Animals," Thord Axelsson said.

Annika stopped for a moment.

"Before the Wild Animals," she repeated, making notes.

The line fell silent again.

"Hello?" Annika said.

A deep sigh confirmed that the man was still there.

"The girls are here," he said, his mouth close to the phone. "I can't talk about this now."

Annika thought quickly for a couple of seconds.

"I'm coming up to Luleå on some other business tomorrow," she said. "Could I visit you at home so we can talk undisturbed?"

"Margit's dead," the man said, the sounds coming out broken and distorted. "There's nothing for her to be afraid of anymore. But I shan't let her down, ever, you need to understand that."

Annika kept making notes even though she didn't understand him.

"I just want to understand the context," she said. "I'm not going to hang Margit or anyone else out to dry."

The man sighed again and thought for a moment.

"Come at lunchtime. The girls have an appointment with the police, so we can be alone then."

He gave her the address and directions and told her to come around twelve o'clock.

Afterward she let the receiver sit in its cradle for a long minute. The angels were quiet, but there was a sharp buzzing sound in her left ear. The shadows in the room were long and irregular, jumping jerkily over the walls as vehicles passed and the streetlight swayed.

She had to find the right way of explaining this to her editors.

She phoned reception and she was in luck, Jansson was on duty.

"How the hell are you?" he asked, blowing smoke into the phone.

“I’m on to something,” she said. “A real human-interest story, a poor man in a nice suburb outside Piteå whose wife has been murdered and the whole town thinks he did it.”

“But?” Jansson said, not sounding particularly interested.

“Definitely didn’t do it,” Annika said. “He was at work sixty kilometers away from the scene of the crime, with three colleagues, at the time of the murder. And the police think they know who was responsible, but that hasn’t made any difference for this man. His neighbors saw him being taken away in a police car early in the morning and they all think they know what happened. The local papers wrote that he was taken in for questioning, but was released due to a lack of evidence. He’ll be known there as the man who killed his wife until the day he dies.”

“Hmm,” Jansson said, “I don’t know.”

“Just imagine what it would be like to be in this poor man’s situation,” Annika said. “Not only has he lost the wife he loved, but he’s lost his reputation among the people he’s spent his life among. How on earth can he go on?”

She fell silent and bit her lip; maybe she was pushing it a bit far now.

“And he’s prepared to talk about all this?”

She cleared her throat.

“Tomorrow lunchtime. Can I go ahead and book a ticket?”

Jansson sighed audibly.

“Okay, okay,” he said. “After all, you are an independent reporter.”

“And this isn’t about terrorism,” Annika said.

The editor laughed slightly sheepishly.

“I heard Schyman had put his foot down there,” he said.

“New day, new byline,” Annika said and hung up.

Then she dialed the number of the paper’s twenty-four-hour travel office and booked herself onto the 9:40 flight to Kallax, and a rental car, and not a small one either.

She had just ended the conversation when the front door opened and the children tumbled in, buzzing with surplus energy. She went quickly over to the computer and switched it off, then went out into the hall.

"Mommy! Do you know what, we got candy for being so good at Grandma and Grandad's, because we didn't run and Daddy bought a paper with naked ladies and Grandad's heart hurts again and can we go to the park, pleeeeease?"

She hugged them both, laughed and rocked them slowly, warm and fragrant.

"Of course we can," she said. "Are your gloves dry?"

"Mine are horrid," Ellen said.

"We'll find another pair," Annika said and opened the pineapple cupboard.

Thomas walked past her without a glance.

"I'm going to Luleå for the day tomorrow," she said as she pulled the gloves onto the girl's spread-out fingers. "You'll have to drop them off and pick them up."

He stopped at the door of the pantry, his shoulders hunched right up to his ears. Looked like he was going to turn inside out and explode; she waited for a blast that didn't come.

He carried on toward the bedroom with the evening papers and *Café* under his arm and shut the door behind him.

"Can we go now, Mommy?"

"Yep," Annika said, grabbing her jacket and opening the balcony door to get the sled they kept out there. "Off we go."

MONDAY, NOVEMBER 23

In front of Annika lay an endless chalk-white landscape with roaring clouds of snow and deep blue sky. She stood naked with both feet frozen solid in a block of ice, sharp wind howling around her and cutting small wounds in her skin. Her entire attention was focused on the horizon; someone was heading toward her but she couldn't see him yet. She could feel his presence as a bass note in her stomach as she peered into the sharp wind.

And then he came, a blurred gray silhouette against the velvet background, his coat swaying slowly from side to side as he walked, and she recognized him; he was one of the presenters from Studio Six; she tried to free her feet from the block of ice that had now turned to stone, the man came closer and his hands were now visible and she saw the hunting knife in his hand and it was Sven; there was blood on the knife and she knew it was cat's blood; he was walking toward her and the wind was blowing and she looked up at his face and it was Thomas, and he stopped right in front of her and said: "It was your turn to collect the children."

She stretched her neck and back and looked past him and saw Ellen and Kalle hanging from meat hooks on a steel beam with their stomachs cut open and their guts dangling down toward the ground.

Annika stared up at the ceiling for a moment before realizing that she had woken up. Her pulse was throbbing hard in her throat, there was a shrieking sound in her left ear, and the covers had slid off her. She twisted her head and in the dark she saw Thomas's back heave in dreamless sleep. She sat up carefully, realizing that her neck was aching and that she had been crying in her sleep.

She crept through the hall on shaky legs, and into the children's room and their living warmth.

Ellen had put her thumb in her mouth, even though they had cajoled, threatened, and bribed her to stop. Annika took the little hand and pulled her thumb out, saw the girl's mouth searching for what it had lost for a few seconds before sleep forgot it. She watched the sleeping child, marveling at her complete unawareness of how precious and beautiful she was, feeling a great loss for the sense of the clarity of life that her daughter still possessed. She stroked her soft hair, feeling its warmth through the palm of her hand.

Little girl, little girl, nothing is ever going to happen to you.

She went over to her son, lying on his back in his Batman pajamas, his hands above his head, just as she used to sleep as a child. Thomas's blond hair, and already his broad shoulders: he was so like them both.

She leaned over and kissed him on the forehead; the child took a deep breath and blinked up at her.

"Is it morning?"

"Soon," Annika whispered. "Sleep a bit longer."

"I was having a nasty dream," he said and turned onto his side.

"Me too," Annika said quietly, stroking the back of his head with her hand.

She looked at the luminous face of her watch; it was about an hour before the alarm would go off.

Knew that she wasn't going to get back to sleep.

She walked like a lost soul out into the living room, the draft from the window was moving the curtains. She went over and peered through the gap, Hantverkargatan was slowly coming to life below, the yellow streetlight swinging in eternal isolation between the buildings. She warmed one foot against the radiator, then the other.

Went out into the kitchen, lit the stove and filled the pan with water, measured four spoonfuls into the coffeepot, and looked out onto the frozen desert of the courtyard as the water came to the boil, the thermometer outside the window showed –22 degrees Celsius. She poured the water on the coffee and stirred, turned on P1 at low volume and sat down at the kitchen table. The burble from the radio drove out the demons from the corners, she sat quietly with frozen feet as the coffee slowly cooled.

Without her hearing or sensing him, Thomas came into the kitchen, bleary-eyed, hair all over the place.

"What are you doing up so early?" he said, taking a glass from the draining board and filling it with water, drinking in deep gulps.

She turned her face away and stared at the radio without replying.

"Okay, don't then," he said, and went back into the bedroom.

She covered her eyes with a hand and breathed through her mouth until her stomach had calmed down and she could move again. She poured the coffee down the sink and went into the bathroom. Showered under scalding water, dried herself quickly. She dressed in her skiing outfit, thermal long johns and vest, two layers of wool jumpers, thick jeans, and a fleece top. She dug out the keys to the cellar and went out onto the empty street and through to the courtyard, down the steps, and undid the lock on their storeroom in the cellar.

Her ski boots were in a Co-op bag next to Thomas's old college textbooks. Her polar jacket was dusty and dirty; it had been hanging abandoned here since Sven died. She hadn't needed it, those endless evenings standing around ice-cold hockey rinks were over for good.

She took the boots and jacket outside and brushed them off, then carried them up to the apartment. She hung the jacket up and studied it critically. It was really hideous, but it was going to be even colder in Piteå than it was in Stockholm.

"When will you be home?"

She turned and saw Thomas standing in the bedroom door pulling on his underwear.

"I don't know," she said. "Do you want to know when to have dinner ready?"

He turned away and walked into the kitchen.

She suddenly felt that she couldn't stay a moment longer. She pulled on the polar jacket, laced the ski boots and checked that she had her keys, purse, gloves, and hat in her bag. She closed the door soundlessly and flew down the stairs, away from the children, leaving them behind her in the warmth, her whole chest thick with loss.

Little darlings, I shall always be with you; nothing bad will get to you.

She walked along newly woken streets toward the Arlanda Express, and took a packed train out to the airport.

There were still two hours before the plane took off.

She tried drinking coffee and reading yesterday's evening papers, but restlessness tore at her stomach until the words and the caffeine felt like they were suffocating her.

She gave up and watched the wings being de-iced.

Made up her mind not to think about the Federation of County Council middle managers planning the day's work, and preparing to deal with a rapidly developing crisis involving one of their employees.

When the plane's howling engines lifted the plane from the ground, her sense of being lost gradually faded. The plane wasn't quite full—she had an empty seat next to her—and she picked up a copy of the *Norrland News* that had been left by a previous passenger traveling in the other direction.

She watched the ground glistening, frozen and rock hard beneath them, farther away with every passing second.

She turned her attention to the paper and forced herself to look through it.

The inhabitants of Karlsvik were demanding more evening buses.

A missing three-year-old had been found in the forest outside Rosvik with the help of a helicopter with thermal imaging equipment, and everyone was happy and grateful and the police had done a wonderful job.

There was the threat of a taxi strike at Kallax Airport after the collapse of wage negotiations and disagreement about the prioritization system at the taxi stand.

Luleå Hockey had lost at home in the Dolphin Stadium, 2–5 against Djurgården; served them right.

She lowered the paper and leaned her head back, shutting her eyes.

She must have dozed off, because the next moment the wheels were hitting the ice and tarmac at the Arctic Circle. She looked at her watch, almost eleven, and stretched her back, staring out of the plane window. Pale dawn was hanging over the frozen heath landscape.

As she walked through the arrivals hall she felt empty and naked, it took a few seconds before she realized what was missing: the horde of chattering taxi drivers in their dark uniforms by the exit.

She went over to the rental car counter and picked up her keys.

"The engine warmer and inside heater are plugged in," the young man said, smiling flirtatiously. "Take the cable with you. You'll need it."

She looked down at the floor and muttered her thanks.

The cold outside was dry as dust and utterly paralyzing. It hit her like a fist. Shocked, she gasped for breath and tried to defend herself against the sharp little knives she was breathing in. The illuminated figures above the door said it was minus 28 degrees.

The car was a silver-gray Volvo, anchored to an electricity post with a thick cable. Without electric engine warmers no car would ever start in this sort of cold.

She took off her polar jacket and threw it on the backseat.

Inside the car it was stuffy and warm thanks to the heater on the passenger side, she started to sweat immediately in all her thermals. The engine started the first time, but the power steering and wheels were sluggish and hesitant.

She passed the fighter plane that loomed over the entrance to the airport, and took the left exit from the traffic circle instead of the right, toward Piteå instead of Luleå. She peered through the windscreen to see if she recognized anything; she had shared a taxi from the airport with Anne Snapphane ten years ago.

The heathland disappeared behind her and she drove into what must have been fertile agricultural land. Large farms perched on the edge of the forest, oblong timber buildings, exuding wealth and influence.

To her surprise she emerged onto a wide expressway; she didn't remember that at all. Her surprise only grew as the expressway went on and on without her seeing another single vehicle on the road. The feeling of surreal desolation took a stranglehold of her neck, she had to struggle to breathe normally. Was this some sort of joke? Had reality slid away from her—was this the road to hell?

Forest flew by on both sides, short, thin pine trees with frozen crowns. The cold made the low sunlight shimmer, just like heat can. She took a tighter grip on the steering wheel and hunched forward.

Maybe your perspective changed at the Arctic Circle. Maybe up was down, right was left. In which case it would be entirely logical to build an expressway through arctic forest where no one lived.

After two wrong turns, one where she discovered she was on her way toward Haparanda and the Finnish border, she reached the center of Piteå. The town was silent, low-built; it reminded her of Sköldinge, a village between Katrineholm and Flen, just colder and barer. The main difference was the central thoroughfare, three times broader than even Sveavägen in Stockholm.

Margit and Thord Axelsson's home was in Pitholm, the same place where Anne Snapphane's parents lived. She rolled carefully along gritted roads until she reached the turning Thord had described to her.

The detached house was one of a row of confusingly identical houses built in the seventies, when the lending rates dictated for home building by the state led to a previously unknown form of construction, the decade of the oversized pitched roof.

She parked the rental car behind a green Toyota Corolla identical to the one Thomas had. She got out of the Volvo, pulled her jacket on, and was struck for a dizzying moment by the notion that she actually lived here, that the children were at university and she worked on the *Norrland News*. She took shallow breaths of the frozen air, looking up at the peak of the roof that was casting a great shadow across the street.

Anne Snapphane grew up just a few hundred meters away, and she would rather die than move back, but it was peaceful here. This driveway was in complete harmony with its time.

"Annika Bengtzon?"

A man with a shock of steel-gray hair had opened the door slightly, his head peering through the gap.

"Come in," he said, "before you freeze to death."

She walked up to the porch, stamped her feet and shook his hand.

"Thord?"

The look in his eyes was dark and intelligent, the set of his mouth sad and watchful.

Annika stepped into a hall with a dark green patterned plastic mat, dating from 1976 or so, from the look of it. Thord Gustafsson took her heavy jacket and hung it on a hanger below the hat rack.

"I've made some coffee," he said, walking ahead of her into the kitchen.

The pine table was set with woven mats and flowery coffee cups and saucers, a birch-bark basket containing at least four different sorts of cookies.

"Oh, that looks good," Annika said politely as she settled onto a chair and put her bag down beside her.

"Margit likes baking," Thord said, biting off the sentence and staring down into his cup. Then he took a deep breath through his nose, clenched his jaw and reached for the thermos he had already filled.

"Milk and sugar?'"

Annika shook her head, suddenly unable to speak.

What right did she have to march into other people's tragedies? On whose authority did she demand to take up this man's time?

She picked up her spoon and unconsciously clinked it against the porcelain cup.

"Margit was a good person," Thord Axelsson said, looking out of the window. "She meant well, but she carried awful secrets. That's why she died."

He took two lumps of sugar from the bowl and dropped them into his cup with a plop. Then folded his arms on the edge of the table and looked out at the street again.

"I've been doing some thinking since yesterday," he said without looking at Annika. "I want to talk about what happened, but I don't want to sully Margit's memory."

She nodded, still mute, and reached for the notepad in her bag. She glanced briefly at the clean windowpanes and neatly wiped orange kitchen cupboards, suddenly aware that there was a smell of antiseptic cleaning fluid.

"How did you meet, you and Margit?"

The man stared up at the ceiling and sat quite still for a few moments, then looked over at the stove.

"She came up to me in the City Pub in Luleå. It was a Saturday night in the spring of '75. I was there with some friends from college, she was standing next to us at the bar and heard me say that I worked in the air force."

He seemed to lose himself in history for a moment, his eyes roaming over some inner landscape.

"She spoke first," he said. "Interested, almost inquisitive."

He looked into Annika's eyes, giving her a small, embarrassed smile.

"I was flattered," he said, "she was a good-looking girl. And smart. I liked her from the start."

Annika smiled back.

"Was she living in Luleå then?"

"On Lövskatan, she was at teacher training college, the nursery course. She wanted to work with children, kept saying they were the future, doing something creative was important to her even back then, both in her art and in her life . . ."

He put his hand in front of his mouth and looked out at the street again.

"Margit was a serious person," he said. "Responsible, loyal. I was lucky."

Silence spread through the kitchen; she could hear a clock tick; the cold was making the walls creak.

"What was the secret she carried?" Annika eventually asked.

He turned his gaze toward her.

"The Beasts," he said, with sudden strength in his voice. "Margit was an active member of a number of groups and associations even as a teenager, one of Norrbotten's best athletes in the early sixties. She joined the Communist Party at an early age."

Athletics, Annika thought, remembering the cutting from the *Norrland News.*

"Did she know Karina Björnlund?"

"They're cousins," he said. "How did you know that?"

Annika started slightly, and looked down to hide it.

"Karina Björnlund was an athlete too," she said. "So they were close?"

"Margit was two years older; she was a bit like a big sister to Karina. She was the one who got Karina started on athletics. But Margit gave up after that, of course."

"Why?"

"She went into politics. And Karina followed her into that as well . . ."

Annika waited for the man to go on, but when nothing came she tried to help him along.

"So what about the Beasts?"

"They were a breakaway group," Thord Axelsson said, rubbing his forehead. "A splinter cell that saw themselves as an offshoot of the main organization, the Chinese Communist Party. They moved beyond conventional Maoism and went the whole hog, or at least that was how they saw it themselves."

"And they had code names?" Annika said.

He nodded and stirred his coffee.

"Not real names but proper code names, animal names. Margit's was Barking Dog, she was really upset about that. The others got political names, but she got a personal one. The men in the group thought she asked too many questions, always debating and criticizing."

Everything in the kitchen was very quiet. The cold held the house in a viselike grip, the smell of disinfectant was suddenly very noticeable.

"What did the Beasts do that was so bad?" Annika asked.

Thord got up, went over to the sink and filled a glass with water, then held it without drinking.

"She never got over it," he said. "It lay like a shadow over us all these years."

He put the glass on the countertop and leaned against the dishwasher.

"Margit only spoke about it once, but I remember every word."

Thord Axelsson suddenly shrank into himself, and went on in a quiet, monotonous voice.

"It was the middle of November. Not too cold, just a bit of snow on the ground. They got in through the back, from Lulviken, by the river. There's nothing but summer cottages there, so there was no one nearby."

He looked up at Annika with empty eyes, his arms hanging by his sides.

"Margit had never been inside the base before, but one of the boys knew it well. They told her not to go near the hangars, so as not to wake the dogs; they were really vicious creatures."

She was taking notes.

"They ran across the heath for a kilometer or so. The boys waited in a clump of trees while she went closer. There was a plane on the tarmac outside the workshop. She took off the safety seal and set off a flare, and threw it into the container of spent fuel behind the plane."

The air was heavy with antiseptic disinfectant, catching in Annika's nose.

"As she watched it burning she saw two conscripts approaching. She ran toward the south fence and they shouted after her. She threw herself behind the workshop, only just made it before the explosion."

Annika looked down at her notes.

It wasn't Karina Björnlund. She had been wrong.

"One of the conscripts went up like a torch. He just screamed and screamed until he finally collapsed."

Thord Axelsson closed his eyes.

"Margit had no memory of how she got out of the base. Afterward they dissolved the group. They never met again."

He walked back to the table, slumping onto his chair with his hands over his face, reliving something he never experienced but which had colored his whole life.

Annika tried to fit the pieces together in her head but failed.

"Why did the plane explode?" she asked gently.

The man looked up and let him arms drop to the table.

"Have you ever noticed that missile that hangs beneath a fighter jet?"

She shook her head.

"It looks like a moon rocket designed by Disney. It isn't actually a missile but an extra tank of fuel. The skin is thin, the explosion in the fuel container pierced a hole in it."

"But why was the plane sitting on the tarmac with a full tank?"

"Fighters are always fully tanked when they're in the hangars—it's safer that way. The gases that build up in an empty tank are more dangerous than fuel. The lad . . . he was standing below the tank when the extra fuel ignited."

The wooden walls of the house creaked and groaned, the sound hissing and bouncing around the electric kitchen. Despair hung in dark clouds between the kitchen cupboards and the pine lamps; she felt an intense and instant desire to flee, to run away, home to the children, to kiss them and embrace their cozy chubbiness, home to Thomas, to love him with all of her body and all of her mind.

"Who else was there?" she asked.

Thord Axelsson's face was completely gray, he seemed on the point of fainting.

"The Yellow Dragon and the Black Panther," he said hoarsely.

"The Dragon was the leader, Göran Nilsson from Sattajärvi," Annika said, and something deep, unfathomable, flickered across the man's face. "Who was the other one?"

"Don't know," he said. "Karina was the Red Wolf, but I don't know who the boys were in real life."

"How many of them were there?"

He rubbed his face.

"I mentioned the Black Panther. The Lion of Freedom was another one, the White Tiger, and the Dragon of course. Yes, that was it. Four men, two girls."

Annika wrote down the names, noticing how ridiculous the silly code names were, but was unable to smile, not even internally.

"Karina wasn't with them that night?"

"She'd finished with Ragnwald, and wanted out of the group. Margit was very angry with her, thought she was betraying them. Loyalty was always very important to Margit."

A clock chimed somewhere in the living room. Annika thought about the marriage announcement in the *Norrland News*—why would you put that in if you weren't going to get married?

She looked at the man thoughtfully, thinking about the huge burden the pair had carried together, and which was now his alone.

"How long was it before Margit told you all this?" she asked quietly.

"When she got pregnant," Thord Axelsson said. "It was an accident; she'd forgotten to take the pill, but when it happened we were both delighted. But one evening she was lying there crying when I got home, and she just couldn't stop. It took all evening to get her to tell me what it was. She thought I was going to hand her in to the police. Leave her and the child."

He fell silent.

"But you didn't," Annika confirmed.

"Hanna did her national service at F21," Thord said. "She's an officer in the reserves; she's studying nuclear physics at Uppsala."

"And your other daughter?"

"Emma lives on the same corridor as Hanna; she's doing a master's in politics."

"You've done well," Annika said, honestly.

He looked through the window.

"Yes," he said. "But the Beasts have always been with us. Margit thought about what she'd done every day. She never escaped it."

"Nor you," Annika said. "You went to work every day knowing what had happened."

He merely nodded.

"Why didn't she tell the police?" Annika said. "Wouldn't that have been better, not having to deal with it alone?"

The man stood up.

"If only she could have," he said with his back to Annika. "When the Dragon disappeared Margit got a package in the post. There was a finger in it, a human finger, from a small child, and a warning."

Annika felt herself heating up; could feel the blood drain from her brain; thought she was about to faint.

"No one ever spoke about the Beasts, not ever. Margit heard nothing from them for all those years, not until this October."

"Then what happened?" Annika whispered.

"She got the call, the symbol of the Yellow Dragon, summoning her to their meeting place."

Annika could see before her the strange drawing the minister of culture had received, in that envelope mailed in France.

"A meeting?" she said. "When?"

Thord Axelsson shook his head and walked over to the sink, picked up a glass but did nothing with it.

"Then they contacted her. One of them called her at work, asking if she was going to the meeting to celebrate the return of the Dragon. She told them to go to hell, said they'd ruined her life, and that she loathed the fact that she'd ever met them."

His shoulders were shaking.

"She didn't hear from them again."

Annika was struggling against a growing, sucking feeling of nausea. She sat for a long while, swallowing, watching the man weep, holding the glass to his forehead.

"I want them caught," he said eventually, turning toward Annika again, his face red and unlike itself.

He sat down heavily on his chair again, and sat still for a while as the clock ticked and the antiseptic smell spread throughout Annika's body.

"Margit never got rid of her guilt," he said. "She paid for it all through her life. I can't go on like this anymore."

"Have you told the police?"

He shook his head.

"But I'm going to," he said. "As soon as the Dragon's been caught and the girls are safe."

"What do you want me to do?" she asked.

He looked at her blankly.

"I don't know," he said. "I just wanted to tell someone."

He looked out through the window and stiffened.

"Hanna and Emma," he said. "They're coming. You have to go."

Annika stood up without thinking, stuffing her pad and pen in her bag and hurrying out into the hall, where she pulled her jacket from the hanger and tugged it on. She went back toward the kitchen, and saw the man sitting there motionless, his eyes blank.

"Thank you," she said quietly.

He looked at her and tried to smile.

"By the way," she said. "Did Margit have very small feet?"

"Size thirty-six," he said.

She left him by the pine table in the scrubbed kitchen with the untouched cups of coffee gradually cooling.

The car had had time to get completely cold; she kept her polar jacket on. For one panicky moment she thought the engine wasn't going to start, that she was going to freeze to stone in her rental car among the identical seventies houses, forever held fast in the life lies of the Axelsson family.

She turned the key so hard that the metal almost snapped, the engine stared with a hesitant rattle, and she breathed out and saw her breath freeze to ice on the inside of the windscreen. She found reverse as the gearbox protested, and backed into the street, hoping she wasn't going to hit anything; she hadn't scraped the rear window.

The two daughters passed close to her side window; she attempted a smile and waved feebly as they looked curiously at her.

The rubber of the tires creaked on the icy road as she rolled toward town. The nausea persisted, the smell of disinfectant still in her nostrils, the thoughts bouncing around her head and chest.

Was Thord Axelsson telling the truth? Was he exaggerating? Was he hiding anything?

She drove past the secondary school and the church and Åhléns department store, and was out of the town center before she even realized she was in it.

He wasn't glossing over his wife's deeds, Annika thought, nor was he making excuses for her. On the contrary, he had stated soberly that she had set fire to the aviation fuel and caused the plane to explode. He hadn't even tried to present it as an accident.

If he had wanted to lie, he would have done so then.

The Beasts, she thought. The Yellow Dragon, ha, what a stupid idea, what a load of crap. The Lion of Freedom, the Barking Dog, the Red Wolf, the Black Panther, the White Tiger.

Where are you now? she thought as she pulled out onto the deserted expressway again, heading toward Luleå.

The Yellow Dragon, Göran Nilsson, homecoming professional hitman. The Barking Dog, Margit Axelsson, murdered nursery school teacher. The Red Wolf, Karina Björnlund, minister of culture, making panicky changes to government proposals.

And the rest of you? Three middle-aged Swedish men, where have you hidden yourselves away? How much have you forgotten?

She drove past the exit to Norrfjärden, feeling the cold whirling around her feet. The temperature had fallen to minus 29 degrees; the sun was already going down, spreading a pale yellow light on the horizon. It was one thirty in the afternoon.

The child's finger, she thought. Could that really have happened?

She swallowed, had to open the window for a few seconds to get some fresh air. Thord hadn't said what the accompanying warning had said, but no one had blabbed about the Beasts, not ever.

She believed the finger had really existed.

The attack itself, three people involved, Margit and Göran and one other man. Did that make sense?

Margit had the same shoe size as the prints found at the site. Thord Axelsson's story included enough detail to make her believe the basic chain of events, even if she would have to check the theoretical possibilities with the press officer at the base. So why should she doubt how many people were involved?

Karina Björnlund wasn't there.

She was innocent, at least as far as the act itself was concerned. Of course she could have been involved in the planning, maybe even assisted in other ways. But, apart from anything else, she must have known about it.

How can you be sure of that? Annika asked herself. If Thord is telling the truth, she may well have been ignorant of the attack. She had split up with Göran and wanted out of the group.

But in that case how could she be open to blackmail? Why was she allowing Herman Wennergren to scare her into changing government legislation?

And why had she put a marriage announcement in the local paper if she had broken up with him?

Maybe Karina herself hadn't put the announcement in, she suddenly thought.

Maybe the announcement was part of the jilted man's strategy either to cause trouble or get her back.

Annika rubbed her forehead, feeling suddenly thirsty, her lips dry. She passed Ersnäs and was back on the huge expressway again. A few frozen houses from the thirties huddled in the twilight, plumes of smoke rising straight up from their chimneys; the wind had given up. The cold was clear as glass.

I have to talk to Karina Björnlund, she thought. I have to set things up so that she doesn't get away. She won't wriggle out of this, lying and protecting herself at any cost.

She pulled her cell phone from the bag, and found she had no reception. She couldn't be bothered to get cross, just carried on toward Luleå, looking forward to being back in civilization again.

By the turning to Gäddvik she picked up her cell phone again, shut her eyes, and replayed her mental video recording.

The Post-it note on the registrar's computer screen, the minister of culture's cell phone number, summoning up the memory.

Twice the number of the beast, and then a zero.

She keyed in 070-666 66 60, stared at the number on the screen for a moment, then realized with a start that she was on the point of ignoring a right-hand bend.

What was she going to say?

Karina Björnlund will listen, she thought. It was just a question of getting hold of her.

She pressed the call button, feeling the warmth of the cell phone in her hand, and pressed in the earpiece as she slowed the car's speed.

"Hello?"

Annika braked in surprise; the first ring had hardly started before a woman's voice answered.

"Karina Björnlund?" she said, pulling up at the side of the road and pressing the earpiece farther in; there was a rushing, humming sound in the background.

"Yes?"

"My name's Annika Bengtzon; I work for the *Evening Post* . . ."

"How did you get this number?"

Annika stared at the red-painted wall of a Norrbotten farmhouse and adopted a neutral tone of voice.

"I was wondering if the Red Wolf had met the Yellow Dragon recently?" she said, and listened intently to the noise on the line, voices talking, a metallic clattering in the background, a public address system announcing something; then a second later the line went dead.

Annika looked at the display. She pressed redial, got an impersonal electronic answering service, and ended the call without speaking.

Where had Karina Björnlund been when she took the call?

What was the metallic voice saying over the P.A. in the background?

She shut her eyes and pressed her fingertips to her temples.

Last call for SK009 to Stockholm, gate number 5?

A flight announcement, that much was certain.

But SK? Didn't that mean an SAS flight?

She called directory inquiries and asked to be put through to Scandinavian Airlines System, business customers.

She waited in a queue for thirty seconds until the call was picked up.

"SK009 is the afternoon flight from Kallax to Arlanda," the sales assistant at SAS told her.

Annika felt the adrenaline pumping.

Karina Björnlund was at the airport just five kilometers away and was either on her way back down to Stockholm, or else she'd just arrived and was collecting her bags.

She considered booking her return flight to Stockholm but decided to wait, said thank you, and ended the call.

Then she drove toward the traffic circle, turned right, and glided along frozen roads toward Kallax Airport.

Because of the taxi strike anyone who didn't have their own car was forced to take the bus from the airport into Luleå. Annika could see the queue trail back outside the terminal, huddled figures fighting against the cold and their own luggage. She was about to drive past the airport bus toward the rental car parking lot when she caught sight of Karina Björnlund.

The minister was at the back of the queue, patiently waiting her turn.

Thoughts ricocheted around Annika's head.

What was Björnlund doing here?

She pulled up by the curb, putting the car in neutral and pulling on the hand brake, stared at the minister and picked up her cell again. She dialed the department and asked to speak to the minister's press secretary.

She was told that Karina Björnlund had taken the day off.

"I have a question about the proposal being presented tomorrow," Annika said, her eyes glued to the woman at the end of the queue. "I have to talk to her today."

"I'm afraid that isn't possible," the press secretary said amiably. "Karina's away and won't be back until late this evening."

"Isn't it a bit odd for a minister to take time off the day before a major proposal is presented to parliament?" Annika said slowly, staring at Karina Björnlund's dark fur coat.

The press secretary hesitated.

"It's a private matter," she said quietly. "Karina was called to an urgent meeting that couldn't be postponed. It's very unfortunate timing, I have to agree with you—Karina was very upset that she had to go."

"But she'll be home this evening?"

"That's what she was hoping, anyway."

What sort of meeting would make a minister abandon her work? A sick relative, a partner or child or parent?

A meeting in Luleå, something she couldn't avoid, something that took priority over everything else.

The Red Wolf.

The meeting to celebrate the return of the Dragon.

Annika's fingers started to tingle, and sweat broke out along her back.

"Thank you," she said, and ended the call.

She drove past the bus, and watched in the rearview mirror as the minister climbed on, then let the bus pass her and stayed a hundred meters behind it.

Just before the Bergnäs Bridge she decided it was time to get closer.

You're sitting in there, Annika thought, staring at the vehicle's filthy back window. You're on your way somewhere that you don't want to be seen, but I'm here.

And the angels starting singing gently to her, slowly and mournfully, *winter month ice crystals . . .*

"Oh, shut up!" Annika yelled, and hit her head with the palm of her hand so hard that she saw stars, and the voices disappeared.

She followed the bus over the bridge and entered the frozen city, driving past paneled houses and banks of snow and frozen cars, and turned off left at a junction by a gas station.

The airport bus stopped just across the street from the City Hotel's heavy façade; she braked and leaned forward to watch the passengers getting off. Her breath misted the windscreen, and she wiped it with the sleeve of her thermal vest.

Karina Björnlund was the second to last off. The minister of culture stepped carefully out of the bus with a black leather bag in her hand; Annika could feel herself on the verge of hyperventilating.

A bag to breathe into, she thought, realizing that she didn't have one.

Instead she held her breath and counted to ten three times, and her heartbeat slowed down.

It was getting dark, but the sunset was as slow and gradual as dawn had been, and she watched Karina Björnlund stand and freeze at the bus stop, a thickset, dark woman in a fur and no hat.

The Red Wolf, Annika thought, trying to make out the features of her face in the shadows, and imagined that she could see a pair of anxious, sad eyes.

What are you doing here?

Her mother lives on Storgatan, she thought. Maybe she's on her way there.

Then realized: this is Storgatan. Why would she be standing at a bus stop to go somewhere else?

She hasn't come to see her mother.

Suddenly her rear window was filled with the headlights of one of the local buses. She put the car in gear and rolled a few meters to let the bus pull in, passing the little gaggle of people waiting in the queue for the bus as she did so, and watched in her rearview mirror as Karina Björnlund picked her bag up and climbed onboard.

I'll follow the bus to see where she gets off, Annika thought, and rolled a bit farther until she realized she was heading into a pedestrianized street. People were walking slowly in front of the car, challenging her with their stares; she looked up and noticed a sign indicating that all vehicles apart from public transport were forbidden. She felt herself starting to panic again, grappled with the gearshift to find reverse, and saw the bus gliding slowly toward her. She turned the wheel as hard as she could and performed an evasive maneuver on crunching tires.

The bus slid past and she felt the sweat sticking her legs to the seat. She was about to lose sight of the minister, and had no idea where she was heading.

Bus number 1, she thought. The bus that Linus Gustafsson usually took.

Svartöstaden.

East, toward Swedish Steel.

And she drove down toward the harbor, turning right toward the ironworks.

On the viaduct over the railway sidings she pulled over to the side and waited; if she was right the bus would have to pass her here.

Four minutes later the bus glided past her and carried on toward Malmudden.

She just had time to register the name of the street, Lövskatan, as the bus turned right; wasn't that where Margit Axelsson used to live? Another sign, Föreningsgatan, and the bus carried on along the edge of a messy and desolate industrial development, huddling in the shadow of an enormous jet-black mound of iron ore. On the left was a row of identical two-story apartment blocks from the forties, and up ahead loomed a huge, abandoned industrial building that seemed to have grown into the side of the mountain of iron ore. Dark windows sent warnings into the twilight, cold cries into the darkness. She followed the bus as the road swung up and left and ran alongside the railway line. An immense steel pipe hung high above, and below lurked a row of graffiti-covered and ramshackle industrial units, surrounded by pipes, steel girders, tires, and pallets. She could see rusting trailers and a beaten-up portacabin, a few overflowing containers, driving past fragments of steel sheeting, sections of piping, and a wooden boat under a tarpaulin. No sign of life anywhere.

The bus signaled and pulled in at a bus stop. Annika braked and pulled up behind an abandoned car twenty meters farther down the hill.

Karina got off, clutching her leather bag; Annika slumped down in her seat and stared at her.

The bus signaled and pulled away, and the minister of culture was left staring out at the railway tracks, her breath drifting like clouds around her. She seemed to hesitate.

Annika switched off the engine and pulled out the key, waiting inside the warm interior of the car without taking her eyes off the woman.

Then Karina suddenly turned around and started walking toward the crown of the hill, away from the industrial units.

Annika stiffened, fumbled with the ignition key, biting the inside of her cheek.

Should she get out and follow the minister?

Drive up and offer her a lift?

Wait and see if she came back?

She rubbed her eyes for a moment.

Wherever Karina was going, she evidently didn't want company.

Annika opened the car door, pulling her hat and ski gloves from her bag, pushed the door shut, and locked the car with a bleep. She gasped for breath, reeling from the cold—how was it possible to live in a climate like this?

She blinked a few times; the cold was making the air incredibly dry, hurting her eyes.

The daylight was dark gray now, almost gone. The sky was distant, clear and entirely colorless, a few stars twinkled above the mounds of ore. Two streetlights farther down the road spread a dull, hopeless light in a small circle around their own feet. Karina Björnlund had disappeared over the crown of the hill, and there was no other sign of life anywhere. The rumble from the steelworks was carried through the cold along the railway tracks, reaching her like a dull vibration.

Walking carefully, she started up the hill, looking hard at every bush and shadow.

At the top of the hill the road swung sharply to the left and led back into the housing development. Straight ahead was a narrow track, tolerably clear of snow and ice and with a sign forbidding vehicle traffic.

Annika narrowed her eyes and peered around her, unable to see the minister anywhere. She took a few steps along the private track, jogging as fast as she dared on the ice and grit along a surface that seemed to consist of earth and ragged tarmac. She passed a bundle of cables leading down to the railway tracks and ran past a brick building with a sign saying SKANSKA on it, an empty parking lot, then the track emerged alongside the railway line again. Far ahead the ironworks, coke ovens, and blast furnaces sat brooding darkly against the winter sky, millions of tons of ore turned into a rolling carpet of steel. To the left was nothing but slurry and snow. The full moon had risen behind the mounds of ore, its blue light mixing with the yellow lights illuminating the ore railway.

She ran for several minutes until she was forced to stop and catch her breath, coughing dryly and quietly into her glove, blinking moisture out of her eyes and looking around for Karina Björnlund.

The track looked as though it was rarely used; she could see just a few footprints, some tracks left by dogs and a bicycle, but no minister.

Sunshine darling, the angels suddenly burst out, *winter chill eternal longing . . .*

She hit the back of her head so hard that the voices fell silent. She shut her eyes and breathed for a few seconds, listening to the emptiness in her head, and in the echo of the silence she suddenly heard other voices, human voices, coming from within the forest up ahead. She couldn't make out any words, could just hear a male and a female voice talking fairly quietly.

She passed beneath a viaduct, either a road or a railway, Annika couldn't tell: she no longer knew where she was. The voices grew louder, and in the light of the moon and the railway tracks she suddenly saw footprints leading into an opening in the scrub.

She stopped, peering through the low trees, just able to make out shadows, spirits.

"Well, I'm here now," Karina Björnlund was saying. "Don't hurt me."

A rough male voice with a Finnish accent answered:

"Karina, don't be scared. I've never meant you any harm."

"Believe me, Göran, no one's ever done me as much harm as you have. Say what you want and . . . let me go."

Annika caught her breath, her stomach turning somersaults, her dry mouth like sandpaper. She took a careful step into the first of the footprints already there in the snow, then another, and another.

In the moonlight she saw the forest open out into a clearing, and at its center was a small brick building with a sheet-metal roof and sealed-up windows.

In the middle of the clearing stood the minister of culture in her thick fur, and a thin gray man in a long coat and leather cap, with a dark duffel bag beside him.

Göran Nilsson, the ruler with divine power, the Yellow Dragon.

Annika stared at him with painfully dry eyes.

Terrorist, mass murderer, evil personified—this was what it looked like, hunched and dull and trembling slightly?

She had to call the police.

Then realized:

Her cell phone was in the bag on the passenger seat of the Volvo down by the abandoned car.

"How can you think I've ever meant you any harm?" the man said, his voice carrying through the still air. "All my life you're the person who's meant the most to me."

The woman shuffled her feet nervously.

"I got your messages," she said, and Annika realized at once why she sounded so scared.

She had received the same warnings as Margit.

The man, the Yellow Dragon, lowered his head for a few seconds. Then he looked up again, and Annika could see his eyes. In the strange light they glimmered red and hollow.

"I had a reason for coming here, and you're all going to hear it," he said, his voice as cold as the wind. "You may have come a long way, but I've come farther."

The woman was shaking under her fur, her voice scared, and she was close to tears.

"Don't hurt me."

The man went up to her; Annika could see him pull something from his coat pocket, black, shiny.

A weapon. A revolver.

"I shan't trouble you again," he said quietly. "This is the last time. You'll just have to wait at the meeting place. There's something I need to take care of first."

The wind freshened, tugging at the branches of the pine trees.

"Please," the woman pleaded. "Let me go."

"In," he said harshly. "Now."

Karina picked up her bag from the ground and, with the revolver aimed at her back, walked inside the little brick building. Göran Nilsson didn't move, watched her go inside, put the gun in his pocket again, turned around and walked over to the duffel bag leaning against the wall of the building.

Annika took a deep breath; she had heard more than enough. She moved softly and carefully back along the trail of footprints and emerged onto the track, casting a last glance at the trees so she could describe the site properly to the police.

Someone was moving, someone was coming toward her.

Her breathing came hard and deep; she looked around in panic.

Ten meters or so behind her was a metal box with a mass of thick cables snaking out of it, and behind it was a thicket of young pine trees.

Annika fled toward them, her feet scarcely touching the crunching surface of the track, she flew into the sharp branches, parting them with both hands, then peered back behind her.

The gray man emerged into the feeble light from the railway tracks, dragging the duffel bag behind him; it was evidently very heavy.

He stood still on the icy track for a few seconds, then put his hand to his stomach and bent over, his breath rising from his mouth in panting bursts. Annika craned her neck to see better; it looked like the man was about to fall flat on his face.

Then his breathing calmed down; he straightened his back and took a few unsteady steps forward.

Suddenly he looked straight at Annika.

Horrified, she let go off the branch she had been holding back, and put her hand over her mouth to muffle the sound and cloud of her breath. She stood completely still in the darkness as the man slowly walked toward her. His panting breath and strained steps grew in her head, coming closer and closer until she thought she was going to scream. She closed her eyes and heard him stop a meter or so from her back, on the other side of the little pine trees.

There was a scraping noise. She opened her eyes.

Metal scraping against metal. She held her breath and listened.

The man was doing something with the metal box. He was

opening the doors of the cabinet containing all the cables. She could hear him panting, and realized that she had to take another breath, inhaling quickly and silently, only to feel a huge and instant desire to throw up.

The man stank. A smell of decay filtered through the branches and made her put her hand in front of her mouth again.

He was panting and struggling with something on the other side of the trees; the scraping sounds continued, then fell silent. There was a squeak, and then a click.

Ten seconds of easier breathing, then some more steps, away.

Annika turned around and pushed the branch aside to take another look.

The man was on his way back into the bushes. The duffel bag was gone.

He put it in the box, she thought.

The undergrowth swallowed him up, erasing his presence in the weak light.

Annika stood up and flew quickly along the track, only pausing at the edge of the forest.

She turned and ran as quietly as she could, under the viaduct and back up to the Skanska building, and past the empty parking lot. Someone was coming toward her.

She stopped instantly, looked around with adrenaline racing through her veins, threw herself down in the forest and sank up to her chin into the snow.

It was a man. He was bareheaded, dressed in jeans and a thin padded jacket. From his stumbling gait and unsteady movements she read the signs of serious and long-term alcohol abuse, a drunk.

A few seconds later he had vanished behind the Skanska building and she was able to get out onto the road again, rushing on without trying to brush off the snow.

To begin with she couldn't see the rental car, and had a moment of panic before she saw it behind the abandoned car. She clicked open the lock and threw herself into the driver's seat, pulling off her gloves and fumbling for her cell phone, her fingers trembling so much that she had trouble keying in Inspector Suup's direct number.

"Karlsson, Central Control."

She had reached the switchboard.

"Suup," she said, "I'm trying to reach Inspector Suup."

"He's finished for the day," Karlsson said.

Her brain went into overdrive, she shut her eyes and rubbed a sweaty palm across her forehead.

"Forsberg," she said. "Is Forsberg there?"

"Which one? We've got three."

"In crime?"

"Hang on, I'll put you through."

The line went quiet and she ended up in a vague cyberspace without sound or color.

After three minutes she gave up and rang again.

"I'm trying to get hold of someone on the Benny Ekland and Linus Gustafsson murder inquiries," she said in a tone of panic when Karlsson answered once more.

"About what?" the young man said, uninterested.

She forced herself to breathe calmly.

"My name is Annika Bengtzon, and I'm a reporter on the *Evening Post*, and I . . ."

"Suup's in charge of the press," Karlsson interrupted. "You'll have to call him tomorrow."

"Listen to me!" she screamed. "Ragnwald is here, Göran Nilsson, the Yellow Dragon—I know where he is; he's in a small brick building next to the ore railway together with Karina Björnlund, you've got to come and arrest him, now!"

"Björnlund?" Karlsson said. "The minister of culture?"

"Yes!" Annika shouted. "Göran Nilsson from Sattajärvi is with her in a small building below the ironworks, I can't explain exactly where, it's close to a viaduct . . ."

"Listen," Karlsson said. "Are you sure you're feeling okay?"

She paused and realized that she sounded like a lunatic; cleared her throat, and forced herself to speak calmly and coherently.

"I know this might sound a little crazy," she said, trying to smile down the line. "I'm calling from somewhere called Lövskatan; it's not far from the ironworks, the railway track runs right alongside . . ."

"Lövskatan, yes, we do know where Lövskatan is," the policeman said, and she could hear that his patience was wearing thin.

"A man you've been looking for for years has come back to Luleå," Annika said, sounding almost normal. "His name is Göran Nilsson, and since he returned to Sweden he's committed at least four murders, the Mao murders, you know, and right now he's outside that building, or at least was very recently, a brick building with a tin roof a short way into the forest below a viaduct . . ."

Officer Karlsson sighed audibly down the line.

"The duty officer is booking someone in," he said, "but I'll pass on your message as soon as she gets back."

"No!" Annika yelled. "You have to come now! I don't know how long he's going to be there."

"Listen," the policeman said firmly. "Calm down. I've just told you: I'll talk to the duty officer."

"Good," Annika said, breathing heavily, "good. I'll wait here by the bus stop until you come so I can show you the way. I'm parked here; I'm in a silver Volvo."

"Okay," the policeman said. "Just you wait there."

And he hung up.

Annika looked at the display on her phone, a glowing green rectangle in the darkness.

She pushed in the earpiece and called Jansson's direct number in the newsroom.

"I might have to stay in Luleå tonight," she said. "Just wanted to check it's okay to book into the City Hotel tonight if I have to."

"Why?" Jansson said.

"There might be something going on up here," she said.

"No terrorism," Jansson said. "I got hauled over the coals this morning for letting you go up to Norrbotten again."

"Okay," Annika said.

"Are you listening?" Jansson said. "Not one single line about another bloody terrorist—is that clear?"

She waited a second before replying.

"Of course," she said. "Understood. I promise."

"Stay at the City," the editor said closer to the receiver in a considerably quieter and friendlier voice. "Call room service. Get pay-TV and watch porn films; I'll sign for all of it. I know how it is: we all have to get away sometimes."

"Okay," she said smartly and ended the call, dialled 118 118 and asked directory inquiries to put her through to the City Hotel, Luleå, and booked a business-class room on the top floor.

After that she sat in the car and stared out of the windscreen. Her breath hit the windows and they soon froze over again.

She could do nothing more. All she could do was sit and wait for the police.

It'll soon be over, she thought, feeling her pulse rate slow.

She saw Thord Axelsson's gray face before her, Gunnel Sandström's swollen eyes and wine-red cardigan, Linus Gustafsson's spiky gelled hair and watchful eyes, and was consumed with burning fury.

You're finished, you bastard.

She realized she was freezing, thought about starting the car engine to heat it up, but opened the door instead and got out, far too restless to sit still. She checked that her cell phone was in her pocket, locked the door and walked up toward the top of the hill.

The arctic night had taken an iron grip on the landscape, as hard and unrelenting as the steel produced in the blast furnaces down by the shore. Annika's breath drifted around her, light veils of frozen warmth.

It's beautiful, she thought, her eyes following the rails and ending up among the stars.

Then she heard a vehicle rumbling behind her, she turned around, hoping it was the police.

It was a local Luleå bus, the number 1.

It drove toward her and stopped, she realized that she was standing at the bus stop and took a few steps to one side to indicate that she wasn't waiting for it.

But the bus stopped a few meters away from her anyway, the back door opened and a thickset man stepped onto the street, moving slowly, heavily.

She looked at him and took a step closer.

"Hans!" she said. "Hans, hello, it's me, Annika."

Hans Blomberg, the archivist from the *Norrland News*, looked up and met her gaze.

"What are you doing here?" Annika said.

"I live here," the man said, smiling cheerfully. "On Torsgatan."

He gestured over his shoulder toward the housing development.

"Do you?" Annika said as the bus pulled away. She took a step closer and looked into his eyes, and at that moment something clicked inside her head—suddenly she remembered when she had seen the drawing of the Yellow Dragon before. All of a sudden she knew where it was. She had thought it was a child's drawing, a yellow dinosaur, on Blomberg's bulletin board in the archive of the *Norrland News*. She took a couple of involuntary steps back.

"Surely the real question is," Blomberg said, "what are you doing here?"

The bus disappeared beyond the crown of the hill and the man walked toward her, his hands in his pockets. He stopped in front of her and in the moonlight his eyes were almost transparent.

She laughed nervously.

"I'm up on a job and got lost," she said. "Föreningsgatan, which one is that?"

"You're standing on it," the archivist said in amusement. "Doesn't anyone have a sense of direction in Stockholm?"

"They'd run out by the time they got to me," she said, realizing she would soon be unable to speak.

"Who are you meeting?"

She shrugged.

"I've already missed my deadline," she said.

"But then you must come inside and warm up," he said. "Can I offer you a cup of tea?"

She searched frantically for an excuse; the man ignored her hesitation and took a firm grip of her arm and started walking.

"I live in a little two-room apartment on the ground floor," he said. "It's not much, but what can you do when there's no longer any room for you in consumer society?"

She tried to pull her arm away and found it was held in a viselike grip.

"It's not often a guy like me gets such a charming visitor," he said. "A lovely young lady all the way from the capital."

He smiled genially at her; she tried to smile back.

"Which one of them are you?" Annika said. "The Panther, Tiger, or Lion?"

He was looking straight ahead, pretending he hadn't heard the question, just took tighter hold of her. The houses were disappearing behind them; they were approaching the NO VEHICLES sign. She glanced over to the left, past the power cables and into the undergrowth.

"So you live out here in the forest?"

He didn't answer, and the next instant she was back in the tunnel; she felt the earth tilt, heard someone breathing hard, panting, and realized it was her, her mouth wide open.

"No," she said. "I don't want to. Please."

Her legs gave way beneath her; Blomberg caught her with a smile.

"You're a reporter," he said. "A proper, inquisitive little reporter. Of course you want to get a good story, don't you?"

She could see the pipes in the roof of the tunnel above her and started to cry.

"Let me go!"

She jammed her feet in the ice and struggled and was rewarded with a ringing blow to the head. She saw stars and Sven was there screaming at her and she ducked, sank to the ground and put her hands over her head.

"Don't hit me."

The world slowed down and paused, the ground stopped tilting and she could hear herself panting. She looked up cautiously and saw Blomberg shaking his head at her.

"God, the way you carry on," he said. "Up you get. The leader's waiting."

She stumbled forward in the moonlight with the lights above the railway tracks swaying far off to the left. The angels were completely silent: where their anxious voices had been was now only dark emptiness.

They passed the Skanska building, and it was completely black.

"We're going to the little brick building, aren't we? The one beyond the viaduct?"

"So you've already found our headquarters," the archivist said in his good-natured voice. "Have you been creeping around in the bushes? Very talented. Then I may as well tell you what to expect. The Dragon has called us together again. I don't think everyone can make it, we've suffered something of a decline in membership recently, but Karina will probably be there, and Yngve, of course. He never misses a good party."

The archivist laughed happily, as Annika struggled against nausea.

"Poor Yngve," the man went on. "Göran wanted me to look after him, but what's a chap to do? To help an addict you have to change the whole apparatus of oppression, and I haven't been able to do that. Unfortunately I have to admit that Yngve no longer has any hold on reality; it's truly tragic. I have failed in my duty . . ."

A moment later she heard something heavy and rhythmic behind her, glanced over her shoulder and found herself staring into the headlight of a huge diesel locomotive coming down the track.

"Straight on," Blomberg said.

Annika obeyed, peering at the great engine as it slowly rumbled past her toward the ironworks with its endless train of fully laden ore trucks behind it.

Her heart was thudding; she tried to see herself from the train driver's perspective, she was dressed in black against a dark background of scrub, only lit by the cold moonlight.

She forced her heart to slow down. Tried to see how long the train was without twisting her head, but couldn't see the end of it.

They walked under the viaduct, the train thundered past—*dunkdunk dunkdunk dunkdunk*—car after car after car, casting black shadows from the railway tracks.

Then the last one disappeared, the end of a long tail heading toward the fiery heat of the blast furnace.

Annika swallowed hard and found that her hands were shaking.

They reached the transformer box where Göran Nilsson had hidden his duffel bag. She glanced at it; it was closed, sealed up.

"Down to the left here," Blomberg said, pushing her toward the gap in the undergrowth.

She slipped and was on the verge of falling down the slope, but grabbed hold of some branches and managed to stay upright.

"Take it easy," she said lamely as they walked toward the brick building.

The windows were sealed with metal shutters, a half-collapsed flight of wooden steps led up to the door, which was slightly open. Annika stopped, but Blomberg shoved her in the back.

"Go on, in you go. It's just an old compressor shed."

She took hold of the door and pulled it open, noting that its lock consisted of two welded metal hasps, one with a rusty old padlock hanging from it.

The same terrible stench that she had smelled behind the pine trees poured out through the door.

Ragnwald was in there.

She stepped into the solid darkness, blinking, hearing people breathing. It was icy cold inside; paradoxically it felt even colder than outside.

"Who are you?" Karina Björnlund said from the far left corner.

"We have an important guest," Blomberg said, shoving Annika farther into the room, then stepping inside and pulling the door shut after him.

The minister of culture lit a lighter—a weak light illuminated the shed, the shadows cast across her nose and eyes made her look monstrous. Yngve the alcoholic was next to her, Göran Nilsson leaning against the wall to the right. On the wall beside him hung a picture of Chairman Mao.

Annika could feel panic rising at the sight of the murderer, the characteristic itch in her fingers, giddiness and numbness.

Calm down, she thought. Don't hyperventilate. Hold your breath.

Karina bent down and lit a small candle at her feet, put the lighter down, then stood up holding the candle.

"What's this?" she said, looking at Blomberg. "Why have you brought her here?"

She put the candle on a piece of rusty machinery that may have been the old compressor. Their breath hung like clouds around each of them.

I'm not alone, Annika thought. This isn't the same as the tunnel.

"May I present," Blomberg said, "Miss Annika Bengtzon, snooping reporter from the *Evening Post*."

Karina started and stepped back a step.

"Are you mad?" she said in a loud voice. "Bringing a journalist here? Don't you understand what you're exposing me to?"

Göran Nilsson looked at them, his eyes cloudy and tired.

"This isn't for outsiders," he said, surprisingly sharply. "Panther, what on earth are you thinking?"

Blomberg, alias the Black Panther, pulled the door firmly shut behind him and smiled.

"Miss Bengtzon already knows about us," he said. "She was standing outside, so I couldn't let her run around telling anyone."

Karina stepped closer to Blomberg.

"It's all ruined now," she said in a shrill voice. "Everything I've worked for for all these years. Damn you all."

She picked up her bag and turned toward the door, and Göran Nilsson stepped into the small circle of light. Annika could see no sign of a weapon. The man's face was sunken and drawn; he looked weak and ill.

Yet Karina still stopped midpace, frightened and uncertain.

"Wait," he said to the minister, then turned to Blomberg. "Do you accept responsibility for her? Do you guarantee the safety of the group?"

Annika stared at the killer, noting his shabby appearance and slow sentences, as if he had to search for the words before he found them.

"No problem," the archivist said enthusiastically. "I'll take care of her afterward."

Annika felt her feet turn to lead and her body grew heavy. Inside her she heard a pleading, whimpering sound grow, but it never reached her throat.

The Yellow Dragon looked straight at Annika; she daren't even breathe.

"Stand in the corner," he said, pointing.

"We can't have a reporter here, surely you can understand that," Karina said animatedly. "I won't agree to that."

The Dragon raised a hand.

"That's enough now," he said. "Our group commander bears the responsibility."

He put his hands in his pockets.

The gun, Annika thought.

"It's very cold today," he said. "I shall be brief."

Yngve the alcoholic stepped forward.

"Great," he said, "but has anyone got something to drink?"

Blomberg undid the top button of his jacket, and from his inside pocket he pulled out a bottle of Absolut. Yngve's eyes lit up, his lips parting in rapture, and he took the bottle as gently as if it were a baby.

"I thought we might have a little celebration," Blomberg said, nodding encouragingly.

Yngve unscrewed the cap with tears in his eyes, Annika looked down at the floor and wriggled her toes to stop them from going stiff.

What were they going to do with her?

It's not like the tunnel, it's not like the tunnel.

Karina put her bag down on the floor again.

"I don't understand what we're doing here," she said.

"Your power has made you impatient," Göran Nilsson said, looking at the minister with his dragon's eyes, pausing until he had everyone's full attention. Then he tilted his head back and looked up at the ceiling.

"I am very aware that some of you were surprised to get my call," he said. "It's been a long time since I gathered you together like this, and I appreciate that it aroused mixed feelings. But there's no need for you to be scared."

He looked straight at the minister of culture.

"I'm not here to harm you," he said. "I'm here to thank you. You became the only family I had, and I say that without any sentimentality."

"So why did you kill Margit, then?" Karina said, her voice tight with fear.

Göran Nilsson shook his head, his Yellow Dragon head, his divine, stinking, ruler's head.

"You're not listening," he said. "You're just talking. You weren't like this before. Power really has changed you."

Blomberg took a pace forward, apparently tired of the lack of focus.

"Tell me what I should do," he said to his leader. "I'm ready for armed struggle."

Göran Nilsson turned to him, sorrow in his eyes.

"Panther," he said, "there won't be any armed struggle. I've come home to die."

The archivist's eyes opened wide, an imbecilic expression spreading across his face.

"But you're back now," he said. "You're here again, our leader, we've been waiting years. The revolution is near."

"The revolution is dead," the Dragon said harshly. "Capitalist society that treats human beings like cattle has won, and with it all the false ideologies: democracy, freedom of expression, justice before the law, women's rights."

Blomberg listened devoutly, Karina Björnlund seemed to shrink with every word, and the alcoholic was completely absorbed in his newfound bottle of bliss.

"The working class has been reduced to a brainwashed horde of cretinous consumers," he said. "There's no desire to improve things anymore. The false authorities herd people into the meat grinder without a word of protest."

He fixed his eyes on Karina.

"The authorities use people up, now as then," he said, his voice clear and steady. "They wring us out like dishcloths and then they throw us away. This is how it has always been, but today it is governments elected by the people that permit the buyers of labor to exploit us until we break. I have accepted that this is the case, and I have fought against it in my own way. Revolution?"

He shook his head.

"There'll never be any revolution. Humanity has bartered it for Coca-Cola and cable television."

Blomberg stared at him, his eyes blank and bewildered.

"But," he said, "that's not true. You're back, and I've been waiting so long. I've trained all these years, just as you said, and I'm ready. It isn't too late."

Göran Nilsson raised his hand.

"I have very little of my life left," he said. "I have accepted my personal condition, and the condition that we are all in together. Fundamentally, there is no difference between me and the lies of the bourgeoisie. I shall live on through my children, and in return I give them their inheritance."

He staggered, clutching his stomach.

"No one will be able to exploit you anymore," he said. "Your days on the hamster wheel are over."

"What do you mean?" Karina said, seeming less scared now.

"He's going to give us presents," Hans said, his voice echoing with astonished disbelief. "It's Christmas for all of us! Or perhaps some postfuneral coffee? The revolution is dead, didn't you hear?"

"Stop it, Hasse," Karina said, taking hold of his arm. "Mao's dead too, and even China is capitalist now."

"You believed as well," Hans said. "You were a revolutionary too."

"But, good God," she said, "we were nothing but children. Everyone believed in the revolution. That was just the way things were back then, but that all vanished long ago."

"Not for me!" Hans Blomberg shouted, and Göran Nilsson took an unsteady step toward him.

"Panther," he said, "you've misunderstood me."

"No!" the archivist yelled, his eyes red and moist. "You can't do this to me. The revolution is the only thing that matters."

"Pull yourself together," Karina Björnlund said, shaking the archivist's arm in irritation, and with an angry tug the man pulled himself free from the minister of culture. The next moment he raised his clenched right fist and punched her hard in the face.

Someone screamed—it could have been the minister or the alcoholic or Annika herself—and then the furious archivist turned to face Göran Nilsson and shoved him with all his strength against the wall with the poster of Mao. The Yellow Dragon fell to the concrete floor with the audible crack of breaking bone, and a hissing sound as the air went out of his lungs.

"You goddamn traitors!"

Blomberg's voice was breaking. He gathered himself and leaped for the door, throwing it open with a crash and slamming it behind him with the same force.

The candle flame flickered but did not go out; the shadows slowly stopped dancing about.

"I'm bleeding," the minister shouted from the floor behind the compressor. "Help me!"

Then silence settled heavily and the cold grew even harsher. Annika could hear the archivist cursing through the brick wall as he disappeared toward the railway line. She went over to Göran Nilsson; he was unconscious by the wall, his right foot twisted at an unnatural angle. His right leg looked a bit shorter than the left. Yngve the alcoholic stared drunkenly and unsteadily at his leader lying there on the floor, his face almost completely colorless and his teeth chattering. Karina struggled to her feet, holding a hand to her face; blood was trickling between her fingers and down onto her fur coat.

"My nose is broken," she howled. "I have to get to the hospital."

She started to cry, then stopped because it was too painful.

Annika went over to the minister, put a hand gently on her arm.

"It's all right," Annika said, inspecting the woman's face behind her hand. "It'll heal okay."

"But what if it's crooked?"

Annika turned away and went back to the man slumped on the floor. He really did smell unbelievably bad, the stench of something severely diseased.

"Göran," she said loudly. "Göran Nilsson, can you hear me?"

Without waiting for a response she leaned over, taking off her gloves, and pulled the man's gun from his pocket, it was heavy and ice cold. With her back to the others she slipped it quietly into one of the outer pockets of her polar jacket; she knew nothing about revolvers and tried to convince herself that the safety catch must surely be on.

The Yellow Dragon groaned out loud, his pale eyelids flickering. She put her hand on the frozen cement floor to see how cold it was, sweat making her fingers stick to it at once. Shocked, she pulled them away.

"You can't lie here," she told the man, "you have to get up. Can you stand on your leg?"

She looked up at Karina.

"We've got to get out of here," she said. "This place is worse than a freezer. Can you help me carry him?"

"But I'm wounded," the minister of culture said. "And why should I help him? After all he's done to me. Can't Yngve carry him?"

The alcoholic had sat down on the floor clutching the half-empty bottle in his arms.

"You can't fall asleep here," Annika said to Yngve, feeling reality letting go of her; the ice-cold room was threatening to strangle her.

"If you knew how much I've suffered over the years," Karina said from over by the compressor. "Always afraid that someone would let on that I knew these fools. But that's what happens when you're young, isn't it? You think a load of crazy things, get in with the wrong crowd?"

Göran Nilsson tried to sit up but let out a little cry and slumped back on the concrete floor.

"Something's broken in my hip," he whispered, and Annika remembered her grandmother's broken hip that winter when there was so much snow.

"I'll go and get help," Annika said, but a second later the man was holding her wrist in a viselike grip.

"Where's Karina?" he muttered, his eyes unfocused.

"She's here," Annika said quietly and wriggled loose in horror, standing up and turning to the minister. "He wants to talk to you."

"About what? We've got nothing to say to each other."

Karina's upper airways had swollen, making her voice sound thin and nasal. She took a few cautious steps toward the man and Annika could see that her nostrils were bleeding badly. Her face was bruised and swollen, from her lips right up to her eyes. Annika met her gaze, reading in it all the bewilderment that she herself was feeling, and inside her a small light went on: she wasn't alone, she wasn't alone.

"Keep him company," Annika said, and the minister went hesitantly over to the terrorist, but as she leaned over him he screamed.

"Not blood," he panted. "Take the blood away."

Something short-circuited in Annika's head. There he was, the mass murderer, the professional hit man, the full-time terrorist, and he was whining like a crybaby. She flew over to him and grabbed him by the coat.

"So you don't like the sight of blood, you bastard? But killing all those people, that was all right, was it?"

His head fell back and he closed his eyes.

"I'm a soldier," he said flatly. "I am nowhere near as guilty as the leaders of the free world."

She felt tears welling up.

"Why Margit?" she said. "Why the boy?"

He shook his head.

"Not me," he whispered.

Annika looked up at Karina, who was standing in the middle of the floor, a look of shock on her face.

"He's lying," she said. "Of course it was him."

"I only strike at the enemy," Göran Nilsson said flatly. "Not against friends or the innocent."

Annika stared at the man's pain-racked face, his apathy, and she suddenly knew that he was telling the truth.

It wasn't he who murdered them. There was no reason for him to kill Benny Ekland, Linus Gustafsson, Kurt Sandström, or Margit Axelsson.

So who had done it?

She was shaking. She stood up on numb legs and walked unsteadily toward the door.

It was shut. Stuck fast, immovable.

She remembered the lock on the outside, and realization hit her like a physical blow.

Hans Blomberg had shut them in.

She was locked inside a freezer with three other people; it was 30 degrees below zero, two of them were wounded and the third was blind drunk.

Hans Blomberg, she thought. Is that remotely possible?

And the next moment the tunnel was over her again, the pipes stretching along the ceiling; she could feel the weight of the dynamite on her back, and somewhere in the distance a woman was crying, snorting and howling with pain and despair and she realized that it was the minister of culture, Karina Björnlund, and she wasn't alone, she wasn't alone.

She let go of the tunnel and grabbed hold of reality; she mustn't fall apart—if she fell apart she would die.

It's so cold, she thought—how long can you survive in this sort of cold?

Her breathing calmed down.

She was in no immediate danger herself. In her polar outfit she could last the night if need be. The minister had her fur coat, but the men were worse off.

The drunk's eyelids were already drooping; he wouldn't last another hour. The terrorist had better clothes, but was lying directly on the cement floor, which was like a block of ice.

We have to get out of here. Now. How?

Her cell phone!

She let out a small noise of triumph as she fumbled in her pocket and pulled out her phone.

No reception.

She held it up in the light of the candle, trying it in every corner of the room.

Not a trace of a signal, fucking Tele2.

She pressed 112 anyway. Nothing happened.

Don't panic.

Think.

The minister had a phone. Annika had called her on it just a couple of hours before.

"Your number starts with six," she said to the minister. "That means you're with Telia. See if you can get reception."

"What?"

"Your phone! You've got a cell phone on you, I called you, didn't I?"

"Oh, right."

The minister carefully searched in her black leather bag, pulled out her cell phone and switched it on with PIN codes and a lot of loud puffing, then held it up in the air.

"I haven't got any reception," she said in surprise.

Annika put her hands over her face, feeling the cold bite at her skin.

It's all right, she thought. I've already called the police, they should be here any minute.

She studied the minister; the woman was bruised and shaken. She looked toward the alcoholic: in the flickering candlelight his lips looked dark blue. He was shaking with cold in his thin jacket.

"Okay," Annika said, forcing her head to think rationally. "We are where we are. Is there any sort of blanket here? A tarpaulin, any insulating material?"

"Where did Hasse go?" Yngve said.

"Did he lock the door?" Karina asked.

Shaking, Annika did a circuit of the dusty little building: a few rusty tins, a lot of dirt, and a rat's skeleton.

"He can't have locked the door," the minister of culture said, going over to try it for herself. "Göran has the key."

"You can just click a padlock shut," Annika said. "So what is this place, anyway?"

She felt the walls, saw that the windows were sealed shut with coarse wooden planks nailed from the inside, and remembered the metal shutters outside.

"It's been derelict for forty years," Karina said. "My father was on the railway; he brought me here as a child."

"What's it for?"

"It was a compression room; they blow the points free from snow and ice with air pressure. They built a new one when they rerouted the railway. How are we going to get out?"

"Are there any tools anywhere?" Annika asked.

"We're stuck," Karina Björnlund said, her eyes now so swollen that they were almost completely closed. "God, how are we going to get out?"

She wouldn't find any forgotten tools, Annika realized; they would have been removed years ago. The walls were of solid concrete, and the door couldn't be forced.

"We have to keep moving," she said. "We have to keep each other warm."

She gulped, feeling panic creeping up on her.

What if the police didn't come?

What if Karlsson in Central Control had forgotten her?

She shook off the thought and went over to the rancid-smelling man below the Mao poster. His breathing was shallow and rattling, a string of saliva hanging from his mouth.

"Göran," Annika said, crouching down next to him and struggling against the stench. "Göran Nilsson, can you hear me?"

She shook his shoulder and the man looked up at her with vacant eyes, his bottom lip shivering with cold.

"*J'ai très froid*," he whispered.

"*Je comprends*," Annika said quietly, and turned to the minister. "Karina, come and sit next to Göran. Put your arms around him and wrap him in your fur."

The minister of culture backed away until she reached the corner behind the compressor.

"Never," she said. "Never in a million years. He's done me so much harm."

Annika looked at the man beside her, his waxy, pale skin, his shaking hands.

Maybe she should let him die?

Wasn't that what he deserved?

She left Göran Nilsson and went over to the man leaning against the wall.

"Yngve?" she said. "Is your name Yngve?"

The man nodded, had pushed his hands up into his armpits to keep them warm.

"Come here," she said, opening her polar jacket. "Come and stand next to me. We're going for a walk."

He shook his head firmly and clutched the almost empty bottle.

"Okay, don't then," Annika said, closing the jacket and looking over to the minister.

"He's got a gun," Karina Björnlund said. "We can shoot our way out."

Annika shook her head.

"The door's made of steel. The bullets would ricochet around the room and kill all of us. Besides, we'd have to hit the padlock on the outside to get out."

"What about the windows, then?"

"Same thing."

Should she say she'd told the police?

How would they react?

"I knew it would turn out like this," Karina said with a moan. "This whole Beasts thing has been a nightmare right from the start. I should never have gone with them when they left the Communist Party."

The minister of culture dug in her bag and pulled out a black garment, it might have been a T-shirt, which she held up to her nose.

"Why not?" Annika said, watching the minister's shadow dance across the wall as she moved around behind the candle.

"I don't suppose you had even been born in the sixties," Karina said, glancing at Annika. "It can't be easy for your generation to understand what it was like, but it was actually fantastic."

Annika nodded slowly.

"I can imagine," she said. "You were young. Göran was the leader."

The minister nodded eagerly.

"He was so strong and clever," she said, "he could get anyone to go along with him. All the girls wanted to be with him, all the boys looked up to him. But I should have walked away when he was thrown out. It was stupid to go along with his idea for the Beasts."

Karina Björnlund lost herself in memories for a moment; Annika watched her with increasingly clear eyes.

"How come you never got caught?" Annika asked.

The minister looked up.

"Well," she said, "I never actually did anything, and Göran was very thorough. We only communicated through symbols, a forgotten old language comprehensible to anyone, across borders, races, cultures."

"So no minutes of meetings?" Annika asked.

"Not even letters or phone calls," Karina Björnlund said. "We were summoned to meetings by a drawing of a yellow dragon. A day or so later came a combination of numbers giving the day and time of the meeting. 23-11-17 meant November 23, at five o'clock. Now, in other words."

"You each had a symbol?"

The woman nodded carefully, still holding the T-shirt to her nose.

"But only the Dragon could call a meeting."

"And at the end of October you got the call again, in an anonymous letter to the department?"

A flicker of fear crossed the minister's eyes.

"It took a few seconds before I realized what I was looking at, and when I did I had to go out and throw up."

"Yet you still came," Annika said.

"You don't understand," the minister said. "I've been so scared all these years. After F21, when Göran disappeared, I got a warning in the post . . ."

She hid her face in the T-shirt.

"A child's finger," Annika said, and the minister looked up in surprise.

"How do you know?"

"I spoke to Margit Axelsson's husband, Thord. The symbolism was crystal clear."

Karina nodded.

"If I didn't keep quiet then not only would I die, but any children I might have in the future, and those close to me."

Göran Nilsson groaned on the floor, moving his left leg in agitation.

Annika and the minister of culture looked at him with empty eyes.

"He's been stalking me," Karina said. "One night he was standing outside my house in Knivsta. The next day I saw him behind a display in Åhléns in Uppsala. And on Friday I got another letter."

"Another warning?"

The minister closed her eyes for a few moments.

"A drawing of a dog," she said, "and then a cross. I had an idea of what it might mean, but daren't actually take it in."

"That Margit was dead?"

Karina nodded.

"We don't have any contact with each other anymore, of course, but I spent the whole night thinking, and in the morning I called Thord. He told me that Margit had been murdered and I understood exactly. Either I came here, or I would die as well. So I came."

Looked up at Annika, taking the T-shirt from her nose.

"If you knew how scared I've been," she said. "How much I've suffered. Being terrified every day that someone would find out about all of this—it's poisoned my whole life."

Annika looked at her, this powerful woman in her thick fur, the girl who had hung out with her cousin, first sports, then politics, who got together with the leader of the gang, strong, charismatic, but then finished with him when he lost his power.

"Shutting down TV Scandinavia to sweep it all under the carpet was a huge damn mistake," she said.

Karina Björnlund looked at her like she hadn't understood what she'd just heard.

"What do you mean?" she said.

"I've got the email that Herman Wennergren sent you; I know why you changed the culture proposal."

The minister of culture got to her feet and took three quick steps over to Annika, her swollen eyes narrow slits.

"You, you shitty little gutter reporter," she said, her bloody face right in front of Annika's. "Who the hell do you think you are?"

Annika didn't back down, and looked into her bloodshot eyes.

"Don't you know?" she said. "We've spoken before. A long time ago, almost ten years now."

"I don't remember."

"I contacted you for a comment about Christer Lundgren's trip to Tallinn the night Josefin Liljeberg was murdered. I told you what had happened to the lost archive at IB. I told you the government was being blackmailed to conduct illegal weapons exports, and I asked you to pass on my questions to the trade minister, but you didn't go to him—you went to the prime minister, didn't you?"

Karina had turned white as Annika spoke, staring at her like she'd seen a ghost.

"That was you?" she said.

"You used the information to get a cabinet post, didn't you?"

The minister of culture gasped loudly, suddenly coloring again.

"How dare you?!" she yelled. "I'll sue you for this."

"I've only got one question," Annika said. "Why are you getting so upset?"

"You come here and make terrible insinuations like that? Am I supposed to have called the prime minister in Harpsund and forced my way into a ministerial post?"

"Oh," Annika said. "So you got hold of him out at Harpsund? How did he react? Was he angry? Or is he really as pragmatic and rational as people say?"

Karina Björnlund fell silent, her eyes bulging.

A moment later the silence was shattered by Yngve's empty bottle hitting the cement floor and splintering into a thousand pieces. The alcoholic slid, unconscious, down the wall and slumped on the floor.

Annika stopped focusing on the minister of culture and ran over to Yngve.

"Hello!" she shouted, slapping him lightly on the cheek with her glove. "Up you get!"

The man blinked.

"What?" he said.

She tugged open her coat, grabbed the man by the armpits and dragged him to his feet.

"Hold on to me," she said, wrapping the polar jacket around him at the same time as she clasped her arms around his back. The man breathed warmly and damply against her neck; he was so skinny that she could almost fasten the coat behind his back.

"Can you move your feet? We have to keep moving."

"You won't get away with this," the minister of culture said, but Annika paid her no attention, putting all her effort into getting the drunk to shuffle across the floor in a macabre and ice-cold dance.

"Which one are you?" Annika said quietly to Yngve. "Lion or Tiger?"

"The Lion of Freedom," the man said through chattering teeth.

"So where's the Tiger?"

"Don't know," the drunk muttered, almost asleep.

"He had the sense not to come," Karina said. "He always was the smartest one of us."

Suddenly, over by the wall, Göran Nilsson moved, attempting to get up, kicking with his good leg, his eyes staring as he tried to take his jacket off.

"*C'est très chaud*," he said, lying down again.

"Put your coat back on," Annika said, straining to go over to him, but the alcoholic had his arms around her and wouldn't let go.

"Listen to me, Göran, put your coat on."

But the man slumped beneath the poster of Mao, his legs jerked spasmodically before settling, and he fell asleep. His chest was fluttering lightly under his ivory-colored linen shirt.

"You've got to help him," Annika said to Karina. "At least put his coat back on."

The woman shook her head, and at that moment the candle went out.

"Light it again," Annika said, hearing the fear in her voice.

"It's burned out," Karina said. "There's no wick left."

And with the darkness came silence; the cold grew sharper and drier.

Annika opened her eyes wide but could see absolutely nothing, she was hovering in an empty, ice-cold space, and was struck with a sense of utter and immense loneliness. Surely nothing in the world could feel worse than this. Anything but isolation.

"We have to keep moving," Annika said. "Karina, don't stand still."

But Annika heard the minister sink to the floor, and a muffled and uncontrollable attack of sobbing rose from the corner.

The woman was crying, wailing, drooling, and Annika and Yngve were moving ever slower in the ice-cold freezer. She held the shivering man in her arms, feeling his limbs getting heavier and heavier, his breathing more and more strained, and she tightened her grip, her arms rigid.

Responsibility for others, she thought, staring into the darkness. Nothing without each other.

And Ellen's and Kalle's soft faces appeared in front of her; she could feel their silky smooth warmth and sweet smell.

Soon, she thought. I'll soon be with you again.

The minister of culture gradually calmed down, her sobbing dying away.

The silence that followed was even deeper than before.

It took a few seconds before Annika realized why.

Göran Nilsson had stopped breathing.

The thought sent sparks through her mind; her fingers itched like mad; a sound emerged: *panic.*

A moment later Yngve slumped in her arms, his legs gave way beneath him and his head fell on her shoulder.

"Shit!" she screamed in the man's ear. "Don't die. Help, someone, help!"

She didn't have the strength to hold the man upright; he slid into a heap at her feet and she was hit by a complete blackout.

"Help!" she screamed at the top of her voice. "Help us, someone!"

"There isn't any help," Karina said.

"Help! Annika shrieked, fumbling forward to where she thought the door was, and walked right into the compressor, her knee striking the metal. "Help!"

Somewhere behind her she heard muffled voices and for a moment feared she was about to suffer a new onslaught from the angels. Talking, cries, the voices were definitely human, and a moment later came a sharp knocking sound.

"Hello?" a male voice called from the other side of the wall. "Is there someone in there?"

She spun around and stared into the darkness in the direction the voice had come from.

"Yes!" she screamed, falling over Yngve. "Yes! We're in here. We're locked in. Help us!"

"We'll have to cut the padlock off," the man said. "It may take a while. How many of you are there?"

"Four," Annika said, "but I think one man is dead. Another is on the point of falling asleep; I can't keep him awake. Hurry!"

"I'll get the tools," the voice said. Then Karina Björnlund came back to life.

"No!" the minister shouted. "Don't leave me! I have to get out, now!"

Annika found her way over to Yngve where he lay on the floor, breathing shallowly. She stroked his rough hair, clenching her jaw, then lay down on the floor and pulled the man on top of her, wrapping the polar jacket around them both.

"Don't die," she whispered, rocking him as though he were a child.

And she lay like that until she heard the cutting torch break the lock and the door was pulled open, and a flashlight was shining right in her eyes.

"Take him first," Annika said. "I think he's about to give up."

A moment later the man was lifted off her, put on a stretcher, and floated out of her line of vision in just a couple of seconds.

"What about you? Can you stand?"

She peered up at the light, could see nothing but the silhouette of a policeman.

"I'm okay," she said, and stood up.

Inspector Forsberg looked at her anxiously.

"You'll have to go to the hospital and get checked out," he said. "When you feel like talking I want to speak to you down at the station."

Annika nodded, suddenly mute. Instead she pointed at Göran Nilsson, noting that her hand was trembling.

"You're so frozen you're shaking," Forsberg said.

"I think he's dead," she whispered.

The paramedics returned and went over to Göran Nilsson, checked his breathing and pulse.

"I think he broke his leg," Annika said. "And he's ill; he said he was going to die soon."

They put him on a stretcher and carried him quickly out of the building.

Karina stepped out from the shadows, leaning on a paramedic. Her face had dissolved in tears, her nose still bleeding.

Annika soaked up her swollen look and stored it away.

Karina stopped right next to her and whispered so low that no one else could hear.

"I'm going to say everything myself," she said. "You can forget all about your exclusive."

And then the minister went out to the floodlights and police cars and ambulances.

Inspector Forsberg had a cramped, messy office on the second floor of the yellow brown monstrosity that was the police station. Annika was dozing off on one of the chairs, but gave a start and sat up straight when the door flew open.

"Sorry you've had to wait. No milk or sugar," the police officer said, putting a steaming hot plastic cup in front of her on the desk, then went around and sat on his swivel chair.

Annika picked up the cup, burning her hands and blowing on the drink. She took a cautious sip.

Machine coffee, the worst sort.

"Is this an interrogation?" she asked, putting the cup down.

Forsberg looked through a drawer without answering.

"Witness questioning, I suppose we should call it. Where the hell have I put it? There it is!"

He pulled out a little tape recorder and mess of cables, straightened up, looked Annika in the eye and smiled.

"You're not too frozen, then?" His gaze held hers.

She looked away.

"Oh, I am," she said. "But I learned to dress properly the hard way. How are the others?"

"Ragnwald is dead, like you thought. Yngve Gustafsson is in intensive care, his body temperature was down to 28 degrees. He'll make it though. Did you know he was the father of Linus, the boy who was killed?"

Annika looked up at the police officer, a lump in her throat, and shook her head.

"And Karina Björnlund?" she said.

"She's having her face patched up, and she's got frostbite in her feet. So what happened?"

He leaned forward and switched on the tape recorder.

"Okay," she said, "do you want the full story?"

He looked at her thoughtfully for a few moments, then looked away and pulled out her personal details.

"Witness questioning of Annika Bengtzon," he said, "of Hantverkargatan 32 in Stockholm; location, questioner's office, conversation begins . . ."

He looked at his watch.

"... at 10:15 PM. How did you come to be in an abandoned compressor shed near Swedish Steel in Luleå this evening?"

She cleared her throat toward the microphone, which was standing on a memo from the National Police Commissioner.

"I wanted to interview the minister of culture, Karina Björnlund, and happened to catch sight of her at Kallax Airport, and I followed her."

The inspector looked at her and smiled.

"Interview her?" he said. "What about?"

She tried to smile back but discovered that she was too exhausted.

"The imposition of the new library regulations," she said.

He sat in silence, pondering her reply for several seconds, then leaned over and switched off the tape recorder.

"Better now?" he said, blinking flirtatiously.

She nodded and reached for the plastic coffee, prepared to give it another chance.

"What happened?" he said

"Just so we get this straight from the start," she said, sipping the drink again and suppressing a grimace, before putting the cup down for good. "I'm a journalist. All my sources are protected by law. You represent an official authority and you would be breaking the law if you made any attempt to find out what I know and who I learned it from."

He stopped smiling.

"And I have a case to solve. Can you tell me why you came to Luleå in the first place?"

"I was here on a job," she said. "I got it into my head to call the minister of culture and ask her about her connection to Ragnwald, and I could hear that she was at Kallax Airport, so I drove off to find her."

"Why?"

"She didn't want to discuss anything over the phone, if I can put it like that."

He nodded and jotted something down.

"And the minister of culture went for a walk in the woods next to the railway and you followed her?"

Annika nodded.

"I drove to Lövskatan, my rental car is still there."

Forsberg reached for a sheet of paper and read it with a frown.

"I've got a report here," he said, "which says that a person with your name called Central Command at 5:12 PM and said that someone we've been looking for was in a brick building, location unknown, near a viaduct. Does that ring any bells?"

"The guy on the phone wasn't exactly Einstein," Annika said, realizing that her whole body was still cold in spite of the ministrations of the hospital staff. "I tried to explain to him as best I could, but the elevator didn't go all the way up."

The inspector studied the report.

"The caller, in other words, you, is described as incoherent and hysterical."

Annika looked down at her hands, dry, chapped, and red, and didn't respond.

"How were you able to identify Göran Nilsson?"

She shrugged slightly without looking up.

"Karina called him Göran, and I knew they were together once upon a time."

"And the revolver you handed to us—he gave that to you of his own free will?"

"I took it out of his pocket when he collapsed on the floor . . ."

All of a sudden she had had enough, stood up and walked nervously around the room.

"I've been digging into this story for a couple of weeks now; everything just fell into place. Have you found Hans Blomberg?"

She stopped in front of Forsberg with her hands on her hips. The police officer paused for a moment before turning away.

"No," he said.

"It was Blomberg who locked us in."

"So I heard," Forsberg said. "As well as the story about the Beasts, and the plane getting blown up at F21."

"Can I go now? I'm shattered."

"We'll have to talk to you in more detail, about what was said and exactly what happened in that shed."

She looked at the police officer from the end of a long tunnel.

"I don't remember anything else," she said.

"Rubbish," he said. "You're going to tell me what you know before you leave."

"Am I being arrested?" Annika asked. "Suspected of some crime?"

"Of course not."

"Right, then," Annika said. "I'm leaving."

"I'm ordering you to stay."

"So lock me up," Annika said, and walked out.

She took a taxi out to Lövskatan to pick up her car, and paid with the paper's credit card, one of the few perks she had been able to keep since she voluntarily stopped being an editor.

As the taxi rolled away she was left standing there, infinite space above her, listening to the rumble of the steelworks.

She had hardly thought about Thomas all day. One of the nurses had called to tell him that she had been taken in for observation in Luleå Hospital, which wasn't quite true: she had just been examined and released, but she wasn't complaining. It wouldn't do him any harm to think she was ill.

She took a deep breath, the air crackled like sandpaper in her throat.

The light around her changed; she lifted her face to the sky and saw a veil drift across the moon, and the next moment a fireworks display went off above her head, the likes of which she had never seen.

From horizon to horizon, a bow of pale blue light stretched across the sky, moving in sweeping ripples, splitting into cascades of luminous colors over the whole sky. She stood there gawking at it.

Pink, white, swirling and twisting, colors and lights and stars tumbling over one another, getting brighter and then dissolving.

The northern lights, she thought, and a second later the sky began to crackle.

She gasped and took several steps back, surrounded by sparkling space.

A streak of purple merged with a semicircle of green, the two playing around each other, cracking and sparking and vibrant.

It's a strange world up here, she thought. When the earth is frozen solid the sky starts singing and dancing.

She laughed quietly, a soft and unfamiliar sound.

It had been a very peculiar day.

She clicked open the lock, climbed in and put the key in the ignition. The engine protested but decided to cooperate, and she found an ice scraper in the glove compartment, got out and cleared the ice and frost from all the windows. Got in again, turned the headlights on full.

There was a glow at the top of the hill where Karina Björnlund had disappeared earlier. On the horizon she saw a ribbon of pink light flicker and die, and suddenly remembered the transformer box and the duffel bag.

Less than a kilometer away, she thought.

She put the car in first gear and drove slowly up the road, as the ball bearings in the wheels protested. She went past the No Vehicles sign, under the power lines, past the Skanska building and the empty parking lot. The track got narrower and narrower, she crept along as the headlights played over scrub and craggy snowdrifts.

She put the car in neutral and pulled on the hand brake shortly after the viaduct, climbed out and walked toward the box.

There was a handle, and a sliding bolt. Hesitant, she took hold of the frozen metal, twisted, and pulled.

The door opened and the duffel bag fell out at her feet.

It was heavy, but not as unwieldy as it had looked when Göran Nilsson was dragging it behind him.

Annika looked around, feeling like a thief in the night. Nothing but the stars and northern lights. Her breath hung white around her, making it hard to see when she crouched down.

Whatever this might be, it was Ragnwald's bequest to his children. He had gathered them together to read them his will. She held her breath and untied the large knot holding the bag closed, then stood up with it.

She peered into it, heart pounding, saw nothing, reached in her hand and found a box of Spanish medicine. She put it carefully on the ground, reached in for the next thing.

A bottle of large yellow pills.

Göran Nilsson had been heavily medicated toward the end.

A packet of suppositories.

A box of red-and-white capsules.

She sighed and reached in one last time.

A five-centimeter-thick bundle of notes.

She stopped and stared at the money, as a light wind blew eerily through the trees.

Euros. 100-euro notes.

She looked around her, the sky was flaming, blast furnace number two over at the ironworks was roaring.

How much?

She pulled off her gloves and ran a finger over the notes, new notes, entirely unused, at least a hundred of them.

One hundred 100-euro notes.

Ten thousand euros, almost one hundred thousand kronor.

She pulled on her gloves again, leaned over and pulled out two more bundles.

She folded down the sides of the bag and looked openmouthed down at its contents.

Nothing but bundles of euros, dozens of them.

She pressed the bag, trying to work out how many layers there were inside.

A lot. An absurd number.

Then she felt sick.

The executioner's death-tainted bequest to his children.

Without reflecting anymore about it she picked up the bag and threw the money into the trunk of the car.

The glass internal doors of the City Hotel slid open with a swishing sound. Annika walked into the candelabra-lit space, blinking against the light.

"I think she's just walked in," the receptionist said into a telephone behind the counter. "Annika Bengtzon?"

Annika looked at the young woman.

"It is you, isn't it? From the *Evening Post*? We spoke when you were here two weeks ago. I've got your boss on the phone."

"Which one?"

The woman listened.

"Anders Schyman," she called across the lobby.

Annika hoisted her bag onto her shoulder and walked over to the desk.

"Tell him I'll call him in five minutes, I just need to check in."

Ten seconds of silence.

"He says he wants to talk to you now."

Annika reached for the receiver.

"What do you want?"

The editor in chief sounded muted and clenched when he spoke.

"The newspaper's telegram agency has just sent out a news flash that the police in Luleå have cracked a thirty-year-old terrorist cell. That the attack on a Draken plane at F21 has been cleared up, that an international hit man has been found dead, and that a suspected terrorist is still at large."

Annika glanced at the receptionist's inquisitive ears, turned around and stretched the cord as far as she could.

"Goodness," she said.

"It says you were there when the hit man died. That you were locked up with some of the terrorists. That Minister of Culture Karina Björnlund was one of the members. That you alerted the police so that they could be arrested."

Annika shifted her weight from one foot to the other.

"Oops," she said.

"What are you planning for tomorrow?"

She glanced at the receptionist over her shoulder, noting from her gold-colored name badge that her name was Linda.

Linda was sorting some papers from one pile to another, trying hard to look as though she wasn't listening.

"Nothing, of course," she said. "I'm not allowed to write about terrorism—that was a direct order. I obey my orders."

"Yes, yes," the editor in chief said. "But what are you writing? We've torn up everything we've got, all the way to the center spread."

She clenched her jaw.

"Not one single line. Not in the *Evening Post*. I've got a hell of a lot of material, but because you've forbidden me to gather it, then of course I won't be using it."

There was a short, astonished silence.

"Now you're being silly," he eventually said. "That would be a very bad miscalculation on your part."

"Sorry," she said, "but who's responsible for the miscalculations on this story?"

Silence echoed along the line. She knew the editor in chief was fighting against a justifiable instinct to tell her to go to hell and slam the phone down, but with an entirely empty news section he couldn't afford to.

"I'm on my way to bed," she said. "Was there anything else you wanted?"

Anders Schyman started to say something, but changed his mind; she could hear his breathing over the line.

"I've had some good news today," he said, trying to sound conciliatory.

She swallowed her derision.

"Oh?" she said.

"I'm going to be the new chair of the Newspaper Publishers' Association."

"Congratulations."

"I knew you'd be pleased," he said. "Why aren't you answering your cell phone, by the way?"

"There's no coverage up here. Good night."

She handed the phone back to the receptionist.

"Can I check in now, please?"

The door of the elevator was heavy, Annika had to strain to push it open. She stumbled out onto the fourth floor, the thick carpet swallowing her steps.

Home, she thought, home at last.

Her business-class room was off to the left; she set off toward it. The hotel corridor was tilting slightly from side to side, she had to put her hand out to steady herself against the wall twice.

She found her room, pushed the card in, waited for the little bleep and the green light.

She was greeted by a gentle hum, and narrow slivers of light creeping around the closed curtains, her safe haven on earth.

She shut the door behind her; it closed with a well-oiled click. She let her bag slide to the floor and switched on the main light.

Hans Blomberg was sitting on her bed.

She froze to ice, her body utterly rigid; she couldn't breathe.

"Good evening, young lady," the archivist said, pointing a pistol at her.

She stared at the man, his gray cardigan and friendly face, trying to get her brain to work.

"What a long time you've been. I've been waiting for several hours."

Annika roused her legs and took a step back, fumbling behind her for the door handle.

Blomberg stood up.

"Don't even think that thought, my dear," he said. "My trigger finger is terribly itchy tonight."

Annika stopped and let her arm drop.

"I can believe that," she said, her voice high and very thin. "You haven't hesitated so far."

He chuckled.

"How true," he said. "Where's the money?"

She leaned against the wall for support.

"What?"

"The money? The Dragon's bequest?"

Her brain rattled into action, her thoughts rushing in a torrent; the day ran past in images and emotions and conclusions.

"Why do you think there's money, and why would I know where it is?"

"Little Annika the Amateur Detective who creeps around the bushes, if anyone knows, it's you."

The man approached her with an ingratiating smile; she stared up at his face.

"Why?" she said. "Why did you kill those people?"

He paused, and leaned his head to one side.

"But this is war," he said. "You're a journalist, haven't you noticed? The war on terror? That must mean armed struggle on both sides, don't you think?"

He chuckled contentedly.

"It wasn't my idea," he said, "but suddenly it was legitimate to eliminate dictators and false authorities, and there are lots of those around the world; they're everywhere."

He looked at her and smiled.

"As a journalist, Annika," he said, "you'll be familiar with the old adage, 'dig where you stand.' There are stories everywhere, why cross the river to fetch water? The same thing applies to false authorities—why look further than you have to?"

"And Benny Ekland was one of them?"

Blomberg took a few steps back and sat down on the bed again, waving with the pistol to indicate that she should sit at the desk. She obeyed, moving through air as thick as cement, and dropped her polar jacket beside the chair.

"You haven't quite understood," the archivist said. "Hans Blomberg is just my alias. I'm really the Black Panther, I've never been anything else."

He nodded to emphasize his words, as Annika searched feverishly for a loose thread, something that could make him unravel.

"That isn't strictly true," she said. "You've tried to fit in as Blomberg as well, haven't you? All those articles about the county council that were always published at the bottom of page twenty-two—was that it?"

A flash of anger crossed his face.

"A way of maintaining my façade until the Dragon came back. He promised, and his return was the signal."

Then he smiled again.

"Benny made sure I ended up in the archive. Not that I'm bitter, because of course I won in the end."

Annika forced back a feeling of nausea.

"But why the boy?"

Blomberg shook his head sorrowfully.

"It was a shame that he had to go, but war claims many civilian casualties."

"Because he recognized you? You used to see the family socially, didn't you?"

Blomberg didn't reply, merely smiled gently.

"Kurt Sandström?" Annika said, fear pounding at her midriff, putting pressure on her bladder.

"False authority," he said. "A traitor."

"How did you know him?"

"From Nyland," Blomberg said. "The big lad on the next farm; he was one year older than me. We were at Uppsala together, and joined the movement at the same time. But Kurt's faith was weak, and he drifted over to the side of capitalism and exploitation, to the farmers' movement. I gave him a chance to change his mind, but he chose his own fate."

She was holding on to the desk.

"And Margit Axelsson?"

Blomberg sighed, adjusting the hair across his scalp.

"Little Margit," he said, "ever lovely, trying to make the world a better place. She always meant so well. A shame she was so loud and obstinate."

"And that's why you strangled her?"

"She deserted."

Annika shifted on the chair and felt that she would have to pee soon.

"So tell me," she said, "why did you blow up the plane?"

The man gave a small shrug.

"It was really just a test," he said. "Of the Dog's loyalty."

"And she did as she was told?"

He chuckled at the memory.

"She was so angry about the Wolf leaving that she would have done anything. The Dog was so disappointed, but you know what girls are like. Popular little Karina was only interested in fucking whomever all the others wanted."

"But," Annika said, "why were they getting married, if that was the case?"

The archivist laughed out loud.

"You really fell for that," he said. "The marriage announcement: I made it up there and then, wanted to give you something to chew on. And, my word, you did chew, didn't you?"

He calmed down and nodded thoughtfully, and Annika stood up.

"I have to go to the toilet," she said.

Blomberg was on his feet with the same speed she had seen when he attacked the minister of culture in the compressor shed.

"Not a chance."

"Then I'll wet myself."

The man stepped back, but hit the bed.

"Go on, then, but no tricks. Leave the door open."

She did as he said, went into the bathroom, pulled down her trousers and underwear, and peed so hard that it splashed.

She looked at herself in the mirror, and in her eyes she could see what she had to do.

If she stayed in the room she would die. She had to get out, even if that meant taking Blomberg with her.

"Who's the Tiger?" she asked as she walked back into the room, concealing her intentions behind dull eyes.

Something needy and lustful had lit up in the archivist's eyes; he was staring at her crotch.

"Kenneth Uusitalo," he said. "Departmental manager at Swedish Steel. A really great guy, active in the Manufacturers' Association; negotiates slave contracts with the Third World. Unfortunately he's been away for a while."

He licked his lips.

Annika went over to the desk again, and leaned over it.

"But really," she said, "you're not much better yourself. You're only after Göran's money."

He flew up like a shot, raced across the room, and pressed the pistol to her forehead.

"For being sarcastic," he said, taking the safety catch off, and she felt fear loosen her bladder and let out the few drops that were in there.

"Good luck with the treasure hunt," she croaked, her mouth completely dry.

He stared at her for a few seconds, then pulled the gun away from her head, pointing it at the ceiling.

"What do you know?"

"I'm not sure," she said, "but I saw Göran Nilsson put a duffel bag in a transformer box next to the railway. Could that be it?"

She gulped audibly; the man raised his eyebrows.

"Oh," he said, "so it's suddenly time to tell the truth, is it?"

"Can I sit down?"

He moved so that he had her in his line of fire as her knees gratefully lowered her onto the chair.

"Where exactly is this box?"

She struggled for air for several seconds.

"Not far from the viaduct," she said. "There's a little clump of pine trees right next to it."

"How come you saw that?"

"I was following Karina, hiding, and I saw Göran put the bag inside the cupboard."

The archivist went up to her, put his hand around her neck, breathing right in her face and staring into her eyes.

"Well, well," he said. "I do believe you're telling the truth. Put your coat on."

Blomberg backed toward the door.

"I'll have the pistol in my pocket the whole time. If you try anything you won't be the only one: you'll be taking the girl in reception with you to Hades. Understood?"

Annika nodded, pulling on her polar jacket.

They stepped out of the room, the corridor was tilting and swaying. In the elevator the archivist stood very close to her; she could feel his chest against her breasts.

"How did you know where I'd be staying?" she asked, looking up at his face.

"Your charming boss told me—I think his name was Jansson?"

The elevator stopped with a jerk.

"I shall be walking right behind you," the archivist said. "If you're a good girl, then the little lady in reception will get a chance to grow up."

He moved even closer to her, his hands sliding into her coat pockets and down toward her crotch.

She kicked the door to open it.

He quickly withdrew his hands from her pockets, and in one hand he was holding her cell phone.

"Nice and quiet, now," he whispered.

They stepped into the lobby; Linda the receptionist came out from the kitchen, talking on the phone, and smiled warmly at them.

Ring the police, Annika tried to tell her telepathically, staring at her with fire in her eyes, ring the police! Ring the police!

But the young woman waved to them and went back into the room behind reception with her phone.

"And out we go," Blomberg whispered.

The cold tore at her skin, and she felt the pistol at her back again.

"And so to the right," the archivist said. She turned and walked unsteadily along the pavement; they passed her rental car with Ragnwald's millions in the trunk. Blomberg pulled her by the arm and steered her toward an old Passat that was parked outside a bookshop.

"It isn't locked," he said. "Jump in."

Annika did as he said; the car seat was ice cold; the man walked around the car and got in the driver's seat.

"Where did you steal this one?" Annika asked.

"Porsön," Blomberg said, hot-wiring the ignition.

They drove toward the water and turned off to follow the railway.

For the third time that day Annika drove through the industrial development on Lövskatan.

"How did you get into my room?" she asked, staring into the rearview mirror, behind them, a long way back, she caught sight of a distant but growing point of light.

The archivist laughed slightly.

"A little hobby of mine," he said. "I can break into anything. Anything else you'd like to know?"

She thought, shut her eyes and swallowed.

"Why did you change the way you killed them each time?"

He shrugged, braked at the opening of the narrow track with the NO VEHICLES sign, craned his neck and peered through the windscreen.

"I wanted to try things out," he said. "At our training camp in Melderstein in the summer of 1969 the Dragon appointed me his supreme commander. I was the one who would lead the armed struggle; we practiced different forms of attack, different ways to take a life, all summer. Over the years I kept up my interest and my education. How far do we drive?"

"To the viaduct," Annika said, glancing in the mirror again, the light was closer now. "Margit Axelsson received a warning after the Dragon disappeared—did you get one as well?"

The archivist laughed again, louder this time.

"But, dear girl," he said, "I was the one who sent them. They all got one."

"Whose fingers were they?"

"A little boy who had been killed in a car accident," Blomberg said. "I broke into the mortuary and cut them off. There's no need to worry; he didn't miss them."

She looked out of the window until she could talk again.

"But why start killing them now?" she said, looking at him. "Why did you wait so long?"

He glanced back at her and smiled.

"You're not listening," he said. "The revolution is here. It was going to start when the Dragon returned. He promised that before he left, and now he's back."

"Göran Nilsson is dead."

Blomberg shrugged.

"Ah well," he said with a sigh. "All false authorities die sooner or later."

He pulled up, put the car in neutral and pulled on the hand brake, leaving the stolen car running. He turned to look at Annika, suddenly serious and thoughtful.

"The Dragon promised that he would come back, and I knew it was true. I waited all those years. Of course I've had moments of doubt, but I'm the winner in the end."

"Do you really believe that?" Annika said.

He slapped her across the face with the flat of his hand.

"So now we go out and find the box," he said, reaching over her to open the passenger-side door, his hand pausing on her stomach.

She heaved herself out, taking a quick glance backward.

Not yet time.

She turned toward the box and pointed.

"There."

"Open it."

She walked slowly forward, lead weights around her feet.

It won't work, she thought. I can't do it.

She listened behind her, thought she could hear the dull rumble, not yet, but soon.

She took hold of the handle, tried to twist, pulled, used both hands, pulled even harder, braced her feet on the ground, and groaned loudly.

"I can't get it open," she said, letting go.

The light was close now, the whistling sound was very clear, merging with the distant rumble of the steelworks. Soon, soon, soon.

Blomberg walked over, annoyed.

"Get out of the way."

Holding the pistol in his right hand, he grabbed the handle with his left, gathered his strength, then pulled. The door flew open, the man's eyes opening wide as he leaned over and stared into the darkness, and Annika shrugged off her heavy jacket and ran.

She threw herself down onto the track, slipping on the railroad ties, running with lead weights tied to her ankles, shouting without hearing.

A bullet flew past her left ear, then another, and then she was bathed in the full glare of the diesel locomotive's headlight; the driver pulled the whistle but it was too late—she was already across. She collapsed on the other side and the train thundered past her with its endless cargo of ore truck after ore truck after ore truck, forming a wall of iron one kilometer long between her and Hans Blomberg.

She got to her feet and ran and ran and ran toward the noise, toward the glowing red eyes at the top of blast furnace number 2. She scrambled up a steep slope and over a mountain of coal, knives tearing at her lungs, and down below the turning circle was spread out and in the distance the sign, West Checkpoint.

TUESDAY, NOVEMBER 24

Thomas put the evening papers down on the desk before he took off his coat and hung it up on a hanger. He glanced at the desk over his shoulder as he hung the hanger on the back of the door. Annika's solemn face stared up at him from the front page of the *Evening Post*, the new byline from after the Bomber, with her looking older and sadder.

"Evening Post Reporter CRACKED TERRORIST GANG," the headline screamed, and his pulse started to race as he sat down and ran a finger over her face.

His wife, the mother of his children, was unique, and not only in his eyes.

He opened the paper: articles about how Annika's investigations had cracked the Norrbotten terrorist cell took up half the paper.

Across the first news spread inside, pages 6 and 7, there was a night picture, taken from a plane, of the Gulf of Bothnia, with someone running within an illuminated circle of light, and the caption: *Terrorist hunt at sea tonight—serial killer tracked by helicopters with thermal cameras.*

A long article described how a single man from Luleå had murdered at least four people in just the last few weeks. Journalist Annika Bengtzon had sounded the alarm at the West Checkpoint of Swedish Steel; the police had sealed off the Lövskatan district, forcing the man out onto the ice. Fortunately police helicopters were already fitted with thermal-imaging cameras, because they had been searching for a missing three-year-old the year before. He glanced through the article, then moved on.

The next spread described how Annika had been locked in an abandoned compressor shed beside the railway in Luleå with members of the terrorist cell, the Beasts, and how she had managed to alert the police before she was captured, and how she had saved the life of pensioner Yngve Gustafsson by keeping him warm with her own body heat.

Thomas felt a jolt in his genitals at that sentence, and had to swallow, he stopped reading and looked at the pictures.

A nice picture of Annika in the newsroom.

Below that was a photograph taken with a flash, of a little red brick building.

His wife could have died there.

He ran a hand through his hair and loosened his tie.

Annika had escaped the killer by throwing herself in front of an iron-ore train, and had run for a kilometer to Swedish Steel and sounded the alarm at the West Checkpoint. The article had been written by a reporter, Patrick Nilsson; Annika herself was interviewed and just said she was fine and that she was glad it was all over.

He breathed out hard. She was mad—what on earth was she thinking? How could she put herself in such a dangerous situation when she had him and the children?

They had to talk about this—she couldn't carry on like this.

The following pages were full of Minister of Culture Karina Björnlund's story of how she was lured to join the Beasts, a Maoist group in Luleå in the late 1960s. After Björnlund left the group it went to pieces and turned to violence, something she deeply regretted. The minister tried to describe the spirit of the times, a desire for justice and freedom that spun out of control. The prime minister welcomed her honesty, and was giving her his full backing.

The truth about the story of the attack on F21 filled the next two pages: the serial killer now in custody had thrown one of the military's own flares into a container of surplus aviation fuel and thereby caused the explosion.

He skipped the article once he'd read the introduction and captions.

The next two pages covered the hit man Ragnwald, one of ETA's most ruthless terrorists, who had evaded the world's police and security services for three decades. He had frozen to death in the compressor shed while Annika and the others had looked on, powerless to help.

He looked at the grainy photograph of a young man, dark and skinny, with nondescript features.

Then Annika was back again, a brief summary of her work and achievements, not unlike the one published after the Bomber, but now including the night in the tunnel as part of the past.

He put the palm of his hand over her face and shut his eyes.

Strangely, he thought he could feel warmth from the newspaper.

A moment later the phone rang, and he picked it up with a smile.

"I have to see you," Sophia Grenborg said, sobbing loudly. "Something terrible has happened. I'm on my way up to you now."

For a moment he was caught up in her panic, his throat constricting, terrorists, hit men, people frozen to death.

Then everything fell into place: Sophia's terrible things were not Annika's. He cleared his throat and looked at the time, trying to think of an excuse not to see her.

"There's a committee meeting in quarter of an hour," he said, blushing at the lie.

"I'll be there in five minutes."

She hung up and he was left sitting there with an unidentifiable summer tune in his head.

On Friday she had been happy as a lark, because she was going to be in an article in *County Council World*. They had asked her what she wanted for Christmas.

"I said you," she had whispered, then kissed him on the ear.

He looked at the front page of the *Evening Post*, one of the biggest papers in Scandinavia, his serious-looking wife uncovering a group of terrorists. She was changing reality, while he and his colleagues were trying to tame it and administer it; she was making a difference while he was putting up smoke screens.

The telephone rang again, an internal call from reception.

"There's someone here to see you."

He stood up and stared out across the churchyard below, frosted and frozen. He rolled his shoulders in an attempt to shake off the disquiet, the clamminess, the feeling of reluctance and obligation.

A few seconds later Sophia Grenborg stumbled into his room, red with crying, her nose puffy and swollen. He went over and helped her take off her coat.

"I don't understand what's happened," she sniffed, pulling a handkerchief from her bag. "I don't know what's got into them."

He stroked her on the cheek and tried to smile.

"What's happened?"

She sank onto a chair, holding the handkerchief to her mouth.

"Management want to move me," she said, breathing unevenly. "Clerk in the traffic safety department."

She lowered her head, her shoulders began to shake. He shuffled his feet a couple of times, bewildered, then leaned over her, paused.

"Sophia," he said. "Oh dear, come on, poor you . . ."

She stopped, looking up at him in genuine confusion.

"After all the work I've done," she said. "I've put everything into this job for five years. How can they downgrade me like this?"

"Are you sure it isn't a promotion?" he said, sitting down on the desk and putting his hand on her back.

"Promotion?" she said. "I'm losing my project management bonus, and I have to clear my room this afternoon and move out to an open-plan office in Kista, and I won't even have my own desk."

Thomas rubbed her shoulders, looking down at her hair, breathing in the smell of apples.

"What reason are they giving?"

Sophia started to cry again, he stood up and pushed the door shut properly.

"Come on, love," he said, crouching down and stroking the hair from her face. "Tell me what happened."

She pulled herself together and wiped her nose.

"We'll sort this out," he said. "Tell me."

"They called me in for a meeting," she said. "I was really pleased. I thought I was going to join the congress group, or maybe one of the committees, but instead this happened."

"But," Thomas said, "why?"

She shook her head.

"They said it was part of the reorganization ahead of the merger with you, and then they sent me out. Thomas, I don't understand. What's going on?"

He kissed her on the forehead, stroked her hair, looked at his watch.

"Darling," he said, "I have to get to my meeting, and I don't have any contacts in the Federation . . ."

The words hung in the air; she looked at him, wide-eyed.

"Can't you pull any strings?"

He patted her cheek.

"Well, I can always try. You'll see, this will all sort itself out."

"Do you think so?" she said, and stood up.

He followed her, breathing in the scent of her apple hair.

"Absolutely," he said, getting her coat.

She kissed him gently before turning around and letting him put her coat on.

"Can't you come over tonight?" she whispered into his neck. "I could cook something Italian."

He felt the sweat break out between his shoulder blades.

"Not tonight," he said quickly. "My wife's home. Haven't you seen the paper?"

"What?" she said, opening her damp eyes wide. "Which paper?"

He walked away from her, went over to the desk and held up the front page of the *Evening Post* toward her. Annika's dark, unseeing eyes stared at them.

"Cracked terrorist gang," Sophia read in astonishment and disbelief. "What does your wife do, exactly?"

Thomas looked at his wife as he replied.

"She used to be head of the crime desk, but that took too much time from the family. Nowadays she's an independent reporter, looking into official corruption and political scandals. She's been working on this terrorism case for the last few weeks."

He put the newspaper down, the picture facing upward, noting the pride in his voice and behavior.

"She was supposed to come back yesterday, but this came up instead. She's flying home this afternoon."

"Oh well," Sophia said. "I can understand that you're busy tonight."

She left without saying anything else, and he was surprised at how genuinely relieved he felt when she had gone.

Annika was staring at the countryside outside the window of the Arlanda Express; frozen fields and icy farms rushed past without her really seeing them. Her eyes were fixed, it felt like they were full of grit and gravel.

The night had disappeared as she had weighed up and analyzed different options and their consequences, piecing together the facts and formulating her argument.

Now the article was in her notepad, ready to be printed.

Home, she thought. It doesn't have to be a place or a house, it's something else entirely.

She shut her eyes and thought through her decisions one more time.

One: the text would be published.

Two: she had lived in the building on Hantverkargatan for ten years. That didn't mean that her home was there. Thomas had never really liked living in the city, for him it would come as a relief.

You have to win, she thought. You have to be stronger. You

can't give your opponent a chance. She must not be an alternative. Thomas will never pick a loser.

Her phone started to vibrate in the inside pocket of the polar jacket; she pulled it out and saw it was Q, calling from his private number.

"Congratulations," the head of the national crime unit said.

"What for?" Annika said.

"I heard you got your cell phone back."

She smiled weakly.

"From your lads up in Luleå. Blomberg had it in his trouser pocket when they caught him out on the ice. What can I do for you today?"

"I was wondering about something," he said. "It's this business of the money."

"What money?" Annika said.

"Ragnwald's money. A bag full of euros."

Annika watched blue-paneled industrial units fly by at 160 kilometers an hour.

"Don't know what you mean," she said.

"How did you find it?"

She shut her eyes, swaying with the movement of the train.

"I was just out taking a walk. I stumbled across a bag of money that someone must have dropped. I handed it over to the police as lost property. Anything else you're wondering?"

"That's Ragnwald's life's work," the commissioner said. "He killed people for money all his life and never used a franc to make his life easier, and because of that he was never caught. He collected it all in his doctor's safety deposit box in Bilbao and took it all out one month ago."

Annika looked through the window again.

"Goodness," she said. "I wonder what happened to it?"

"Perhaps he dropped it? In a transformer box, perhaps?"

"Perhaps, but I don't suppose we'll ever know."

The commissioner chuckled, admitting defeat.

"Do you know how much it was?"

"I'd guess about 12 million."

"Almost 14; 128 million kronor."

"Wow."

"No one has reported the money as missing. If the owner doesn't come forward within six months, it goes to the person who found it."

"But?" Annika said.

"But," Q said. "Because the chief prosecutor in Luleå suspects that the money was the result of criminal activity, he's considering impounding them."

"That's bad luck," Annika said.

"But hang on a moment, I haven't finished. So that you don't fight for the money, the prosecutor has decided to give you the customary ten percent finder's reward."

The carriage, and the world, suddenly went very quiet. Annika saw a shopping center and a garden center swirl past.

"Really?" she said.

"You'll have to wait six months. Then it's yours."

She did the calculations in her head, stumbling over the zeros.

"What happens if someone claims it?"

"They'd have to describe the object the money was in when it was found, describe roughly where it was found, and naturally how they came to be in possession of it. Are you fond of money?"

"Not particularly," Annika said. "It's really only exciting when you haven't got any."

"True enough."

"By the way," Annika said, opening the newspaper on the seat beside her. "Who said Blomberg blew up the plane at F21?"

"He did, he confessed to it. Why? Do you know otherwise?"

Annika saw Thord Axelsson in front of her, his face turned gray by lifelong secrets.

"No, no," she said quickly, "I was just wondering how it all fitted together . . ."

"Hmm," Q said, and hung up.

She was left sitting there with her phone, weighing it in her hand.

Twelve point eight million.

Kronor. Almost 13 million kronor.

Thirteen.

Million.

In six months.

Was anyone likely to claim the money? Could anyone? Who could describe the bag it was found in, the place it was found?

Ragnwald and her. No one else.

And who was going to stick their hand up and say: the serial killer's money is mine?

Thirteen million kronor.

She rang Anne Snapphane.

"What was the apartment on Artillerigatan like, then?"

Anne sighed, only just awake.

"What time is it?"

"Quarter past something. Was it stylish, then?"

"Pure pornography, I had an orgasm the moment I entered the building."

"Put in an offer. You can borrow four million from me. I've found a load of money."

"Hang on, I need a pee . . ."

Annika heard the receiver hit Anne's bedside table out on Lidingö, as she watched the inner city rear up with its brick buildings and traffic-packed streets, swirling traffic fumes and processions of human lemmings.

"This train will reach Stockholm Central in three minutes," a metallic voice announced.

Annika pulled the polar jacket up over her shoulders.

"What did you say?" Anne said, back on the line. "You found a load of money?"

"Well, I'm not exactly going to broadcast the fact, but around about midsummer I'm going to get a reward of several million for handing it in. You can have four of them to help you move to Östermalm."

She bit her lip, waited. No one needed to know exactly how much she was going to get.

There was a clattering sound on the line.

"You're mad, you do know that, right?"

The train slowed down, the rails fanning out as it approached the station.

"Okay," Annika said. "Then I'll buy it and you can rent it from me."

"Look," Anne said. "I can't let you do this."

Annika stood up, hoisting her bag onto her shoulder.

"You haven't read the papers, then?"

"You woke me up."

"It says in the *Evening Post* that Karina Björnlund isn't planning to resign, she wants to carry on as a minister."

"What are you talking about?"

"That's wrong," Annika said, bracing against for the jolt as the train stopped. "She'll resign tomorrow."

"What? Why?"

"I've got to go . . ."

She ended the call, jumped down onto the platform and walked back toward the Kungsbron exit. The air was cold, but still milder and softer than in Luleå; she filled her lungs greedily. The bag slapped against her back; the ground was solid and even.

She would do some shopping, write up the article, email it to Schyman, and pick up the children early. They would have time to bake something and rent a film and watch it together as they waited for Daddy. Maybe some potato chips, just this once, and a big bottle of cola. Have a meal with an appetizer, homemade béarnaise sauce, and a dessert.

She emerged onto Kungsbron, and walked off toward Fleminggatan. The angels in her head were completely quiet. The space they had occupied was now available for real thoughts, but right now she was using it to take a break from thinking.

Maybe they were gone for good.

Maybe they were only hiding for a while.

The most important thing is having somewhere to belong, she thought.

Thomas stepped off the bus outside their door and looked up at the façade.

There were lights on in all their windows; he could see an Advent star and a Christmas candlestick in the living-room window, and felt a warm, soft glow in his chest.

It was good to have her home again.

He flew lightly up the stairs, rang the bell cheerily before opening the door, and was met with the children's happy cries, he could hear them before he even stepped into the apartment.

"Daddy!"

They leaped into his arms and showed him drawings and told him about outings and the film they had watched which was really good, they asked about the computer, and Mommy had given them chips, and cola, and Ellen had made the salad and Kalle had made a Swiss roll with buttercream that they were going to have for dessert.

He hung his coat up, put his briefcase to one side, loosened his tie, and went into the kitchen.

Annika was frying steak; had opened the window a little to let out the smell.

"Oh good, you're here," she said. "We're ready to eat."

He went over and put his hands on her shoulders, kissed her neck and pressed his crotch hard against her buttocks, wrapping his arms around her.

"You need to be careful," he whispered. "Don't you realize how precious you are to us?"

She turned around, looked up into his eyes, kissed him gently.

"I've got something good to tell you," she said. "Sit down."

He sat down at the table, already laid for dinner, poured some mineral water and looked around for the morning paper.

"I've found a house," she said, putting the sizzling frying pan on the designer trivet. "In Djursholm. Newly built, only 6.9 million."

He looked up at her, at her blushing cheeks.

"What?" he said.

"Sea view," she said, "so you'll be able to see the sea again. Vinterviksvägen, do you know where that is? Big garden with fruit trees, oak floors throughout, open-plan kitchen and dining room, Mediterranean mosaic in both bathrooms, four bedrooms."

Her eyes were excited and glowing, but there was something dark and mysterious swimming about in there, and he felt an inexplicable chill run down his spine.

"How can we afford that?" he said, staring at the basket of bread, then picked up a slice and took a bite from it.

"Ellen and Kalle, it's ready!" she called out into the hall, and sat down opposite him. "I found a load of money: I'm going to get a huge reward."

He took the slice of bread out of his mouth and looked up at her.

"What do you mean, found?"

She smiled into his eyes without blinking.

"Seven million."

He stopped chewing and frowned.

"Found?"

"A sack of money."

"Money?"

She smiled and nodded.

"That's crazy," he said, putting the bread down. "Really?"

"I have to head over to the paper for a while after dinner," she said, and helped herself to a baked potato.

"That doesn't matter," he said. "I'll sit up and wait."

She leaned over and stroked his hair and cheek.

"Don't," she said.

"Seven million," he said. "Where did you find it?"

The children rushed into the kitchen, fighting over who was going to sit next to Annika.

"I'll tell you later," she mimed.

"And we'll make a huge profit on the apartment as well," he said.

She stood up to get the sauce, and he had a sudden giddy sense of incomprehensible reality. She was a little green woman from another planet. There was nothing soft or malleable or negotiable about her; she was simply her own solid core.

The next thought hit him from out of the blue.

There's no one else like Annika.

The realization made his throat tighten, with something that might have been happiness.

Annika was sitting outside Anders Schyman's office and felt like she was falling. She was gliding slowly down the wall and had long since passed the basement. The sounds from the newsroom were muffled and thin; the day crew had gone home and the evening gang were still waking up; the recessed lighting in the corridors was throwing irregular dancing shadows across the floor.

Her workplace. A context in which she belonged.

"You can go in now," Schyman's secretary said as she emerged from her alcove with her coat on and locked the door.

Annika stood up shakily, walked into the editor in chief's office and shut the door firmly behind her.

The editor in chief was sitting at his desk, staring at a printout. His face was red, and his neck looked sweaty.

She took several tentative steps forward, glancing at the printout. It was her article, of course. She sat down, her back stiff and straight.

"What are you playing at?" he said without looking up, trying to sound derisive but concerned.

She stared at him, the feeling of falling still within her, her tiredness throbbing.

"I've written an article that's going to be printed in the paper tomorrow," she said in a voice that lacked all emotion.

He picked up a pen and tapped it against the printout.

"It will hardly come as news to you that I am legally responsible for what gets published in this paper," he said. "The decision on whether or not the article gets published is down to me."

She swallowed hard.

"And?"

"And I'm saying no," he said.

"Then I'll take it elsewhere."

"You can't," Schyman said.

"Of course I can," she said quickly. "The *Worker* wouldn't say no. They published Vilhelm Moberg's articles about corruption in the legal system in the fifties; they'd snap up the article like a shot."

"I forbid it."

"Freedom of expression," Annika said. "Ever heard of that? The free world, democracy? If my employer—the *Evening Post* in this instance—says no to an article I've written, then I have the right to offer it to someone else."

She felt her pulse quicken; the air was full of his doubt and repudiation. There were several seconds of silence.

"I had a very unpleasant conversation today," he said. "Who's Sophia Grenborg?"

The floor opened up beneath her, she gasped as all color drained away.

"What do you mean?" she said.

"How do you know her?"

"She's my husband's . . . colleague."

"Aha," Schyman said, a glint in his eyes. "So she worked with your husband. Closely?"

Thoughts swirled, spinning and dancing.

"Did she call you?" Annika said, and heard how shaken she sounded.

"No," Schyman said, "not her, but her boss at the Federation of County Councils. Do you know what I'm talking about?"

She shook her head, her mouth dry.

"They're saying you called and made insinuations about this woman to various departments within the Federation. Is that correct?"

Annika took a deep breath.

"I had a tip-off," she said.

Anders Schyman nodded and looked down at his desk, tapping his pen again.

"Okay," he said. "You got a tip-off that this woman had fiddled her tax, used to be a right-wing extremist, and had exaggerated her expenses?"

Annika squeezed the arms of the chair; this conversation wasn't exactly turning out as she had imagined.

She nodded.

"How closely did she work with your husband?"

"Not too close; they were in the same working group."

"Much overtime?" Schyman said, leaning toward her. "A lot of late nights?"

Annika stretched her neck.

"Some," she said.

The silence in the room grew thick and heavy; she gulped audibly.

"They've seen through you at the Federation of County Councils," the editor in chief said slowly. "I just thought you should know. They realized that you were just trying to throw mud at her. But they're letting her go anyway. Do you know why?"

Annika stared at Schyman, shaken and confused—they were letting her go? She's been fired? She's disappearing?

"They're merging with the Association of Local Councils in the spring," the editor in chief said, his voice utterly cold. "They daren't risk a dirt-throwing campaign in the *Evening Post* right now, would do anything to avoid it, in fact. A crisis of confidence in the Federation would sabotage the merger they've spent four years preparing for."

The editor in chief could sit still no longer and stood up to pace the room, then leaned over her.

"Do you imagine I don't understand? She got too close to your husband, didn't she? How close? Were they fucking in your bed?"

She put her hands over her ears and shut her eyes.

"Stop it!" she shouted.

"How dare you?" he shouted back at her face. "How dare you exploit your position here at the paper for your own sordid purposes?"

She let her hands drop, her eyes opening wide.

"You're a fine one to talk," she said in a cracked voice.

His face was quivering with rage and fury; he stared into her eyes as though he were trying to find an explanation.

"You're not going anywhere with that article," he said eventually, then stretched and walked back to his desk. "The moment that text leaves this building I'll report you to the police."

She felt her brain explode, and flew up, setting her face ten centimeters from his, and saw him flinch.

"Okay," she said hoarsely. "I'll be fine. Because you know what? I'm right. I can't lose."

He was dumbfounded.

"I see," he said. "What will you say to your husband when the police arrest you for grave defamation and arbitrary conduct? How will he react when he finds out why she was fired? Who will get custody of your children? And what do you think will happen to your job? Surely you don't imagine you can stay here if you publish that article in the *Worker*?"

Annika felt the adrenaline pumping, tore her eyes away from him and walked giddily around the desk, stopping right in front of him.

"And what do you think will happen to you?" she said in a low voice. "Do you think you'll still be sitting at this desk after I explain how it all happened, including your threat to crush me because of my desperate attempt to save my marriage? Do you imagine that you'll have an ounce of credibility left once you block an article that reveals the worst abuse of media power in modern times? How you've exploited unpublished information about a minister obtained by the paper in an attempt to blackmail her into destroying a business competitor? And what about the Newspaper Publishers' Association? Do you imagine for a moment that you'll get to be chair? You're finished, Schyman. I might go down with you, but you're going to fall a hell of a lot harder."

He stared at her; she felt her eyes burning and returned his gaze.

There was something dark and unfathomable in there, shadows of desire and ambition and social conscience, in an unholy and powerful alliance, a pure and conscious awareness that had been shaped and misshaped by time and experience. When thoughts and problems were poured into the editor in chief's head, they didn't run smoothly in straight lines. They jolted and twisted along the tracks carved by previous experiences, but their path was still logical.

Schyman was a pragmatist. He would do whatever was required for him and his pet project to escape as unscathed as possible.

She suddenly had to smile.

"So what would happen if we ran the piece?" he said quietly, doubt rising behind his larynx.

She felt her eyes calm down.

"The *Evening Post* reinforces its position as the last outpost of freedom of expression," she said, "stifling any doubts about what we stand for these days. We alone stand for truth and democracy. Without us the barbarians would run amok."

"Thin," he said.

"Depends entirely on how we present it," Annika replied. "People will believe us if we believe it."

He had to sit up, and reached for a bottle of mineral water, drank some, and looked at her under his brow.

"You're bluffing," he said, once he had put the bottle down. "You'd never do this to the paper."

Annika thought for a moment.

"Not before," she said, "but I won't hesitate now."

"You've gone mad," Schyman said.

She sat down on the desk, rested her elbows on her knees, put her hands together and leaned forward.

"Do you know," she said quietly, "you might well be right, but only you and I know that. If you try to stop me publishing this because you think I'm mentally ill, you'll make things even worse."

He shook his head.

"If I were even to contemplate publishing this, I'd be finished, utterly finished," he said. She could hardly hear him.

"But don't you see how wrong you are?" Annika said. "If we get this right you can sit at that desk forever, completely untouchable."

He looked at her, the abyss dancing inside him, a battle of shadows.

"Just think," she said, feeling her eyes narrow. "We tell it exactly how it is, the whole story: how we discovered that Karina Björnlund was a member of a terrorist cell, how I told you, you told the chairman of the board; he sent an email to the minister and demanded an urgent meeting—I've got the register number of the email—how he exploited what we knew, you and me, to blackmail the minister into changing a government proposal in order to close down a television channel that posed a threat to the interests of our proprietors. But now we're revealing the truth, in spite of the danger; you had the nerve to do it; you're legally responsible for what we publish, and you're the chair of the Newspaper Publishers' Association, and you took your responsibility, in spite of all the pressure."

"It won't work," he said quietly.

She gave a thin smile.

"Yes, it will," she said, "and you know why? Because it's true."

"It isn't worth the risk," he said.

"If this isn't," she said, "then what is? What are we for? To provide a dividend on our proprietors' shares, or to protect democracy?"

"It's not that simple," he said.

"You're wrong," she said. "It's precisely that simple."

She stood up, picking up her bag and hanging it on her shoulder.

"I'm going now," she said.

"But it was only a crap American commercial channel," he said.

"That doesn't make any difference," she said.

She saw the air go out of him as he slumped back.

"Wait," he said, holding up one hand. "Don't go yet. You're not serious?"

She swayed a little.

"Yes, I am," she said.

Silence spread out around her, large and heavy and dark. She stood there, halfway to the door, and looked at him, saw the doubts and various alternatives coursing through him.

"The owners would have the whole edition withdrawn," he said.

"True," she said.

"This mustn't leak out," he said.

"No, it mustn't," she said.

"So we can't run this through the newsroom."

She didn't reply, allowing the dizzying conclusions to settle in his head.

"All the work will have to be done in here," he went on. "That means you and me. Can you do layout?"

"More or less."

He shut his eyes, and covered them with his hands for a few seconds.

"How many pages are we talking about?"

"Four spreads," she said. "Plus the front and the leader."

He sat silent, thinking, for an infinitely long minute before he spoke.

"I'll call the printers and tell them to shift half the news section."

"Extra pages?"

"Two plates is enough," Schyman said, "eight pages."

"Is there anyone we can trust to keep quiet at the printers?"

"Bob. He can set the plates. How quick are you with Quark?"

She dropped her bag on the floor.

"Not very."

She looked at his eyes; concentration had drawn a veil of decisiveness and determination over them. The shadows had stopped dancing, and were lining up ready to march.

"It's going to be a long night," he said.

"I know," she said.

ACKNOWLEDGMENTS

This is fiction. I want to emphasize that all events and characters are entirely and only the product of my own vivid imagination. Like everyone else, however, I have memories, experiences, and impressions that I make use of as I find necessary.

I spend a lot of time on research for my books. Even though every line is fiction, I take care that the details of places, activities, and phenomena that do exist in the real world should be as accurately described as possible. This means that people sometimes recognize some elements, which is entirely proper. Everything in this book *could have* happened.

However, I sometimes make use of the author's prerogative to change details of existing bus routes, the location of certain compressor sheds, the use of various sites, etc.

The interior of the Norrbotten Air Base, which is closed to the public and must not be photographed or otherwise documented, is my own invention.

Neither the *Evening Post* nor the *Norrland News* exists, but they bear traces of many different actual media organizations. *Katrineholms-Kuriren* does exist, however, but all references that my characters make to the newspaper and its organization are completely fictitious.

Both the Swedish Association of Local Councils (*Kommunförbundet*) and the Federation of County Councils (*Landstingförbundet*) exist, but I would like to point out that I in no way claim to be providing a documentary depiction of the employees or inner workings of these organizations.

A project aimed at threats to politicians, involving among

others the Association of Local Councils and the Federation of County Councils and the Department of Justice, did actually take place during 2003 and 2004, but Thomas's working group and its members, methods, discussions, and consequences are entirely imaginary.

This is, in other words, a novel, and it could not have been written without Torbjörn Säfve's incisive analysis of the rebel movement in his book *Rebellerna i Sverige* (Författarförlaget 1971; The Rebels in Sweden)—thank you Jan, for the tip, and Matthias, for finding a copy in a secondhand bookshop in Vadstena!

Further essential reading was provided by Björn Kumm's documentation and summary of the history of terrorism in the book of the same name (*Terrorismens historia*, Historiska media; I have editions published in 1997, 1998, and 2002).

I would also like to thank the following, without whose tolerant assistance this project would never have been successfully completed. They are:

Dan Swärdh, theatrical manager of *Teater Scratch* in Luleå, and a dormant Maoist going by the code names of "Greger" and "Mats," who initiated me into both the public and hidden activities of Maoist groups in Luleå in the early 1970s.

Mikael Niemi, author and old acquaintance from Pajala, for discussions of the backgrounds of various characters, and for an introduction to Læstadianism in the Torne Valley.

Christer L. Lundin, public relations manager of Teracom, who provided information about the technical and political development, marketing, and situation of digital television, and with whom I discussed and analyzed the consequences and plausibility of various fictitious political decisions.

Stefan Helsing, public relations manager of the Norrbotten Air Base, F21, in Luleå, for facts and discussions concerning the history of the base and scenarios of possible attacks.

Anders Linnér, public relations manager for the Air Force, for discussion of the political and military complications surrounding an attack against a military target, and for information regarding flying routines and the security arrangements of air bases.

Peter Svensson, personal adviser to the Supreme Commander of the Swedish Armed Forces, for ongoing invaluable collaboration.

Thorbjörn Larsson, chair of the board of the newspaper *Expressen* and TV4, and a colleague on the board of publishing company Piratförlaget, for valuable discussions concerning media issues.

Per-Erik Rödin, chair of the executive committee of the Uppsala Student Union, for assistance with local knowledge and contacts.

Sakari Pitkänen, editor in chief of the newspaper *Metro*, for information regarding newspaper technology and other matters.

Peter Rönnerfalk, chief medical officer and health adviser to the Stockholm County Council, for information regarding the diagnosis and treatment of ventricular cancer, frostbite, etc.

Lotta Snickare, head of management training at Förenings-Sparbanken, for constructive discussions on all manner of subjects, from capitalism to ceramics courses.

Lena Törnberg, head of the lost property section of Stockholm Police, Niclas Abrahamsson, police inspector with the Norrmalm Police in Stockholm, and Tor Petrell, detective inspector with the Stockholm Police, for theoretical discussions concerning lost property.

Tove Alsterdal, dramatist, who follows me every step of the way and reads everything first of all. Without you there would be no books.

Any mistakes or errors which have crept in are entirely my own.